2/1

LOOK LIVE

Caught Dead in Wyoming, Book 5

Patricia McLinn

❖ ❖ ❖ ❖

Caught Dead in Wyoming Series

Dear Readers: If you encounter typos or errors in this book, please send them to me
at Patricia@patriciamclinn.com. Even with many layers of editing, mistakes can slip
through, alas. But, together, we can eradicate the nasty nuisances. Thank you! –
Patricia McLinn

THE BEGINNING

MY PHONE RANG as I neared the doors to the KWMT-TV newsroom that Tuesday morning. I didn't even check the number. That's how good I felt despite the early hour.

"E.M. Danniher, KWMT-TV's 'Helping Out!' reporter." Usually I answer with my name alone, but I was feeling chipper after surviving a long weekend of wild animals at Yellowstone Park—that was two-legged wild animals. The four-legged ones had been well-behaved.

"Elizabeth?"

"Yes." Belatedly, I recognized the voice, though not the phone number. "Dell? Why are you whispering? How was the B&B? Better than the Haber House Hotel?"

"Elizabeth," he said, still whispering. "There's a body in my bed."

I rolled my eyes. "That kind of bragging is crass, even for you, Dell."

"I'm not bragging. It's... It's a dead body."

"Right. So now you're calling to give me first-thing-in-the-morning grief about dabbling in murder investigations? You didn't do enough of that over the weekend? Really? You're as bad as the new sheriff. I should—"

"*Elizabeth.*"

I stopped. The plea in that one word—though still a whisper—was more compelling than just about anything else he could have said.

"You're serious? There's a dead body in your bed?"

"*Yes.*"

I turned and headed back across the parking lot toward my SUV for the privacy.

"You're not pulling my leg? Because if you are—"

"*No.*"

He meant it. There was a dead body in Wardell Yardley's bed in the new bed and breakfast in Sherman, Wyoming. The one KWMT's owner had wanted me to do a piece on.

My first thought was not for the person—and I had a good idea who it was—who had been demoted to dead body.

That first thought also wasn't for Dell, a network White House correspondent, my former colleague, and most-of-the-time friend, despite his predicament.

It wasn't for my job, either, though that, too, might be affected.

Or for the owners of the not-even-officially opened B&B, who were unlikely to agree right now with the maxim that bad publicity was better than no publicity.

No, my first thought was for the brand new Cottonwood County sheriff.

Now, we'll see, I thought. *Now we'll see.*

But that is getting way ahead of the story.

Because a story is supposed to start at the beginning.

THE PREVIOUS THURSDAY

Chapter One

ONCE UPON A Time. That's how the stories of my childhood memories began.

The newsroom equivalent is "I got a phone call." Or, these days it might be a text or an email or a photo or a video.

Whatever the form, it starts with communication to a reporter or editor from that big, wide, crazy outside world where news is born.

Some stories are recognizable from that first instant.

For others, it takes a while from the Once Upon a Time/I got a phone call start until the story truly takes recognizable shape. A gestation period of sorts.

For some stories you only realize that a phone call, text, email, photo, or video was the beginning when you reach the end of it and look back. Rather like those women who say they had no idea they were pregnant until, oops, out pops Junior.

I certainly wasn't expecting much when newsroom dogsbody Jennifer Lawton called out, "Someone on the main line wants to talk to you, Elizabeth."

She called out rather than transferring the call to me because I wasn't at my desk, but instead, about eight feet from her, with my head in the mini-fridge in the bump in the hallway that masquerades as a staff break room at KWMT-TV, Sherman, Wyoming.

I could have sworn I'd left some peach yogurt in that mini-fridge.

Of course that was before I'd bought the latest package of Pepperidge Farm Double Chocolate Milano cookies. Had to eat the cookies first. Yogurt will last for centuries, but I hear Pepperidge Farm Double Chocolate Milano cookies will go stale.

Never experienced that myself, because who'd want to risk it?

Apparently yogurt, however, *can* go missing.

Since the search was for yogurt and not Pepperidge Farm Double Chocolate Milano cookies—which I never would have trusted to the communal fridge, because I am not stupid—I was willing to walk over to the nearest empty desk and ask Jennifer to transfer the call to Line 4.

"E.M. Danniher, KWMT," I answered.

"Ms. Danniher, I am calling from Sheriff Conrad's office. He would like to see you."

Hot *damn.*

News, especially TV news, obsesses about what's happening now. What's right in front of it this moment—especially if there's good video.

It's all about the pointy tip of ice showing above the waterline, not the iceberg holding up that pointy tip. Even though it's the iceberg below, not the pointy tip, that always gets the Titanic no matter how many times you watch the movie.

I'll admit it. I wasn't looking around for icebergs when I took that call. I was focused on the story's pointy tip.

And the pleasure of getting in ahead of anchor Thurston Fine.

There was a new sheriff in town and I'd been trying to get an interview with him even before he arrived in Sherman.

Of course that was only yesterday, and he'd been officially named sheriff only a couple days before that. But still, I'd placed a lot of calls, both directly to him, at his previous home and new office, and indirectly, working sources to see if any knew anyone who knew anyone who knew him.

I'd come up blank.

Cottonwood County had been without a sheriff or a county attorney for more than five months. Some say I instigated those departures.

I prefer to say their actions were responsible. I just reported what they did. Mostly.

"When?" I asked the caller.

"Three o'clock. At his office."

Not much time. Good thing I was prepared.

It would cut it close to meet a friend and former competitor who was arriving in town on assignment—much to his chagrin. Still, it was do-able.

"We'll be there. Thank you."

We hung up. I immediately called the assignment desk.

Yes, I could have walked over to talk to Audrey Adams directly with little chance of being overheard.

That's why I called.

"Audrey? It's Elizabeth. I need Diana for an assignment at three."

"Today? She's already assigned and—"

"We have the sheriff."

Heads popped up around the newsroom like prairie dogs out of their holes, though few were anywhere near as cute. I took note of which heads emerged.

It's a valuable journalistic skill to be able to leave your eavesdropping frequency open for names and terms associated with hot stories while otherwise going about your business. Those head-poppers had that skill. They were people I'd want to work with in the future.

Well, most of them.

Two of the head-poppers were minions of our unesteemed anchor Thurston Fine. But they, too, were useful, because they would carry the news that I had the first interview with the new sheriff to Fine.

"You got the sheriff?" Audrey spoke into the phone, but was audible across the small newsroom bullpen.

"But you did not shoot the deputy," sang a familiar voice from right behind me.

Michael Paycik, KWMT-TV's Eye on Sports, had demonstrated truly impressive head-popping, since he'd been editing in one of the mini-bays around the corner when I'd last seen him ... unless he'd taken a break from editing and had been right behind me because he was on the hunt for food, as he so often was.

"You're channeling Bob Marley now?" I asked Mike as he sat on the edge of the unassigned desk I'd commandeered for my short-distance phone call.

"Never heard of him, but I know that song," Jennifer said. "I'm sure I heard it recently."

"Probably the Eric Clapton version," Mike said.

"Never heard of him, either. I think it was on a commercial."

Stabbed in the heart by the generation gap. As if being a television journalist weren't a strong enough reminder that *tempus fugit*, classics have become soundtracks for commercials.

"Back to the sheriff." Audrey's voice came in stereo, live and through the phone. "Are you sure?"

More heads had joined the initial popping-up crop. Since they could hear both sides of my conversation with Audrey, the head-swiveling rivaled the grandstand at a tennis match.

"Yup. His office called and wants us there at three."

"Isn't your reporter friend flying in around then? I could take the story for you," Mike offered. The same way someone offers to take those stray hundred dollar bills off your hands.

"It is when he's flying in—but to Billings. He's renting a car and driving here."

I was looking forward to seeing Dell.

Wardell Yardley—yes, *that* Wardell Yardley, the leader of the White House press corps who's been on your TV more times than you can count—was a long-time colleague, buddy, and competitor. Since circumstances in my life and former marriage had conspired to banish me from news mecca New York to lead-with-the-cow-in-the-highway Sherman, Wyoming, I no longer constituted much in the way of competition for Wardell Yardley, which had strengthened our buddyness quotient.

Dell was among the last half dozen people on the planet I would have predicted would come to Cottonwood County.

But a bright idea by an exec at his network had brought about the unpredictable.

Dell wasn't taking it well. I tried to restrain a tendency to view it as a spectator sport.

"So that gives me plenty of time to do *my* story," I said. Emphasis added for Mike's benefit. "Well, with Diana, of course."

"You know, more and more stations have reporters do their own filming. Especially stations our size. Video journalists or multimedia journalists, they call them," Audrey said.

"Has Haeburn programmed you?" Mike asked incredulously, citing our News Director Les Haeburn, as unesteemed as anchor Thurston Fine and nearly as irksome. We didn't have to see him butcher the news on TV, but we all got caught in the vise of his penny squeezing. "Besides, have you ever seen Elizabeth's video?"

"Hey," I protested.

"I bet she could do it if she put her mind to it, like she'll get the hang of horseback riding eventually." Jennifer's effort at supportive loyalty fell a tad flat to my ears.

"My talents aside, I'll tell Diana you suggested I handle her camera," I said into the phone.

From her desk Audrey waved a one-handed surrender. "Never mind. Bad idea. Never said it. Thought never crossed my mind. I'll juggle the schedule."

"That's all I ask. Thank you." I'd captured Thurston Fine's intonations well enough to draw chuckles from several in the newsroom, even though none of us had ever heard him use those last two words.

We hung up and most of the heads returned to their burrows. A few, apparently inspired by seeing the break room in the background during their tennis-match head swiveling, ambled over toward where Mike and I were.

The two Thurston minions stood.

They looked at each other. Minion in the white oxford shirt started a zig-zag path between the desks that might take him toward the men's room. Or might not.

Minion in the brown plaid shirt started toward the hallway, casually mentioning to no one that he was going to the editing bay because—wait for it—he needed to edit.

That caused a flurry of look exchanges, since he usually edited only under duress and if he couldn't foist it off on someone else.

White oxford shirt didn't fall for the ploy. He zagged more than zigged, changing his trajectory from the men's room to the hallway, which led to the editing bay, but also to Thurston's private office.

Thurston's office is in the quietest spot and has the best furniture in the building, complete with a comfy couch and full-sized fridge for his sole and exclusive use, while the rest of us piled into the mini version chugging along on its third or fourth decade. He keeps a nanny cam in the studio so he can watch over the door to his office when he's in the studio.

Both minions picked up the pace, throwing aside pretense, as they raced for where the hallway began just past Les Haeburn's office door.

They jostled each other, and brown plaid shirt banged an elbow into the closed door. But he regained his momentum and they were in a dead heat when they disappeared from view.

"Maybe you should get out of here before the eruption," suggested Audrey. "I can send Diana after you."

I shook my head, listening.

Another thud echoed to us from deeper in the hallway, then absolute silence.

Mike looked at his watch, tapped it, and looked around. He and several others nodded wisely as he said, "Afternoon nap time."

The minions apparently were demonstrating their good judgment by restraining themselves from thundering into Fine's office during the most important part of his day.

Haeburn's door jerked open, he glared out, and said, "What?"

"What what?" Jennifer asked.

"Who knocked on my door?" There it was, the Les Haeburn management style distilled to a closed door and a hostile question.

Nature, apparently recognizing it had shorted Les on sincerity, shoulders, honesty, hair, charm, and chin, had opened full throttle on ambition. Until he assessed how helpful or unhelpful any event might be to him, he moved cautiously.

He also kept Thurston Fine happy. Because if Thurston moved up,

Les was not releasing that coattail.

The sad thing is, Thurston might do it.

Isn't television grand?

"Nobody knocked," Jennifer told Haeburn.

"I heard it. I said come in, even though I'm busy. Then, nothing. So who was it? One of you people playing a joke? Real funny. Ha. Ha."

"Nobody knocked," Jennifer repeated. "Somebody was going down the hall and bumped into it."

Haeburn glared suspiciously at Mike and me, but since we still stood in front of him he'd be hard-pressed to accuse us of being the door-bumpers who'd gone down the hall.

He growled, turned around, and slammed the door.

With that done and the diversion of minions reporting to Thurston on hold, we turned to more important matters.

The fridge.

I wedged in next to Leona D'Amato, who covered Cottonwood County social doings part-time. Mike hung over us and I felt the hot breath of other fridge-lookers.

As I pushed aside a plastic container of what was either chili or sludge, I asked, "What happened to my yogurt? I had some in the fridge."

"Was that yours? In the back right-hand corner of the second shelf?" Leona asked.

"Yeah. It's gone."

"What flavor?"

"Peach." I should have chipped the darn thing so I could ID it later.

"Then it's good that I threw it out, because it was green."

That started the kibitzers.

"Roquefort yogurt?"

"Can't you scoop the moldy part off and eat it anyway?"

"No. It can make you sick."

"Sure you can. I do it all the time."

"Proves my point."

"I just put that in there," I protested.

Leona shook her head. "You couldn't have just put it in there. I saw it at the beginning of the summer."

"Oh." Okay, there might have been more than one package of Pepperidge Farm Double Chocolate Milano cookies inserted between putting the yogurt in the fridge and now. Time flies when you're eating cookies.

"The question," Mike said, "is whether someone threw it out to protect you from your self-destructive tendencies or if they absconded with it."

Everyone looked at me. "What do you think?" Jennifer asked.

"It's clearly a case of absconding, since I do *not* have self-destructive tendencies—"

"And if you did, who here would protect you from them except Mi—"

I talked over Leona. Loudly. Covering society did not mean she had a license to broadcast gossip about my supposed social life. "—so we need to look for someone who's been sick lately. Also if they had a peach-colored crust around their mouth."

"Green-colored," Leona corrected.

"If you pursue the case of the peach- or green-colored clue with the refrigerator door closed the rest of us might be able to skip a dose of food poisoning," said a familiar voice from the back of the group.

I looked over my shoulder, but couldn't spot Diana Stendahl, KWMT-TV's best cameraperson, for the peering-in-the-fridge crowd behind me. "Diana? You heard about the assignment?"

"Yes. Are you ready?"

"Just about. I—"

A shout came from the direction of Thurston's office, complete with comfortable couch and regulation sized fridge. It was a shout in an overly stylized broadcast voice.

I came up out of my crouch, elbowed my way through those assembled, shot to my desk, where I grabbed my bag, a new notebook (just in case), and three new pens (triple just in case) and met Diana at the door.

In tandem, we pushed through the first set of double doors that led outside as an oral eruption that seemed to consist mostly of "She can't" wails bubbled to life at the opposite side of the newsroom.

"Perfect timing," Diana said as we reached the parking lot.

Chapter Two

DIANA DROVE THE Newsmobile, a four-wheel drive van that looked as if it had been buried for the past two decades, while I took my new—and recently returned from body work, which is a whole other story—SUV so we could part ways after the interview. She had another assignment after this. I would return to the station to put together packages for the five o'clock news before meeting Wardell Yardley.

Assuming he survived the rigors of driving from Billings, Montana to Sherman.

The guy had experienced third world backwaters amid war, famine, and flood—sometimes all three simultaneously—but you should have heard him on the phone from Billings Logan International Airport whining about a few mountains to get over and a less than spectacular rental car.

Maybe that network executive who'd sent Dell out into the real world had a point.

I could hardly believe that thought formed in my head, considering another member of the network executive guild had torpedoed my career, landing me in Sherman earlier this year. That exec also happened to be my ex-husband. At the time of the torpedoing, my very recently exed husband.

That wasn't a coincidence.

Still, Wardell Yardley might benefit from returning to his journalistic roots. To where he had to dig deep to pursue a story. I mean sometimes our cell phones didn't get reception out here in the Wild

West. *That* is getting back to your journalistic roots.

As I pulled onto the highway outside KWMT-TV, my phone proved it had reception by ringing.

It was my agent, Mel Welch.

Actually, he was a member of the extended Danniher clan first and my agent second, stepping in when my long-time agent chose to stick with my ex and dropped me. Perhaps there'd been more than one torpedo strike.

We exchanged pleasantries—not that kind, the real kind.

"I don't suppose you called to update me on the health of everyone in the clan, did you, Mel?" In addition to stepping in as my agent, he was a highly regarded lawyer in Chicago. He had better things to do than tell me how my father had arranged all the comforts around the couch where he spent most of his time since breaking his ankle in a recent fall from the roof of my childhood home in Illinois.

"I wanted to drop a word that KWMT-TV management would like you to do a story."

"KWMT-TV management, in the person of News Director Les Haeburn, has assigned me a story in the past in addition to my 'Helping Out!' duties," I pointed out. "He usually comes out of his office and shouts my name. So why have you call this time?"

"Yes. Well, this is higher."

Ah. The invisible Heathertons.

Val Heatherton owned the station. Her son-in-law Craig Morningside was the only absentee General Manager I'd ever encountered—or *not* encountered in this case—in the business. I'd never met them. I'd never seen them.

But Mel had talked to them, at least long enough to negotiate my new contract.

Wes, in his pre-ex days, had lined up my contracts and I'd signed essentially without reading them. Wes had known those contracts inside and out, so why should I look? Yes, that's how he knew about the clause he'd turned into my Exile in Wyoming.

But that contract was nearly over and I had agreed to a new non-Wes one with KWMT-TV.

It offered a minimal increase on an annual salary that wouldn't have paid for my car service in New York. But in addition to the "Helping Out!" gig, it gave me considerably more elbow room to pursue stories that interested me than any previous contract I'd had or dreamed of.

There was one caveat...

"They want you to do a piece on a new bed and breakfast in Sherman this weekend. The, ah, Wild Horses Bed and Breakfast."

...that I take occasional assignments from upper management.

It had seemed like an acceptable deal at the time Mel raised that stipulation, since I hadn't heard a word from the owners or general manager in the nearly seven months I'd been here. But this call, with the contract not even in force yet, wasn't good.

I thought about it. At least for a second and a half. Maybe two. "No."

"No? But—"

"It's not the kind of story I do here. Unless they want me to do an expose' or warn people how not to be ripped off by bed and breakfasts."

"Good heavens, *no.*"

"That's what I thought. So this is a promo job for some personal connection."

"I, uh, I can't say." As if he needed to at this point. "But, Danny, you did agree to the contract and it does say with occasional requests for stories from ownership-slash-upper management."

"If this is what they mean by that it's good this is happening now. Good grief, Mel, the contract's not even signed and they want me to do PR puff pieces? No. Tell them never mind. We'll talk to the other people who were interested in me. If those jobs aren't still open—"

"Now, now, don't be hasty. Let me see what I can do. Give me some time."

"Okay. But make it clear I am not doing puff pieces under any circumstances. On top of that, I'm off this weekend—Friday through Monday. A friend's coming in from D.C. today and we're going to Yellowstone for a long weekend."

"Oh? Anybody I know?"

"Yes. But retract your gossip radar. Wardell Yardley is a friend. Strictly a friend."

We wrapped the conversation up then. As I said, he's a busy lawyer in Chicago. And I was driving in Sherman, Wyoming.

One of the dichotomies of Wyoming is that within its towns, distances are measured in units of five minutes. If you get above four—in other words, twenty minutes for those who learned to use a calculator but never learned math—it's considered far flung. But outside of town, distances are measure in units of hours, where a "couple, three hours" is considered practically next door.

In other words, I had already arrived at the sheriff's department at the back of Courthouse Square in the center of town.

The courthouse itself, a venerable, turreted building that could claim the Nineteenth Century by the skin of its teeth, claimed the center of the square. From its broad, shallow granite steps to Cottonwood Avenue, the original park-like setting remained.

The half of the square behind the original building, however, was all business, with a more recent addition, parking lot, and buildings that house the Cottonwood County Sheriff's Department, the smaller Sherman Police Department, and the jail.

Diana had pulled into the parking spot next to me and was getting out her equipment. At least it wasn't the load it had been when I first arrived at KWMT and she and the other shooters used cameras practically carved out of rock.

Inside the sheriff's department a familiar, unfriendly face greeted us from behind the counter.

"Sheriff Conrad is expecting us," I said, prepared to head straight back down the hall that led to the sheriff's office.

Ferrante stepped in front of me.

"The sheriff is not available right now."

"He called and asked us to be here at this time."

"I know. I'm the one who called. He'd like you to go on over to the county attorney's office. Unless you'd prefer not to meet Mr. Abbott, too?"

His self-satisfaction with his wit revealed that he knew I'd do cartwheels from here to the courthouse for the opportunity to add the new county attorney to my trophy case.

Thurston Fine was going to have apoplexy.

It was a good day.

"Got anything prepped for the county attorney?" Diana asked as we walked from the sheriff's department toward the back entry of the courthouse. We'd taken this walk before. I far preferred it in daylight, even on this raw, first-week of November day. "You've been prepping for the sheriff, haven't you?"

"I can wing it. And I've got those questions viewers sent in."

Thurston had refused to have anything to do with the viewer questions, so Les had somehow decided they belonged in my consumer affairs segment "Helping Out!"

We reached the third-story office in the old building with a new nameplate announcing "County Attorney Jarvis Abbott."

Just inside the hallway door, a trim woman in her fifties typed rapidly at a computer. So he'd kept his predecessor's assistant.

"Hello, Mrs. Martin. I had a message that—"

"You're expected." She stood, tapped on the door to the inner office, and swung it open.

I looked back at Diana.

To my knowledge, neither of us had been in this office since a singularly unpleasant spring night.

She gave a quick, grim smile, acknowledging the moment. "You first," she said wryly.

I went.

I'll admit to a little jerk when Mrs. Martin closed the door behind us with a snap.

The room looked out the back of the courthouse. Its occupant literally could keep an eye on the comings and goings at the sheriff's department and Sherman Police Department.

County Attorney Abbott, who stood at our entrance, was not quite my height. He was shaking hands with sixty—a fit sixty. He had neatly trimmed white hair, a neatly trimmed white mustache, and a neatly tucked in white shirt. It was tucked in to jeans, which we saw when he stood for introductions and handshakes. The jeans topped cowboy boots, which we saw and heard when he moved his chair to a better position at Diana's request.

His black cowboy hat hung from a line of pegs on the wall next to a dark gray jacket.

Whether the western wardrobe was authentic or a costume would be revealed over time. I'd seen plenty of the former in Sherman. But, then again, I'd seen Thurston Fine in jeans, so there was also the cautionary tale of the latter.

Except for Mrs. Martin, all signs of his predecessor were gone. The pegs had taken the place of a coat rack. Leather-bound law books were whittled to a few. The shelves otherwise held—from a one-second survey—books on Wyoming and the West. A throne-like red leather custom chair was gone from behind the desk, replaced by a caramel-colored chair that matched all the others in the room.

If his clothing and office hadn't already told me, his even tone announced he would not give much away.

We covered the basics in two minutes flat, with about ten seconds of usable video, since he rarely changed expression.

Don't get me wrong. He wasn't wooden or unpleasant. Simply extremely self-contained.

One example. I asked what goals he'd set for his office. His answer? "Justice."

I had a sudden urge to ask if he was related to Thomas David Burrell, a local rancher who'd—reluctantly—been drawn into some of the stories Mike, Diana, and I had pursued.

Not because Abbott and Burrell looked alike, but because of that shared Western economy of speech and expression.

They were the essence of bad video.

There was no choice. I went to the reader questions.

The majority of the questions centered on whether a husband, wife, son, daughter, or honey could be released from jail well before they were scheduled to be. The reason put forth for these requests? Just because.

I skipped those and picked my way through questions about his stance on the enforcement of hunting, driving, and drug laws—in that order of importance to the writers, and with the subtext strongly being don't bother with enforcing these petty matters.

Before I started the next question a knock came at the door, then it opened immediately.

"Russ, come in. Meet Elizabeth Margaret Danniher," the county attorney said.

My antenna went up.

Not only because he didn't mention the station or fill in any other background, which indicated he expected the sheriff to already know who I was, but also because of a look that flashed between the two men that said they understood each other well. That was fine and dandy for them, possibly even for Cottonwood County.

It might not be so hot for me, because that look also said the sheriff *did* know who I was and they had a plan for how to handle me.

"Sheriff Conrad." I started to stand. He waved me back and took a chair at right angles to mine.

That gave Diana only his profile, backlit from the window. It was a decent profile with a straight nose and a good chin, but TV viewers tend not to be fans of silhouettes unless the voice is disguised, a hat or wig is added, and the silhouette tells juicy secrets.

"If you'd like us to come to your office now, Sheriff Conrad…" An office I knew had minimal natural light to cause these issues.

"No. Don't let me interrupt your discussion here."

"Ms. Danniher was relaying questions from viewers of her TV station." That was the most discursive the county attorney had been yet.

The sheriff made up for it with a grunt of acknowledgement. Great. Yet another Tom Burrell type.

The sheriff was somewhere in his forties. Dark, deepset eyes under dark brows and a strong brow line gave the impression of intensity. How many wrongdoers had squirmed, thinking he could look right through them?

"Call me Elizabeth, please." I added my most winning smile.

It was lost on Sheriff Conrad, clearly, since he said, "Let's hear the next question, Ms. Danniher."

Call me suspicious, but how did he know we were between questions?

I decided to shake things up by including a question I'd previously vetoed.

"Will this office continue to—and I'll quote here to ensure I have the viewer's words exactly—'make defendants sit through listening to people whine about how rough they have it because of some penny-ante something that happened to them.' Which I interpret as meaning Victim Impact Statements."

"It depends."

"On?"

"For crimes in which the victim can speak directly to the impact the crime has had on him or her, yes, there will continue to be Victim Impact Statements."

A small part of me rejoiced in a complete sentence from Abbott. Most of me was occupied with my jangling news story nerves.

The origin of that jangling emanated more from the stillness of the sheriff than the sudden verbosity of the county attorney.

"And those crimes in which the victim cannot speak about the impact? For example murder."

Diana might have picked up on my reaction or, more likely, her instincts kicked in. She shifted around so she had a better angle on the sheriff while still being able to shoot the county attorney—photographically, of course. No county attorneys or sheriffs were harmed in the making of this news package.

The sheriff's frown deepened, but he didn't look at her.

I focused on the county attorney and continued, "Many, if not most, prosecutors are fully supportive of Victim Impact Statements, to bring home the emotional impact of the crime, how the loss of that person affects the lives of those left to mourn."

Silence.

I glanced toward the sheriff. A pulse ticked at the ridge of his jaw. It seemed to keep time with the jangle of my news nerves.

"As Cottonwood County Attorney, Mr. Abbott, will you support Victim Impact Statements in murder cases?"

"Victim Impact Statements, my ass."

My head snapped up, especially since it was the sheriff who'd spoken. "Excuse me?"

"The way they're done now, they're not the statement about what impact the crime had on the *victim*. It's all about what impact the murder had on the victim's relatives—*I'll* never dance with her at her wedding. *I'll* never have grandchildren. *I'll* never get another birthday present from him.

"What about the person who died? What about what was denied to that person by this asshole murderer? *She's* denied a chance to have a wedding because of the self-centered, immaturity of an asshole who couldn't let her love somebody better. *They'll* never get to have kids because this jackass who'd had his license taken again for drinking and driving still had the arrogance to think his belting back bourbon then getting behind the wheel was more important than their right to keep breathing. *He'll* never get to make a saucer in kindergarten for his grandfather because his mother found a kid put a cramp in her social life, after the father skated away without the tiniest dent in his life except that he saved himself the cost of a condom."

I felt as if I'd been blasted by a wind tunnel.

"So you don't think the families and loved ones of murder victims suffer?"

"Sure they suffer. But they don't lose as much as the one who died. It's *my* job to make sure the person who had his or her life wrenched away gets justice. It's my job to make everybody remember that a living, breathing, laughing, crying, human being is now in the ground because of some asshole."

I quickly looked at the county attorney. After a statement like that, the sheriff expected the spotlight. The county attorney didn't.

A hint of satisfaction slid across his eyes before he contained that, too.

"I understand you made bringing in Sheriff Conrad a condition of accepting this job, so—"

"What are your sources for that supposition?" he inserted. He did it extremely well, talking over enough of my introductory phrase that I couldn't use it if I'd wanted to. I didn't want to. Had no intention of using it. But he clearly had dealt with reporters who would have included that introductory phrase in a piece and make it sound like his not challenging it turned it into an accepted fact.

But I had a more direct question. I purposely restated it so the entire question was on the record. "Do you agree with Sheriff Conrad's view of Victim Impact Statements, Mr. Abbott?"

"Sheriff Conrad is excellent at his job, including testifying when called on to do so. It's my job and responsibility to draw from him and other witnesses the whole story. If Victim Impact Statements get that across better than I can, I should hang it up. Perhaps some prosecutors rely too strongly on Victim Impact Statements because they don't think juries or judges have the imaginations to remember the dead person, because they want the crutch of crying relatives in the court, because they fear they don't have the ability to present the real victim so compellingly that everybody remembers him or her."

"As you can do?"

"I hope so."

I faced the sheriff again. "As you can do, Sheriff Conrad?"

"As I can do."

Much ego? "What about the need of the family of a murder victim to be heard?"

The sheriff made a sound.

The county attorney said, "That's valid. But our first responsibility is to get justice for the people of Cottonwood County and for the victim."

"Okay. You've certainly answered our viewer's question."

"Good." The sheriff leaned forward. Ah, here came the main course of the meal they'd set the table to serve up. "Then let me be equally clear about this, Ms. Danniher. Stay out of the sheriff's department's business."

"The sheriff's department's business is the business of every citizen of Cottonwood County. And the business of journalists bringing news to those citizens. If you think people like me or Needham Bender—"

"The editor and publisher of The Independence—" That was showing off that he'd done his homework and knew who Needham was. "—doesn't stick his nose in to murder cases."

"We've *solved* murder cases," I snapped.

"Almost got yourself killed a couple times and—"

"By murderers."

"—got your brand new vehicle wrecked."

I smiled. I hoped it wasn't a pleasant one. "The death of a deputy in this department was not solved by your predecessor, Sheriff. In fact, the department was prepared to dismiss it as an unexplained disappearance. Reporting by KWMT-TV solved the case and led to the openings you and Mr. Abbott have filled."

"Are you threatening—?"

"Russ," the county attorney said. "She stated a fact."

Good to know the county attorney had some control over this guy.

"Well, here's a fact you need to know, Ms. Danniher," the new sheriff said. "I don't want you around any crime scene in Cottonwood County."

But clearly not sufficient control.

"Tell me, County Attorney Abbott, can the sheriff bar an individual member of the media from covering a story? Can the sheriff unreasonably restrict the access of any members of the media to information to cover a story?"

"There are times when, for the sake of the investigation—"

"Unreasonably restrict," I repeated. "We can, of course, test that in court. I would imagine many news outlets in the region and beyond would be interested in a new sheriff and county attorney attempting to block freedom of the press and First Amendment rights."

The county attorney looked at me for a long moment, then turned to the sheriff. "Sheriff Conrad will not unreasonably restrict access of the media or any individual member of it."

The sheriff growled.

He might have thought it was an acknowledgement or even agreement, but it was a definite growl.

"You catch a killer, I'm all for that," he said, not sounding like he was for it at all. "As long as you catch them in a way that I can make a good arrest and County Attorney Abbott can put him or her away. You've been playing fast and loose and that ends now. You ever put your damned story ahead of getting one of these assholes and you're done for. One of them goes free because of your screw-up, and you're done for."

Now he was making me mad. I leaned forward.

"Agreed—and you'll be held to the same standard. You screw up a case and someone goes free who shouldn't have and you're done for."

He nodded. Once. "I expect no less."

"Fine." I slid my notebook into my bag. Some introductory interview this had been. I'd be surprised if there was much we could use after *Hello.* "Anything else?"

"Yes," the sheriff said in the same tone. "What's your camerawoman's name and is she married?"

After a half beat of gaping, I jerked my head around in time to see Diana turn off the camera and slowly lower it.

"Her camerawoman can speak for herself," she said with her usual calm.

"Good. Will she?"

The pause was long enough for me to zip a glance at him, then back to her, catching a view of Jarvis Abbott looking as inscrutably calm as ever.

"My name is Diana Stendahl. I am a widow." Her evenness turned slightly flinty. "With two children living at home."

He nodded. "Understood."

Abbott stood and we exchanged bland good-byes.

Then Sheriff Conrad stood and extended a hand to me. "It was good to meet you, Elizabeth."

I studied him for hints he was mentally adding, "And setting you straight."

I saw no hint of it.

That might mean that in the moment he said the words, he meant them.

Then he crushed my hand in his and I wasn't so sure.

He released my hand and turned to Diana with his hand out once more. I felt I should have warned her about the crushing, but she was already stepping forward and putting her hand in his.

His face was impassive. I couldn't see hers because of the angle. But the handshake appeared even ... and definitely was longer than his had been with me.

But that might have been because he recognized I'd been about to whimper in pain. While Diana, with all that hay-bale tossing she did in her off hours, appeared to hold her own. Or maybe it was kid-wrangling that let her stand still those extra beats with her hand in his.

All the rest of the good-byes were crisp and dry.

Wordlessly, we headed for the Newsmobile for a post-interview debrief before we went our separate ways.

When we were safely back in the KWMT vehicle—telling that *safely* was how I thought of getting out of Sheriff Conrad's territory and into this extension of mine—I finally exhaled. "Well, that was interesting."

"Uh-huh."

"Quite a change from Sheriff Widcuff. Even Deputy Shelton. I know, I know," I said as if she'd protested, "he hasn't officially been the acting sheriff, but everybody knows he's been in charge."

"Uh-huh."

Oh, no, she wasn't getting away with that. "What did you think of him?"

"What do I think of Wayne Shelton?"

I glared. "The new county attorney." I put him first to warm her up, get her talking.

"Seems decent enough. Not a glad-hander like Ames Hunt."

"Thurston will hate him."

"Uh-huh."

She was back to that.

"What did you think of the new sheriff?"

"Interesting."

"I could see where some women would consider him quite attractive, though I couldn't imagine..." A strong reluctance to solidify any imaginings into words stopped the sentence.

"No, you two wouldn't be a good match."

"Match? I don't mean—"

She talked right over me. "You were caught off guard today, but next time I expect you'll give as good as you get. You two are far too much alike."

"Alike? I am *not* like Conrad. I did not come into this county rolling over everybody and everything. Good grief, this guy has the ego that ate Wyoming."

"No, you didn't do that when you first came, but you were at a disadvantage when you arrived—still recovering from a major life attack."

"A what?"

"A life attack—it's when a major malfunction does to your life what a heart attack does to your body. So, you weren't at full capacity. But you're getting there, and the more you do, the more you'll be like Russ. So you two would tear each other apart. And I don't mean in bed. Or at least not just in bed."

I gaped at her. "This is a side of you I've never seen before, Diana."

"No, you haven't." She met my eyes for a second. "Haven't you ever wondered why I don't resent hanging around on the sidelines while Mike Paycik and Tom Burrell both pursue you?"

"That is not at all what's—"

She laughed. "Go ahead, delude yourself, but you're not fooling me. Or them. Or a fair number of other people. Anyway, right now, we're talking about *me*."

"Yes we are," I agreed. "If you're ready to date and get back out there socially, I think that's terrific."

"Oh, I'm not ready to date. Or to get out there socially."

I thought I'd known what she was saying, but now she'd lost me. "So why are you smiling?"

"Because Sheriff Russ Conrad is going to call me. Soon. And we're going to do a lot more than date."

Chapter Three

I'D BEEN WRONG. We had plenty of usable video for packages at five and ten.

Of course they'd be introduced by Thurston, who would mess it up somehow, but I was becoming inured to that. The trick was to include all necessary information in the package itself, leaving nothing for the intro, so viewers could go "La-la-la" with their fingers in their ears while Thurston spoke and still get the complete story.

I'd decided by the time we'd reached the station not to use any of the harsh bits.

Part of my reasoning was fairness—let the people of Cottonwood County form an impression of these two officials from what they did rather than what was said to a reporter. Part of it was so they couldn't pull out the trite blame-the-media excuse. Part of it was reserving my ammunition. Part of it was because they never expected reasonable from me.

Their goal in giving me these first interviews was to smoke me out as a troublemaker so they could dispose of me right at the start.

So I put together a piece introducing the two, with more background than Thurston had ever bothered with, then showing County Attorney Abbott as contained and thoughtful, and Sheriff Conrad as passionate about doing right for the victims of crime.

It was no puff piece, but it was even-handed and open-ended. Implied, but not said that we—the great people of Cottonwood County—would reserve judgment until we saw how they performed.

Knowing I'd done good work, with the added benefits of surprising the sheriff and county attorney while driving Thurston Fine bonkers, I zipped up my Fine-proof pieces for five and ten, and went to meet my buddy, sometimes-competitor, and colleague who'd just arrived in town.

And who looked more than a little shellshocked when I walked into the Haber House Hotel's lobby. It might have been the red flocked wallpaper.

Or the lack of TVs.

MRS. PARENS, A former teacher and principal as well as an expert on the history of Wyoming, had told me about a period in the 1870s when a spattering of offspring from English gentry were sent to Wyoming to make their fortunes in the cattle business.

I could imagine what fish-out-of-water those young men must have looked like on their arrival in the then-territory of Wyoming.

Wardell Yardley—tall, elegant, African-American, and metrosexual down to the soles of his pedi-pampered feet—standing in the Haber House Hotel lobby must have made the most outlandish of those English would-be cowboys look like fish splashing around the pool they'd been born to.

He stood in the middle of the compact lobby, with his two carryons at his feet and an old-fashioned key held pointing out like a weapon.

I pushed the key to one side, put my arms around him, and hugged. "Dell! It's so good to see you. Welcome to Sherman and Cottonwood County." Then I added in a whisper, "Be careful what you say. Think of this as a foreign country."

"It is. It. *Is.*"

The listeners—who didn't bother masking that they were listening—clearly took it to be Dell's way of saying it was good to see me, too. Not knowing he was emphasizing the foreignness of his surroundings.

He looked around.

"It truly is."

The stretches of red flocked wallpaper were intercut by three tall mirrors framed lavishly in wood and flanked by drapes—red velvet, of course. Unfortunately for Dell's taste, rather than interrupt the red flocked wallpaper, they reflected it back. Then they caught mirrors behind the heavy wooden reception counter, which reflected the reflection. Everywhere you looked, red flocked wallpaper.

"This is unlike—"

I interrupted. "You're all checked in? Let's go up to your room. No one will mind." That wasn't what he'd been about to say. "We'll have a chance to catch up some, then a few people are joining us for dinner here to get to meet you."

"I am told I will carry my own luggage."

"I'll help."

"There's no elevator."

"Be grateful you're not hauling equipment."

He gave me a look that was not grateful.

It was only on the second floor. When he opened the door with the old-fashioned key, he muttered, "More red velvet."

Did I know Wardell Yardley or what? I would have objected to the patterned carpet competing with the patterned wallpaper, which both competed with the patterned bedspread and would have forgiven the solid color drapes.

I deposited his bag by the foot of bed. "It's not so bad. If this were in Paris you'd consider it charming."

"If it were in Paris, it would *be* charming."

"Don't tell me you've become a snob. I've known you to stay in a lot worse."

"I paid those dues. I'm past that now. It smells as old as it looks."

Now he sounded like my mother, who had not thought highly of how the Haber House Hotel handled its linens. "Unpack and let's talk."

"I'm not unpacking. We're leaving in the morning for this trip to Yellowstone and I hope to find other accommodations when we return."

"About that... There are no other accommodations except a motel you *really* don't want to stay in. If I had room—" But I didn't since I lived in Diana's bunkhouse/studio apartment after my unlamented rental house burned down. "I have heard of a bed and breakfast that's not quite open yet, but perhaps they could be persuaded..."

"Sold. I will be the most persuasive man on earth if it relieves me from this. Now, tell me what has possibly captivated you about this rock-infested landscape punctuated by far-flung outposts that appear to have no connection at all to civilization."

He put his rollaboard on the bed, opened it, and took out a lavish leather Dopp kit. Wardell Yardley had never done the quart-sized plastic bag for liquid toiletries that we mere mortals must submit to.

"Couldn't get a signal for your phone?" I guessed.

"Not once between Billings and here. Not. Once. At least this place has free Internet."

As he headed for the bathroom, I said, "Indoor plumbing, too."

"Not funny, Danniher."

He shut the door.

It would take more than a few humorous comments to get Dell out of this mood. He was the acknowledged king of the White House press corps, a top-line network correspondent, and well enough known to be a draw on talk shows.

And I owed him—not as much as he thought, but I did owe him.

He'd dug up background information that had helped in a murder case that had also resulted in the recovery of historic gold coins. To say there was a dispute over ownership of the coins was a major under-statement. That legal wrangling had barely begun.

A network exec—a BBB according to Dell, which stood for Baby Big Boss—had the brainstorm to send Dell to do a feel-good, atmosphere piece on the story, since he was already connected to it through me. This would humanize Dell with the audience, the BBB had said.

That had made Dell like the assignment even less. He preferred being a god to his audience.

Add in an ambitious coworker jumping on the chance to fill in for him and my pal was not happy.

He emerged looking refreshed, but no happier. Especially when he looked at the horn-adorned chair covered in cowhide.

"You sit on that thing," he ordered. "It's probably got enough allergens to cause my throat to spasm."

"No problem. I'm tough." I took the offending chair. "Hey, it's a rocker. This is—What are you doing?" Actually, I saw what he was doing—peeling the bedspread and blanket off the bed.

"Haven't you seen reports on the bedding in hotels? That's in *good* hotels. At least they have to wash the sheets sometime. Even in a place like this."

I laughed.

He glared at me momentarily before resuming his bed unmaking.

"Oh, Dell, I *am* glad you decided to come in early for this trip to Yellowstone."

"As long as I'm being sent to hell. I opted to add these extra days to my sentence in hopes of lightening the torment of someone who appears damned to this existence for the foreseeable future."

"You do know I've agreed to this contract extension willingly, don't you? No gun to my head. No extortion forcing me with trembling hand to sign."

"I'll never understand it. Don't tell me it's the sky. Yes, it's big. Yes, I saw plenty of it driving here. But, really? If you want sky, you can rent a luxury yacht and take a short cruise from D.C. or New York. There's no reason to go to these extremes."

"When Easterners talk about Wyoming's big sky, they seldom understand the term the way people living in Wyoming do. Mind you, *Easterners* are not just those clinging to the Atlantic Coast. Easterners are anyone east of Pierre, South Dakota. Those Starbucks swillers in the Pacific Northwest need to prove themselves, too. And the entire population of California is suspect."

"Big sky is—"

"Yes, everyone knows—it's Montana that's the Big Sky Country. It says so on the license plate. But Hollywood people have been moving in at such a rate that it seems the only open sky left is here in these ninety-seven-thousand-plus square miles of Wyoming."

"Good Lord, you sound like you're a native."

"Merely well-informed. As I was saying, the thing about the sky that Easterners seldom comprehend while they write poetry about pure light is that the Wyoming sky can be cruel. The weather, sure—but other places have weather, too. It's something else."

"Hah, so now you're one with tumbleweed? A Wyomingite to the core?"

"No. I'm neither fish nor fowl." I heard myself sigh, didn't like it, and hurried into more words. "Just a few observations."

"How is it cruel?"

"It exposes. It reveals. It wears away. Like the wind and water do to the mountains."

"Charming. I can hardly wait for—"

The alarm on my phone rang, cutting him off.

"Time for dinner," I said cheerily.

Chapter Four

MIKE AND DIANA arrived as we came down the stairs. I introduced Dell and we all walked into the dining room together.

His eyes lit up when he saw Diana.

In fact, he was so occupied looking at her, he hardly seemed to notice that this room, too, featured red velvet. Though here it was dwarfed by a sequence of heavy wooden arches enclosing mirrors, which lined the bar down one side of the large room. The red velvet and dark wood were lightened by the wide windows along the street-front and white cloths on the tables.

The dining area was separated from the bar by a velvet rope—red, of course.

But Dell wasn't looking at décor. He was still on Diana.

"Do. Not. Touch," I growled into his ear.

His eyes widened in would-be innocence. Right.

Standing at the reserved table, waiting for us, were Thomas David Burrell, with his cowboy hat, Clara Atwood, curator and director of the Sherman Western Frontier Life Museum, plus Leona D'Amato from KWMT-TV.

Clara knew a lot about the history of the coins. She was also an interested party in their final disposition, making her a must-meet for Dell. At the same time, he could see how normally rational people slipped the surly bonds of sanity when it came to these antique gold coins.

In addition to her coverage of Cottonwood County's social life, Leona was Thurston's most frequent fill-in at anchor because he considered her unthreatening. Another example of his lack of insight. She'd raised the possibility of interviewing Dell about his visit for a piece next weekend.

Tom was the gold standard for laconic that I'd compared County Attorney Abbott to. He owned a ranch and a highway construction company. He also had a daughter named Tamantha, who is in third grade. Give her another year or two and she'll run the world.

Back in the day, Tom was Cottonwood County High School's basketball star when Mike, several years younger, contracted a major case of hero worship for him. But Tom's college athletic scholarship was cut short by personal matters. Ever since, he'd run the family ranch and a road construction business.

Mike had become a football standout at the University of Wyoming. He went on to play several years for the Chicago Bears. When his knees dictated retirement from the NFL, he returned to Sherman to learn the ropes of TV journalism. Eventually he would return to the broader world, and he'd do great there. Tom would never leave Cottonwood County.

Considering all that, there was something impressive about the way Mike respected Tom.

There also was something annoying about the way the two of them got along, considering each had indicated interest in me. Why weren't they decently at each other's throats like ordinary men?

No, I had a pair of brothers-in-arms, all full of mutual respect and friendship whenever they encountered each other, which all the time.

My feelings about each of them were tangled. (Hey, at least I didn't say complicated.)

Tom, along with Jennifer, had been part of our investigating team. I knew Dell would enjoy their company.

I'd also invited Emmaline Parens and Gisela Decker. Mrs. Parens was a retired teacher and principal. Gisela was her next door neighbor in the town of O'Hara Hill, Mike's Aunt Gee, and the head of dispatch for the sheriff's department in the north part of the county.

They'd declined because Aunt Gee was working a rare night shift to let a subordinate celebrate his anniversary. We'd offered to pick Mrs. P up and drive her home, but she wouldn't hear of it.

One does not argue with Mrs. P.

We were scheduled for lunch Wednesday with both ladies in O'Hara Hill, although the time they'd set was more brunch by my standards.

Deputies Shelton and Alvaro, who would have been good connections for Dell's reporting, also declined. Young Richard Alvaro had shown a lot of promise—as a sheriff's deputy and a source—until Shelton stepped in. Now Richard was only a promising sheriff's deputy.

The introductions were still going around when Jennifer Lawton hurried in. She'd been touchingly thrilled to be included. I hoped some of Wardell Yardley's journalistic knowledge would rub off on her.

But nothing else.

I growled into his ear, "Her, too. Do. Not. Touch."

This time he looked genuinely injured. "She's a child."

I gave him a stern side-eye, which would translate into "I mean it" in every known language.

We settled in with Dell in the middle on one side of the table, Mike across from him, and Tom and me at opposite ends.

"I hear you're going to Yellowstone this weekend," Tom said into a momentary lull that allowed full-table conversation. "Surprised you got lodging this time of year, Elizabeth."

"She didn't. I did." Dell grinned. "Pulled some strings."

"He insisted. You know these big shots from out of state, gotta throw their weight around." Since that was a mild version of what they'd all thought of me when I arrived, there were chuckles. "But why does it require string-pulling this time of year? I'd think there wouldn't be many people wanting to go with it so cold."

That drew more chuckles.

"Cold? Just wait, dear," Leona murmured.

Mike said, "This is the last weekend the roads will be open. That's usually a pretty good draw. It's late this year, too. Mid-October's more common."

"They consider this winter," I told Dell morosely. "And spring isn't until June."

"Your choice to be here." Dell had no sympathy. He asked Mike, "They close the whole park for half the year?"

"Nope. It opens in December for overroad use."

"Overroad?"

"Snowmobiles and such. Couple of the lodging places open for winter, too. That's not usually until mid-December, though. Got to have enough snow first. This patch before the snow really falls and again in the spring before the roads are clear are the quiet seasons."

"Spring's worse," Tom said. "Avalanches."

"*Avalanches?*" Dell and I repeated. Everyone else looked nonchalant.

"Heavy, wet spring snow can bring down a slide easy," Mike confirmed with unseemly cheer. He faced Dell, "Surprised you could get us into Lake Yellowstone Hotel for the weekend, since it officially closed to tourists today."

"Hmm," was all Dell said.

He wasn't going to tell how he'd gotten us rooms there. Not without a lot of pressing. I didn't press.

He was already suffering from feeling like he'd stepped into an alternative universe. One where Wardell Yardley didn't know the maitre'd.

Even more unimaginable, one where there wasn't a maitre'd.

A familiar voice came from behind me. "Heard there was a disturbance. Can see this table is trouble."

I twisted around to see Deputy Shelton, with Richard Alvaro behind him. "Won't you join us for dessert and coffee?"

"I suppose that can't hurt too much."

The conversation flowed easily, lubricated by coffee and the Haber House Hotel dining room's acclaimed chocolate pie.

At one point I took the opportunity to say in a low voice to Richard Alvaro, "I'm surprised and impressed that you're willing to risk the ire of your new sheriff to consort with the media."

"Deputy Shelton thought coffee and pie…" He let it die as color bloomed in his face. The unspoken "couldn't hurt too much" hung in the air.

I heard Dell say, "Did Elizabeth ever tell you about the hotel we holed up in in Istanbul?"

"No, no, no, that's not a story they're interested in." My effort to stem the memory-blabbing was the equivalent of the band playing on the Titanic deck as it sank. Valiant, but not going to change the course of events.

A chorus of "yes, we ares" rose.

"Actually, Elizabeth's right. The much better story is how much we drank while we were holed up in that hotel."

I held my head.

The story was coming whether I liked it or not.

TUCKING THE LAST few things into my bag—years in TV news had made me a fast packer—I picked up the ringing phone.

The phone number on the display was the first one I'd ever learned, but even as I answered the call, I had trouble believing it.

Mom, calling after the sun had risen? Was the earth still spinning the right way?

"Hello."

"You never told us!"

Not Mom. Dad. Yet nothing about his tone said *emergency.*

Confused, I stammered out, "I—I didn't?"

My mouth was on its own. My father's accusation had started the mental equivalent of pulling out a directory and scanning a yard-long list headed "Things I Never Told My Parents."

I was barely through the A's under "The Big Ones" when he went on.

"Michael Paycik. Good heavens, *Michael Paycik.*"

I stopped. Because I was entirely innocent on that topic. Well, innocent as far as actions. Because surely a kiss or two didn't count toward not-innocent.

When it came to thoughts, no female with eyes and a solitary drop of hormones could be entirely immune to the potential of—

Nope. Not thoughts to entertain while on the phone with my father.

"What about him?" I asked.

"He played for the Bears."

"Uh-huh." I awaited the punchline, but apparently that was it.

"He was great. A great, great player."

"Really?" I knew he was decent, but he hadn't been famous enough for a desultory fan like me to know his name before I came to Sherman.

"Never gave up on a play, always tenacious. Didn't have the best physical skills but made the absolute best use of everything he had. Thinking all the time. A true student of the game, always learning. I thought for sure he'd be a coach. He'd've been great."

I recognized many of those attributes in Mike's approach to reporting.

Then it hit me. Dad had said "us," but Mom wasn't on the phone. That was downright weird. It was like the parent contract said all phone calls would be initiated by the mother. Mother could call solo, Father never did. Yet, here he was, on the phone, talking to me. All because Michael Paycik had played for the Bears.

You know, the pundits are right, sports *can* bring families together.

"I don't know why I didn't recognize him right away. I mean, of course he wore a helmet on the field, but after all the interviews I saw with him I should have. I didn't make the connection until he mentioned the Bears. Stayed totally professional, but gave a little smile, and *bam*! I knew. I can't believe you didn't tell us."

My father—all of my family—qualified as rabid Bears fans. I'd lost my rabid status a few moves ago, like a carton of mementos left behind in some basement. I recalled the memories the mementos represented, but their direct impact had faded.

What else had I left behind?

That might be a topic to consider. Later. For now, something else had caught my attention. "How did you see Mike's sportscast?"

"Mel. I've been catching up on them since I broke my ankle."

I knew Jennifer was sending Mel copies of broadcasts that included stories I'd done. Apparently he was sharing them with my parents. *God, please don't let him have shared the special reports.*

Oh, wait, of course he hadn't shown them those, or I'd have had Catherine and James Danniher on my doorstep—broken ankle or no broken ankle—instead of Dad solo on the phone.

He was still talking. "Mel said you're interested in somebody out there, and she had to see what he's like—you know your mother."

I did. But I couldn't say it or otherwise comment, because if I did, I'd shout, "Mel, said *what?*"

"Don't be upset with your mom. She's concerned about you, Maggie Liz. We both are, but your mom's protective—"

So said the man who'd blatantly tailed me on every first and second date through high school, and even later was known to flash flood-lights into cars he thought had been parked too long with my date and me inside.

"—especially when that jerk who swore to love you turned around and hurt you that way." If he'd used that tone on my high school dates, it would have cleared my social calendar permanently. "But with you seeing Mike Paycik, I'll tell your mom what a great player and upstanding man—"

"No!" I toned down my next words, even though my pulse had picked up, because Mike's SUV had pulled up in front of the bunkhouse. I did not want him to hear my side of this conversation. Not to wonder why I didn't answer his knock. "Dad, don't tell Mom anything. I'm not seeing Mike that way. Not at all. We're colleagues. Friendly colleagues. He's a great guy, but we've just worked on a few stories. Like I do with that shooter I told you and Mom about, Diana Stendahl."

"I wish you wouldn't use that term."

"Excuse me?"

"Shooter. It sounds so … grim. My little girl…. Couldn't you say camerawoman?"

I'd distracted him inadvertently. I'd take that. "That's a mouthful, Dad. Shooter's part of the lingo. And speaking of Diana, she's about to knock on the door." That was only a little fib. I'd spotted her heading this way from the main house, though Mike was well ahead of her.

"Okay. I just wanted to—"

"I know," I interrupted. I did not want him back on the topic of Mike. "We'll talk more. Later. Give my love to everyone and I'll call you soon."

He clicked at the same time Mike knocked. I swung the door open fast enough to catch both him on the outside and my dog Shadow on the inside by surprise.

"Am I late?" Mike asked, apparently trying to find a rational explanation.

Shadow didn't bother. He gave me a more-nutso-behavior-from-her look and sauntered outside, getting a pat on the head from Mike on his way.

Shadow stayed out most of the day, apparently patrolling the nearby areas of Diana's ranch. She rented out most of the land and Shadow seemed to know the boundaries as if he'd read the lease agreements. He watched the renters at work on the land, but barked only if someone he didn't know—or someone he did know and didn't approve of—came onto the property around the house.

The first several times he'd barked had made me jump, because he'd done so little of it before we'd moved to the bunkhouse.

Rail thin and standoffish, Shadow had lurked around my previous abode. He gradually started coming closer as I put food and water out for him. Until, eventually, he'd thrown his lot in with mine.

We were a couple now. Heck, we'd moved in together with the switch to Diana's bunkhouse. Though he was gone all day patrolling, he slept on the bed I'd bought that sat in the middle of the bunkhouse floor between my bed and the door.

"No, you're not late. I'm eager," I told Mike.

"Oh-*kay*," he said skeptically. He went past me and grabbed my bag, then we headed out.

"Don't worry about Shadow," Diana said from the bottom of the wide porch steps. "I have all your instructions posted on the fridge for Gary and Jess. Though they did complain that they were so long they covered the handles."

"I wanted to be thorough."

"Uh-huh. Jess had a good idea—we're going to let Shadow come in here each night, check around so he knows you're not here, then we'll take him to the house. That way he shouldn't fret that he's being kept from you."

"I doubt he's attached enough to me to worry about that."

"Right. Just like you're indifferent to him. There's a pattern there. A definite pattern." Her gaze slid meaningfully toward Mike's back.

"See you Monday night," I said cheerfully. "You have my number if there's an emergency."

"I do," she said solemnly. "And if I can't reach you immediately because Shadow has a bad dream, I'll call the head ranger to get you a message."

"Smart—"

"You, too. Have a great time." She waved us off with a smile.

Shadow, accustomed to my leaving most days, barely lifted his head from where he was examining the vegetation between the bunkhouse and barn.

Dell was waiting on the sidewalk outside the Haber House Hotel, even though we were early.

Based on his sour expression, I figured it was because he'd wanted to shake the dust and other allergens of the Haber House's hospitality off as soon as possible.

Being no fool, I wordlessly handed a clean cup and the coffee thermos Mike had brought to Dell in the back seat.

"I want to stop at the new bed and breakfast before we leave town," he said after about half a cup's worth. "This is good coffee. The stuff at that Hoover House—"

"Haber House," Mike said.

It was a testament to the quality of Mike's coffee that Dell ignored the interruption. "—tasted like what you get out of hospital machines. If you don't mind stopping," he added, harking back to his request.

"No problem. But I don't know where—"

"I do." I gave him the address.

Upon arrival, I chose to stay in Mike's SUV. Dell had a better chance of getting what he wanted by not being associated with the person who'd refused to do a story on their new enterprise.

That gave me plenty of time to look over the two-story frame house with fresh light gray paint, a dark gray roof, white trim, and a red door. It looked welcoming, with broad steps leading to a wrap-around porch. A discreet woodcut sign announced it as the Wild Horses Bed and Breakfast.

When they came out, Dell was in a visibly better mood, so I knew he'd gotten what he wanted.

"So you talked them into letting you stay there even though they're not officially open."

"I did." He opened my door. "Now I'm going to talk you into letting me sit in the front seat. Because I'm the guest, because I have longer legs, because you'll have other opportunities since you live so close, but I am unlikely to return."

Grumpily, I got out. "We can trade off during the trip," I said as I got in the back seat.

"We'll see," was all Dell would commit to.

Mike went west out of Sherman, past the rodeo grounds, past the turnoff to O'Hara Hill, past Burrell Road Construction.

"Your friend's?" Dell asked, nodding toward a trailer standing guard in front of blocky vehicles and machinery.

Dell had aimed the question over his shoulder at me, but I was content to let Mike say, "Yeah," then explain how Tom's father had started the business to help smooth out ranching's erratic income.

Not long after that, Mike turned south onto a road I'd never been on before. He continued roughly west-southwest, with lots of turns from west to south and south to west.

"Whoa," Dell said after one turn. "It looks like we've landed on the moon."

"Alkali springs, rock formations, not worth irrigating. That'll do the trick," Mike said.

I leaned forward with my chin on the back of Mike's seat to see through the windshield, then nudged his shoulder to get a better angle.

"Want me to drive from outside?" Mike asked.

"It would help. Or let me drive, then I could see."

"No way." He turned to Dell. "You know she wrecked her brand new SUV?"

"*I* wrecked it? *I* wasn't behind the wheel."

"She let her brand new SUV get wrecked," he amended. "In the pursuit of justice."

"Do you two wear capes when you go crusading for truth and justice?" Dell said to me, "You never showed interest in dead bodies in D.C. or New York, well, other than Wes."

"Hey, that's right. You know her ex. What's—"

I interrupted Mike, along with giving him a quelling look via the rearview mirror. "I wasn't allowed to pursue interesting cases the way I've been able to here." Not because the news director encouraged it, but because my official beat left me so underemployed I had plenty of time. "To get in early and dig into what's really happened."

That started a strange combination of murder investigation details, grief from Dell about what he called my new hobby, historical factoids courtesy of Mrs. Parens, and exclamations at natural wonders.

We joined up with the highway heading west out of Cody. In an efficient use of pavement, that highway was U.S. Routes 14, 16, and 20, all rolled into one.

First, we twisted and turned in a complicated game of tag with the north fork of the Shoshone River amid rock formations that would put any wedding cake to shame for elaborate detail. Gradually, we experienced the simultaneous sensation of rising as the road climbed, yet feeling as if we were sinking as rocks and ground beside us climbed faster.

At the East Gate to Yellowstone Park, we eased up to a short line before it was our turn to drive under the peaked gable roof.

As driver and thus closest to the ranger, Mike won a short scuffle to pay the entrance fee.

The ranger handed over flyers along with our pass, cautioning us to read the safety information and take it seriously.

Mike asked about the roads and was assured they were in good shape.

"How many channels do the TVs pick up?" Dell asked, apparently still smarting from the Haber House Hotel's limited repertoire.

"There are few TVs in the park to pick up any stations. Most rooms don't have phones, either," the ranger said to Dell.

"That's okay I have my own."

The ranger chuckled. "Good luck with that. You might get some service in the villages, but that's a small part of the park."

He waved us on our way.

"No TV, no phones, probably no internet, *and* no TV cameras, Dell. Think you can survive?" I asked.

"How little you know me," he said with grandiose dignity.

Mike said he'd mapped out an itinerary if it was all right with us. It was. Especially when he said our first stop would be the Grand Canyon of the Yellowstone, including lunch.

Seeing the canyon was my top priority. Dell wanted lunch.

The road we took twisted like that curly ribbon you pull against a scissor blade to make ringlets to decorate a package.

Dell said, "Amazing country, though I keep thinking there might be IEDs or tribal warriors coming over any ridge."

"You have never encountered IEDs or tribal warfare in your life."

"I have had a varied and dangerous career—"

"Dangerous from traffic on the Beltway and infighting in the White House press corps."

Dell gave in with a chuckle.

Chapter Five

THE GRAND CANYON of the Yellowstone is ... well, grand.

There's a huge painting—seven feet by twelve feet—of the canyon by Thomas Moran, who'd been on an 1872 expedition to what became Yellowstone. It hangs in the Smithsonian's American Art Museum near Federal Triangle in D.C. I'd looked at that painting in awe many times.

The real thing brought tears to my eyes.

The gleaming fortresses of rock formations, the unceasing thread of water that slowly carves its sculptures, the ten thousand shades of gold and green and blue—Okay, enough waxing enthusiastic. I will say only two more things:

Go see it.

It brought Wardell Yardley to silence.

Though that miracle wore off as we ate lunch.

Back in the SUV—me still in back—we made a short stop at Roosevelt Lodge to see where Teddy hung out in 1903. We also saw the Petrified Tree—the lone representative of an ancient redwood forest caught in volcano eruptions.

Dell leaned over and jabbed, "A murdered tree. Going to find the volcano responsible?"

The drive to Mammoth Hot Springs included cutoff drops that provided overlooks of the Yellowstone River to rolling sweeps with mountain vistas beyond to stands of fir trees, including a patch burned apparently in a wildfire. Yes, Dell made another crack about finding the murderer—this time with Smokey Bear as our co-detective.

Mike kept telling us this was a prime spot for seeing black bears, but we saw none. Though a substantial herd of deer crossing a valley was breath-catching.

Once at Mammoth, I wanted to see historic sites, including what was built as Fort Yellowstone when soldiers guarded the park in the late 1800s. I was outvoted, so we went with the stink of sulfur.

The otherworldliness of the hot springs, with calcium deposits looking like ice and snow, and the venting steam from geothermal "features" were fascinating. If only I'd worn a gas mask.

"We'll try to come back and see your historic stuff tomorrow or Sunday," Mike said when we were back in the SUV. Sure, he and Dell had sated their alien-world thirst, not to mention the male if-it-smells-bad-it-must-be-great bent, but my interest was a "we'll try."

I was contemplating a second—idyllic—trip to Yellowstone in which I planned everything, when Dell said from the front seat, "Unbelievable."

"What?" I swiveled from my side-window viewing to out the front as Mike applied the brakes to bring us into a long, slow glide behind a lineup of vehicles.

"So few cars, so much space and people still manage to gridlock traffic with accidents," Dell said. "It's the Beltway with mountains."

Mike put his window down and leaned out, trying to see past the camper in front of us.

I shook my head. "No way this is as bad. Don't have nearly as many out-of-staters here. And—" I added the *pièce de résistance*. "—there are no diplomatic corps drivers."

"Diplomatic plates on any vehicle are the unquestionable sign that the devil exists," Dell agreed. "Yet, without the horrors of D.C., here's the incontrovertible proof of gridlock from an accident."

Mike pulled his head back in. "I don't think it's an accident."

I grinned. "Hah! You've been controverted, Dell."

"Looks like a bear jam." Mike sounded pleased.

"A what?" Dell asked.

"Possibly a bison jam. But in this location, I'd say bear. Tourists spot bears and leave their cars wherever they are to take pictures."

"Sounds like the Beltway in a snowstorm," I said. "Same happens with bison?"

"Bison jams happen usually because they take over. They'll amble along, blocking both lanes. Can back up for hours. I've seen rangers herd them using pickups."

"Shouldn't it be a buffalo jam?" Dell asked.

"There are no buffalo in Yellowstone," Mike and I said in unison. He chuckled. "Go ahead, show off your new-found bison knowledge."

I didn't need a second invitation. "Not only are there no buffalo in Yellowstone, there are no buffalo on this continent. The buffalo roam in Asia and Africa, but we have bison. The early settlers got it wrong and it stuck. They should have looked at the horns—curved for buffalo, straighter, like cows, for bison."

We'd reached a curve to the right. Mike edged his SUV close to the center line and peered around the camper.

"Ah. People have been waiting to get into an overlook parking area. That must be where the bears can be seen. Somebody's pulling out. Want to grab the spot?"

His eagerness came through clearly. I supposed it was understandable. After all, the man had played for the Bears.

"As long as we've waited this long, might as well see what the hold up's been about," I said.

"You're the driver," Dell added.

He easily maneuvered into a spot opened by the departure of a lumbering bus.

"Hey, it looks like elk." He pointed through the windshield. All I saw were trees. "Not bear, but I like elk. You should see a herd going across a valley, jumping a fence. They line up all neat and patient then go over it one by one like water on four legs."

We all got out. "Great line, Mike," I said. "Poetic. Use it in a story."

He looked pleased and embarrassed.

We'd started along a path away from the parking lot when a clot of people came toward us, led by a couple in Seattle Seahawks jackets. "I *told* you it was too late in the season to hear them," the woman said to the man. "But you *had* to stop. Now we'll never make Old Faithful in time."

"It's not like a train schedule, Doris. It blows when it blows."

"I am seeing Old Faithful if we have to sit there all day and all night." Her threat continued as the moved out of earshot.

"Sounds like Doris is about to blow," Mike said in a low voice.

"Why is it called Old Faithful if it's not on a schedule?" Dell asked.

"I've got this," I said to Mike. "Old Faithful blows regularly, but not on a schedule. The gap varies from about thirty-five minutes to two hours. Rangers can estimate the next eruption based on how long the previous one lasted."

"That—" Dell started.

"—was a total waste of time," said another guy heading toward the parking lot. "I thought—."

"—is frightening. The Elizabeth I knew—"

"—they were supposed to be getting it on. Those animals were standing there."

"—would never know such details."

We came around a curve and saw a half-dozen elk clustered on a rise across a stream ahead.

"There's the male," Mike said.

"What a rack." Dell made eye contact with me as he said it in a low voice. Neither of us giggled. We were professionals, after all.

"Antlers, you greenhorns," Mike said.

"You'd think he'd have a headache." I said.

"Must get used to them as they grow."

We'd come up now to other people gathered to watch the animals from a reasonable distance. Most had their phones out, taking photos or video.

"The one with the horns is the male," a young man said loudly. He was part of a group, all about the same age, mostly guys, none looking like the outdoors was their natural habitat. More like the only light their skin received was from the glow of a computer screen.

None of his group looked particularly impressed by his knowledge, which he'd clearly cribbed from Mike's comments.

However, a gray-haired man beside a worried-looking gray-haired woman stiffened and turned on him.

"Antlers," the man intoned, far more severely than Mike had. "*Antlers*. I learned the value of distinguishing words carefully while attending Harvard Law school. Horns remain, antlers are shed each year. Elk display antlers. As that magnificent creature manifests. We are privileged, absolutely privileged to witness these great and noble animals in a sacred ritual from time immemorial."

Two other couples, one middle-aged, one slightly younger, who did look like outdoors people, pulled their heads deeper into their jacket collars, rather like turtles.

"That animal's not thinking of sacred or ritual," Dell murmured. "He's thinking of getting some action."

The male made a sound. Something that combined a keening cry and a football stadium's unified exhalation of dismay. It ended with yipping chuffs that sounded suspiciously like "Yuck, yuck, yuck."

The group of young not-outdoors types shuffled with chuckles that edged toward titters.

Something about them caught what I call my Go Fish attention.

When I was a kid, games in my family stayed just this side of cut-throat only because we didn't dare spill blood in Catherine Danniher's clean house.

Some members of the family specialized in certain games.

One excelled at Monopoly. I was bankrupt far too often to ever consider a career in finance.

Another played Scrabble like the right combination of letters for the highest score might open the gates to Nirvana. I frequently came in second in Scrabble, but always maintained a Zen calm, because it was a game. It didn't matter, it really didn't that I never—ever—won. Zen. Calm.

Unlike two of my brothers, whose Battleship encounters made a couple of world wars look like tiffs.

With this background, you can imagine that the first contest was to determine what game we'd play.

Mom solved one such eruption during a rainy summer day with the

Solomon-like solution of locking the closet where the games resided, and handing us a deck of cards.

First, we tried Slapjack. After the third timeout for howl-worthy injuries, Mom outlawed that.

That's how we came to Go Fish.

I learned an invaluable lesson playing Go Fish with my siblings. I learned to look beyond the person being asked the question— "Elizabeth, do you have any sevens?"—to the people listening to the question.

Sure, the question told you something about the questioner, and the answer told you something about the answerer. But you could also glean information by watching the other reactions. Did they have sevens? Did they want sevens? Were they so close to going out and winning that they squirmed at every move before it became their turn.

That lesson has stood me in good stead in journalism. I make it a habit to look beyond where the camera's focusing, to broaden my field of vision beyond the person I'm interviewing.

It also let me win enough rounds of Go Fish that I finally had a game of my own.

In this instance it made me look at the backup band first—the young guys shuffling around.

They all wore sloganed t-shirts, jeans, and sneakers. Not a hiking boot among them. A few had layered in hoodies under their jackets. Three of the guys appeared to be wearing the same style of black framed glasses. A bulk discount?

But I could separate a few out as individuals, mostly by hairstyle. There was a guy with the sort of super-short haircut usually reserved for new boot camp arrivals and prisoners. Another had a balding spot at the crown of his head that the wind played peekaboo with as it tossed hair styled to swoop over it. The third—the one who'd incorrectly repeated Mike's info about the antlers—attempted the classic compensation for a receding hairline by letting the sides and back straggle long. A fourth had a bowl cut.

Only one had a classic Ivy League cut. He was older and stood slightly separated from them, yet connected by the same kind of not-an-outdoorsman clothing. He had a neatly trimmed beard, which made his square jaw even squarer. He wasn't enough older to be a parent, but was a definite step up in maturity, like a resident assistant in a college dorm. Though the others seemed older than college age.

Unlike the elk band, which included six calmly munching females and the solitary alert male, this human group boasted a solitary female.

She was the diva. Her dark, straight hair and the epicanthic fold of her eyelids pointed toward Asian heritage. She wore the same outfit as the others, but hers fit entirely differently. And she knew it.

"Elaine, can you see it?" the guy with a bowl cut framing a pale, pudgy face asked solicitously.

She didn't even bother to look at the asker as she tossed her long hair back over her shoulder. "I can see it, hear it, and smell it."

The gray-haired man puffed up with indignation. "The elk's bugle—"

"My grandmother used to eat those." By Elaine's tone, she had not signed on to the ethnic stereotype of respect for her elders.

"Bugles. Ha, ha, ha." The super-short haircut guy said the words, rather than actually laughing. "I remember those."

"Quit sucking up to her," receding hairline said to Ha Ha Ha. "Because her presentation tops the rankings doesn't mean it will stay there. Not when I do mine."

"—can be expected to be heard in Yellowstone Park," the older man droned on, "in prime rutting—"

"Rutting?" demanded receding-hairline with a smirk. "Is that the same as f—?"

"Shut up, Kelvin," the RA interrupted.

"—season, which is September into early October. But to—"

"What is he, Smokey the Bear or something?" a voice asked from the back of the group. Another icon misidentified, since our pontificator wasn't talking about forest fires.

"—hear it now, so late in the season, is, indeed, an unexpected delight."

One of the younger group, I wasn't sure which, muttered an oath that indicated a state well south of delight.

It might have been the peekaboo-baldspot. He hadn't said anything loudly enough that I could identify his voice. Possibly because he kept his head down as he flexed his hands and starting to reach toward his pocket repeatedly, the way some trying-to-quit smokers do.

We moved past. The group of younger people was also trying to get away from the pontificator, but we had better position. The wisdom of age.

"They are great and noble creatures." The man's would-be whisper was not only audible to us, but, judging by his ear-twitching, to the bull elk. "When I was at Harvard Law School, I gained an appreciation for such marvels of nature."

"At Harvard Law?" Dell whispered in my ear. "That's a surprise."

"Shh."

"Surely his companion—wife?—knows by now where he attended law school. Yet he's still saying Harvard Law every ten words."

"Are you getting good shots, Joel?" the gray-haired woman asked anxiously. "You don't want to miss this."

"Of course I won't miss it. I shall preserve these memories forever." He manipulated his phone as if it were a squirmy toddler. "I shall now review the photos I have taken so far. When we attend the next Harvard Law School reunion, I will be able to share this moment with—Oh, my God."

The elk lowered its head, appearing to momentarily forget even its mating drive, and stared toward the man.

If the elk decided he was a threat and charged him, I doubted Harvard Law would provide much protection.

"Someone has intruded on every photo with his finger. A *finger*. In every photo!"

"Talk about bugling," Dell murmured.

"Whatever do you mean, Joel?" the gray-haired woman asked.

I was keeping an eye on the elk. But apparently feeling it was no longer being appreciated, it ambled toward the edge of the woods.

"I mean, Ariel, that a finger has been place over the aperture, marring my photos. I said *his finger*. But it could have been a female finger."

Poor Ariel. She now received the full force of a Harvard Law glare.

But she was rescued by the group of bored younger people bursting into laughter. "Idiot doesn't even know it's his own finger over the lens," one said loudly enough that Harvard Law couldn't miss it.

He didn't, judging by the red surging up the back of his neck and staining his ears.

One of the female elk passed in front of the bull on her munching path and he started after her.

The male picked up speed, coming in behind as she paused at a tempting bit of vegetation. He gave a sort of cry. The female moved forward. His cry started high as he followed her, his head on her moving rump. As she broke contact and trotted away, he let out a shuddering squeal.

"I know just how he feels," Mike muttered.

Dell looked from him to me, then covered his mouth.

"Thanks a lot," I grumbled, not sure which of them I was responding to. "She needs more time. She's an evolved, thoughtful creature—" With both of them guffawing, I had to talk louder to be heard. "—not prepared to fall for the first male making sounds like bad plumbing."

"Bad plumbing? *Bad plumbing?*"

Joel had rounded on me, transferring his ire from the phone, Ariel, and his finger. The younger group cravenly stepped aside to let him through.

He puffed out his chest. "Only a heathen would describe it thus. The rutting male elk's bugle is the clarion call of nature. One of its wonders. Awe-inspiring. To demean it as resembling bad plumbing displays a lack of knowledge, a lack of understanding, a lack of taste that—"

"Hey, aren't you ... somebody?"

The question came from Elaine and redirected the attention of everyone—even Joel—past me.

They weren't looking at me, or at Mike, who had stepped beside me in protective mode.

They were looking farther back, where Dell had found a patch of sunlight to pose under. It wasn't a key light, but it would do in a pinch.

Don't misunderstand about Dell. At one level he can't help it.

Some of us on the lens side of the camera don't particularly like to be recognized, especially not when we're not on the job. I hardly recognize myself on screen, so I think no one else will either. Some psychiatrist could probably have a field day with this, but it seems as if the person on that screen is someone else, someone separate from me. That might be what makes me a bit edgy about being recognized.

That and the fact that some broadcast journalists are actually rather shy. Besides me, at least another five, six broadcast journalists I've met in my career are.

Then there are the Thurston Fine types, who get huffy unless every soul he encounters not only knows who he is, but can recite all his self-styled career highlights by heart.

A fair number of that type would get sarcastic, cutting, or ironic about someone asking if they're "somebody."

Wardell Yardley is that rare well-adjusted (in this area) combination who doesn't have a shy bone in his body yet whose ego can grab the cut-you-down-to-size "Aren't you somebody?" line with aplomb and julienne it into something tasty.

"Aren't we all?" he tossed back to Elaine with just the right wryness.

My preliminary assessment was that Elaine was the kind of woman that other women mostly don't like, while men do. The women who don't like Elaine prototypes are looking at the personality. The men are looking at the body.

She trilled a laugh now. It was fake and annoying. No one with a Y chromosome recognized those two elements.

It made the men around her now stir like a shiver of sharks.

Yes, a group of sharks is called a shiver. Or a frenzy. A school, too, but that's pretty tame. Or, a gam. That one makes *me* shiver, considering it's a synonym for leg and... Well, you get the point.

Dell focused in on her with a look I'd seen before from him.

Really, Dell?

"You're on TV, right?" asked bowl cut.

"I am, now and then," Dell said with believable but false modesty. Along with counting no shy bones in his body he also counted no modest ones.

"That must mean you're not used to being around everyday people." Elaine couldn't have been more obvious if she'd handed Dell a card that said, "Your next line is: *I'm certainly not around an ordinary person now because you are clearly extraordinary.*"

No way this woman had ever had a female friend in her life.

Also, she didn't know Wardell Yardley.

"You are correct," he said. "I am rarely around everyday people."

"Don't you like everyday Americans?" Receding Hairline demanded, trying to put Dell on the defensive.

Good luck, kid.

"I do my best to avoid ordinary people of any nationality. Everyday Americans? No way. Why do you think I work in Washington?"

"You're saying we're not as a good as—"

"You're not." The collective sucked-in breath should have pulled Dell off his feet. But he was in his element. "Not as good at breaking laws. Not as good at creating scandals. Not as good at making news." He grinned crookedly, inviting them all in to his world. "Not as good at raising ratings. No, you're definitely not as good as the people I cover."

Elaine snatched the punchline away before Dell could deliver it. "Because we're better people."

She smirked, looking up at him through her eyelashes.

Before I could get a reading on Dell's reaction, the two genuine outdoorsy couples turned and walked through the group, dispensing disgusted looks universally as they headed toward the parking lot.

The older woman said, "People come out here to enjoy the wildlife, to experience nature, not to listen to your big mouths."

"So look at the stupid, smelly animals. Nobody's stopping you," Elaine snapped.

"We are looking at stupid." The younger man's pointed gaze swept over the young group, the gray-haired couple, then Dell, Mike, and me.

The RA guy laughed, which drew a glare from Elaine.

I looked over my shoulder and realized the elk—the bull and the females—were gone. I had missed their departure, my attention grabbed by the human herd.

Chapter Six

"COUNT ON YOU to find a place like this in Yellowstone Park," I said to Dell as we started into the wide entryway at Lake Yellowstone Hotel.

You hear Yellowstone Park and you think lodge, lots of wood, dark colors. Lake Yellowstone Hotel was a rambling Colonialish structure with porticoes.

"No need to rough it in order to take in nature," Dell said.

But by that time Mike and I had both come to a complete stop.

"What's all this?" I asked.

"What's all what?" Dell looked around, apparently unable to see posters plastered with the VisageTome logo clustered in the lobby and strategically placed at each intersection of corridors.

That logo was everywhere. Not just in this hotel, but in the world.

VisageTome had risen at a dizzying pace among social media platforms in the past few years. Everyone had a "Leaf" in "The Tome." Some were basic, some were gilt-edged, either way, they connected with family, friends, mates, colleagues, and employers. VisageTome's advantage was rolling functions previously dispensed separately into one package.

You started with a free account, but once your community was established and you didn't want to lose it, you had to pay. Like several of its brethren, this burgeoning social media company was doing its best to take over the world.

A hostile takeover in my opinion.

"Looks like there's something going on with VisageTome here,"

Mike said.

"Huh," Dell grunted in would-be surprise.

I groaned.

"What?" Mike asked me.

"He's up to something."

"I got us into this warm and presumably comfortable hotel when all the lodging in Yellowstone has officially closed for the season, didn't I? Or, my assistant said—"

"*How* did you—or was it your assistant—get us into this hotel?"

Dell ignored my questions and sailed on. "—we could camp. *Camp.*"

He shuddered before continuing.

"Or, we could have driven another three and a half hours to Jackson Hole and stayed at one of the big hotels there."

Mike shuddered.

"Exactly," Dell said. "On top of all the driving you've done today. Yet Elizabeth would have had you push on."

"Mike was shuddering at the idea of big, posh hotel," I told him. "So, exactly what did you do, Dell?"

"Seems like everywhere you turn there's something to break," Mike muttered.

"I don't know why you would think—"

"Give it up, Dell." I turned to Mike. "I'll bet you a drink he told them we were covering VisageTome. Bet?"

"They'd believe we were covering when we don't have a camera crew or—"

"You're overthinking it. So settle the bet, Dell. What did you do to get us in here?"

"I didn't agree—" Mike tried.

"I might have let them think we were part of the VisageTome group."

"Part of... Good grief. That's *worse* than I thought."

"You lose the bet," Mike said.

"You didn't agree." After that quick aside, I focused on Dell. "How do you expect to pull that off? They're going to know we're not with VisageTome."

"How would the hotel people know? Nobody's checking IDs. Hotel people will think we're with VisageTome, VisageTome folks will think we're walk-ins. It's only three nights."

"Getting the bill straightened out will be a pain."

"Hmm."

"Dell, we are *not* riding on VisageTome's financial coattails. I will personally out you for this little escapade to the New York Times, Washington Post, and CNN. You would never live it down, much less be able to report a story on VisageTome."

"These people do not come to the White House."

"Facebook's Mark Zuckerberg has been there." Both Dell and I looked at Mike after that contribution. "What? I know more than scores, you know."

"Yes, I do know. I didn't expect that to be one of the things you knew, however." I returned to my point. "We're paying our own way, Dell. That's final."

"Fine. Can we check in now? You could be a little grateful we're not camping."

I WAS THE first downstairs.

The bar was clogged, mostly with young males. A few had taken seats in groupings of chairs and loveseats near where a man valiantly played soft piano music against the rising voices of a dispute in a language that sounded like English but wasn't.

It was Tech Talk.

I wandered away from the noise, taking in the empty sunroom. With daylight gone, its windows showed only darkness. I kept going and had a view down a wide, open alley between two sections of the dining room.

At a distant table sat three uniformed employees, apparently finishing their dinners.

A guy approached them. I recognized him as one of the non-outdoors guys from the elk bugling incident this afternoon. The one with the retreating hairline and the smirk.

"Are you ladies on VisageTome?" He put his hands on the table and leaned in.

The closest girl turned away, wrinkling her nose.

"I'm unveiling the new feature you're all going to be using on VisageTome next year." He clearly expected that to impress.

With their heads down, but exchanging covert glances, the girls said nothing.

"I could give you a preview if you're nice to me."

"We've got to get back to work," one said.

They stood, picked up their plates and headed toward the kitchen. So did the smirker, talking all the while. One of the girls moved ahead fast, entering the kitchen.

Before the other two and the smirker reached the door, a guy came out of it with the first girl hovering in the background.

The kitchen guy didn't say a word, just stood there. The smirker stopped, the girls kept going into the kitchen.

I continued, heading out to a porch sheltered from most of the wind, though not the cold. With light from inside reaching this spot, the night sky put on a show.

Wyoming skies have wowed me before, but this one benefited from inky darkness possible only with minimal imposition of civilization. It also had the silky ripples of the lake reflecting it back. A sky in motion that slid from rhythmic to syncopated as the wind furled the water.

A woman's harsh whisper sliced into my awareness.

"—and I'll do what I said I would."

"I have no idea—" It was a man's voice. Regular volume.

They were at the end of the porch, past where a light was out, making them darker patches against the night. A solitary glowing dot provided the best guess to their positions.

"I'll leave the money, then you leave—" The harsh whisper from the woman swallowed words. "—forever."

"—what you're talking about."

Her voice rose. "Why are you doing this? You said—"

"I don't know anything about this. I never said anything to you. I have no interest in any of you. None. I made that clear."

He turned and started toward me.

"You can't—" The woman's voice broke off, most likely when she spotted me.

She must have retreated, because in a second there was only the normal darkness where they'd been.

As he neared, I saw it was the older guy from that group at the elk bugling. The one I had thought of as the resident assistant to their geeky undergrad-ness.

He shifted his left arm behind him. Too late. I'd seen the cigarette. Not to mention the smoke trailing lightly over his shoulder. His right hand held a glass of red wine, which he made no effort to hide.

"Good evening," I said.

He looked toward me, then toward the door beyond which, presumably, he saw his fellow VisageTomers gathered around the bar.

He released a short, somewhat disgusted breath, and leaned against the nearest pole.

"I know," he said. Was he going to bring up the odd exchange I'd heard? "Who smokes in a wilderness area?"

"Someone who can't shake the habit."

He huffed. "Actually, I had. Until this trip."

"You're supposed to relax in nature, not get more stressed."

"Yeah. Until someone has a great idea… Dysfunctional, but brilliant."

"You're not a fan of VisageTome sending its staff to the wilderness?"

"Oh, that. That's survivable with a good dose of humor and cabernet sauvignon." He drew in for a long moment, expelled it strongly, dropped the butt to the porch floor then ground it out thoroughly with his heel. "Ready for the next round."

He was halfway to the door when he turned back, a silhouette against the interior lights. "I'd appreciate it if you didn't tell the rat pack about the smoking."

"Unless you start a forest fire, it's between you and your lungs."

He nodded a quick thanks and was inside.

After a deep lungful myself of non-nicotined air, I followed more slowly.

"Finally," Dell said when I joined them in the lobby. But I could tell he was in a much better mood.

"I've already toured this floor and been outside to enjoy the night life. How are your rooms?"

"Nice," Mike said, which I took to mean potential breakables were kept to a minimum.

"Acceptable, considering the alternative was camping," Dell said.

I couldn't resist poking at him. "Does that mean you didn't un-make the bed?"

Mike required an explanation.

"It's an ordinary precaution to pull down the bedspread," Dell maintained.

"What happened to the Wardell 'Wild Thing' Yardley I once knew and loved?"

"He learned to value his health and cleanliness. It appears that they have begun seating people for dinner. We don't want to be late—"

"Or they might realize we're not part of VisageTome," I said under my breath.

Dell gestured me to precede him, but I didn't miss his grin. He did love getting away with things.

Chapter Seven

AFTER DINNER, EATEN at a table Dell chose because it straddled the murky line between being part of the VisageTome group or outside it, we were standing to leave as a large group of VisageTomers who'd been seated farther into the room came past.

"Hey. You're that guy."

It was Elaine making that announcement to Dell. She stood directly in front of him in the wide aisle through the dining room, taking an almost aggressive stance. Certainly her tone was meant to draw attention.

Mike and I exchanged a look. Yup. He, too, would have preferred to leave the dining room without being noticed.

But it didn't seem to bother Dell.

Looking around, I spotted several of the non-outdoors guys who'd been with her this afternoon among a wider fraternity of similar males. A few females were sprinkled through the larger group, which streamed around our island.

"I am," Dell said with a smile that only someone who didn't know him would consider self-deprecating.

"You're famous or something."

"I'm famous *and* something."

Elaine giggled. Nope. She'd never had a female friend in her life.

"And you were that woman all those people got pissed at."

That announcement came from the smirker with the receding hairline. Kelvin, that's what the adult had called him. I thought he was referring to Elaine until I realized he was looking at me.

Now everyone turned toward me.

"Those people out at that place who got all excited about ... something," the guy said.

Yeah, that was precise.

Before I had to come up with a response, Elaine said, "About that moose trumpeting, you moron."

"Elk. Bugling," said the one I thought of as the resident assistant.

She glared at him. "Who cares."

Some people don't like being wrong, whether they find it out themselves or someone else calls them on it. For them, it's the inaccuracy that's the offense.

Other people have no problem with being wrong as long as no one catches them at it. For them, it's the reminder of fallibility that's the offense.

Taking a wild guess here, but Elaine came out of Door Number 2.

"You don't care because it's not all about you," said the smirker. "When the topic's you it's fine with you if the talk goes by way of Altoona."

For half a breath I thought she would launch herself at him. Instead, she said, "Another of your stupid sayings nobody understands."

Now he seemed prepared to launch himself at her.

Dell prevented that by stepping between them, extending his hand to her, and saying, "Wardell Yardley."

"Elaine Malsung."

Neither bothered to widen the introductions.

Mike was the one who asked the group of guys, "What are you all doing here?"

"Team building." That was the bootcamp super-short haircut guy. He couldn't have sounded more morose if he'd said "Pre-Execution Protocol."

"We have a meeting now. But I'll be in the bar afterward." Elaine directed that information to Dell only.

"We have to get up early tomorrow for the tours," said the bowl cut.

She didn't even blink in his direction. She kept looking at Dell. It struck me as less sexy than predatory. Maybe it was all the wildlife around us that had me thinking in those terms.

"I'll remember that," Dell said.

"Let's go. Now," ordered the cigarette smoker from the porch. He was across the lobby, impatiently waiting.

"God, Justice is on our case again," muttered peekaboo bald spot. If he raised his head the spot wouldn't be as visible, but he kept his focus on the floor. "What's with him?"

No one responded.

Elaine strutted off, the others following.

Mike, Dell, and I got drinks—yes, I paid for Mike's—and took seats not far from the now-deserted piano and settled back comfortably.

"This is so peaceful and—"

My phone interrupted me by ringing.

"Ah-hah! Connection." Dell crowed. He immediately pulled out his phone and headed a short distance away. I don't know if he'd had it in his pocket from optimism or habit.

"Actually," Mike said in a quick, low voice, "they added cell service and internet to this hotel a while back. I thought you'd rather Dell didn't know."

I grinned at him as I went in the opposite direction to answer my call—from Mel—on the third ring.

"I've been trying to reach you," he gently complained.

"I'm at Yellowstone," I reminded him. "Not a bastion of connectivity."

I agreed with Mike. The fewer people who knew we were reachable the better.

"Oh. Right. Well, I wanted to let you know, you're off that story on the bed and breakfast."

"I was never on the story, Mel. And if they think I'm going to do it when I come back—"

"They don't. That's all settled. Here's the proposed new language."

He read me a long paragraph packed with legal language. I wasn't sure I had it all, and he agreed to email me a copy.

"It sounds good, but how did you pull this off, Mel?"

"I pointed out that your effectiveness with the crime stories and special reports you've done would be greatly diminished if your authority is diluted by, ahem, puff pieces. They have enjoyed the enhanced status of the station as a result of your reporting. They wouldn't want to lose that."

"Way to go, Mel. Hit them in the ego."

He chuckled with satisfaction. "I must go now, though. We have an early morning. By the way, we're going to see your parents in the afternoon. Anything you'd like me to tell them?"

"Just that I'm working on another murder case."

"You *are*—? But you know I can't tell them."

I laughed at his initial excitement so quickly drowned out by the well-known Fear of Overprotective Parental Units. That fear is on many people's Most Scary lists, ranking above spiders and below public speaking. But for those who dealt with Catherine Danniher, it was a clear No. 1.

"Oh. Not funny, Danny. Decidedly not funny. But are you really—?"

"No, Mel. I was joking."

"Definitely not funny."

But we were both chuckling when we disconnected.

COMING BACK INTO the main lobby, I spotted Mike out on the porch, about where I'd stood earlier with the VisageTome closet cigarette smoker whose name—first or last?—apparently was Justice.

Dell was halfway down the hall where the VisageTome people had gone, separating into a number of rooms on either side.

He saw me looking his way and tried to look innocent.

He failed.

I headed for him.

I could see he wasn't pleased to have my company and he could see I was coming anyhow. He gestured with palms patting down the air in front of him, ordering me to tread lightly. I complied.

The door to a room a bit farther down the hall was partially open and voices could be heard coming from it.

Dell pointed.

Not at the door, but at a mirror above a side table on the opposite side of the hall. The mirror showed a slice of the room.

It took me a moment to realize it was actually reflecting a reflection from inside the room. A mirror inside the room connecting to this one outside the room.

Dell couldn't possibly have planned this. But he'd found it. And he'd found it because he'd walked down the hall to see what there might be to see.

It was one of the things that made Wardell Yardley such a good reporter.

I heard a voice droning on about gigamadewsitz and alphabet soup. Shifting a bit I saw the reflected reflection of a guy standing by a screen, though I could only see a corner of it. It was the smirker who'd failed so completely earlier at trying to charm the three employees finishing their dinner.

At his age, a hairline that far back did not hold much promise for its golden years. Or next year. And he clearly didn't have the character to embrace his future.

His voice rose, apparently reaching the climax of his presentation.

"... so this will change VisageTome forever. It is without president." He spread his thin arms wide, as if expecting thunderous applause.

"That's wrong." Elaine Malsung sounded gleeful.

"Precedent. Not president," came the calm voice of the adult.

"That's what I said, Justice."

"No, it's not. You said president." I couldn't see Elaine from where I stood, but her tone had an eye-roll in it.

"Besides, it's written there." An arm cut across the view, apparently pointing toward something on the screen out of my view.

"Great. Fine. Precedent. Give me a break. Like there aren't more important things in the world. Don't you know terrorists are killing people and children are starving and people get shot all the time for no reason and you're up in arms about some *word*. Talk about screwed up. Screwed *up*. Your priorities are totally screwed up."

There was a half beat of silence. I shifted and got a view of Elaine sitting at a conference table beside the grown up named Justice.

Laid-back, almost bored, except for his eyes, he said slowly, "Gordon Kelvin, you're an asshole. A defensive asshole. Like what you're doing—what any of us are doing here—is going to cure terrorism and starvation? You're just pissed that you made an error and somebody pointed it out."

Bingo.

"It's not the freaking end of the world," Kelvin screamed. "How many other words were in this presentation and they were all right, but—"

"Actually—" Elaine subsided at a sharp gesture from Justice, but not with good grace. She pushed her chair back and slumped nearly out of my view.

"—you're ranting and obsessing like it's the end of the world."

"You're the only one ranting," Justice said calmly. "Elaine pointed out your error. Quit being a defensive asshole and fix it."

There certainly was nothing touchy-feely about Justice's management style. And I had my doubts that this was the recommended way to build a team.

"You're totally off the deep end. Frothing at the mouth. About one stupid word in the whole thing."

"Because it's a stupid mistake. Because it makes you look stupid. Because it's the last word of the presentation. Because you look like a moron. Because you *are* a moron. Next."

"Wait—what? What about my presentation? So I had one f'ing word wrong. The rest of it—"

"—was worthless. Unoriginal and uninspiring. Next."

"You can't—"

"I have. Shut up and sit down." He sat back, out of view.

At the same time, Elaine sat upright, into the center of my view again. I remember seeing a fox once that had spotted some chickens out in the open. It had the same expression as Elaine did now.

I'd hooted and hollered, startling the fox away—after it gave me a snarling glare. I rather wished I could do that now.

I LEFT THAT hallway and went out to join Mike, who'd taken a seat in a cozy alcove.

A few minutes later, Dell arrived.

"They got all technical about an algorithm." He sat on my other side. "Might have been a story in it, but I didn't understand a tenth of it. Hope I got enough to feed our tech guy and see if he can make heads or tails of it. Sure was boring after the fireworks ended."

"Fireworks?"

Dell filled Mike in, though only about the interpersonal wrangling. Nothing technical. That he was saving.

He'd nearly finished, when Mike's phone gave the alert that a text was coming in.

He read it and groaned.

"Sorry. I thought the lineup was straight for tomorrow's coverage of high school football, but a hole's developed. I've got to calm Pauly down and give him ideas for a stringer. This might take a while. See you at breakfast?"

We said goodnights and he went.

Dell and I sat in silence for a moment. I was aware of him studying me.

He said, "What's with you? That look. Is it because Mike disappeared?"

"Of course not. If I have any look at all, I suppose it's reflecting the atmosphere."

"The atmosphere? You mean the great outdoors? The fresh air and natural wonders? The—what did our Harvard Law School expert call them this afternoon?—great and noble beasts?"

"Also magnificent creatures. But I was thinking of the human animals."

"Ah. Well, at least there's one interesting one."

"Why do I have the feeling it's not her brain you find interesting?"

"Because you have the type of brain that can form such conclusions, which is why I find yours far more interesting. More's the pity. It condemns us to a lifetime of friendship."

"When we could have had a wild weekend fling instead? Thanks. I'll take the lifetime of friendship."

"You don't know what you're missing."

I grinned. But it faded quickly. "Seriously, Dell, can't you feel undercurrents here?"

"You've become so enamored of solving mysteries that you see them everywhere. I saw your reports. Where others thought accidents, you've proved murder."

"It's not for fun."

"Maybe not, but it's a mental challenge, which you've always liked. And you want to show that new sheriff that you are a force to be reckoned with. That you could run rings around him solving a murder, say one here at Lake Yellowstone Hotel."

"A murder here would be handled first by the rangers with assistance from an FBI agent assigned to the park. Plus they have mutual support agreements with surrounding jurisdictions, but Cottonwood County is not among them. And on top of all that, we're in the Lake District, which would almost certainly call on law enforcement from Teton County."

"Good God, you've got it worse than I thought. You're becoming obsessed."

"It was in research material Mrs. P—that's the former schoolteacher I told you about—gave me for this trip."

"And there among the lore on elk and buffalo—"

"Bison."

"—you managed to find out how a murder would be handled in Yellowstone. But there's not even an accident this time, Elizabeth. Nobody's dead. Simply a bunch of ambitious, geeky guys spinning around one female. Whom I'm about to sweep away from under their noses." He grinned devilishly. Then he cocked his head. "If that sound is what I think it is, they're pouring out of their meeting rooms, and Elaine is looking for the incomparable Wardell Yardley. Sure you don't want to come watch the dance?"

"Thanks, but no thanks. I've seen that circus before. Think I'll go to bed. Early morning tomorrow, remember. Lots more elk and bison to see."

SATURDAY

Chapter Eight

WE WERE ON our way to see Fort Yellowstone and the other historic sites I'd been denied the day before. The guys were metaphorically dragging their feet.

"Oh, look." Dell pointed to dark, lumpish shapes congregating at the lower edge of a hillside. "We could pull over and—"

Mike kept driving. "Nah. There are better things to see."

Dell looked out his side window, keeping his gaze on the creatures as we rolled past. "What have you got against buffalo?"

"Bison," Mike and I said together.

Then Mike continued solo. "Skinny legs, oversized, barrel chests, big ugly heads. They drool and spit, their coats are always molting, like a shaggy snake. They make this grumbly noise. They don't smell good and neither do the bison pies they leave."

"They're a powerful and beloved image of our American West," I quoted Emmaline Parens. "What's not to love?"

"They can sprint three times faster than you can run and they have horns. What's *to* love?"

"Are you sure this isn't a carryover from your NFL days and playing the Buffalo Bills?"

Mike grimaced. "I refuse to answer on the grounds that it might tend to incriminate me."

"I notice you didn't contradict Mrs. P to her face. Didn't dare."

Dell chuckled. Mike shot him a look. "Wait til you meet Mrs. P. As for you—" He made eye contact in the rearview mirror. "—you didn't fare real well with the new sheriff—"

"What does that have to do with—"

"—who made it clear Elizabeth's to stay out of law enforcement's business."

Dell shook his head. "I wish she would. She should be reporting national stories again, not these little murders."

"They're not little to the people who are murdered," I protested. "Or—"

"She'll go back to the big-time eventually," Mike said confidently.

"—the suspects. Hey, who's the one who egged me on at the start? And who's been part of every one of these?"

"Yeah, but Dell's right. You belong back at the top of TV news. Maybe we'll move on together." He grinned into the mirror.

Dell pivoted to look at me. "A package deal? I could see a Chicago station pouncing on that."

I ignored him. "You've been all gung ho until now, Paycik."

"I'm not saying that if something came up I wouldn't be interested. But Sheriff Conrad isn't going to make it easy, that's for sure."

"Diana, the traitor," I mumbled. "She's been involved in these, too."

"Diana didn't say a word. I saw the raw footage. This sheriff's tough. Hey, this is more like it," he added, slowing the SUV to look at a park sign. "Norris Geyser Basin. We can take a short stop here."

"We saw geysers yesterday," I protested. "You promised we'd see Fort Yellowstone today."

He turned in anyway. "We didn't see *these* geothermal features yesterday. Plenty of time for old buildings. Did you know that more than half of the world's geysers are here in Yellowstone? All the other geysers in the world put together don't equal what Yellowstone has."

We swung our doors open and gulped in the fresh, bracing scent of rotten eggs.

"Phew. The rest of the world can have these," I complained.

"A little smell," Mike mocked. "C'mon."

Under the power of his enthusiasm, we followed a path that changed to a boardwalk. Eventually it opened to a circular area where we joined a group gathered around a ranger talking about early mountain man John Colter, a veteran of the Lewis and Clark Expedition, who had spent the winter of 1807-08 trapping in what was now southern Montana and northern Wyoming.

Apparently it was a parlor game among historians to map his possible route and declare whether he had or hadn't entered current-day Yellowstone Park.

"Earlier historians believed Colter's Hell—the name he gave to an area of geothermal features—was in Yellowstone but—"

"It's actually near Cody," Mike and I muttered to each other, parroting Mrs. P's teaching in time with the ranger saying the same thing.

"A few years later," the ranger continued without us as a chorus, "mountain man Jim Bridger came through here. His stories of streams that boiled and black glass mountains were scoffed at as tall tales until more and more accounts confirmed what he'd said."

Mrs. P would approve of this ranger. He was probably about the same age as the VisageTome crew, though with his robust build, tanned skin, and confident delivery, he seemed older.

Then he started in about how some of the geysers and their pools featured most un-spa-like hydrosulfuric acid, producing the not-so-calming rotten eggs scent. Oh, yes, and temperatures exceeded 200 degrees Fahrenheit and all the boiling water made the ground unstable.

Happy thoughts.

"Do not leave the boardwalks," he said sternly. "They are here for your safety."

A puff of smoky steam rose abruptly, making a dramatic backdrop.

"A guy went off the paths a few years ago and there wasn't anything left of him to recover," a man's voice said from behind us.

The ranger turned toward him. "A tragic accident. Don't let it happen to you. Stay on the boardwalks."

Certainly no one wandered off as the ranger began explaining how these stinky, steamy pools came to be.

My attention wandered a bit. Partly because I'm not a big fan of geology—layers of stones. Been here so long I can't get my mind around it. Seem solid, but doing tricky stuff that could suddenly eat part of the planet—but also because a dart of light drew my eyes across the way. Between bodies, I could see a phone being thumb-typed on, but people in front blocked my view of its holder.

Then a glimpse of someone caught my attention.

Somewhere in the depths of my mind, I thought the someone I'd glimpsed on the opposite side of the circle was familiar. But the figure was not only on the opposite side, but in the outer ring of the listeners. Masked by the people between us, I couldn't get a clear view.

"Down! Down" demanded a toddler sitting on his father's shoulders in the front row opposite me.

The man complied.

"Keep a tight hold on his hand," the ranger interrupted himself to say.

Everyone looked to see if the father was doing as instructed. That caused enough shifting that I had a new view of the people on the opposite side of the circle and spotted familiar faces from VisageTome—Justice the adult, Elaine, Gordon Kelvin, Peekaboo Bald Spot, Boot Camp, and Bowl Cut.

Could any of them be the possibly-glimpsed-and-recognized figure? It was a reasonable explanation. Was it the right one?

No.

The answer sounded in my head, fast, firm. But an answer without supporting explanation, no matter how fast and firm, isn't proof. It's gut. A good journalist needs two independent sources to confirm gut.

What happened next happened fast.

There was another shifting, though this seemed to come from the back of the group on the opposite side of the circle. I caught lateral movement from my right to left.

For a split second everything seemed to still, then Justice—the adult—went sideways to the left.

In the first heartbeat, I thought he'd fallen over. In the second, I thought he'd pushed someone, someone blocked from my view. Until I could see around people's legs that a form was down and—yes, the person was at least partially off the boardwalk.

"Out of the way," the ranger ordered, moving toward the action.

Others backed up to make way for him, revealing Justice on one knee, his other leg extended for balance, while he gripped the waist of Gordon Kelvin's jeans, half suspended over the ground past the boardwalk. It was a good thing the guy was skinny.

"I've got him. I've got him."

The ranger ignored that and kept going. He had to push past Elaine, who hadn't given way like everyone else. He gripped Kelvin around the torso, muffling the high, squeaky sounds from the VisageTomer, and dragged him back onto the boardwalk.

Without even losing his ranger hat. Impressive.

"You have to be more careful." The ranger spread his glare to all the VisageTome group, but brought it back home to Kelvin. "Horsing around out here can be dangerous."

"Horsing a—I didn't—Somebody pushed—It wasn't my fault. I know somebody—"

"Shut up," Justice said without heat.

"I'm telling you, somebody pu—"

"Quit being a whiny crybaby," Elaine said.

"I will as soon as you stop being a heartless bitch. I'm telling you—"

"We're going," Justice said to the ranger. His calm voice topped Kelvin's high, thin exclamations. He looked at his group. "Now."

After that, geology seemed even less interesting. At least to me.

Mike appeared to be having a fine time.

So was Dell. The man with the toddler had recognized him.

I ENJOYED THE historic sites. The guys were most taken with a pair of bear cub statues at the old post office that held the spot flanking the steps usually reserved for lions.

After lunch, we explored an area recovering from a forest fire, hiked for a view across a fabulous valley, and—yes—walked through more stinking, bubbling thermal features. Always staying on the boardwalks.

Returning to the hotel, we ate dinner like famished teenagers. Dell said he was going to his room to make phone calls, but would be back down later and see us then.

In other words, he was going to squeeze in work while the Vis-ageTome people were in their nightly meetings. And he'd see us if it suited Elaine.

I had no issue with him pursuing, ahem, his interests. It was Elaine I objected to.

I said as much to Mike as we strolled along a path near the lake, catching the last of the day's sun. With daylight's savings ending tonight, it was the latest in the day we'd see the sun for months and months.

"Look at the bright side," he said.

"Which is?"

"She doesn't want to spend time with us. You know how some-times a buddy finds a woman and she wants to hang out with the whole team? And you can't stand her, but you don't want to ruin it for your pal?"

"Not being a guy or on a team, I haven't experienced that."

"Okay, okay. But you get the gist."

"I get the gist. And you're right. That's definitely the bright side."

We enjoyed the rest of the walk, pointing things out to each other and sometimes standing in silence. And then it was dark with a completeness that caught us both by surprise.

Half-stumbling, chuckling, and warning each other about pitfalls, we made our way to the closest doors, rather than back to the main entrance. It was muddier, but it was faster.

"Phew. Not locked." Mike held the outer door for me.

Entering the area between the outer doors and glass inner set, I could see all the way down the long corridor. It was the one where the VT people were meeting and was unoccupied except for one woman, who appeared to be bending over a closed trash can.

She didn't wear a hotel uniform. In fact, she had on a full-length coat, with the collar pulled up. Below the hem showed something I hadn't seen at Yellowstone—nylons and heels.

Mike pulled open the inner door, which gave a discreet groan.

The woman's head came up, then she froze. She looked behind her, where people were emerging from a meeting room closer to the lobby, then straightened and started walking toward us.

As we passed her, I did a double take.

My first instinct was to pretend I hadn't recognized her. She'd certainly given no indication of recognizing me.

Maybe I only *thought* I'd recognized her. After all, she had the collar of that coat up, revealing only a slice of her face. A large part of me hoped I hadn't.

But two things spurred me to not let her pass.

The first was the impression that she was awfully eager to not let me get a full view of her face.

I stopped and said, "Bunny?"

Mike looked around. "A rabbit? Inside?"

I whacked his arm in passing as I turned and caught up with the woman. She didn't look toward me until I had passed, turned, and stopped in front of her, forcing her to halt not far from the double set of doors to outside.

"Bunny Ramsey? It *is* you. I thought… Hi."

Her face went white.

I have that effect on some people. I didn't expect it, though, from someone I used to play with as little more than a toddler.

Then she'd favored Barbies. Now she looked like one. From the frosted hair, right down to the feet deformed in order to wear high heels.

"Elizabeth Margaret Danniher," I said with a hand on my chest. "Catherine and James' daughter. From Maple Street."

"Oh. Yes. How nice to see you." Could anyone have meant those words less? "You used to be on TV."

"I'm still on TV."

"Are you? I don't see you anymore."

"That's because you don't live in Wyoming."

She stared at me uncomprehendingly. "Of course I don't."

"But you're here now." That drew another blank stare. "Here in Yellowstone Park, I mean."

"You said Wyoming."

"Yes, it's—Never mind." I indicated Mike, who had joined us.

"This is Michael Paycik, a friend and colleague. Mike, this is Bunny Ramsey from Maple Street and—"

"Sterakos."

That sounded vaguely familiar. From deep, deep in my memory vaults a fragment of conversation in my mother's voice seemed to float to me. Something about Bunny getting married while I was still in college. "A real catch. All sorts of money."

Was that Sterakos? Or was she minted as Mrs. Bunny Sterakos more recently?

Some of the color had come back into her face, though she still wasn't operating at full mental capacity.

I based that on the fact that she'd glanced at Mike as if he were a potted plant.

Women don't look at Mike Paycik that way. At least not women who like men. And if I recalled correctly, Bunny Ramsey had liked males from a remarkably young age.

"It's Bunny Sterakos now," she said. "Mrs. Sterakos."

It's too bad she couldn't have gotten it worked in to the marriage ceremony that her first name changed, too. Because Bunny was her legal name, not a nickname. Even as a kid I'd thought it was weird.

"But what's her dad call her?" I'd asked my mom, thinking of how my dad inverted my names and called me Maggie Liz, and how special that always made me feel. "Rabbit?"

My dad had sputtered a laugh. Mom scolded us both and ordered me never to share that with any of my friends. I think I held out until sixth grade, when the raging hormones of puberty simultaneously unlock the lips and drain the pool of compassion.

She was known as Rabbit for the next three years. Then her hormones settled in to a comely order well before most of the rest of us and she began her string of Misses and Queens. Miss Cornfest, Homecoming Queen, Miss County Fair, Watermelon Day Queen. You name it, she had a tiara for it.

All that hardware gave her the clout to insist on being called Bunny. At least to her face.

"Pleased to meet any friend of Elizabeth's," Mike said. "So you knew her as a kid? What was she like?"

She blinked at him twice, looked at me for a moment, then back to him. "Difficult."

He chuckled.

I could have told him Bunny Ramsey had never had a sense of humor and I saw no sign that adding Sterakos to her name had changed that. She'd meant it literally.

Clearly she held a grudge, because a few of her Barbies were mussed up in the making of dashing, globe-spanning stories of adventure and heroism. A totally acceptable sacrifice.

"What are you doing here, Bunny?"

She looked around vaguely. "To see, uh, nature."

"Were you out at the geyser today, Bunny?

And that was the second reason I hadn't let her pass by without stopping her.

Could *she* have been the tantalizingly familiar, but unidentified figure who'd been there—who I thought might have been there— before Gordon Kelvin nearly took a tumble into the Instant Stew You waters.

It made a kind of sense. My brain could have registered her as someone I knew, yet not picked her out because it had been so long since I'd seen her and it was such an incongruent setting.

"No," she said abruptly. "I'm sorry, Elizabeth, but I have a … an appointment. I have to go now."

"If you're staying through the weekend, I'm sure we'll see each other again. Perhaps we can have a meal together, catch up…"

"Perhaps. Good-night."

"Where are you staying? Or give me your cell—"

"Have to go."

She was off quickly enough that the good-nights from Mike and me echoed after her departing back.

"You recognized her out at the Geyser today, but didn't say any-thing?" Mike asked as we passed the once again cracked open door to the Elaine & Co. group's meeting room. No sound came from it or any of the still-closed doors.

"Not really. I had the feeling I'd recognized *somebody*, but it was too fast to be sure, and I didn't know who."

He looked puzzled. "You were close friends?"

"No."

"You seemed awfully eager to see her again."

"Only because she wasn't."

"That makes sense to you?"

"Yup."

What didn't make sense was Bunny going out those doors to that rough track in those heels.

Chapter Nine

MIKE AND I returned to the lobby simultaneously, having gone to our rooms to change into shoes that weren't dragging half of Yellowstone Park along with us.

Dell and Elaine were at the bar along with maybe another two dozen VisageTome people.

They'd just come out of their meetings, yet a stunted forest of shot glasses already littered the bar top. The besieged bartender tried to retrieve them, even as calls for more came from three directions.

Mike and I settled into a seating area nearby.

Almost immediately, Gordon Kelvin came over carrying a bottle of tequila and trailing half a dozen other guys, who seemed drawn to the bottle, rather than the company.

When he sat on the table in front of us, the others landed in chairs nearby, some reaching for the bottle. He curled his arm into his body to protect it.

"I almost died today. Didja hear about it?"

"We were there," Mike said.

"Glad you're okay," I added.

"Okay? *Okay?* I'm not okay. I nearly died."

"Have another drink," advised Peekaboo Baldspot. At least that's what I think he said, since he was in his usual head-down and hand-twitching mode.

"Shut up, Nelson," Kelvin said, apparently picking up Elaine's role in her absence.

"Or let us have another drink, not with that stuff that knocks out girls." Bowl Cut snatched the bottle away from him to laughter.

"Yeah, take a dose of that stuff you brought back from Mexico so we can stop hearing about this," muttered the guy with the super-short haircut. He had a long, narrow face, with a particularly long chin.

Kelvin dove for the bottle. "Give it here, Hart."

Hart of the Bowl Cut held it aloft, then drank. "To VisageTome. The home of the open exchange of ideas for the planet."

The response mixed celebration with grumbles.

"It's a great place to work. Great, great, great place," Hart said. "They brought us here, didn't they?"

I caught mumbles, but not enough to form a full, meaningful sentence.

"No place better." Kelvin lunged and grabbed the bottle back. Seventh-eighths was gone. "To the open exchange of ideas." He put the bottle to his mouth, tipped it up and his head back, and made a dent in the final eighth.

I snorted.

"You got something to say?" Gordon Kelvin demanded of me belligerently.

"Open exchange of ideas? Customers have to pay you before the expression of their ideas can reach the people who have signed up saying they *want* to hear them. As long as they pay, VT has no problem with what is spouted, much of which has nothing to do with ideas."

Long-faced Nelson of the super-short cut started in a bored voice, "We have guidelines and Terms of Service that—"

"That don't do a darned thing. Not about the serious abuses. Want to do a search and see how many times VisageTome and murder come up together? Because someone's used your platform to lure a victim despite—and this will shock you—the fact that doing so might break the Terms of Service."

"We're not responsible—"

"No, you're not. You're irresponsible."

"—for what people choose to do on our platform any more than a highway is for a bad driver who causes a crash."

"If that highway is a for-profit toll road and lets people drive as fast as they want or purposefully hit other cars or car jack or any of a thousand other things, the administrators of that highway sure as heck have a responsibility. VisageTome certainly has proved capable and eager to police whether people pay, but not whether they're using your platform to prey on others. Sounds like you need to tweek your algorithms."

They hooted at that. "Algorithms are to make money. Can't waste algos on customers."

Why didn't it feel better to have my suspicions about VisageTome confirmed?

"The least you could do would be to offer a real customer service department. A—"

"We do," Hart said.

"—phone number. Someone to answer it."

"You email and we—"

"Never answer. I know. Or it's answered by sadists who repeat the same canned script over and over no matter how little it has to do with what the user's actually asked."

Gordon Kelvin chortled. Honest to God chortled.

I glared at him. "You think it's funny?"

"I think it's hilarious. Pathetic little people whining to us all day, every day about how this is screwed up and that is broken and none of it makes sense. Like *we* have to make sense to them. We're *VisageTome*. We don't need them, they need us. Demanding we fix things or they'll leave? Right. Like that will happen. Damn right it's hilarious when we get a chance to mess with their minds."

The others were giggling or grinning.

Someone from the other side of the group said, "Messing with accounts and ads."

Without acknowledging the source, Kelvin said, "Not to mention messing with their accounts. I can get into anyone's account any time. And they won't even know it."

"*You?*" The sharp scoff came from Nelson. Muffled because he had his head down. Of course.

"They can't figure out a damned thing. Makes people run around screaming. Total panic hysterics like girls in a slasher movie. It's the best damned job perk there is and we get a ton of them, along with making a shitload of money. You're all jealous."

"Jealous of you?" Mike said. "Listen you little twerp, this woman has interviewed presidents and ambassadors and prime ministers and—

Kelvin laughed, which ended in a belch. "Oh, you think they're better than us? Shows how little you know. Those guys—those presidents and ambassadors and shit, they think they have power? No way. *We* have the real power."

"She interviewed presidents?" demanded one of the guys on Mike's other side. Mike turned toward him.

Kelvin kept going. "They have nothing. Because we have the data. All the data." He sounded exactly like my nephew, who as a toddler would grab a toy away from his little sister and exult, "Toy mine. Toy mine."

"Oh, yeah," I said, "the much-touted big data—you all love big data and you cannot lie."

"What the f—does that mean?" He gave me the you're-as-crazy-as-you-are-old side-eye, clearly not getting the reference. "We love our data all right. And it's not all big, randomized. We know shit *you* can only dream about. About every one of you." He smirked. Smug and self-satisfied. "All sorts of shit. We can ruin your life. All your lives."

He gestured widely with the bottle.

I'm no expert, but he seemed to me to have reached the throwing up stage. And I was sitting directly across from him.

I stood. "Good for you," I said placatingly.

At the same time, I tapped Mike on the shoulder. He appeared to be in meaningful conversation, though somehow it had shifted from presidents to weak-side draws. Count on Mike to find a tech geek who loved football.

"I'm going out for some non-tequila scented air," I said to him. With a significant look toward Gordon Kelvin, I added under my breath, "Beware projectile vomiting."

✧   ✧   ✧   ✧

OUTSIDE THE AIR was evergreen-scented and cut to the bone. I drew my sweater tighter around me. Caught in the porch lights, mist swirled erratically past the roof. I shut the door on the tequila-fueled noise behind me.

When my eyes adjusted, I saw Justice back in the same spot as last night, cigarette in one hand, glass of red wine in the other.

He hadn't turned when I came out and I could have walked past.

I didn't.

"Do you mind company?"

He flicked me a look. "No."

"I'm Elizabeth Margaret Danniher."

"Darryl Justice." He shifted the wine glass to his left hand with the cigarette and we shook.

"That was frightening this afternoon," I said.

He turned to me with blankness in his eyes.

"At the Norris Basin Geyser."

"Oh. That. Scary? For you?" He actually sounded slightly curious.

"Well, scary for everyone. When your, uh, coworker almost went over. Scariest for him of course."

Slowly, he said, "Oh. Yeah. When Kelvin almost went over."

He breathed in and out, in and out, in and out. Then seemed to remember I was there, glancing toward me and shifting his feet.

I said, "If you hadn't reacted so quickly, it could have been a whole lot worse."

"No big deal. What could have been really scary was if I'd done this—" He held up the cigarette, nodding toward the glowing tip. "—out there. There's sulfur right under the surface in a lot of those thermal areas. If they catch fire, the fumes can kill you."

"Not a pleasant thought." I didn't remember the ranger talking about that, but I couldn't swear I'd listened to every word.

After a pause I tried another tack. "Interesting group you've got here."

"Each one of them smarter than the next in their specialties."

"Which are?"

"Landon Hart and Gordon Kelvin algorithms. Brant Nelson security. Alan Varney big data. Elaine Malsung end-user behaviors. If they'd work together, they could serve end-users. Or they could manipulate the hell out of them. Depending on what task they were given."

"But all that's if they work together?"

"Yeah. That's the problem, isn't it?" He stubbed out his cigarette on the pole and flicked it into the grass.

I doubted Smokey the Bear would have approved, but considering the mist it probably wasn't an issue.

He nodded, said good night, then went past me and inside.

That wasn't an issue, either. Yet I couldn't shake the feeling that *something* was an issue.

The sound of the door opening again made me realize I'd been staring into the mist without a conscious thought for some time. Also that the tip of my nose had gone numb.

Wardell Yardley came over to me. "Mike and I were wondering where you got to."

"I thought you were fully occupied with Elaine."

"She had to do something for a presentation tomorrow. Apparently she's a finalist for this elimination bracket of presentations."

"Huh."

Only when he said "Penny for 'em, Danniher," did I realize I'd lapsed into silence.

"Wish I could collect, but I have no idea what I was thinking."

"Okay, then tell me what the hell you were thinking to agree to stay here in the wilds of Wyoming?"

"I agreed to stay in Sherman, not here in Yellowstone Park," I protested.

"Same difference. Wilds. Wyoming."

"It's only six months at a time, either side can opt out then."

"I don't care if it was for six minutes. What were you thinking?"

I looked back to the mist. "Maybe about that."

"What? Darkness?"

"The unknown. Maybe the magical unknown. Isn't that what the future is? The magical unknown."

"Yours sure is. Unknown, anyway. And it didn't have to be." He held up a hand to stop me from replying. "I'm not arguing that there's not some appeal. If I batted for the other team, I'd be all over your swain Michael."

"He's not—"

"If he's not, it's not because he doesn't want to be."

I had nothing to say to that.

"Is it the cowboy?" he asked abruptly.

"What makes you think—? He's not—" It was like trying to stop after I'd already crashed into the other car. Useless. "A cowboy," I finished lamely. "He owns a ranch. And the road construction company. And there's nothing between us."

Not that would make me stay in Cottonwood County.

Though, yes, there was chemistry.

As there was chemistry with Mike.

Sometimes I felt like one of those science experiments where magnets are pulling an object opposite directions at the same time. Scooting a bit this way, then being tugged the other. Possibly until it's pulled in two by the force.

"He's not your type, Elizabeth."

"How can you know that? First, I don't have a type."

"Little Lord Fauntleroy."

I ignored that reference to my ex and kept going with my protest, "Second, you don't know him. Either of them."

"I'm getting to know Mike. And you could remedy that situation with the cowboy when we get back to Outer Podunk. Perhaps by having another gathering where you do not purposely seat us at opposite ends of the table."

"I did not purposely—It made more sense for you to get to know Mike before this trip and you needed to get to know Clara for the story. Besides, third, is that there's nothing between me and anyone. Not here. Not anywhere."

"Then I come back to, why are you staying?"

"It's interesting, Dell. I have time. Unlike anywhere else. You know how it always is, rushing from one assignment to the next, always thinking you could have given that package a little more polish if you'd had more time."

"Mine are always perfect. Speak for yourself."

He kept a perfectly straight face when I grimaced at him. I continued my explanation. "I have time here. I'll admit I don't devote all of it to 'Helping Out!'—"

"Because you keep finding dead bodies. What is that, Danny?"

"I don't know."

"And it doesn't bother you?"

"They're stories, Dell."

"I'm not so sure."

I groaned. "Now you sound like the new sheriff, accusing me of trying to take over his job."

"Are you?"

"No way."

"What?" His demand was sharp enough that I jolted a bit.

"What what?"

"You went away there for a moment. What were you thinking that time?"

"I was thinking about that episode at the geyser."

"That idiot nearly going in because he was trying to be so cool?"

"He said he wasn't. He said he was pushed."

Dell rolled his eyes. You have not been eye-rolled until you've been eye-rolled by Wardell Yardley. "Sure he did. Self-aggrandizing, immature jerk."

He had a point. A good point. The guy was an attention seeker. And yet...

"You didn't get any sense out there today of something ... weird?"

"Only you. You're making mysteries where there aren't any. All the free time that rinky-dink station is giving you is going to your head."

I chuckled. Mostly because he wanted me to.

"Elizabeth," he said in a new tone. "How much did all this hurt you? Really?"

"A lot."

"Wes or the job?"

"They're rather bound together. Those first months… But I've been better lately. Maybe," I said slowly, finding the words as I went, "better than I've been in a long, long time."

The door opened again. It was Elaine.

"Dell. I want that drink now. Upstairs." Her tone was just short of rude. The fact that she gave no sign that my existence was worth noting went well past rude.

"And you will get it," he said to her smoothly. Then he turned to me and winked.

Yup, I was enough of one of the guys to be included in the Dell's-gonna-get-lucky-tonight inside scoop.

SUNDAY

Chapter Ten

SUNDAY MORNING, I saw no sign of Mike or Dell when I came downstairs.

I had zonked out the moment my head hit the pillow and slept straight through, even with the extra hour of sleep from the end of Daylight Savings overnight. They should combine chilled fresh air with a dose of hiking and sell it as a sleep aid.

That chilled fresh air and dose of hiking could also be used as an appetite stimulant.

I took a seat at what I was coming to think of as our table, then went to a buffet station for eggs, bacon, and melon.

When I returned, five VisageTome guys had pulled up chairs to the table and were deep in conversation.

They'd left my place empty, so I slid into it without comment. It couldn't hurt our cover.

None of these people appeared to be tuned in to the oddness of Dell, Mike, and me being part of their group for meals, but not their meetings or outings. Better not to do anything that might cause that to change.

One guy—Varney, they'd said his name was—moved his elbow so I could put down my plate.

Gallantry is not dead.

Two sniffed in the scents of my breakfast and immediately left to fill their own plates. The other three reacted more slowly but also got some breakfast.

All the while, the multi-sided debate went on.

I ate breakfast amid a barrage of terms like SoLoMo, deflection rate, competitor sentiment, SOV, and creep. Eventually, I concluded they were talking about something to do with algorithms and brand-jacking. That was specific enough for me.

Mike showed up with a quizzical look, went through the buffet, and sat at the next table over. Dell joined him shortly.

I stayed where I was until they got up to leave.

As I stood, one the VT guys I hadn't seen before said to me, "Good input, man. See you later."

You can't ask for more than that from a breakfast meeting.

MIKE GOT TO see a bear Sunday, which was appropriate, because he kept trying to get connected to check the Bears' game.

As we observed the animal from a good distance, Mike chatted on about bear-human interaction being harmful … to the bears.

"They start thinking humans are the source for food," he said. "Once they do that, they're not going to give up trying to get it from humans, but they aren't the best guests. They take what they want. Ever seen those claws?"

Dell yawned. A lot. And a raw rain took the pleasure out of it for me.

When the bear finally wandered out of sight, it was my turn to suggest a stop. I opted for lunch and a gift shop.

"Not enough sleep last night?" I asked sweetly after another huge yawn from Dell.

"Better things to do than sleep," he murmured.

"You were insulted when I warned you off Jennifer. Elaine's not much older."

"Elaine was born older than Jennifer. And more than able to take care of herself."

"Maybe it's you I'm looking out for."

He laughed and kissed me on the top of the head. "This western sky you talk about has rattled your brains."

In that gift shop, I found Mike the perfect memento—a sign that read "A fed bear is a dead bear."

Then it was Dell's turn to pick a destination. He chose the hotel and an afternoon nap.

BUNNY WAS BACK in the same hallway outside the VisageTome meeting rooms.

So was I, but I wasn't rooting around in a trash can.

After dinner, I'd excused myself to Dell and Mike by saying I'd be right back—a euphemism for going to the toilet that few men ever question.

I was in the hallway because I'd wondered if she would be. What was her excuse, other than having a thing for that trash can?

"So we meet again," I said.

She reacted better tonight.

Sure, she jumped and her expression first squeezed into a scowl. But then she smiled broadly. Falsely.

"Wonderful to see you again, Elizabeth. But I need to go right now. Such a shame I can't linger, but…" She shrugged at the futility of fighting the fate keeping us apart.

The door to the meeting room for the VisageTome group we'd come to know best clicked closed. We hadn't been that loud.

"Of course. It's great to see you, too, Bunny." The only question was which of us was the bigger liar. "It's amazing that we meet out here at Yellowstone after all these years. And then twice. Right here in the same hallway. In fact, right by the same trash can if I recall correctly."

She laughed.

At least she tried. It sounded more like gargling, which can happen when your throat clamps closed.

Like the woman I'd heard talking to Darryl Justice Friday night.

I'll leave the money, then you leave—forever.

"Bunny, I asked you yesterday, but I'm asking you again, were you at the geyser yesterday?"

"What? No. What geyser?"

That answer was so wrong in so many ways.

The "what" to gain time. The "no" when there wouldn't have been any reason for an emphatic denial unless she was there and knew what had happened. The "what geyser" unbelievable and weak, considering she was in Yellowstone Park. Even if she didn't know it was home to more than half of the world's geysers, surely she hadn't come here without knowing it had a geyser or two.

"I'm sure I recognized you." I amped up my certainty to try to rattle her.

"No." She shook her head. Then said again, "No."

I stepped toward the trash can.

She stepped in front of me, barring my way.

"Go away. Just go away." Her voice was low and harsh. "You're as bad as him. Never leaving me alone. Leave me alone."

It was the same voice as the whisperer I'd heard the first night out on the porch. It was the same tenor. Some of the same words. The same distress.

"Just go. Now. We have to."

"Bunny, are you in trouble? Were you—"

"*Mom?*"

Chapter Eleven

I'D THOUGHT HER face had lost color when I stopped her yesterday, but that was merely pale. *This* was white.

It was like seeing her makeup under a blue light. Contouring here, blush there, and, oh, yes, concealer lots of places.

The young, male voice that interrupted me came from behind me, from the end of the hallway near the lobby. I turned toward it. She pivoted the opposite way and started to walk away toward the outside door.

I hooked my hand around her elbow. She stepped out of that, but I still had a hold on the strap of her designer bag and she wasn't going to let that go.

It swung her around, so she was looking down the hallway toward the owner of the voice.

As I completed my turn, more slowly than she had, because I hadn't been slingshotted around by a purse strap, I saw surprise—no, shock—on her face.

A figure stood frozen there in mid-step.

I was reminded of a wild animal prepared to turn and run, but the surroundings might have suggested that impression.

"Hi." I held a hand above my eyes as if to improve my distance sight.

The figure hesitated another breath, then began to come toward us.

A sense of familiarity struck me.

At first we couldn't see details, because of the shadows in the corridor in contrast to the stronger light behind him.

He was about fifteen feet away when enough light hit him to know that the young man walking toward us wasn't anyone I'd seen before.

Middle teens. Nice looking.

"Mom." This was considerably flatter than the genuine surprise of that first call-out. "It *is* you. What are you doing here? How'd you know I was here?"

Now, I might lose all color if someone addressed me as Mom. But I don't have any kids.

She did.

And this was almost certainly one of hers.

Put a wig, some makeup, and high heels on him, and he could have been Bunny at the same age.

No wonder he'd seemed familiar.

Her lips didn't move, but a breath came through them that I thought was his name.

Hoping I had the name right, I said, "Christopher?" He nodded. "Hi, I'm Elizabeth Margaret Danniher. I'm an old friend of your mom's. We went to school together."

"College?"

"Kindergarten. Then all the way through high school."

His face brightened, which made him look less like Bunny, who was still white. "Then you know my grandma."

"*Granmama*," she muttered.

"Sure do. Mrs. R. used to give away popcorn balls on Halloween. Never missed going there."

"I loved those." His enthusiasm dimmed. "She doesn't make them anymore."

I hoped he meant because homemade goodies are now frowned on for Halloween because of the actions of whackos.

He saved me the trouble of tactfully moving away from Mrs. Ramsey's possible fate by asking, "You and Mom came here together—?"

"No, no. We ran into each other here. You know, they say if you stay in Yellowstone long enough you'll see everyone you ever knew."

Actually, that was about a café in Paris, but I was struggling here, what with Bunny standing motionless and bloodless, while Christopher darted anxious looks at her and the floor.

Turning to Bunny, I asked as if I were teasing her, "You knew your son was here at the hotel and you never mentioned it?"

She looked blankly at me, then down at her hands.

Maybe the Sterakos family had a complex about running into people unexpectedly.

I said to him, "What are you doing at Yellowstone, Christopher?"

Before he could answer, she said, "A program." She cleared her throat, but the words didn't come out much better. "A special program for school."

"Yeah," he said.

I might not have kids, but I've been one. This kid was lying.

Weirder and weirder.

"You shouldn't be here," Bunny said, low and vehement. "You're staying at that other place. Wooly."

"Geeze." That sounded like normal teenager annoyance at a parent. "Not wooly. Mammoth. Mammoth Hot Springs. They closed it up. Repairs or something. So I'm here."

"What kind of program?" I asked, again brightly.

Now they both looked at me blankly.

"One for school," he said, impatient.

"Doing what?"

"Working at the park."

"Where?"

He was getting annoyed. "Here. At the hotel. In the kitchen."

If he didn't make that up on the spot I don't know liars.

There were mysteries here. She'd known he was at Yellowstone, but hadn't sought him out. He'd clearly regretted calling out her name. She wanted us to get away from that trash can. He was lying about this so-called program. She was too oblivious to realize it.

"Ah, well, that must be fun," I said.

"If you call cutting up potatoes fun. But I'm broke, so…"

I didn't believe it. Not any of it. Right down to this kid cutting up potatoes.

My instinct was to keep digging to get to the root of this weirdness.

That warred with my instinct to minimize my time with Bunny Ramsey Sterakos, an instinct I'd been listening to since childhood.

"Well, I wish you lots of success with the program, Christopher. It was nice to meet you." I put out a hand. He met it with a passable handshake. "And good to see you, Bunny. Two nights in a row, right here—" I glanced toward the trash can and her returning color ebbed a bit. "—in the same spot after all these years. But I better go now."

"Yes, yes, we all should." She tried to take her son's arm. He shook her off. "We have to all go. Now."

I started off. They were following, but so slowly that I'd reached the exterior door—the one to the porch—before anyone emerged from the hallway.

It was Bunny, alone. She headed for the back entrance, her heels tapping on the floor.

Chapter Twelve

THIS EVENING WHEN I went out on the porch later I was hoping to find Darryl Justice there. And I got my wish.

That didn't mean I plunged into what I wanted to know about.

He was leaning against a roof post, looking toward the skies and smoking. No glass of wine in sight this time.

He slewed his eyes around to see who had joined him.

I took up a similar position, leaning back against the next post. This time I'd been smart enough to wear my jacket.

"Awe-inspiring," I said.

He grunted agreement.

"Interesting juxtaposition, isn't it?" I elaborated before his lack of response could become too obvious. "High tech team-building and wilderness, I mean. What benefits does Yellowstone Park offer?"

He jerked his head toward the skies. "Perspective of where we fit in the universe."

"It does do that, doesn't it? However, I notice you're the only one from the teams—" I'd almost said *from VisageTome*. Referring to the teams was better, leaving open the question of whether Mike, Dell, and I were here as part of VisageTome, though we clearly weren't with a team. "—out here soaking up that perspective. So that doesn't seem to apply."

His eyes came to me again. "You'd know better than me why teams from different divisions are sent here first thing in the spring, last thing in the fall."

You'd know better than me. That sounded as if he'd concluded I was higher up in VisageTome. Someone keeping a distant eye on the team-building exercises.

That explained his confidences about his team members last night.

But then what did he make of Wardell Yardley being here? Surely, he'd picked up on his identity from the others. Did that make Mike and me some sort of media handlers?

This might work to my advantage. "I'd like to hear what you think," I said.

"VisageTome accounts include more than half the world's population, with a new leaf sprouting every second. So people are naturally going to be interested. That means there's always a spotlight on VisageTome people."

He said all that almost in a monotone, as if he'd said it before, said it many times, and hadn't been particularly interested the first time he'd said it.

With only marginally more animation, he added, "For programs like this team-building it takes some doing to find a venue where our team members can work together in a relaxed atmosphere."

"Seems like you have your hands full with your team."

He jerked a shoulder. A shrug or a tic?

"Is there as much friction on other teams as your group?"

"What do you mean, friction?"

I nodded. "Fair question. Let's start with competition."

"Sure."

"So members on other teams are as competitive with their team-mates as your people are?"

"Yeah. It's the culture. VisageTome encourages internal competition." He paused, and I had the feeling he was thinking something through. "Probably also the nature of the people who do the kind of things we do."

I nodded acceptance of his observations, then added, "What about animosity?"

"That can arise from competition."

"It can. It doesn't always. And sometimes it arises without any competition. Which of those is the case with Gordon Kelvin?"

His brows rose. "Why him?"

"He didn't take it well when Elaine pointed out his president/precedent error."

He looked faintly surprised, but it disappeared fast.

He hadn't known anyone outside the room knew about that. Yet he had rapidly accepted that someone could know about it. Because he expected VisageTome higher management to spy on the teams?

"That was two wrongs make a worse. Gordon doesn't like having his errors pointed out and Elaine loves to point out anybody else's goofs, large or small, important or not. It's ego. They've all got egos. Big egos. Egos get them here. Egos can kick them out. They've always been ahead of the pack, but now they're surrounded by people just like them, so that *is* the pack."

"Doesn't sound like the best raw material for a team."

He smiled briefly and without amusement. "That's why we're here. To make it better."

"Is that truly why you're here?"

"Why else? VisageTome sent us here for team-building sessions and that's why I'm here. I'm the ego-wrangler." He challenged me with a why-else-would-I-be here look without saying it.

"The only reason?"

"Yes."

"Yet you seemed to know Bunny Ramsey—Sterakos," I added belatedly. "In fact, you seemed to have some conflict with her."

He came up slightly on the balls of his feet. His hands flexed. "You know her? She's some friend of yours? That's—"

"Not really."

"—great. Then *you* tell her I don't want anything to do with her. Nothing. I said it nice, now I'll say it flat out. It's all settled and done. Leave it alone. Maybe she'll listen to you."

For a moment that wrong-footed me, since Bunny—assuming it was Bunny I'd heard that first night—had indicated *he* was the one who wouldn't leave *her* alone.

I recovered enough to go along with his version. "She doesn't seem willing to accept that."

"That's not my problem. And it doesn't have anything to do with—She's going to have to accept it. She can't make anybody—" He looked off across the dark lake, then turned back toward me.

Before he came face to face with me, though, something past me caught his attention. He lifted his head, acknowledging someone. I turned and saw a guy in jeans and a jacket walking slowly toward us. But that was all I could make out, since he was in a pocket of shadow cast by that porch light still being out.

Darryl repeated, "Not my problem. Not VisageTome's business. Nothing to do with my job. Gotta go."

He walked past me. I watched as he met up with the other man still in the shadowy area. The other man turned and matched his pace as they continued away from me down the porch at a good clip.

I watched until they turned a corner, going out of sight.

MONDAY

Chapter Thirteen

WE LEFT THE hotel Monday morning without seeing any of the VisageTome people. So there was no big, emotional farewell with Justice, Kelvin, Hart, Nelson, Varney, or the others.

As for Elaine, Dell wasn't volunteering and neither Mike nor I asked.

I got to sit in the front seat for the trip back—not the driver's seat though. Dell occupied himself in the backseat by reading aloud from a book he'd purchased on deaths at Yellowstone Park.

He kept stopping to quiz Mike and me. "Murder or not murder?"

Our percentage would have been better if Mike hadn't kept saying that no one who went over a cliff was murdered. He'd been impressed by the precipices at the Grand Canyon of the Yellowstone.

We stopped for a great lunch in Cody. Back in Sherman. we dropped Dell off at the B&B.

I asked if he wanted to get together for dinner, but he said he was going to have a quiet night doing prep work for the story, since his crew was coming in Friday.

At Diana's ranch, Shadow greeted me with effusive joy.

In other words, he showed up when I arrived and came within petting range—briefly.

Mike hung around long enough to be invited for dinner by Diana when she came in from her day at KWMT-TV. We had pot roast with her and her kids and told them about our trip.

Gary and Jess told me about how great Shadow had been for them. I swear, between Diana's kids and Tom Burrell's third-grade daughter, Tamantha, I was getting a real inferiority complex about my dog.

He clearly liked them better than me. *Well, Shadow, unless I discover the secret to getting younger, you're stuck with an adult—and one of a certain age.*

I was in the bunkhouse with said traitor dog, feeling downright sentimental about sleeping in my own bed when my phone rang.

It was a local number I didn't know.

"Elizabeth Margaret Danniher."

"Oh. Hi." Not Dell. A woman's voice. I'd guess a young woman. "This is Krista Seger from Wild Horses Bed and Breakfast. I, uh, know you said you couldn't do a story on us for 'Helping Out!' unless someone lodged a complaint against us, but really, Ms. Danniher, I think you'll be interested in this." Her voice dropped to the conspirator's register. "We're full."

"I'm sure that's good news, but—"

"No, no, that's not it. They're all part of a group. Most of them anyway. From…"

"What? I couldn't hear you."

She mumbled something again.

"Sorry. I still can't—"

The third time I thought I had it, though I wouldn't have guessed it if it hadn't been for the past weekend.

"VisageTome? People from VisageTome are staying at your bed and breakfast right now?"

"Yes. I can't—It's better if I don't."

I thought I recognized the hand of Wardell Yardley in this.

Quiet night and catch up on prep work, my ass. He'd had plans of an entirely different kind for this evening.

"Is Elaine Malsung there?" I asked.

"Yes. How did you—?" She cut herself off.

Simple math. VisageTome people being in the B&B where Dell was staying, plus Dell's most recent play partner, plus Dell planning a quiet night. The answer was Elaine.

But this young woman had said a group.

Krista's voice was different when she continued. "That's great. We appreciate your interest."

"Got it. You can't talk. There's someone there who might hear and you don't want them to know that you're telling me the name of the company they work for?"

"Yes. Thank you. We've worked hard."

"How many are there?"

"Yes, the fifth should work fine."

"Five?" I confirmed with her.

Since Elaine was there, it made sense it was her group. But they were one short of the group, since there'd been four guys, her, and their leader, Darryl Justice. Besides, why on earth would they be with her? Her presence in Sherman could be explained by Dell, but not theirs.

"That's perfect," Krista said.

"Do you think there's something going on?"

"Absolutely." Her voice was as certain as the word.

"What? No—never mind. I know you can't say now, but if we meet—"

"I'm so sorry. I can't help you with that. We're full right now. But I'm sure we can work it out for your later visitors."

"Is there a time we could talk?"

"I'm afraid not. I have to grocery shop tomorrow afternoon." She wasn't bad at this spy stuff. After a brief pause she added, "That's right, I'll be leaving here around one. So, perhaps Wednesday?"

"Got it," I said. "I'll look for you at the Sherman Supermarket tomorrow afternoon."

"Fine. Then you can come by Wednesday about noon. See you then."

She hung up.

TUESDAY

Chapter Fourteen

MY TUESDAY GOT an early start.

Not from an alarm going off, but from the ringtone that said my parents were calling.

This time it was my mother on the line. At that hour it figured.

I don't know if she truly can't remember that it's an hour later in Illinois than it is in Wyoming, or if she's reliving the days and months and years of waking me too darned early to go to school.

Some of it was her internal clock. Some was because she'd get all us kids ready and fed at the same time. Since older siblings started school earlier than I did, I got shoveled out early.

Once, in kindergarten, I was there before the teacher. The room was still locked, heck, I don't think they'd turned the heat back up from the weekend. The teacher arrived to find me huddled by the door.

"Are you still *asleep?*" she demanded after my groggy hello.

"Not anymore."

"I told you, Cat," I heard Dad say in the background.

She didn't respond to him, but said to me, "It's high time you were up. The day will be half over."

"Not in Wyoming."

"That's why we're calling. If you insist on roaming around that unsettled state, you could have at least let us know you came out of the wilderness safely."

"I got home fine, Mom." She released a sigh at my referring to anything other than their house as home. "And I had a wonderful time.

You'll never guess who I ran into at Yellowstone Park."

"Bunny Ramsey," Mom said.

"How on earth did you know that?" This was impressive, even for her.

"Because Bunny calls her mother every Sunday and she told me when I was out walking this morning."

"Your mother's started taking a walk every morning. She comes back with more news than any two newspapers combined." Dad sounded proud of her accomplishment. Or perhaps that was delight that she was bringing back tidbits that kept him interested while he was confined to the house.

"She lives over in those condos by the lake now, you know. She hates it. Misses her house. Gets teary every time she sees me, like I remind her of the old neighborhood. Course then she cheers herself up by telling me all about Bunny and what a catch her husband is. He's from one of the top one hundred richest families in Illinois. The Sterakos family."

So Sterakos was likely the "catch" I'd heard about back in college.

"Do you know what she was doing at Yellowstone?" I asked.

"Taking a vacation. Looking at the scenery and animals, I suppose. Didn't she tell you?"

Dad rescued me from that question. "Everyone should get to our National Parks. They're a remarkable resource. We're fortunate to have them."

"Uh-huh. But doesn't looking at the scenery and animals, you know, *outdoors* seem like an odd things for Bunny Ramsey to do?"

"I'm past assessing what's odd. Not when my daughter chooses to remain thousands and thousands miles from home—"

"About twelve-hundred miles. For the job, Mom," I reminded her.

"You could have had a job here—well, in Chicago. And then you could have come home every weekend, been much more involved in your family's lives. It's not too late—"

"Speaking of late. I will be if I don't hang up now. Glad you're healing well, Dad. Give my love to everyone."

As I was reaching to click off, I heard Mom said, "I knew it was a good thing to call. And you wanted to wait, Jim. See? She'd have been late to work."

I sat on the side of the bed with the phone.

No way was I going to fall back to sleep.

Mom was sending me to school early again. At least I knew the early crew would have the doors to KWMT-TV opened when I got there.

✧   ✧   ✧   ✧

BUT I DIDN'T get there—not all the way inside, anyway.

Because of Dell's phone call.

Realizing he wasn't pulling my leg about there being a body in his bed had started me back toward my SUV.

By the time I grappled with my unworthy reaction of thinking of Sheriff Russ Conrad and *Now, we'll see. Now we'll see*, I was turning onto the highway, heading west toward the center of town.

"Dell, we need to hang up and you need to call the sheriff's department."

"But—"

"Now. Immediately. I'm on my way, but you need to call them. Don't talk to anybody else. Don't let anyone else in your room or the bathroom. Understand?"

"Yes."

"You stay in the bathroom. Don't go in the bedroom. Where's your room?"

"Third floor. Turn left. Second on the left."

"The bathroom?"

"Next door. Last on the left."

"I'm on my way."

He clicked off and I let out a breath. He'd sounded more like himself at the end.

Even as a best-case-scenario, this could get very nasty very fast for Dell. He'd fare better if he was firmly in Wardell Yardley mode.

Calls to Mike and Diana went to voicemail. I told them both to call me as soon as possible. That's all I said.

I didn't break the speed limit by much. I let out another breath I hadn't realized I'd been holding when I saw no official cars around the place.

I breezed through the front door, saw a woman I assumed was owner Krista Seger putting plates on a table in the dining room in front of a gray-haired couple. I raised a hand in greeting at her surprised look and kept going, mounting the stairs just short of a run.

Acting like someone *should* recognize you and you belong where you're going is usually enough to prevent them from trying to stop you. They might be puzzled, but not enough to act at the moment.

The moment was what I needed right now.

As I chugged up the second flight I listened for following footsteps. None.

At the third floor, I wasn't completely winded, but I was grateful there wasn't a fourth floor to reach. I hurried down a hallway with all the doors closed, a window with sheer white curtains at the end, a sliver of a table with a phone on it on the left side, and a carpet runner down the middle. It didn't stop the floor from creaking. I slowed my pace.

Nearly to the second door on the left and telling my hand not to reach for the knob, I heard a low voiced, "Elizabeth."

Dell's voice came from the next door down the hallway. I passed the bedroom, glancing at the doorknob, wishing I had instant-fingerprint-identifying vision, and used the narrow opening Dell left to slip quickly into a good-sized, old-fashioned bathroom.

A door that presumably connected to the bedroom was closed. Dell's hair was damp. He had that fresh-scrubbed look, but his clothes were seriously rumpled, especially by Wardell Yardley standards.

"You called the sheriff's department?" I asked.

"Yes."

"When?"

"A minute, maybe two after we hung up. I needed … I had to sit down."

"Okay." That probably gave us a few minutes still.

Officially, the tiny Sherman Police Department had jurisdiction here. But Sherman P.D. and the Cottonwood County Sheriff's Department operated on the basis of who was closest and who was available. If the police were otherwise occupied and the call had to go to the sheriff's department, which covered a lot of territory, their arrival time would depend on how close the first responder had been when the call went out. "Tell me from the beginning."

"I was in the bathroom and when I went in to the bedroom I saw... I found..."

"Elaine," I supplied, trying to make it easier for them.

His eyes went wide. "How did you know she—" Then he shook his head. "No. It's not Elaine."

Chapter Fifteen

"NOT?" I BET my eyes were wide now, too.

"It's not Elaine," he repeated. "He's—"

"*He?*"

"It's that guy. From Yellowstone."

"Kelvin? Nelson? Varney? Uh, Hart?"

"No. The one you were talking to on the porch. The older one."

A pang passed through me, abrupt and sharp. Darryl Justice. He'd been an okay guy. Worried and harried, but more mature and sensible and ... *normal* than the others.

"You don't know his name?"

"I suppose I heard it but—oh, no, Elizabeth." A distant glimmer of amusement edged into his voice. "It wasn't like that. You should know better than to listen to those rumors."

"I wasn't judging—"

"Wouldn't matter if you were. I wasn't here last night." His voice was strengthening as he spoke. "I, uh, slept elsewhere. Then came back early to get ready. I—"

"So you weren't in your room last night?"

He shook his head.

"Not at all?" Another head-shake. "From when to when?"

"A little after seven last night to, I don't know exactly, maybe seven-thirty?"

I breathed a little easier.

Finding a dead body in your bed was never going to make you a favorite with law enforcement, but it was several steps up the ladder from finding your sexual partner dead in the bed you'd spent the night in together.

"Okay. Open the door for me, will you?"

He did not want to. "Why?"

"Because your fingerprints are already on it. And there's good reason for them to be. Mine aren't and there isn't."

Reluctantly, he opened the door. I nudged it wider with a shoulder, pulled out my cell phone, and started recording. It was dark in the room, with the curtains drawn and no lamps on.

No way was I going to disturb the scene by going in and opening curtains. Nor was I going to let anyone who happened to be driving up know that I was looking into the room by turning on the lights.

I'd have to hope that the camera on this phone was not only good in low light, but good in low, low, low light.

Rather than focusing on the screen, I watched where I was recording, letting my eyes take in the scene first-hand.

Staring at the screen narrowed your focus too much. Doing it this way would help fill in details that the camera didn't catch. And, at the same time, what the camera did catch would spark my memory.

Most of my non-visual attention was on Dell. "So you get back here and…"

He'd retreated to near the hallway door. "I came straight to the bathroom to shower. Then—"

"Why?"

"I needed a shower."

"It would have been normal to go through the bedroom."

"Oh, that. I'd forgotten my key and the lady here showed me where they kept a spare key for the bathroom on top of the door-frame." How original.

"When did she do that?"

"When she was showing me the room."

"Was anyone else around?"

"Why—? Oh. Yeah. Everybody, I think. That group from Vis-ageTome. Elaine's group."

"Darryl Justice, too?"

"Not that I saw. Didn't see him at all. Not until … well, you know. In my bed. But the others—Elaine, Gordon Kelvin, Alan Varney, Brant Nelson, Landon Dart—were all in the hallway when she told me. They were getting ready for some meeting."

They hadn't had enough of that at Yellowstone over the weekend?

I wanted to know more, but VT would have to wait.

"Okay. Now, this morning. You've showered and whatever and you still haven't been in the room?"

"Right."

"This is a private bathroom? Never mind. Of course, it is. What was I thinking? How long do you think you were in here?"

He tipped his head. "More than half an hour. I caught the half-hour news when I first got in here and could turn on my phone. WTOP." That meant he was listening to D.C. all-news radio station WTOP through the internet on his phone. "I'd showered and shaved and was at the sink, brushing my teeth when the top of the hour network news came on. Then I went in to get clothes and … He's there. In the bed. *My* bed."

"Did you—" Footsteps on the stairs announced the first arrival of law enforcement. "In the hallway. Fast. Let me handle this, Dell. Not a word."

We were in the hallway with the bathroom door closed and the cell phone along my thigh, masked by my hand.

Only then did I remember I'd asked Mike and Diana to call back. It was one of the few times in my life I prayed to not get a call back. Not yet. Not now.

A head appeared well before the skinny body wearing the uniform of the Sherman Police Department. I'd met him before. Andy? No… got it. Randy Hollister.

From what I've seen, the town police department takes a back seat to its county counterpart in investigations and recruiting.

In other words, Randy Hollister was the first responder, but he wouldn't have been Sheriff Conrad's first choice to be on the scene.

This was a bit of luck.

He stopped when he saw me, apparently recognizing me. "They

said a man called."

I might have given him too much credit.

He might have simply recognized I was female, rather than my individual identity.

"Hi, Officer Hollister. Yes, my friend Dell called the police. I told him to when he told me what he found when he returned to his room this morning. I just got here myself and the scene hasn't been secured yet. We'll keep an eye on things from out here until reinforcements come, but you better check the back stairs." I gestured down the hallway to a shadowy door. "Anyone could get in or out that way. The murderer could still be here. Maybe hiding in the stairway."

I seriously doubted that, considering what little I'd been able to see of the body and what looked like blood, but I wasn't going to get into those details with him.

He didn't ask for any more details. He put his hand on the butt of his gun, nodded solemnly and headed for the back stairs.

Keeping my voice low, I said to Dell, "We won't have much time now."

I slipped back into the bathroom to the door to the bedroom, which I'd left partway open. Quickly, I caught the last part of the room.

Dell had stayed in the hall, but now widened the opening of the door and put his head in to say in a low voice, "I hear someone at the door downstairs."

I ignored that. "Where exactly did you go in the bedroom, Dell?"

"Nowhere."

"But your clothes—"

"I had to put on the same clothes as last night. I wasn't going in there. No way."

He put dirty clothes back on after showering?

It would never stand up in court, but anyone who knew Wardell Yardley well and quite a few who knew him only in passing would swear that if he'd killed a man in the apparent circumstances before us, he'd have made sure to have clean clothes available first.

Quickly, I added video of the bathroom, noticing for the first time that the shower still showed water on its walls. Backing toward the door, I kept shooting.

I could hear sounds from below, too.

"We better get in the hall. Close the door," I added when we were outside the bathroom. I turned off the phone so it couldn't ring or make any telltale sounds and slid it into my back jeans pocket, then pulled my shirt, light sweater, and jacket down over it. God bless layers. I had only my keys, having left my purse in my vehicle. I put them in a front jacket pocket. "Don't lock it and leave the key in the lock."

"What if—"

The sounds were identifiable now as footsteps coming up the final stairs at a good clip.

"Don't worry about what if. I know you didn't do this, Dell. Only an idiot would think you had anything to do with—"

"Get out of my crime scene." Sheriff Conrad's growl came from behind me.

Having delivered my statement in such a way that he might think I didn't know he was there, I was determined to play nice. For now.

"Dell, this is Sheriff Russ Conrad. Sheriff, this is Wardell Yardley. That's his room where the body was found, but he did not spend the night there. He—"

"Get out of my crime scene."

"I'm not in your crime scene, which is in the bedroom next door. Though the body might have been moved there from—"

"*Out!*" he roared.

Behind him, Richard Alvaro looked faintly apologetic, but Deputy Shelton looked satisfied.

"Okay. C'mon, Dell." I took my keys out of the pocket of my jacket, knowing the pocket would lie flat, making it clear nothing thicker than a piece of paper was in it.

"Not him. He stays."

Sheriff Conrad was giving me a quick once-over.

Not that kind.

If I'd had a purse he might have asked to look in it. If I'd had visibly lumpy pockets, he might have asked me to empty them. I'd left him with nothing to suspect.

I squinted at the sheriff. "Wardell Yardley is a respected and admired journalist. He had absolutely nothing to do with the death of that man. You had better treat him with every courtesy."

"I treat everybody with courtesy," he snapped. Probably because he knew he hadn't.

I raised one eyebrow. Satisfied I'd made my point, I turned to Dell. "I'm going straight to the office of a lawyer I know. Do not say a word to anyone—*anyone*—until he says you can. His name is James Long-baugh. Ask for photo ID, in case they get any tricky ideas."

I had the satisfaction of hearing the sheriff grind his teeth. Satisfaction that was short-lived because of the worry in Dell's eyes.

"It'll be okay, Dell. I swear to you."

Then, before the sheriff could issue any more edicts, I made my way past the other representatives of law enforcement arriving at the landing, and headed down the stairs, where I received another surprise.

Chapter Sixteen

I SHOULD HAVE caught it on my way up the stairs.

Even with my attention focused on getting to Dell as fast as possible I truly should have caught it.

But only as I came down the stairs, saw movement in the dining room, and focused on the woman clearing the now-empty table did what I'd seen earlier register.

The gray-haired couple eating their breakfast.

The bugle-lover and his wife.

Joel and Ariel.

What were the chances?

True, Sherman was somewhat on the way to—or, in this case, from—Yellowstone Park, but the majority of visitors using Yellowstone's East Gate stayed in Cody if they wanted someplace close.

And to be staying *here*, a bed and breakfast not even officially opened yet?

I detoured from the direct route to the front door, passed through the dining room, and followed Krista into the kitchen, where she deposited a tray of dirty dishes beside the sink.

"Where are the man and woman who were eating breakfast?"

She turned around, a hand to her throat. "Oh, you scared the life out of me." Color drained out of her face. "I shouldn't... That's awful... I didn't mean..." She blinked hard, like she was fighting tears.

"You can't blame yourself for a figure of speech, Krista. You are Krista Seger, aren't you?"

"Yes. And you're Ms. Danniher from the TV station, right?"

"I am. Elizabeth Margaret Danniher." I switched the keys to my other hand and extended for a shake she returned. "So you've heard what happened upstairs?"

She nodded. Her eyes were wide, but dry. There was a puffiness around them I associate with a night-before crying binge. On the other hand, the woman had been up early enough to prepare and serve breakfast, which is an entirely valid cause for eye puffiness.

"I went up the back stairwell just now to start on the rooms, but there was a policeman there. He said... He said..." Her eyes went wider and tears came into them. "He's *dead.*"

Interesting. Not "someone's dead" but "he's dead" with the emphasis on "dead." But which "he" did she mean?

Randy Hollister hadn't known who was dead in that bed. He hadn't seen him and we hadn't named him. So he couldn't have told her who was dead.

Of course he'd seen Dell, so he did know Dell wasn't dead. But with the other men staying here there were still options.

"Yes. Did you see or hear anything last night or this morning?"

She began shaking her head before a long "noooo" came out. "Nothing."

"What time did you come downstairs this morning?"

"Quarter after five."

"You do that every day?"

My horror might have come through, because her mouth shifted. Nowhere near a smile, but at least remembering the concept. "Every morning. But when I'm in the kitchen anyone could go up the stairs without my seeing."

She said that so quickly she must have been thinking about it. "What about hearing?"

"Oh, I wouldn't hear anything, not through that heavy original door. We had a bell installed so that when I'm in the kitchen I'll know if guests come to the front door."

That might be worth testing down the road. "Are you alone in the kitchen from quarter after five on?"

"Yes—well, no. My husband will help with the cooking, the tables, serving."

I'd seen no sign of a husband, though my passage had been brief. "Every day?"

"Most days."

"Today?"

"He was up late," she said defensively. "He was settling the group from—A group."

"I know where they're from. Not only from your ca—"

"No." She looked around quickly, then directly at me as she said, "Please don't bring up that I called you trying to get you to do the story on our opening. I, uh, shouldn't have done that."

"Okay." I gave a small nod, letting her know the message had been received and understood—I was not to reveal that she'd called pitching a story about the VisageTome people. That also meant I couldn't ask her about what she'd thought was going on—not until I had her alone and away from here. "But getting back to what happened, uh, upstairs, I recognized people you have staying here as people from VisageTome whom I met over the weekend at Yellowstone Park."

That was a fib, since I hadn't seen them here. But I trusted Dell's reporting.

Her mouth formed an "O" with no sound coming out.

Still, my lying sentence accomplished what I'd hoped it would—it put her more at ease. She was no longer on the hook for my knowing the VT people were here.

"Including, uh…" I tipped my head back, indicating somewhere above us.

"But *he* wasn't staying here."

"He didn't come with the other VisageTome people?"

"No."

"You're sure?"

I wanted to kick myself for asking that. Ask it of someone who sounds unsure, okay, maybe. But to ask it when the person sounds positive solely because it's surprised me is useless. "Never mind. I can see you're sure. What was Dirk doing to settle them?"

"They wanted to use the second parlor for a meeting last night and to have takeout, so there was all that to set up and clean up after. Dirk worked late on that."

I nodded. "I wonder if he might have seen or heard anything? Perhaps last night. If I could talk to him—"

"He's not here. He left early."

Up late and left early. Hmm.

I shifted gears. "I noticed that older couple eating breakfast a bit ago. I was so distracted, but I think I know them. Joel and Ariel?"

"Oh, you know the Williamses." She happily shifted gears, too. She was fine with swapping them for her husband as a topic when the core of the conversation was a dead man upstairs in one of their guest beds.

I let her think that I did know them by not contradicting her, then added in absolute honesty, "I had no idea they'd be staying here."

"They got the last room. To be filled up and even have another inquiry and all before we officially open was more than we could have hoped for—and now this."

I could see that murder might not be great for their business. On the other hand, considering some people's tastes, they might be able to charge a premium.

"Are the Williamses in their room?"

"Oh, no. They left right after you went upstairs. I think…" She frowned. "I think they were talking about birding. They didn't even finish eating."

"But you're sure they'll be back?"

She looked puzzled. "Why wouldn't they be back?"

"Any idea where they might have gone, uh, birding?"

She shook her head.

I heard footsteps on the stairs.

She'd said she couldn't hear anything from here. True, the door was open now. Could the door make that much difference?

That might be worth testing if it became significant. But not now. Because these footsteps were coming down, and they had the sound of the heavy tread of law enforcement, who thought I'd left the premises a while ago.

✧ ✧ ✧ ✧

I DROVE STRAIGHT to the center of town and waited to take out my phone until I had pulled into one of the diagonal parking spots that are a sure sign of an advanced civilization.

First thing I did was send copies of the video to myself, Mike, and Diana. Their subject line said Do Not Open Until You Talk to Me.

Then I called Mike.

"Where are you?" he added. "I called you back, but got your voice mail. I thought you'd be at the station this morning."

"Something came up. Dell needs our help."

"Dell does? He doesn't like the B&B, either?"

"You could say that. Don't use his name anymore and be careful with your reactions. Okay?" Newsrooms are notorious for eavesdropping and other snooping.

"Yes."

"He returned to his room after spending the night elsewhere and found a dead body in his bed."

Mike said a word he'd better hope he never says on air. "Who? What are you going to do? Have the p—" He stopped himself.

"The police have asked him to remain on the scene to answer questions. I'm on my way to James Longbaugh so Dell has a lawyer. But he's going to need more than a lawyer to keep his reputation. We—"

"Have to find the—find out who did this." Mike's amended statement told me other people were around who might be interested to hear him mention finding a murderer.

We'd had some success at tracking down killers and Sheriff Conrad wasn't the only one not pleased by that. Thurston Fine's veins were threatened by skyrocketing blood pressure any time we came up with a major story.

That was only a side benefit to tracking down the truth about murder, though a lovely one.

"Yes. Don't say anything more there, but see if you can corral Diana and Jennifer and meet me at Hamburger Heaven. An hour."

"Better make it ninety minutes. I have to finish something up if I'm going to be doing other things today. But even then it's kind of early for Hamburger Heaven. They don't open until—"

"It's not for food, it's to talk."

"Right. Of course. But Diana's not here. She's out on assignment."

I swore. My turn to hope I never say that word on air.

"See what you can do to get her out. Tell her not to open a video I sent to her, not to let anybody see it until we talk. You, too. Don't open it."

"You sent me a copy? I don't see it. Oh, wait. Here it is. It's a huge file. I'll—"

"I said don't open it."

"I was making sure it had come in." From his sheepish tone I knew he'd been about to open it.

"When we're together and nobody else is around."

"Okay. Got it. You want me to call Tom or will you?"

I hesitated. "I will."

"Elizabeth."

"I know, I know." He was going to say Tom Burrell added important local insight to our inquiries.

He did.

He could also be like an anchor holding us down every step of the way. At first I'd thought it was because he couldn't believe people he knew could be entangled in a murder. But I'd begun to wonder if it was something deeper. Or wider. Or just confusing.

"I'll call him," I said.

As we disconnected, I caught a glimpse of two people walking into the Haber House Hotel.

That's all it was. A glimpse. I couldn't be sure I'd actually seen Bunny and her son.

The most likely explanation was that thinking about Dell's mess brought to mind the weekend at Yellowstone, which greased the synapses in my brain to connect Bunny and Christopher to a pair of strangers who happened to be walking into the Haber House.

Even if it had been worth trying to track down the pair to definitively prove to my synapses that they were wrong, there wasn't time.

I needed to get Dell a lawyer.

Perhaps it was an excess of caution, but I approached James Longbaugh's office by a route that didn't take me right past the sheriff's department.

In case Sheriff Conrad had changed his mind and thought he wanted to question me, too.

But there was no sign of the sheriff or any deputies, so I walked in to Longbaugh's offices unfettered.

The receptionist took my message that I had to see her boss immediately on an emergency matter with aplomb. I suspected a lot of people who stepped into this waiting room in the restored house-turned office had the same message.

She emerged from a side door to his office after a moment. "He's finishing a call. He'll be right with you."

It took three minutes and forty-seven seconds. Plenty of time to imagine lots of things I should have, could have done differently since I'd arrived at the Wild Horses Bed and Breakfast.

The door from his office to the entryway opened and James Longbaugh said, "Elizabeth. Won't you come in?"

Chapter Seventeen

As soon as he closed the door behind me, I said, "A friend of mine named Wardell Yardley found a dead body in his room at the new B&B this morning. Likely a murdered body. Dell has an alibi. He spent the night out of his room with a woman. You might have to make him cough up the name because he likes to think he's a man of mystery."

He paused partway across the office.

Then he earned my deepest appreciation by avoiding cracks about my relationship with murders, instead, saying, "He wants to hire me?"

"Yes. He's with the sheriff right now and he doesn't know anyone in town except me and a few people I've introduced him to. I want to hire you on his behalf."

He resumed his path to the chair behind his desk.

"Won't you sit down—" He gestured to a chair on the visitor's side of the desk. "—and tell me everything. Right after you've given me a dollar to put me on retainer. We'll sort out later whether you or Mr.—Yardley, you said, I believe—will be paying my bill."

I put a five on his desk. "That's what I've got. I don't know everything, but I'll tell you what he said before Sheriff Conrad showed up."

I did. I also told him about the people staying in the B&B with a sketch of the back story from Yellowstone.

He looked at me for a moment after I'd finished. "It sounds like cooperating with the sheriff's department might be in my client's best interest."

"I won't argue, as long as you're there with him while he's cooperating."

"Of course. I need to juggle some things, then I'll get to wherever he is, the scene or the sheriff's department. Do I want to know what you're going to be doing?"

"No." I stood.

At the door I turned back. "Oh, yeah, ask him where his bedroom key is. The key from the hallway to the bedroom. If he'd had it with him, he wouldn't have gone into the bathroom first or needed to use the spare key all those VisageTome people know about. I'm betting the room key is still in the room of the woman he spent the night with. That will help back up his alibi—and hers."

TOM BURRELL TOLD me on the phone that he was at the office of Burrell Road Construction on the edge of town. That meant a much shorter drive to see him than if he'd been working at his ranch northwest of Sherman.

His attitude about our previous looks into murder cases was the reason I wanted to see him, not tell him over the phone. He was hard enough to read when I could see his face. I was not about to include anyone who might damage Dell with reluctance or divided loyalty.

I knocked on the door.

His "come in" was accompanied by his opening the trailer door.

"How was your weekend at Yellowstone?" he asked before I could say anything more than "Hi."

He was alone. That might make this discussion easier. Or not.

"Good." I amended that by adding, "Interesting."

"As interesting as your interview right before you left?"

I grimaced at him. "You're slipping, Burrell. When you have to resort to watching KWMT-TV to know what's going on it leaves you on an equal footing with all the other residents of Cottonwood County."

He grunted an acknowledgement of my words without agreeing with them. "Did hear some things that weren't on your TV news."

"Like what?"

"Heard you and the new sheriff didn't get off to the best start."

"Of course you did. Probably heard blow by blow as it happened. When it comes to a spy network you rank up there with my mother."

"Not spies," he said mildly. "Anyway, you'll like him better when you get to know him better."

"I doubt that. And now it appears Diana has—Wait a minute. Why would you think—? Do *you* know the new sheriff?"

"Yeah." Or it might have been "Yup." I'm giving him the benefit of the doubt.

"Oh, my God. I thought since he came in from another state we were safe from the Thomas David Burrell spider web of connections. I should have known better."

"Suppose you should have. Didn't you check up on him?"

"He was sheriff in that county in Idaho. Decent record. Before that, he'd worked in jurisdictions in Colorado and Wyoming along the border. Again, no record of issues, no complaints, no major controversies. Graduated from the FBI training at Quantico after a bachelor's degree from the University of Wyoming where—" I stopped. "Football. He played football. You were on the basketball team while you were there."

"Yep."

"But you knew him from college." I don't know if it was something in his on-its-way-to-craggy face or pessimism that made me sure of that. "What were you? Best friends? Roommates?"

"Nothing like that. Just knew him." He gave me a level look. "Respected him. Kept up with his career. Touched base now and then."

"Touched base," I repeated, then switched sarcasm with "Right. You probably were the one who got him hired here."

"Well, I knew he wanted to get back to Wyoming. He and his—"

"You *are*. You *did*. You're the one who got him here—and the county attorney, Jarvis Abbott—and—"

"Russ had worked with him off and on, thought they'd be a good fit."

"Conrad thought—Oh, my God. Everybody thought it was the county attorney who'd brought the sheriff in. It was the other way around. And you were behind it all. And—"

"Said a word or two to folks making the decisions."

"—you never told me about it."

"Wasn't my place to be telling people."

"Not people—me. *Me*."

He leveled those eyes at me. "You got a reason I should view you as different from other people, Elizabeth?"

I was breathing hard. Anger. Anger and irritation. That's why I gave him back look for look, too.

Except it wasn't.

We were at a turning. I wanted...

Wanted.

Yes, I wanted. But I wasn't ready to want. Not this way. Not yet— not *now*.

Hell, I couldn't even say if "yet" might ever come.

I didn't know. Couldn't know.

And I wouldn't be pushed.

Not by him, not by Mike.

Not even by myself.

"No reason except I thought we were friends, Tom."

He looked at me for a long, lung-burning instant. "No you didn't, Elizabeth."

"I've got to go."

His gaze remained level, unwavering. "That's all you came for? To talk about Sheriff Conrad?"

"What else would I have come about?"

He didn't accept the challenge. "Okay. See you 'round, Elizabeth."

MIKE, WITH JENNIFER in the passenger seat, pulled up in the Hamburger Heaven parking lot behind me.

Since it was two to one, I transferred to the back seat of Mike's SUV. It was beginning to feel like a second home.

"When's Tom coming?" he asked before I'd even pulled the door closed behind me.

"He's not."

"Elizabeth—"

"He's buddies with the new sheriff. God, he's the reason the new sheriff is here. He's behind the whole thing. Conrad and Abbott." I reported what he'd said.

"Wow," Mike said.

"I don't get it," Jennifer said.

"Tom Burrell knew Conrad in college and—"

"I get *that*. And he recommended this guy to be sheriff and this guy wanted the other guy and everybody said yes because Tom usually knows what he's talking about. What I don't get is why that would have anything to do with helping us."

"Because he has divided loyalties."

"You think Tom would *snitch* on us?"

"It's more complex than snitching, but basically..." With the two of them looking at me that way I couldn't bring myself to say *yes, hell, yes.* So I went another direction. "We don't want to put him in a situation where he has to decide."

Mike released a breath in a sigh. Resignation, I thought. He truly wouldn't want to put Tom in that sort of situation.

I wasn't that altruistic.

"But—"

"She's right, Jen—Jennifer."

He recovered too late and received a lecture on how she was a grownup and trying to maintain a professional image so she could advance her career and it didn't help one bit when people couldn't even remember a simple thing like calling her Jennifer instead of the dreaded nickname of Jenny.

I appreciated every word of it. First, because I wasn't on the receiving end this time. Second, because it put us farther and farther away from the topic of Thomas David Burrell.

When she ran out of steam and Mike ran out of apologies, I swept in.

"What about Diana?"

Mike shook his head. "I tried, but she's booked solid. She said for all of us to come to her place tonight."

I was disappointed, but not too surprised. Even at KWMT-TV, Diana's ability was recognized. Not rewarded, not by management, but recognized by her coworkers. It kept her busy.

"Jennifer, I sent video to Mike and Diana. I'm going to send it to you now. I'd like you to back it up someplace. Someplace where we can get to it, but where no one would think to look for it, even if they know I took it and that you all have copies. Even if they decide to take it away from us and think they need to know where all the copies are."

"Sure thing."

"You understand that—"

"Got it."

"One more thing. I don't want you to look at it."

"But—"

"No. Not yet. It's … I may never want you to look at it. But for sure I don't want any of you three to look at it until we know how the sheriff's going to play this. If he's going to be a hard ass and come after us—me… Well, I want you to be able to honestly say you never saw the video and to have no expert looking at your devices be able to say otherwise."

"If that's all you're worried about, I can—"

"No, that's not all I'm worried about," I interrupted Jennifer. "Remember. Being able to honestly say you haven't looked at it."

"All right, all right."

"Okay. We don't have much time, because I've got to be somewhere. So listen closely."

I filled them in on everything that had happened since I answered Dell's call as I walked toward the station that morning—seemed like a whole lot longer ago than it had actually been. I didn't give Jennifer the Yellowstone background—except in the briefest form so she knew who the VisageTome people were—because we'd have to repeat it tonight for Diana.

When I got to the part about recording the crime scene, Mike whistled and Jennifer's eyes widened.

He whistled again at the news that Joel and Ariel, the elk-bugle-loving couple had been at the B&B.

At the end, they each said, "What do you want me to do?"

I had to swallow past a throat-lump to answer.

"Mike, the first thing for you is to clear the decks as much as you can for as long as you can. We're going to have to work fast and hard. Also, if you can find out if there's a connection between Krista and Dirk Seger and someone at the station."

"I'll see what I can find out. And I'll call you when I'm free."

"Good. I'll have to come by the station at some point, too. So we'll touch base then. Jennifer, I'd like you to find out everything you can about Darryl Justice."

"That's the dead guy?"

"That's the name of the man who was murdered."

I said it mildly, but her cheeks pinkened. "Got it." I wished she reacted that readily to my warnings about not hacking or otherwise stepping into murky online behavior. "Also Elaine Malsung, Gordon Kelvin, Landon Hart, Brant Nelson, and Alan Varney. But don't let that mire you down too much."

"Not really. With the algorithms—"

"Don't explain," Mike begged. "Please, don't explain."

She grinned at him. "Chicken. Afraid of a little algorithm."

"There's no such thing as a little algorithm," I said, remembering the Sunday breakfast table discussion at the Lake Yellowstone Hotel. "We need more background, too. Jennifer, what do you know about VisageTome?"

Her eyes widened. "You don't know what VisageTome is?"

"Of course I know what it is. I'm not that tech backward. I'm not," I repeated to her skeptical look.

"You have a Leaf?"

"I think the network had one set up for me."

"You don't have a *personal* one?" She rolled her eyes. "Do you even know what happened to the pro one when you came here?"

"I have no idea."

She gave me the Big Gulp sized eye-role. "Even *Mike* has one. I keep it up for him."

"Hey," he protested.

"What I'm hoping you can find out, Jennifer, is more about working there, if there's anything about this team-building exercise that took them to Yellowstone. Do you know anybody who works there?"

"No."

My hopes began to deflate. Then she added, "Not anymore. But I know people who have quit VT."

"Even better." Former employees wouldn't guard their tongues. "Start with the most recent one to leave and work your way backward, see what they have to say in general, ask about this Yellowstone event, see if they'd have any idea why this group would have had a meeting afterward on their own, and if any of your contacts knew any of the folks who came here to Sherman. Also anything about Darryl Justice's career there." When she nodded, I added, "I'm going now. I've got to get to the Sherman Supermarket."

"I know you're out of cookies at work, Elizabeth," Mike started, "but don't you think—"

"I am going to see if I can catch up with Krista Seger," I said with great dignity. "She said she would be there today after lunch. On the chance that she still needs groceries, I'll hang around, see if I can connect with her."

"And find out what Penny knows," Jennifer said.

Penny Czylinski is the head cashier at the Sherman Supermarket. She's also an information hub for the entire county. And unlike others, say some tall ranchers who resembled Abraham Lincoln's good-looking cousin, she talked.

"Yes," I agreed. "That, too."

Mike surrendered. "Okay, okay, so you're going strictly for information."

"As long as you realize that and are sorry for implying otherwise."

I exited with dignity, and pretended I didn't hear the sniggering from Mike's SUV as I walked to mine.

I DROVE DIRECTLY to the supermarket, but did not go in right away. I parked in a distant corner of the parking lot—and let me tell you, there's plenty of room for parking lots in Wyoming, so the distant corner can be quite a distance—and checked my phone.

Needham Bender, editor and publisher of the Sherman Independence had texted me: Tell me all.

I texted back: Sorry, not this time.

I could practically hear him snort that I hadn't told him all any time.

Then I made a phone call.

"Dex? It's Danny."

I had started using that nickname when I called my source in the FBI lab years ago, to minimize the chance that anyone listening would connect his phone caller with the reporter Elizabeth Margaret "E.M." Danniher." Now, it hardly mattered, since I wasn't breaking stories any of his superiors would care about.

"Danny. You could have come back to D.C."

I started from the end. "I will come back to visit, Dex. Maybe in the spring. We can have lunch outside and feed the squirrels. But, yes, I did stay here."

"You're doing good work."

Totally unexpected tears spurted into—but not out of—my eyes. "Thank you, Dex." I cleared my throat. "That means a lot to me."

"You've made people mad. Mad enough to want to kill you. That shows you're doing good work."

That was a benchmark I didn't expect to show up in management guides anytime soon, though it certainly had some merit.

It also made me curious. "Has anybody been mad enough to want to kill you, Dex?"

"Oh, yes. Mostly my supervisor." After a short pause during which I fought to hold in my laughter, he added, "And lawyers."

"They're idiots," I said loyally.

"Oh, yes." He dismissed that as so clearly true as to be uninteresting. On to the puzzle to solve. That's always what mattered to him. "What murder do you have now?"

I told him.

"Every indication is that Wardell Yardley is a good and truthful reporter," he said when I finished.

"He is. He's also my friend."

He released a small sigh. "You have a lot of friends."

I hadn't thought so. Not eleven months ago when my ex's machinations brought my career down in flames and then—But, no. That had nothing to do with his comment.

"I'm very fortunate in the friends I have. Friends like you, Dex. Who have remained my friends, even though I pulled away from them for so long."

"Because you didn't have a question to ask."

That wasn't why I'd pulled away from my friends. But it was what he understood. "Exactly."

"But now you do have a question, because you have a murder to solve." It was half order, half invitation to get on with it.

To him, these were all puzzles to be solved, and his fingers constantly itched for new puzzles because he went through them so quickly.

I told him about the video.

"You sent it? I don't have it yet," he said.

"No, I haven't sent it. I wanted to be sure you'd want to receive it before I sent it. You heard what I said about the sheriff? I don't want to get you in troub—"

"Send it."

"Dex, don't you think I should at the least use your personal email address."

"I can open it right away here, so that's okay."

"I want you to think about this. If your bosses—"

"Send it. I'll call you."

He hung up.

I sent it.

Chapter Eighteen

WHEN I ENTERED the Sherman Supermarket after my virtuously long walk across the parking lot, I did happen to go down the cookie aisle first.

Not that I needed to ever tell Mike Paycik that.

Besides, when I caught sight of Krista Seger, I did not hesitate. I left those cookies behind and took off after her with my empty shopping cart.

She was in the canned vegetable aisle when I caught up. I looked away from a nightmare wall of lima beans and kidney beans on one side, and was greeted by ranks of stewed tomatoes on the other.

When I said her name, Krista whipped around as if I were a hound from hell. True, I'd been deprived of my cookie fix, but I wasn't that bad.

"Oh, it's you."

I think her tone meant I wasn't as bad as she'd feared pre-whipping around.

Clearly she'd forgotten about telling me she'd be here at this time. Nothing like a murder to drive all sorts of things out of your mind.

"Yes, I spotted you and wanted to know if the Williamses had returned."

The surface of her eyes went blank, while the depths kept churning with worry. "Who?"

"The couple who went birding. The older couple who stayed in your B&B last night. You served them breakfast. They left right after."

"Oh. Right. Them. No, they haven't come back yet. God, breakfast feels like a century ago."

"At least with them out you can get into their room, get on with your cleaning routine. It must be difficult with all your other guests sill there—aren't they?—so you can't get in their rooms to clean up?"

"They're still there, but not in their rooms. The sheriff's questioning them one at a time, letting the others go ahead with their meetings in the second parlor."

"What?" I'd thought a lot of things about Sheriff Russ Conrad, but not that he was stupid. It was Investigating 101 to not let potential witnesses talk to each other.

"They questioned all of them once already." She clearly had no idea she was rescuing the sheriff from an accusation of stupidity. "They were raising a fuss. So he said okay and has Richard Alvaro in there with them to make sure they don't talk about anything but, uh, business."

If they did, Deputy Richard Alvaro, young but sharp, would catch it.

Not so stupid, Sheriff Conrad.

"With those guests busy with meetings, that lets you get on with your routine. That's good," I said brightly. Then I let my face fall. "Oh, unless the sheriff's department has made another room off limits."

Off limits sounded so much better than *a crime scene.*

"Off limits?"

"Well, they must have searched all the rooms…" She nodded, an automatic response to that hanging-in doubt sentence. "And if they found something, they would have to keep you out of wherever they found it. I mean along with Wardell's room."

"They're keeping me out of all the rooms upstairs. They're going through them really, really carefully."

That meant the sheriff had a good chance of finding anything there was to find, which I wouldn't mind if that pushed him to realize Dell hadn't done this.

It also meant Krista hadn't been in any of the rooms today, so pumping her for information wouldn't do any good. That well was dry.

Except for possibly one drop…

"That's got to be hard on you with so much cleaning to do and blood being so hard to get out, and with it being in more than one room…"

"Blood? I haven't heard anything about blood. How did you hear—?"

I'd hoped to learn if the sheriff had homed in on any room or rooms beyond Dell's, but she'd given me a different piece of information.

She was scared. Deeply scared that law enforcement had—or *could?*—find blood in a room that wasn't Dell's.

As long as she was this rattled, it was worth pushing on another front.

"Why did you call me about the VisageTome people being there?"

She was staring at the stewed tomatoes, as if they would give her the answer. Stewed tomatoes diced. Stewed tomatoes organic. Stewed tomatoes whole. Stewed tomatoes with onion. Stewed tomatoes with garlic. Stewed tomatoes with special spices. Stewed tomatoes with garlic, onion, and special spices. Stewed tomatoes original recipe.

"I told you, I thought it might be a story for you."

The stewed tomatoes had let her down.

Because that also made me realize how interesting it was that when she'd called she'd known the gist of what I'd said to Mel, which presumably he'd told the Heathertons, about why I wasn't going to do a story on the opening of the bed and breakfast.

It wasn't as interesting as it might be in other communities outside everybody-knows-everybody Cottonwood County, but, still, interesting.

Plus, there was another element:

She'd thought that the fact of a group of VisageTome people holding an apparent secret meeting had potential as a news story.

How many people in this county would recognize the potential in that situation for a good news story? Certainly not Thurston Fine.

Was she particularly acute about news? Or did she know more about what was going on with that VisageTome group than she was letting on? If she had knowledge that made the story big, she wouldn't need to be as acute in spotting potential news.

"Why?" I asked.

Her gaze jerked from the stewed tomatoes—who knew stewed tomatoes came in that many varieties?—to me. "Why what?"

"Why did you think it might be a story that VisageTome employees were meeting at your bed and breakfast?"

"Oh." Was that relief? Yes, I thought it was. "Well, there's a lot of interest in VisageTome. More than half the world is on VisageTome and it sprouts a Leaf every second of every day."

That was almost word for word what Darryl Justice had said at Lake Yellowstone Hotel. Not that the concept was fresh or new. VisageTome pounded away that message all the time.

"People on VT are interested in their own Leafs and Branches, not what a group of employees is up to." Unless the group of employees was plotting to make the system even more frustrating and rule-bound than it already was, and in that case any rational person would have wiped out all the VisageTome people.

"Uh. I didn't think about that," she lied.

Yup, lied through her teeth, right there with all the diced, whole, organic, onions added, garlic added, special spices, and original recipe stewed tomatoes looking on.

"What did you think was going on?" I saw she was headed for general denial and added, "I asked on the phone last night if you thought something was going on and you said *absolutely*. So, what was it?"

"I just meant I had a feeling. A bad feeling. Because there was a lot of ... tension."

"About what?"

"I didn't know—don't know. I don't."

"Do you still want me to do a story about those VisageTome people being at your B&B?"

"No." Then a light went on behind her eyes. An I've-got-an-idea light. "To tell the truth—" An intro that heralds a lie more times than not. "—I thought it might intrigue you. You know, get you to do a story anyway. I suppose I was just being silly. Having nerves about opening and everything. And when they all arrived together, I was overwhelmed. I panicked. Now, with what's happened… well, they can't leave. I'm sorry. I shouldn't have tried to get you to do a story after you'd said you wouldn't. Oh, gosh. Look at the time. I, uh, got to go. I promised Dirk I'd be back by now."

She left at full speed, without even a good-bye to me or the stewed tomatoes.

I returned to the cookie aisle.

✧   ✧   ✧   ✧

WITH A NO-LONGER empty cart, I approached the checkout line in a pensive mood.

That is not good.

When you get in Penny Czylinski's checkout line you need to be pumped up, senses alert, adrenaline high.

Think of football players bouncing up and down to get the blood flowing, chanting, and pounding each other on the shoulder pads. That's what's needed before entering Penny's line.

Because once you're in it, your task resembles trying to pan for gold in the stream from a fire hose.

And here was I strolling up to the line without any pre-game pumping-up. This wasn't going to be pretty.

"Well, hello there, Elizabeth. Shame about your friend being locked up for murder when he's visiting—"

"He's not locked up and—"

"—such a short time. Why—"

As if finding a dead body in his bed would have been okay if Dell were going to be here for a month.

"—that new Sheriff Russ Conrad's going to have to answer to Emmaline Parens if he doesn't have your friend out in time for the lunch she and Gisella have planned out for Wednesday."

My arm jerked as if someone had walloped my funny bone. Sensation jangled through me. I'd totally forgotten. If Dell was still being held and we had to cancel…

Penny was right. The new sheriff would get a well-bred, soft-voiced welcome to the county from Mrs. Parens that would blister his hide. He wouldn't fare well with Gisella Decker, either.

So at least there'd be *that* compensation.

"Saw you talking with Krista Seger. Must've said something that set her topsy-turvy because—"

"I didn't—"

"—she bought the big jar of chunky peanut butter when she knows it's one of those things where the bigger size costs more than two of the smaller ones. And that husband of hers won't let her forget it. Wouldn't be surprised if he marched her back here and made her exchange it like he did with the detergent. Last March that was. Not long after they moved here. Wasn't caring who heard him dressing her down for that, either. Thirty-seven cents."

Her snort of disdain—I thought it was for him, rather than the thirty-seven-cent savings—barely slowed her.

"Touchy that one is, especially as the opening kept getting delayed and delayed. Now, don't be thinking he hits her, because that's not so. More like he's afraid she'll fly away so he holds on tight out of fear. Had a neighbor boy like that with birds. He'd catch hurt ones, but he held them so tight so they couldn't get away that he up and killed them."

In assuring me Dirk wasn't hitting Krista, Penny had likened him to what sounded to me like a serial-killer-in-training.

"Got the hang of it eventually. Now he works down around Cheyenne rehabilitatin' those big wild birds when they get hurt. What do they call them? Copters? Captors? Something like that. Works wonders according to his sister, who's married to Clyde who works out at the airport."

Okay, maybe not a serial killer.

But it didn't mean Dirk holding on to Krista so tight wouldn't hurt her—physically or emotionally.

"Trouble. All they've had is trouble with that place. Don't suppose you can blame the house, not when the Quinns lived there all those years, and a nicer family you'll never find, though not the best at keeping up with repairs and such, much less the fashions. Krista and

Dirk fussed and fussed about the place. Well, it wasn't ready to be on any TV show about fashionable houses, and I'm sure it needed fixing up, but you'd think the Quinns had been animals to hear them—well, mostly him—tell it. Like they'd been living in filth instead of having about them the things that reminded them of their friends and their good, long lives. That doesn't make anybody a hoarder, even if a pile of paper or two shows up at the house. When you've lived—"

Penny's cheeks had gone pink and her eyes flashed. Dirk Seger's take on the Quinns had hit a nerve.

Just guessing here, but I'd put down money that Penny was a pack rat—at best.

"—a good long while in a house that sort of thing happens unless you're one of those neat freaks who're forever sorting and throwing out and such. Mind you, they had died in the house, the two of them together in the bed they'd shared all those years and nobody knows exactly how long they'd been there. Wasn't more than two weeks, because when Vera missed her shopping I called Gisella right off and she got Wayne Shelton over there. There's some say I should have called the town police, but Vera Quinn didn't know any of those boys and she—"

"The Segers bought the house and—"

"—wouldn't have liked them seeing her in bed. Hector wouldn't't've cared a bit. Out in the garden in his underwear if she didn't keep an eye on him and that wasn't from getting old or anything, my momma used to say he ran around naked as a jaybird from a baby on whenever he got the chance. Bought it up before it even could be put up for sale. Heard they got a good price, too." She snorted, giving me a significant look. "Connections. Got in there first—"

We'd switched to the Segers. I thought.

"What connections—?"

"—and had help with paying for it. Bye, now. Well, hi there, Karen."

Too late. My question was lost in my being ejected out the end of her line and a newcomer brought in.

I started the trek to my distant corner of the parking lot mulling if

I'd picked up any golden nuggets from Penny's fire hose delivery.

The one question that kept coming back to me was whether there was something I'd said that had made Krista so unsettled that she'd bought the giant size of peanut butter.

If so, I wish I knew what it was.

I JUGGLED THE shopping bags against the side of the SUV to fish out my ringing phone.

I did not want to miss a call from James Longbaugh, or Dell, or—

It was Emmaline Parens.

After proper hellos, she said, "I expect you here tomorrow, Elizabeth, accompanied, of course, by Michael and your friend visiting you from Washington, D.C."

"Mrs. Parens, that might not be possible. There's been some trouble—"

"I am aware of the events at the Segers' bed and breakfast."

"How did you—? Never mind." Asking Mrs. P how she knew something was useless. If she'd wanted me to know how she would have told me. "Do you know Krista and Dirk Seger?"

"I have known her since she was a child. I had met him once, that being on the occasion of their wedding. Since their return from the Pacific Northwest to open their bed and breakfast, Krista and I have conversed about her experiences working for VisageTome and the exigencies of a small startup firm that becomes, ah, gonzo."

My back teeth about dropped out. Not because Mrs. P knew what VisageTome was, nor at her using startup—though gonzo being in the same sentence could loosen anyone's molars—but at Emmaline Parens volunteering information about someone she knew, someone involved in a murder investigation.

After that, the fact that Krista Seger had worked at VisageTome was barely a blip on the surprise-o-meter.

Though a very interesting one.

Especially since she hadn't mentioned it.

Was that why the VT people had gone there? Did they know her?

Or had they gone there because Dell had talked about it to Elaine and then been surprised to see a former fellow employee?

"I, uh, I'd like to hear your thoughts on VisageTome." What I'd really like was a word for word report of everything Krista had ever said. "However, I'm not sure when Wardell will be available."

I refused to even think *if.* It had to be *when.*

"He will be available to visit as we have planned. You bring him to see me tomorrow. The sheriff's department is no longer questioning him," she said. "However, he—"

"How—No longer being questioned? Are they holding him? Or—"

She sailed on as if I hadn't spoken. "—is likely to be quite tired tonight. You will, naturally, have a good many questions to ask him, however, be sure to let him get a good night's rest. Tomorrow morning will be satisfactory. Ten-thirty."

"Ten-thirty?" That was barely brunch territory to me. But Mrs. P and Aunt Gee were early birds.

"Gisella will have lunch for us at eleven-twenty. That intrusive gap in the transmission of our voices indicates you have another call so I shall say goodbye now, Elizabeth."

Marching orders delivered, she hung up.

I clicked to switch to the incoming call.

"Elizabeth? It's James Longbaugh. I thought you might like to talk to your friend—" Mrs. Parens was right again. "—they never arrested him. He's at the sheriff's department and—"

"How much long—"

"—I don't expect it to be much longer, but he'd like to see you now if you're available."

"I'll be right there."

Chapter Nineteen

WHEN I ARRIVED at the sheriff's department, the deputy behind the counter was our old unfriend Deputy Ferrante.

"Sheriff wants to see you." This statement was totally out of character for his communications, which usually consisted of his telling me who couldn't or didn't want to see me.

My heart jumped. Could he have found the murderer already? That would clear Dell. But then why...?

"Where's James Longbaugh?"

"Dunno," he lied. He didn't even try to do it well. "Sheriff's office is at the end of the hall."

I went down the hall, past the two interview rooms—catching a murmur of voices from Interview Room Two, though I couldn't identify the people behind the voices—on beyond the restrooms and break room to the sheriff's office.

The walk gave me a chance to consider how to approach him. Adversarial might be more honest, but less effective. For Dell's sake, I was a big fan of effective right now.

The door was open. I tapped on the frame.

He looked up from the desk and gave a curt nod. I stepped in to an office that made Spartan look like an overdose of frou-frou. The only remotely humanizing effect were two photos of dogs on the bulletin board behind him. One was all or mostly border collie. The other was a blender dog in which German Shepherd was the only identifiable ingredient.

I was *not* going to say, *You wanted to see me?* That put the ball too much in his court.

I also was not going to ask if he'd solved the murder. Law enforcement tends to answer that question before it can be asked if the answer is yes and get peeved when the answer is no.

Nor was I going to ask if he had a prime suspect. I didn't like the possible answer to that one.

"I appreciate your reassessing your stance on my involvement in this inquiry," I said. Might as well swing for the fences.

He grinned. Genuinely grinned. "Good try."

Without being invited, I sat in a chair that consisted of nothing but right angles. It didn't encourage lingering. "I've proven I'm not trying to cut out law enforcement. I told you what I knew. At least—"

"You went into the scene of a murder."

"I did not. I went into the room next door. I didn't go in the bedroom. And I'm the one who made sure the sheriff's department was called."

"The murder victim was found in your friend's room. His locked room."

"Accessible through the bathroom."

"Which was also kept locked."

"But had a spare key on top of the doorframe, which Krista told Dell about with all the VisageTome people and a couple more guests within hearing. So everyone staying there knew about the key, plus anybody any of them told, along with who knows how many people who've done work on the house while they've been preparing to open."

"They couldn't know your friend wouldn't be using his bedroom, as he claims."

He was putting up obstacles, but not with any firepower between them. Call me wildly optimistic, but I think he'd taken several strides along the path of reason that said Dell wasn't the murderer.

But Sheriff Conrad had reasons to go cautiously. Because his priority was to build a solid case to put a murderer in prison.

I had reasons to go fast. Because my priority was to find the murderer so *that* was the story, rather than Wardell Yardley's involvement in it.

Having a brush with a named murderer made him interesting. Being part of an unsolved case made him vulnerable to all the whisperers and gossips who would get a lot more attention if they speculated about his role than if they acted responsibly.

"They could if they had eyes and knew anything about people." Come to think of it, that might rule out the VisageTome people. Better not elaborate on that. Let him assume for a while longer that they could tamp down their egos long enough to notice other people and then could exercise sufficient empathy to recognize the emotions of those other people. "Or if they could knock on a door. That's all they had to do. Knock, get no answer, grab the bathroom key and voila—a place to stow a dead body." I watched him carefully as I added, "Or to lure someone in order to make them a dead body."

His face gave nothing away. "The victim would have known it was Yardley's room. Why would he go in there?"

"Why would Darryl Justice have any idea whose room it was, since he wasn't staying at the B&B?" The tiniest flicker of annoyance, so I knew he wasn't happy I knew that fact.

Instead of addressing it, though, he asked, "How do you know the victim's name?"

"Dell told me. No, I take that back. I told him the name after Dell described him. But what would it matter if Darryl did know whose room it was? All his lurer had to do was assure him Dell was elsewhere for the night or lie and say it was his room. Either way, it worked."

He huhhed. Half accepting, wholly skeptical. His eyes narrowed. "You said before that you told me what you know. Then you said *at least* ... At least what?"

"At least what you let me tell you before you told me to get lost." I said immediately.

His eyes went to slits. "Tell me now. The facts," he added as I drew in a breath.

I told him what facts I knew about the people who had ended up at the B&B.

First, I related encountering the VisageTome people and Joel and

Ariel at the Elk Jam at Yellowstone. Our meeting again at Lake Yellowstone Hotel. The incident at the geysers. Bunny at the hotel. Then her son's arrival.

My impressions and viewpoints on atmosphere or relationships were not facts. Nor were my memories of conversations that could be called ambiguous at best.

He circled back around to Darryl Justice. That was normal procedure—study the victim in hopes of getting a whiff of the murderer.

"You said you talked to him on the hotel porch Saturday night. Why was that?"

I'd actually said I'd talked to him each of the three nights. I had a feeling I knew where the sheriff was going, and it meant I had no obligation to tell him about that snippet from Friday night's encounter. I was relieved. Because it was the sort of did-I-hear-what-I-thought-I-heard, vague, garbled mess that could lead any investigator down a rabbit hole.

Perhaps because of that relief, I let my eyebrows hike. "I was there, he was there. It seemed polite. They were brief interactions."

"Why were you both there?" That was decidedly testy.

Here to help, Dell, I reminded myself.

"I was there for the view and a bit of fresh air. I can only speculate that he was there to smoke a cigarette." He opened his mouth. Before he could ask the pin-it-down question, I said, "Yes, he smoked a cigarette on the porch. I saw him smoke exactly one each time, but I can't say one way or the other if he had more than that."

He couldn't complain about the thoroughness of that answer. Of course, he didn't know I was happy to answer questions about cigarettes all day. Questions about half-heard voices on Friday night were another thing.

He didn't laud my thoroughness, however.

He grunted. Then asked, "Did he give any indication he considered what happened at the geyser significant?"

"No. The opposite, in fact." He gave another *huh*—this one acknowledging my words while apparently joining in with Darryl Justice's assessment that the incident had no significance.

I did not volunteer my differing assessment.

"That's it?" he asked.

"That's all the facts," I said.

A glint in his eyes said he knew what I was saying, but he was sticking to his guns—and his facts.

"There is one more thing about Darryl, Sheriff. He seemed like a nice guy."

"Doesn't matter whether he was or not. Could be the worst of the worst. He gets the same justice."

"It makes it sadder."

Behind the narrow-eyed don't-mess-with-me-lady concentration I saw a flicker. Damned if we didn't almost connect there for an instant.

He rocked forward a bit and started to stand. "I suppose you want to see your friend now, Ms. Danniher."

"You suppose right."

WARDELL YARDLEY SAT in Interview Room One with Deputy Lloyd Sampson.

Since they usually filled Interview Room One first, whoever was involved in the murmuring voices I couldn't make out from Interview Room Two likely had been brought in after Dell.

Outwardly Dell appeared composed and at ease. A little relief showed in his dark eyes at seeing me.

"I was telling the deputy here how during the past hour since he replaced his fellow deputy, I have looked with increased longing at his crisp, clean uniform. I would give a great deal to have access to my clothes."

He was wearing sweat pants, a shirt, and sweater that he had never in a million years purchased.

"I'm sorry, sir—" started Sampson.

"Wardell." He was corrected.

"Don't mind that, Dell," I said. "He also insists on calling me ma'am."

Sampson doggedly continued, "You can't have your clothes for some time yet. The room's a crime scene and your possessions must remain there until the entire room is completely examined."

"Bringing in the DCI folks, huh?"

He didn't fall for my casual question about the state Department of Criminal Investigations. "I'll leave you alone. The sheriff said he'd be in presently."

"You aren't going to go around to where you can listen to our conversation now, are you, Lloyd?"

"Of course not." He sounded insulted.

As the deputy exited, I caught Dell's eye and said, "Nevertheless."

He nodded. Message received. No revelations while in the sheriff's department.

But he did have something to say.

"Elizabeth, that thing you were saying about the sky out here..." Dell was pensive—a sure sign of how shaken he was.

"What thing?"

"About it not being the weather. About it being something else. That first night I was here you were saying it. About the light and poetry, but about it being something else."

"Oh, yeah." Gradually, the conversation reconstituted itself in my memory.

"What is that something else? What do people from elsewhere not understand about it?"

I huh'd an acknowledgement of his question, but I needed some time to put my mind back to that night, to the point I'd been heading for.

"Visitors talk about what the vastness and the pure blueness of the Wyoming sky *does* to people. But that's missing the core. Because it's not what the Wyoming sky does to people, it's what it shows about them. Leaving them no place to hide who they are and who they aren't. Some folks stand tall under that. Some scuttle as close to the ground as they can get. Some sink out of sight. But whatever they do when there's no place to hide, it's real."

Staring straight ahead, he said, "I wonder what it's going to show about me."

Chapter Twenty

"IT'S GOING TO show you're the man I've always known you to be, Wardell Yardley. Smart and tough and caring even when you like to pretend you're not and above all…"

He looked up when I didn't finish it.

"…a smart-ass to the core."

One side of his mouth lifted. "Thank you, Elizabeth. I needed to get back in touch with the real me."

"And the real you is a reporter, so get ready to start reporting. As soon as we leave here, I want to hear everything."

"But I wasn't there."

"I know *that*. But before and after, you surely saw things."

He released a gust of a sigh. "I've been over and over that with the sheriff."

"And soon you're going to go over and over it with me and a few others."

"I put my things away and—"

"Not yet."

"Right. Sorry."

Wardell Yardley not only taking correction without complaint, but saying he was sorry. It was rather like the British Army musicians playing "The World Turned Upside Down" as they surrendered at Yorktown, essentially acknowledging they'd lost the Revolutionary War and the colonies had become a nation.

Like Dell, the British Army had had more than its share of ego and arrogance, so they weren't figures most viewers would feel all warm and cuddly about. But you could sort of see their point about how the rug had been pulled out from under them.

I had no idea how the British Army bounced back from being defeated by a bunch of pesky rebels, but I prescribed a dose of tough love for Dell.

"Don't get all mopey and sorry for yourself. There's a lot of hard work ahead and we need you to be alert and—"

"I am not mopey or sorry for myself. You try going through a day like this and see how you come out of it, Ms. Delicate Flower Danni-her." The Yardley snap was back. Also, he'd sat up and his eyes sparked. "I can tell you—"

The door opened. "Sorry to interrupt if this was a private quarrel," the sheriff said dryly, reigniting my never extinguished suspicions that they would listen in. "Thought you'd want to know that you can go now. Both of you."

He made the *both* pointed enough to add a glaze of *and good riddance* to it.

If there was a charm school for sheriffs, this guy needed a remedial course.

"Go?" Dell repeated, looking from the sheriff to James Long-baugh, who had come in behind him.

"You were never under arrest. We would have questioned you at the scene, but—" The sheriff cut me a hard look. "—since you declined to answer there, we brought you here. Now that you have answered our questions and more facts have come to light..."

"Your alibi has been confirmed, Mr. Yardley," the lawyer said.

His alibi. Of course. Or I wouldn't have been allowed in.

So Dell's status had already been established, if not completely pinned down, when I was called to the principal's office. That meant Sheriff Conrad had been digging at me to get what he could get, not to assess Dell's situation.

It didn't endear him to me, but it didn't irk me, either. All's fair in love, war, and asking questions.

✧　✧　✧　✧

Outside the sheriff's department, James made sure Dell had all his contact information and vice versa. They spoke a bit more after I tactfully got into my vehicle and out of hearing range.

While I watched through the windshield, I called Mike with the news and was told they'd already planned a gathering at Diana's, so I should bring Dell there in ninety minutes.

Lawyer and client parted with a firm handshake and Dell got in the passenger seat as James walked off toward his office.

"I'm not to leave the county," Dell said.

"You weren't going to anyway, so that's nothing. We're going to get some people together tonight," I told Dell as he fastened his seatbelt, "and go over what's happened. We'll have lots of questions."

"I told you—"

"Specifics. Like when did you leave your room? When did you get back? Who knew you'd be gone? Did you hear anything? See anything? Go back to—"

"Now?"

"No." I shouldn't have jumped the gun. "When we get to Diana's. We have some time, so I can get something from the supermarket and we can microwave it in the bunkhouse—my sort of studio apartment. That way you can eat in peace without strangers ogling at you."

"I need clothes first. They took mine for evidence."

Of course. What was I thinking?

For Dell, clothes were essential, eating was an afterthought. Not that he didn't enjoy his meals, but they were a distant second on his hierarchy.

And people ogling him was never a bad thing in his view.

"You are not going to like the choices, Dell."

"Clean will be a good start."

"Clean we can do."

Wait until he saw what Sherman's men's clothing stores couldn't do.

Chapter Twenty-One

I COULD HAVE stayed with Dell and served as an audience for his inevitable complaints about the clothes or I could try to do something useful. Like possibly take a step toward keeping him on the air as a White House correspondent.

I dropped him off and started toward the Wild Horses Bed and Breakfast.

A call from Jennifer though, prompted a U-turn on a side street, and a return to the station.

Mike and Jennifer came out of the double doors and got into my SUV as soon as I pulled up. Jennifer had her jacket on, but Mike was in shirtsleeves. Even for a hardy Wyomingite, that was pushing things with the sun setting fast on a none-too-warm November day.

"I have to go back in for a final intro and then I should be done," he said. "But Jennifer wanted to update us both."

She gave an impressive rundown of Darryl Justice's life, from his birth in a Portland hospital as the second of three kids, to his college education at Stanford, to his employment at VisageTome almost four years ago. All in a cadence that resembled Edward R. Murrow, if he'd been a young female from Wyoming.

Maybe I needed to lighten up on her history of journalism lessons.

"Two of my sources," she continued, "had something to say about him. Only one had ever met him, but the other one had heard about Darryl Justice from three people who'd worked with him in two positions."

"And?"

"Everybody agreed he was an okay guy. Carried his share of the load, looking out for the overall project instead of just himself." She looked up from the screen where she was checking notes. "They all said that's real unusual at VisageTome. Everybody who works there thinks they're the smartest person in the room, so there're full-blown ego wars. My sources say it's encouraged.

"Oh, and he's one of the few people who resisted the pressure to accept housing on campus. My sources say VT likes workers to live on campus so there's more control over them. It's like this cult," she concluded in her more natural voice.

"Good work, Jennifer."

"Oh, I'm not done. In fact—Darn. I have to go back inside for a minute. I want to switch a search to my server at home. In case Thurston or one of his trolls gets curious about what my computer's doing."

"Mike?" I stopped him as he was about to follow her. "I'll take Jennifer with me and see if I can find Krista Seger again to follow up on a couple points. Could you get Dell and bring him to Diana's?"

"Sure. But why did you get that look while you were listening to that stuff about VisageTome. Something strike you?"

"No. Not about VisageTome. It was Jennifer, talking about her sources. Our little news aide is growing up."

He snort-laughed. "Don't let her hear you say she wasn't grown up before. Or your Leaf will get blight."

YOU WIN SOME, you lose some.

You make the best of what you get.

What we got at the B&B was the win of not being spotted by Officer Randy Hollister, who was sitting on a chair in the front entryway. We spotted him through the half-glass of the double doors as we drove past.

So we parked around the corner and then walked back, turning into the driveway, while keeping vehicles parked there between us and the front door. We came out past the front corner and walked along the north side of the house, with a straight shot to the back door, which was at the northeast corner.

What we lost was an opportunity to talk to Krista alone to find out what had rattled her into buying the more expensive peanut butter.

The man who answered the back door was medium build, medium height. His buzz cut didn't hide that his hairline came down in a low V. That, along with a prominent brow bone and horizontal lines in his forehead gave him a faint resemblance to a caveman.

"What do you want?" His gravelly voice matched.

"Hi. You must be Dirk Seger. I'm Elizabeth Margaret Danniher and this is Jennifer Lawton from—"

"We're not interested."

He started to swing the door closed. Krista's voice came. "They're from the station, Dirk."

"Yes, KWMT-TV," I said.

He'd stopped closing the door and his expression lightened. He looked over his shoulder, presumably toward his wife, though I couldn't see her.

When he turned back, he opened the door.

"C'mon in." He looked beyond Jennifer. "No cameras?"

His tone left it up in the air whether that was good or bad, so I just said, "No."

He let us by, so there was a moment for Krista to give me a puzzled, pleading, displeased look that I hoped I responded to with neutral calm.

Then there were introductions—as if Krista and I hadn't met before and as if I hadn't already given our names—and handshakes all around.

"We hoped to get some background. You have a beautiful place here." If that led him to think the background was for a piece on the B&B and not the murder, that might help.

Krista knew better, but if she gave us away I could snitch on her buying the wrong size of peanut butter.

"It didn't look like this when we started. Took a lot of work. Had a lot of setbacks. The plumbing—"

His wife groaned. It felt rehearsed. Like they'd worked on the timing of that response.

"—teased us that it could be repaired, then gave up the ghost the minute we'd paid for the repairs. We had to start all over. Did the plumbing all over. The electrical system, too. But we got through it. We got it done."

They looked at each other.

The scene directions could have said: Exchange of looks that says this couple battled obstacles together and is united in the accomplishment of overcoming them.

"Now that you're opening, you can start to reap the rewards of all that work," I said.

Their sense of accomplishment seemed to deflate.

"Can we? After this?" Her tone said she already knew the answer and it wasn't a happy one.

"It'll be forgotten eventually."

"If we'd opened when we should have we'd be established and this wouldn't hurt so much, but now…" Dirk shook his head.

I was tempted to say it hadn't turned out well for Darryl Justice, either, but kept quiet.

"We should have opened months ago." His voice was angry. "We were ready. We'd pushed and pushed and we were ready. All ready. We had it all set to open early enough to get fall traffic to Yellowstone, but those assholes at VisageTome messed up our ads."

"You can't know that, Dirk."

"I do know it. And so do you." He glared a challenge at her. She folded. With some satisfaction, he continued. "First, someone changed the targeting for all our ads to people living in China and Nepal. When I caught that and corrected it, they put in a redirect on our url that sent any traffic to a porn site. I caught that, too, but it could have been going for a while. Their next game was using one of their click farms to make it look like we were getting lots of traffic—driving up the cost of the ad. It took longer to recognize the clicks we were paying for weren't real traffic."

I nodded with what I hoped looked like comprehension and sympathy.

"That sucks," Jennifer said with enough of both to cover me, too.

"You probably think I'm paranoid—"

"No," Jennifer and I said in unison.

She had no trust in any big Internet businesses. I had understood enough to get the gist and, remembering Gordon Kelvin's rant, I found it entirely believable.

"That's got to be illegal," I said.

"Yeah," he said bitterly. "Try catching them."

"Try even talking to them," I added. Because their sadistic customer service was something I *did* know about.

"That's right," Dirk said. "Even with Krista being a former employee, we couldn't get any satisfaction."

"Oh? You used to work at VisageTome?" You'd be surprised how much you can find out by asking a question you already know the answer to. For starters, you find out if the person considers it an answer worth trying to hide with a lie.

"A while ago."

"How'd you like it?"

"It's a huge place. A lot of turnover. You barely get to know the person working next to you before they're gone. And that's if there's time to talk to them for all the work."

A non-answer from top to bottom. And interesting that she'd already set up a defense about not knowing people there.

"Yeah, that's one of the reasons Krista and I decided to move here and open the B&B. To get away from that. Overtime. Weekends. Nights. Never predictable. It was killing her. Turning her into somebody she wasn't."

I caught what might have been a wince from his wife.

Had he known yesterday that the group arriving at the B&B was from VisageTome? And what difference could it make if he did? Surely he didn't hold a murderous grudge because it had been a lousy work environment for his wife.

"So, had you met any of the people from VisageTome who are staying here?" I asked her.

She shot a look at her husband. "Uh, a little. In passing."

I'd simply asked if she'd met them, yet she'd played it down even more.

"Small world, huh," I said. "Which ones had you met in passing?"

"Elaine Malsung. Alan Varney. Gordon Kelvin. I didn't know their names, but I recognized the other two from seeing them around—Brant Nelson and Landon Hart."

"And you, Dirk?"

"I never met any of the people she worked with at VisageTome."

"Until last night."

He shrugged at my addendum. "If you can call it that. Like I told the sheriff, they wanted stuff and I got it for them. Wasn't like they bothered to introduce themselves to the help."

"What stuff?"

"Furniture moved in the second parlor. A couple extra chairs. Extension cords. Pizza. Drinks. Stuff like that."

"For their meeting."

"Yeah. Their super secret decoder ring meeting," he sneered. "They stopped talking every time I walked in. And they'd start again as soon as the door closed behind me."

I wondered how they operated with Richard Alvaro in the room. "So they stayed in the room the whole time?"

"With the amount they were knocking back? No way."

"Who spent time out of the room?"

"All of them." He said it, as if he'd been waiting to get it in. "More than once for each of them."

"When?" Would it matter since we didn't know a time of death? At least not yet. If Dex got back to me…

"I wasn't taking notes," he said.

"When did their meeting start?"

"About seven."

"And went until?"

"No idea. Fell asleep on the couch in the front parlor."

"When?"

"You and the sheriff," he complained. "When you fall asleep on the couch do you know what time? After midnight, but beyond that, no idea."

He had a point. He also had a very loosey-goosey account of his movements.

"When did you go to bed?"

"Never did. Woke up when I heard all those deputies tramping through the house. Went up to see what was going on and there went my day."

So Krista had lied about Dirk being up late and leaving early. And neither had an alibi.

"What about the older couple? What did they do last night?"

"Your friends, you mean?" Krista sounded confused.

So was I for an instant, then I remembered. "Right, the Williamses. They're more like friendly acquaintances. Did you talk with them?"

Dirk shook his head. "Only saw them this morning before breakfast when they asked about birding. Like I'd know."

Warm and welcoming did not describe his manner.

"I checked them in," Krista volunteered. "They insisted on carrying their own bags up, so there was no reason to disturb Dirk. They went out to an early dinner, came back and stayed in their room. Not a peep out of them."

"Wish they were all like that," Dirk grumbled, as if he'd been host to thousands already. "Told the sheriff all about that, too."

"As all good citizens have to do in situations like this," I said, insincerely. "Be perfectly open with law enforcement and tell them everything you know. For example, where you went this morning."

"No big mystery. I went to our storage locker to check if we had chairs that would suit the little princes from VisageTome, who complained about the seats being too hard. And then I went to the liquor store because they're going through it like crazy." He grinned. Not nicely. "You should have heard them whining when the sheriff said they had to double up tonight because they aren't done with the rooms on the third floor yet."

✧ ✧ ✧ ✧

"**WHAT HE SAID** about VisageTome. He sure didn't like the company," Jennifer said. "Or…"

"Go ahead, say it."

"He was griping about the ads, but it seemed like he thought they were out to get him personally."

"Yesssss," I drew it out, pleased she'd picked up on that and without my suggesting it. "Not to say that he was wrong about that, because I often feel VisageTome is on a vendetta against me." She grinned. "There's a saying about not attributing to malice what can be explained by stupidity. And if you say my issues with VT can be explained by *my* stupidity, you're in big trouble. Besides, even you say it can be difficult."

Her grin dimmed. "True. Who said that about malice and stupidity?"

"I have no idea. But I do know there's a final part to it—*but don't rule out malice.*"

"You think VisageTome was really out to get him?"

I'd been thinking it was more likely out to get *me*, but okay, I'd go along with her. "Or someone at VisageTome. There was definitely marital tension when the topic of Krista working there came up."

"She was probably making more money than he was. That's one thing everybody says about VisageTome. They pay well. Makes you miserable, but pays a bunch. You don't think that's it?"

"No way of knowing. But he went on about the long, long hours, the working weekends, the unexpected overtime. Does that make you think of anything?"

"No."

"We'll see if the others have ideas," I said as we got in the SUV.

Chapter Twenty-Two

DELL WAS ON the couch by the fireplace in Diana's living room, in conversation with Mike about the state of men's haberdashery in Sherman, Wyoming.

Actually there wasn't much conversing about it. Dell was complaining and Mike was listening between bites of generous roast beef sandwiches provided by Diana. She'd piled on enough greens and tomatoes to qualify it as a salad.

Jennifer was also by the fireplace, tapping away at a keyboard between bites. She didn't even pretend to listen to Dell.

Diana and I were at the kitchen counter on the opposite end of the great room, finishing our sandwiches. Also making coffee and gathering snacks for post-sandwich gobbling.

Her kids, Gary and Jess, had taken their sandwiches to their respective rooms. Both said they had homework. Judging by the volume of what was coming out of the earbuds dangling around their necks while they mingled with us, neither their homework nor the rest of their lives required unimpaired hearing.

Yes, I'm getting old.

I watched their impressive juggling to get the earbuds back in place before they'd even left the kitchen, while also carrying plates and glasses.

Beside me, Diana sighed. "I'm told I should be grateful they take them out at all. I hold my fire for Internet sites I don't approve of."

"They're good kids, Diana. But speaking of not approving... Is your new friend going to approve of you hosting this gathering?"

She didn't pretend not to know I meant Sheriff Conrad. "Don't be pettish, Elizabeth."

"Pettish? Where'd you get that word? Have you two been reading love poems to each other?"

"I seriously doubt pettish appears in much poetry, especially love poems. And that is not how we've spent our time together."

That calm final sentence stopped me in my tracks. "So you did spend the weekend together?"

"Hardly. Remember me? Mother of two? Not to mention he's starting a new job. But we did spend time together."

Was I surprised?

No.

She had said to me not long ago that she missed sex. She'd been a widow for a decade with two kids to care for and to consider in any potential liaison. In a community like this her opportunities had been limited.

And the crackle between her and Russ Conrad in the county attorney's office had been unmistakable.

It was going to happen. I got that. I couldn't even have blamed the woman if they had fallen into bed this past weekend.

Although I wished it had been someone else. Short of Thurston Fine or Les Haeburn, almost anyone else.

"We talked, Elizabeth." She grinned wryly. "Get your mind out of the bed. Just because you'd like to be doing sheets gymnastics and aren't because you can't decide on a partner—"

"That's not even—"

"—doesn't mean I would jump right in with a man I just met. After all, I have impressionable minds around here—the kids and yours."

"—funny. Also not funny," I added for the crack about my impressionable mind. "Seriously, you just talked?"

"There was no just about it. But, yes, we talked. A lot."

"Which brings me back to how he's going to feel about this gathering at your house and your involvement in—" I stirred my hand around to include the two of us and the trio at the fireplace.

"That was one of many things we talked about. I told him I wouldn't quit doing this. It's too important. You—we—have done good work in finding the truth. As long as we're doing that, I'm part of it. He understood."

I raised my brows.

She chuckled slightly. "He accepted. At least provisionally."

"And he's okay with you not telling him things. Or showing him things."

"I did not tell him about or show him the video you sent earlier today, Elizabeth," she said calmly.

I swallowed back a gust of relief.

"For one thing," she continued, "I haven't seen him today, since he's been busy with this murder thing."

I could have jumped on that, said *would you have shown him if you had seen him?* But I know a trap when I hear one.

I made a face at her.

She laughed.

"Is this meeting going to be called to order?" Dell pitched his voice to reach us in the kitchen. "Or are you two going to keep gossiping in there?"

"I didn't think you'd finished complaining about the clothes." But I picked up a basket of chips and two coffee mugs, while Diana followed with a carafe, more mugs, and the usual coffee additives on a tray.

"Lack of clothes," he corrected. "Besides, there are priorities."

"I didn't think anything came ahead of your wardrobe." I poured coffee into the mugs.

"In most circumstances you would be correct. In this instance, it would be beneficial to have it resolved quickly."

A slight strain in his broadcaster's voice brought my head up.

There was even more strain in the lines of his face. Something different from the strains of the hours since he'd called me this morning. "Why?"

"This might not be an opportune time to have my reputation or my credibility, uh, tarnished."

"Your reputation and credibility? Nobody's ever—" I stopped. I needed to pull in another breath to go on. "Dell, are you on the bubble?"

"Of course not."

I didn't buy it. A quick glance said the others had doubts, too.

Or they might have been confused by the term, a theory that got stronger when Jennifer said, "On what bubble?"

"It's from sports." Good start, but then I stalled. I didn't want to say it. I didn't want it to be true for Dell and I didn't want to embarrass him.

I glanced at Mike. He didn't want that hot potato, either.

Dell picked up smoothly. "A competitor who is currently in a position to advance to the next round of competition or to make—or remain on—a team, yet could be knocked off if someone better comes along is said to be on the bubble."

"Huh." Jennifer appeared to be working her way through Dell's explanation.

He looked at me. "It is true that one obstreperous Baby BB is agitating against me. This annoying infant—son of a BB, of course, because he'd never have his current job title without nepotism—has a *vision*." The disdain packed into that final word had made many a presidential spokesperson shudder. "It involves turning the White House assignment into a bastion of what he insists on calling the *New New Journalism*. As if his little ideas could leap past Tom Wolfe, Truman Capote, Gay Talese..."

I took advantage of his being overcome for a moment by the effrontery of that Baby BB, and said to Jennifer, "New Journalism took hold in the Sixties and Seventies, introduced fiction techniques of style and voice and structure to investigative journalism."

Dell recovered sufficiently to say, "Ah, but to this imbecile, he will be outdoing that by bringing in an empty-minded stick figure to babble empty-minded trivia about—heaven help us—the social life of the White House. *Young! Upbeat! Fashion! None of that dreary stuff.*" He dropped from a chirpy falsetto to his normal voice. "In other words, none of that dreary *news.*"

"But…" I scrambled to sort through a plethora of objections.

"Exactly," Dell said. "He wants the White House to be covered like a second-rate entertainment gossip show."

"But…" The sorting hadn't made much progress amid my horror.

"Oh, yes, I retain support. Certainly from the intelligent viewers. Also from those among the news division BBs who are more aware, since they would be swept aside, too, if this new approach came in. They've proven time and again that they know little about news, so they don't recognize what a travesty this approach would be. But the one attribute they all have in abundance is low cunning when it comes to their own positions, and they recognize that they—as part of the current regime—would be out on their well-padded rears if a new regime takes hold. Even beyond the news division, several BBs have said I have nothing to worry about." He snorted. "I should think not, since I'm the best White House correspondent of any on the air and I won't argue if you said the best ever."

"No," I murmured. "I know how you hate arguing."

The others covered their laughter as best they could.

"Ah, the old Elizabeth Margaret Danniher hasn't been totally drowned in sweetness," Dell drawled.

"Are you saying she used to be less sweet?" Diana asked.

Now Dell chuckled. It was good to hear the sound.

"Okay, okay," I said. "Score's even. But you're right. We need to get to work."

With even more pressure.

A scandal like this might be the opening that idiot BBB needed to undermine Dell.

"I have no idea what getting to work constitutes in this case," he said, "but if it stops people from being able to say 'Where there's a dead body in his bed, there's a murderer,' I'm in favor of it."

"That's the goal," Mike said. "Where do we start, Elizabeth?"

"With Dell telling his story, so you all can hear it first-hand."

He gave it clean, as if he were doing stand-up on a news story. Hours of repeating it for the sheriff had smoothed out the rough edges of recency.

I closed my eyes, trying to call up what I'd been looking at, what I'd seen as he recounted the same facts. Sometimes almost word-for-word.

I hadn't taken the time to notice the bathroom this morning, but now I mentally scanned it, seeing the towel dropped to the floor, two socks under the bench beside the shower, the open shower curtain with faint rivulets still running down the inside, toothbrush extended partway out of the Dopp kit because it was still wet. Other signs of a man getting out of a shower, brushing his teeth, shaving, then heading to the other room for clean clothes.

The shock. Retreating to the bathroom. Scrambling into his discarded clothes. It all fit.

Not that I'd expected that it wouldn't.

I was just relieved that it did.

Also relieved that I'd recorded the bathroom. In case Sheriff Conrad changed his mind about feeling Dell wasn't worth holding.

Dell was telling about returning to his room, discovering he'd left his key somewhere, and using the spare that Krista had told him about.

"I took a shower—"

"Wait. Tell them about when she told you about the key," I said.

"Right. Sorry. That group of VisageTome people were there." He looked at Mike. "Elaine and the guys in that same group as at Yellowstone. Except for Justice. I didn't see him. But there was an older couple on the back stairs, too. I saw them for an instant before the landlady's husband came up that way with—"

I opened my eyes. "You didn't tell me about them. Three more people who were there when she told you about the key."

"Four," he said. "The guy from the B&B was showing your friend around the place. They—"

"My friend? *Bunny*? She was there?"

"—and the couple sort of jumbled up together on that back landing. Is that her name? Bunny? The one you ran into at Yellowstone?"

"That's her name, but how did you know about her? You were otherwise occupied with Elaine when I ran into her."

"Mike pointed her out to me."

Bunny Ramsey Sterakos was at the Wild Horses Bed and Breakfast yesterday. That glimpse I'd caught of two people going into the Haber House Hotel this afternoon probably *had* been Bunny and Christopher. And I'd let them go.

"Was her son with her?" I asked Dell. "Mid-teens, looks a lot like her but with a Y chromosome."

"I saw only her."

"What was she doing there?"

He shrugged. "I have no way of knowing. As I said, the husband of the landlady seemed to be showing her around. I figured you'd told her about the place."

I shook my head. "She didn't stay there?"

"Not that I know of. Kristi mentioned they were full when I checked in."

Interesting. Two people who didn't stay at the B&B showed up there, and one ended up dead.

"Be sure to tell James Longbaugh about these other people who overheard you being told about the key. Okay, back to your account." I closed my eyes again as Dell resumed.

Nothing else made them open until he finished.

"Wow," Jennifer said. "That must have been a shock."

"One hell of a shock," Mike emphasized.

"What next?" Diana asked.

"The alibis. Dell has one, thank heavens, which means Elaine has an alibi, too, but what about—"

"Elaine doesn't have an alibi," Dell interrupted.

My stomach sank. "If she doesn't, you don't and the sheriff thinks—"

"No, he doesn't. He knows I wasn't with Elaine last night."

Chapter Twenty-Three

"YOU HAD TO be. You said you were with someone. Don't tell me you lied to the sheriff, to your lawyer, to—"

"I didn't. I was with someone. But it wasn't Elaine."

"Who?"

"I don't know that you have the right to ask—"

"Wardell Yardley, you are mixed up in a murder case. We're trying to keep this from flushing your career down the toilet. Not to mention that you jump right back into the frying pan of being the prime suspect if the alibi this woman provides doesn't hold up. And on top of all that the sheriff's department already knows who it is because she gave them a statement."

"How do you know—?"

"Because James Longbaugh said it was confirmed and Conrad never would have let you go if it hadn't been. That means it's going to be all over Cottonwood County in a heartbeat, if it's not already. So spill it."

"Clara Atwood," Dell said almost meekly.

Clara from the museum.

"Good Lord. You only met her at dinner Thursday with all the rest of us."

"Well, we talked a couple times, before I came and after."

"*That's* why you wanted cell service at Yellowstone. And here I thought it was for work. I should have known better."

He ignored that completely. "I asked her to have dinner last night, for background on the piece, and…" He raised his hands at the inevitability of it all.

They must have gone to her house, since they certainly weren't in Dell's room at the B&B.

Mike said, "But that's good, right? Elaine's not eliminated as a suspect and Dell's covered."

Yeah, it was good—great, in fact, for Dell.

If the sheriff had a lick of sense, and for Diana's sake I had to accept that he did, Clara Atwood was a stronger and likely more stable alibi for Dell than Elaine would have been. Plus, unlike Elaine, she had no apparent vested interest in the case.

But was everyone in Cottonwood County, Wyoming having a sex life except me? Mind you, there weren't all that many people in Cottonwood County to start with, but still, it was depressing that I was the only celibate one around.

Except maybe Mike and Tom.

At least I hoped so.

And wasn't that stinky of me?

"Right, Elizabeth?" Mike said.

I blinked back to the conversation. "Right. But how did this happen?" I demanded of Dell.

"Like I said, I asked her to dinner and we, ah, yes, we hit it off." he had regained his usual manner. "We returned to her house afterward. She had photos of the gold coins and a video of the recovery."

"Come up and see my etchings" was so passé. Now it was "Come see my photos of gold coins."

"Were you supposed to see Elaine? Did you have plans?" If she'd gone to his room, discovered him gone ... and what? Had a berserk jealous reaction? Not to mention how did Darryl Justice happen to be there for her to vent her murderous rage on?

"No."

"But you were the reason she and her cohorts came to Sherman, to stay at the B&B?"

"I suppose so. She asked if I was going back to D.C. after the weekend. I said, no, I was staying in Sherman on an assignment. She wanted to know what assignment. I said only that it was a story that reached back into the history of Wyoming. That led to my describing the Hoover House—"

"Haber House," the rest of us corrected.

"—Hotel, which led to my telling her about staying in the B&B."

"Did she say they were staying there, too?"

"No. She only said it sounded promising."

"Promising? She used that word."

He frowned at my questioning his reporting. "Yes."

"That sounds like they'd decided to have the meeting, but possibly not where to have it."

"What meeting?" Mike asked.

I quickly filled them in on what Krista and Dirk said.

"Ah, that explains it," Dell said.

"Explains what?"

"Why Elaine didn't pursue spending the evening with me."

"Disappointed?" I asked pointedly. That ego would get him in trouble… if it hadn't already.

"Relieved. I had the dinner date with Clara and, as it turned it out, it was far more enjoyable than I could have expected with Elaine."

"So you *did* sleep with her. Elaine, I mean. It's clear you did with Clara."

"A gentleman doesn't—"

"But you do. And even if you didn't, this is about murder, Dell, so quit being coy."

"Yes, I slept with her. Both of them. Or I should say each of them since it was one at—"

"At Yellowstone?" After his nod, I added, "Her room or yours?"

"Hers."

"So you could get away." I waved off his drawn-in breath in anticipation of responding. "Never mind. It doesn't matter—except, yes it does. Tell us about her room."

"What about it? It was a hotel room. There was a bed."

I rolled my eyes. "Tell us about *her* in the room—neat, messy, personal effects around."

"Not neat. Clothes on the bed, on the bench at the foot of the bed, on the chairs by a round table by the window. Toiletries over the bathroom. Mixed brands." He squinted, remembering. "No photos or anything of that ilk. I thought when we came in she would show me something on her computer, but she didn't."

"Why'd you think that?"

"She went right to it, where it was sitting on the small table, and picked it up. I thought she was going to bring it over. But she closed it."

"Did she do anything with the computer later?"

"No. She was otherwise occupied," he said with a bit of his usual smugness.

I considered what he said.

"What is it, Elizabeth?" Diana asked.

"Elaine knew where Dell would be staying in Sherman. It all adds up to her getting her group to stay there, too. But then, when they're both there, she spends all evening in a meeting, making not a peep about letting Dell go off to have dinner and more-than-dessert with another woman. That doesn't fit. Dell, did she say anything to you at Yellowstone about being together in Sherman?"

"No."

"Did she know you went out last night?"

He nodded. "She said they'd have pizza later and invited me to join them, though she said I'd have to leave when they told me to get out." That sounded like the Malsung charm. "Some of the others made vague sounds of protest, but no one confronted her about inviting me. When I said I couldn't, the others appeared relieved."

"How about Elaine?"

"She asked why. I said I had a business meeting for dinner."

"Without saying with whom."

He raised his hands. "It didn't come up." A muscle twitched by his mouth. "Something she said gave me the impression she thought it was with you, Elizabeth."

I closed my eyes. "Go ahead, I know you're dying to tell us."

"It was a phrase about bad plumbing."

Mike's laughter drew demands from Diana and Jennifer for an

explanation.

With that—and their subsequent laughter—over, I said, "Let's get back to alibis. Dirk doesn't think any of the VisageTome were clear. What do you think?"

"No idea. I didn't talk to any of them today. And no one at the sheriff's department confided in me."

"Right. Mike, you met all those guys, can you get yourself over there and get them talking?"

"Sure."

Jennifer then reported what she'd already told Mike and me about her first pass on Darryl Justice and VisageTome information.

"You do still have a Leaf, Elizabeth, but it hasn't been touched since you left the network."

Dell groaned. "Are you deliberately trying to disappear off the face of the earth, Elizabeth?"

"I'm still on the face of the earth, just not on VisageTome. What's the big deal?"

"The big deal is that the first thing every person I talked to about you as a prospective hire did was look you up on VisageTome."

"Don't worry, Dell," Jennifer said, "I'll make sure she catches up with the rest of the world. Her account's frozen—"

"That's why I'm not on there. I tried to get it fixed, but their customer service—"

"—which means you can't get any of your pollinators to come to your Leaf. But I've opened a personal Leaf for you and transferred the Tree Rings over from the network one."

"Tree Rings?" I asked before I could stop myself.

"Historical posts and photos," Dell said. "Excellent, Jennifer. That will add history and depth to what otherwise would be a pitiable Leaf."

"I appreciate Jennifer doing that," I said, "but in the meantime could we get back to this little issue of a man being murdered and his body found in your bed?"

Jennifer was the grownup, saying magnanimously, "Sure."

"So what else have you found out about VisageTome?" I added.

"Every second of every day has to be about VisageTome. They

want people to live on campus. They say it's a benefit, but it's so they'll have no other life and will be available to work all the time. They send a few teams to this retreat to Yellowstone twice a year. Each member proposes a project, the team picks the best, then they're all supposed to work on it together. It's usually really good teams or really bad ones. Darryl Justice was known for taking on problem groups."

"This was considered a problem group?"

She shrugged. "I haven't pinned that down yet. I'm just starting to get the work records for Malsung, Kelvin, Nelson, Hart and Varney—"

"You're not breaking into the VisageTome system, are you?"

"Their security's not that tough."

"Jennifer—"

"I know, I know. I'm looking at public stuff. People don't realize how much is out there. I think I can dig back and get earlier versions of their Leafs, too. That might be interesting.

"Good idea." She was making progress in thinking more like a journalist and less like a hacker. "Let's go back to why Elaine let Dell go without even a complaint."

"Maybe she wasn't that in to Dell," Jennifer said.

I had to cover my mouth at his look of astonishment.

"Dell, your alibi from Clara, is it rock solid?"

"Yes."

"You didn't get up during the night? Come back to bed to find her asleep?"

"Well, uh…" It was one of the few times I'd heard him stumble. "Never long."

I think Mike stifled a groan.

I know I sounded grim when I said, "You can bet Sheriff Conrad is going to dig into all those circumstances. Because if she was in the bathroom for forty-five minutes or she woke up at some point and can't swear how long you were gone or she fell asleep while you were gone, those are all circumstances where he can say you could have slipped out, gone back to the B&B, which was—how far away?"

"Four blocks," Diana said.

"A matter of minutes at a normal walk, much less at a jog or a full-out run. It won't take long for him to discover you're a runner—you would have to show off and interview the president during a jog, wouldn't you? Wait until Conrad digs up that footage. By the way, can you prove you didn't move your rental car?"

"Prove a negative? No."

"Okay. First thing is to gather as many possibilities as we can, including the possibilities the sheriff's department will look into, so we know how to respond to them."

"That's what happens in court," he said grimly.

"Yes. But it's also what happens as we look at the case law enforcement might be building to take to court. Let's start from the top again, Dell. When you arrived at the B&B, who you saw, what you heard, where people went. Every move, every word, every nuance you can remember."

He'd met Krista when he and Mike went in Friday morning. When he'd arrived Monday afternoon, she'd gone through the formalities with him quickly, including showing him to his room and where the spare bathroom key was kept.

Apparently the VisageTome group had traveled straight through from Yellowstone, while Mike, Dell, and I stopped in Cody for a leisurely lunch, because they were there already.

They came out of the room across the hall from his when he and Krista came upstairs. He hadn't noted if the guys were surprised to see him.

When the others returned to that room—he didn't know whose it was—and Krista Seger went downstairs, Elaine came into his room after him. Not invited, but not over his objections, either.

They had a few kisses. "She said she had to go to keep The Geeks in line. She appeared anxious—not eager, but anxious—to return to the group across the hall."

"What do you mean not eager, but anxious?" Jennifer interrupted.

"Anxious is worried, uneasy about something. Eager is you're looking forward to it. You're anxious about something difficult ahead. You're eager about something fun or exciting," Dell said, with more energy than he'd shown since he'd started this recital. "If you say you're anxious to see a friend that means you're not expecting that meeting to be good. Usually you'd be eager to see your friends."

"Huh." The same response she usually had to my lessons.

Back to his account, Dell said that with Elaine gone he unpacked, took a quick shower, then dressed for his dinner.

"Your sheriff, seemed to think—" he started.

"Don't look at me." I pointed at Diana. "He's her sheriff."

He turned toward her. "—seemed to find it highly suspicious that I took a shower then and again when I returned—this morning. God, that was just this morning."

"He suspected you were showering off blood," Mike said.

"But his clothes weren't bloody," I protested.

"And he's not my sheriff," Diana said. "Not yet, anyway. I'll let you know when that changes."

When, not *if*.

"You might want to more thoroughly explore his views on showers," Dell said.

Jennifer giggled first, then we all chuckled.

The rest of Dell's story came quickly. His dinner with Clara at the Haber House Hotel dining room—he'd wanted more chocolate pie—was confirmable first-hand by the staff and other diners. Second- and third-hand it could be confirmed by much of Sherman.

The rest of the night relied solely on Clara.

That left the holes I'd already pointed out, but those were lower down our priority list than other questions.

Dell skipped to when he'd left Clara's house and drove through the quiet streets of Sherman. He had no recollection of meeting or seeing anyone. Including when he'd entered the B&B by the unlocked front door and gone up to his room.

"You know what I saw there," he said.

"We'd know better if Elizabeth would let us look at the video she sent us," Mike groused.

"We'll talk about that in a minute. First, I have some questions, Dell."

"Go ahead. You can't be any worse than the sheriff. Sorry, Diana."

"No problem."

"Did you see Dirk—the husband half of the B&B owners—this morning?"

"No."

"Hear him? Have any indication he might be around?"

"No."

He went through the rest almost mechanically. After calling me, he'd returned to the bathroom, dressed, listening for any stirring in the house and not hearing it.

"Now we can see the video." Mike pulled his phone out.

"Wait a second." I faced Dell. "Did you see Joel and Ariel again after they witnessed you being told about the key to the bathroom on top of the door jamb."

"Who?" Jennifer demanded.

"The older couple Dell saw on the back stairs."

"You're kidding," Mike said.

Dell looked mildly perplexed, which told me how out of it he was.

"Remember?" I prodded. "Harvard Law School from the bugling elk."

"That was the same gray-haired couple as on the backstairs? They were at the B&B, too?"

I pulled in a breath to say yes, then hesitated. "It seems likely. They were certainly there this morning for the second B—breakfast— because I saw them at a table eating on my way up to see Dell. But I have to admit it didn't register then. I saw a gray-haired couple eating. It didn't hit me who they were, not until I came downstairs and saw they were gone."

I repeated what Krista had said, concluding, "So, I not only let them take off without questioning them, seeing me might have scared them off."

"Give yourself a break," Diana said. "You were focused on getting to Dell."

"I wonder if the bed and breakfast people got their car license number?"

"Good thought, Mike," Diana said. "Any chance your aunt…"

He shook his head.

Jennifer said, "I can get into their system and—"

I stopped her with, "Let's ask first. You know, if Aunt Gee could give us anything, what I'd most like to know is if Darryl Justice was drugged."

Mike shook his head. "Don't hold your breath. This new sheriff is watching everybody like a hawk. It would be worth Aunt Gee's job to slip anything to us now."

"I know, I know. I wasn't scraping at her or you. Just wishing. Because if he was drugged, that could open the field."

"You think if he wasn't drugged a woman had to lure him to the bed."

"I wouldn't say had to. Just raises the odds."

"But couldn't one of the guys have caught him unaware, whacked him in the head, then deposited his dead body in the bed?" Diana asked.

"Yes to the first part, but not the dead body part."

"Huh?" Jennifer asked.

"I think there was too much blood in the bed. I'm trying to get that confirmed by a source. But it sure looks to me like the bed is where he did most, if not all, of his bleeding. Not to mention there was no sign of blood anywhere else in the B&B."

"According to Krista," inserted Diana.

"Yes. It would be good to get that confirmed. If we can. I know, I know," I said as Mike's mouth opened. "We can't expect your aunt to tell us. But there have to be other sources. Does Krista Seger have anybody helping her besides her husband? Someone cleaning for them, perhaps. Or maybe she's talked to a neighbor. Or—"

"I have assignments tomorrow, but I know some folks who live around there. I'll see what I can find out," Diana volunteered.

"Good. In the meantime, our working theory is that he was alive when he got into that bed."

"Alive doesn't mean he had to be conscious, right? What if someone stunned him, dragged him to Dell's bed, and finished the job there?" Mike asked.

"No drag marks. At least not that I saw. And before you say he was carried, think about the people we're talking about. I can't see any of them carrying him on his—or her—own, can you?"

"No," Mike conceded. "It would take a couple of them."

"Right. Which means working together. Can you see any combination of the VisageTome gang working together long enough to pull it off?"

"That would be an issue," he agreed. "But, Elizabeth, what about that video? Can we watch it now? Maybe we'll get ideas."

"It's pretty grim. And once any of you watch it … well, the sheriff won't be happy about this. Right now it's only me he won't be happy with."

"We might as well face it from the start." Diana patted my arm. "I'm a big girl. I can make my own decisions."

"Me, too," Jennifer said.

"You've safely backed it up the way—?"

"Exactly the way you asked. Somewhere I can access, but that nobody would associate with me." She was triumphant.

But I had one more caveat.

"I haven't looked at it either. It might be worse than I remember, and that was pretty bad."

Chapter Twenty-Four

THE VIDEO WASN'T going to win awards for lighting or composition. It did convey what I'd seen, which was mostly dark and dim. Though the huddled body could be made out against the white bedclothes.

Watching over my shoulder, Dell agreed it showed what he'd seen, too. "But I didn't look as long as you did."

Mike, Diana, and Jennifer viewed it on their individual phones in silence.

At the end, Mike and Diana immediately restarted it. Jennifer looked up for a moment, a sheen of tears in her eyes.

"Poor guy," she said in a small voice.

I withstood an urge to pat her shoulder. I was proud of her for focusing on the victim. It was important. As a person and as a journalist. But any sympathy or even support might tip her into the tears she was fighting.

Sometimes you had to learn to control the tears before you learned that letting them flow was fine.

"Yes," was all I said.

She swallowed, blinked hard, then restarted the video.

I did the same. This time, though, I handed the phone to Dell and I was the over-the-shoulder viewer.

The perimeter of the room showed no sign of disturbance. Dell's two bags sat on a bench under the window.

"Is that how you left them?"

"Yes. Sheriff gave me an inventory before I left and everything was on it."

"Laptop?"

"He didn't let me look at it, but it's got security measures and I clear sensitive material before I travel."

"That reminds me, what about your phone?"

"Not long before you got there he asked if he could look at it and I said yes."

"Your sources—"

"Coded. Names and Numbers. My personal code. They're protected. My recent calls aren't anything special. He took down some numbers, then gave it back."

Returning to the video, the camera covered the perimeter of the room, which held a dresser and desk painted white, plus an easy chair. Framed western prints hung on the pale walls. The one window looked toward the street.

The wooden bed was large, but its cleaner lines made it significantly less massive than the one at the Haber House Hotel. Light colored bedclothes with a simple red quilt folded at the foot also helped.

Yes, I'm putting off describing what was in the bed.

Darryl Justice.

It looked as if he might have dropped back onto the bed, with his head propped up on stacked pillows, judging by the dent. But his head wasn't on the pillows now.

The mattress had shifted, so from the viewpoint of the bathroom and this video, the head of the mattress was pushed away and the foot had pivoted closer.

Darryl Justice had curled up, perhaps in an instinctive defensive effort. It left him in the darkest shadows of the video.

His head rested down where the pivoted mattress had revealed the box spring.

The dark stain on the light bedclothes was concentrated where his head was, though there was a mark showing on the floor under it.

"Is that blood on the floor?" Diana asked.

"Yes."

"If he was beaten, he must have been unconscious after the first or second blow, because the bed coverings aren't messed up much," she said.

"Probably even less than you think. Dell, did you pull down the bedspread before you left?"

"Yes."

Diana looked up, a frown tucked between her brows. "I'd've expected the bed linens to be pulled around more from a beating like that. And shouldn't there be more blood?"

"And blood spray," Dell added.

"The blood seems to be directed down." I squinted back at the screen to confirm my visual memory. "So it was caught by the bed, rather than spattered. Though with a beating, you'd expect some castoff. Maybe he was stabbed." Or his throat cut, and he'd bled down into the bed.

"Looks like the blood was still dripping." Mike said. "So it couldn't have happened long before Dell got there?"

"I wouldn't say that. The blood had pooled where the mattress was pulled aside, leaving only that fabric-covered area of the box spring. But that pooling must have happened earlier. New blood wasn't being added to the pool."

"But it was dripping on the floor, so that has to mean it was fresh." Jennifer's voice sounded a little strained.

"It was dripping to the floor, yes, but not directly from the body. What was dripping was coming from where it had pooled, working its way through the fabric. Like if you take a towel and fill it with water. Eventually the water will soak the towel and start dripping from it, even though no new water's added."

"Hard to tell on the video, but that makes sense. Glad you were there to see it," Mike said.

"Yeah," I said dryly. "I'll see if I can find out how long it would take to get to this state. Could give us approximate time of death."

I wasn't naming my source in the FBI crime lab. Sure Wardell Yardley was deeply worried, as well as shocked, but that didn't mean his source-poaching instincts were dead. No pun intended.

"No sign of a fight, so he probably wasn't expecting it," Mike said. "Though it takes some force to move a mattress like that."

"Depends on the mattress," Diana said. "Jess has one of those puffy, soft mattresses and we had to Velcro it because it slid around so easily."

"Even with a good-sized guy in it?" I asked.

She nodded. "Though, again, I'd think the covers would be more messed up."

"I know. But there's the video as proof. I wonder if that means the murderer didn't get much blood on his clothes, either. I'm sure the sheriff's department is searching for bloody clothes, but that could make it harder."

Which would make the process slower, which was bad for Dell.

"That would be one lucky murderer," Mike said.

"Yeah. Already had to be pretty lucky to beat someone to death in a house full of people and no one heard a thing." I looked around. "Okay, where are we?"

"You said you were going to ask the others about what Dirk said and what it made them think of," Jennifer said.

I'd forgotten about that.

We repeated his comments, ending with Jennifer saying, "He was talking about her really long hours, working weekends, getting all this overtime, and Elizabeth asked what that made me think of, but—"

"An affair," Mike said.

I raised an eyebrow. "That answer came fast, Paycik."

"I had a teammate who shall remain unnamed who used to tell his wife we had three-a-day practices several days a week all season long."

"He got caught?"

"Oh, yeah. Big time. Not only by the wife, but by his second girlfriend. But the wife got all the money. And I do mean *all* the money. He was driving a used Ford the next season."

"Interesting."

"He didn't think so. He hated that car."

"I meant the idea of an affair."

"So was Krista having an affair or working overtime?"

"You want answers and we're still trying to figure out the questions. Like who are our suspects?"

Diana said, "The suspects are an elderly couple staying at the B&B that we know nothing about, including whether they have any connection with any of these people."

"The B&B owners," I added.

"Again," Diana said, "no known connection."

"The VT people. They were all pretty annoying. Though I would have picked any of the others as a victim before that guy," Mike said. "He did have that dispute with Gordon Kelvin you told me about. Seems kind of weak for motive."

Dell was not entirely numb. He gave me a sharp, critical look for having shared what we'd seen and heard from that meeting room with anyone.

"They're not going to steal your story," I told him.

"People have been murdered over less," he said pointedly.

I ignored that. "There's another possible angle." I wasn't quite ready to say *suspect*. "Bunny Ramsey Sterakos."

"Your childhood friend we met in the hall?" Mike sounded like I'd both lost my marbles and had stabbed someone in the back. "I know Dell says she was at the B&B, but…"

"She wasn't exactly a friend, more like a toddler colleague. And then acquaintances through school."

"You said your mothers know each other and you went to her house for Halloween."

"Yeah, but, she wasn't a *friend* friend. We—"

Jennifer cut through my excuses for committing the social solecism of tossing the name of a frie—acquaintance into the ring for murder suspects. "Why would she kill this guy?"

"Why would any of them?"

"We don't know that yet. Dell said Bunny was getting a tour of the B&B, but is there more, Elizabeth?" Diana asked.

"Yeah. I heard Darryl talking with someone on the porch Friday night—neither of them was happy." I relayed that conversation, admitting I couldn't swear I'd heard Bunny's voice.

After I told them about the hallway meeting when Mike was there, I prodded him with "Didn't you think she was acting strangely?"

"I thought you both were strange," he said promptly.

"Well, it got stranger." I reported seeing her the next night in the same place.

"You just happened to be there?" Mike asked.

"No. I went to see if she'd return. And she did. And then her son, Christopher, showed up."

I told them about that, too.

"You're thinking the trash can was a drop," Dell said. "Blackmail."

"Yes. Or... At least Bunny thought it was blackmail." That brought me to my final conversation with Darryl Justice. "Both then and now I think he was telling the truth when he said he wanted her to leave him alone."

"So Bunny got it wrong? Is that possible?" Diana asked.

"Oh, yes. With Bunny? Yes."

"I don't get it," Jennifer said. "Okay, if he was blackmailing her maybe she'd kill him. But you said he probably wasn't blackmailing her. And why would he blackmail her in the first place? Over what?"

"Exactly," Mike said. "There's not even any proof they knew each other. She's from Illinois, right? And he lives—lived in Seattle. How would their paths have crossed?"

"How old was he?" Diana asked.

"Exactly," I said to her.

The rest of them stared at us. "I *really* don't get it," Jennifer said.

"There were rumors. Bunny was away for a special program for most of a school year when we were in high school," I said. "Nobody had heard about the program ahead of time and nobody could figure out why she would have been picked. She didn't excel at anything except being Miss This or Queen That. Yet she was gone for months and months and months."

I saw the light go on for Mike and Dell, but not Jennifer.

"What?" she demanded.

Appropriately, Diana, mother of two teenagers, explained. "When Elizabeth and I were in high school, girls who got pregnant didn't always keep going to classes, Jennifer. Some families sent them away to where they weren't known to have the baby and put it up for adoption.

Afterward, they returned, pretending nothing had happened and there'd been no baby."

"Geeze. Why didn't they stay home? They didn't have to go away to put it up for adoption. A bunch of girls in my class did that."

"A bunch?" I asked.

"Well, two."

"It was considered more, uh, embarrassing then," Diana said. "It still is for some, but that reaction was more widespread then."

"Elizabeth? What are you thinking now?"

I blinked and turned to Mike.

"I'm thinking about 'special program.' That was what Bunny's family said when she was gone that school year. And then her son used the same phrase about his visit to Yellowstone."

"Ah. Like mother like son?"

"Maybe. I don't know… Neither was happy about the other one being at Lake Yellowstone Hotel. She knew he was at Yellowstone, yet she didn't make any effort to see him. Apparently not even to let him know she was there. In fact, I'd say she was clearly dismayed that he wasn't clear at the other end of the park.

"And then there's Christopher." I was thinking out loud. Closing my eyes, trying to see the scene again. "He called out her name in surprise and then … yes, he regretted it. I'm almost sure he did. I *am* sure he was lying about his special program. I don't believe his program was real any more than Bunny's was years ago. They were lying and lying and lying."

"You think their lies are related?"

I opened my eyes and looked at Diana. "Related. That's interesting."

Could his special program have been a blind for another trip related to the one his mother had taken all those years ago?

She said, "Definitely related if Darryl's her illegitimate son. If he is, her other son, Christopher, is also related. He and Darryl Justice were half-brothers."

"Yes." I drew it out. "If he found out somehow that he had a half-brother there'd be lots of powerful emotions. Happy? Sad? Angry?

Certainly curious.”

“If he found out,” Mike pointed out. “We have no proof he did.”

“No proof. But it’s a suspicion worth keeping in mind and seeing what we can track down. Jennifer—”

“Yeah, I’ll see what I can find out.”

“And I’ll see if my mother remembers anything that might help. What?”

Jennifer had given a subdued yelp after checking the time.

“I gotta go.” She stood, gathering her belongings. “I’m connecting with a guy in Australia who’s going to teach me—” Her eyes cut to me and away. “Uh, something.”

“Jennifer, no—”

Diana spoke across my remonstration. “It’s time for all of us to end this.”

Her warning look advised not hitting Jennifer with my oft-repeated warning against hacking.

“I’ll send my notes and see what else I can get about VisageTome and the dead g—Darryl Justice.”

We all called out good-nights. Diana added a motherly, “Drive safe.”

“So what do you want the rest of us to do, Elizabeth?” Mike asked.

“We need to narrow the timeline. Right now the murder could have happened from right after Dell left until he got back, though possibly less likely after Krista was in the kitchen at quarter after five.”

“The blood not being dry would probably favor early morning over the night before, right?” Mike asked.

“That’s a reasonable assumption, but it is still an assumption. Diana, since I’m persona non grata and you’re apparently persona grata, see what you can get on that or anything else from the sheriff’s department, in addition to checking with people who live around the B&B.”

“I’m not going to try to get him to tell me things he shouldn’t.”

“I said the department, not the sheriff.”

Her suspicion didn’t drop, but she nodded.

“Mike and Dell and I have to be in O’Hara Hill at ten-thirty.”

"With the two ladies? Surely that's canceled," Dell said.

"Command performances with Aunt Gee and Mrs. P are not canceled. Unless they do the canceling," Mike told him.

"But with me a prime suspect…"

"Hah. Wait until you meet them. That will get you over thinking of them as delicate flowers, fast enough," I said.

"Sometimes they have real good information, too," Mike said. "Even with Aunt Gee needing to be cautious, considering…" He glanced at Diana then away. "Changes in the sheriff's department."

Abruptly, Diana said, "Dell, you look beat."

"I am." For Dell to confine himself to two words meant he was exhausted.

"God, I never thought about where you'd stay tonight," I said. I must be tired, too. "Your room at the B&B is still a crime scene and the place is full up. You'll have to go back to the Haber House."

He groaned.

"Unless … Diana could I sleep on your couch? Then Dell could have my bed in the bunkhouse and—"

Mike stood. "Forget it. He's coming home with me."

Diana and I exchanged a look.

"What?" Mike said. "It makes sense. I've got a spare room and any guy stuff he needs. I suppose you'd make him shave with a razor you use on your legs. Besides, we have that command appearance at Mrs. P and Aunt G's tomorrow. We'll pick you up on the way to O'Hara Hill."

"I can drive and bring Dell—"

"I come right by here."

"I know, but—"

"It's settled," Mike insisted.

I walked Dell to the door, while Mike made a pit stop.

"I'm proud of you for acknowledging what's going on at the network, Dell. I know it couldn't have been easy."

His mouth twisted. "If I've learned anything from you and your travails it's that facing the truth with dignity is the smartest course."

"Thank you."

Then I had to fight a grin as I remembered that the truth he was facing included, according to him, being the best White House correspondent, possibly ever.

Pure Dell.

"Needing the help of these people to be sure you don't get charged with murder might have had something to do with it, too," I said.

"That, too. Though if the same scenario were transplanted to D.C., I would not have said a word."

Absolutely pure Dell.

WHEN THE DOOR closed behind Mike and Dell, Diana and I looked at each other. I'd been careful not to make eye contact until then.

She was grinning. "I thought you were going to wrap your arms around Mike's knees and beg him to take you to his place instead of Dell."

"Believe me, I was tempted. Dell could have stayed here in the bunkhouse. And I would have gotten to see Mike's house—finally."

"That's what's so funny—or sad, depending on how you look at it—you weren't even thinking about being alone with him in a place with beds."

I ignored that. "At least we know his house exists. I was worried he was living in his SUV or something and that's why he never invites us."

"Oh, I knew it existed. The previous owners had a big house built out there, replacing the original ranch house, maybe six, seven years before they sold the place to Mike."

Actually, I knew it existed, too. Because I'd driven past his place—solely to check out the GPS on my new SUV. For that brief, sparkling time before it had needed reconstructive surgery at the body shop.

Trouble was, you couldn't see the house clearly from the highway. I'd've had to drive onto his private road. And I'd been unable to think of an excuse to give if he'd spotted me, which would have left only the truth of burning curiosity.

"I suppose it can't be too bad if he has a spare room to offer Dell,"

I said.

"The place had something like seven bedrooms and as many bathrooms, if I recall."

"So the big mystery remains—why has Mike never had us out there? I used to think he didn't want anyone there, but Tom's been and now Dell. Girl cooties?"

"More likely something about it makes him uncomfortable?"

"What? He's running a bordello? Don't you think we'd have heard about that? It's falling down around him? But then he wouldn't have offered Dell the room. I don't get it."

"Me, either. But I think it's one of those mysteries we're going to have to live with until he sees fit to let us see his home."

"Or we figure out a way to weasel our way inside."

"Or that," she conceded. "But right now I need sleep before any weasel figuring."

AS TIRED AS I was, I wasn't quite ready to sleep.

Without much hope, I sent a "Still up?" email to my friends Matt and Bonnie Lester, living outside Philadelphia. Matt and I bonded over brutal assignments at the start of our journalism careers. He and Bonnie and Wes and I had been close. I'd stayed close with them, while Matt stayed in newspapers and I moved to TV. Wes had pulled away from all of us.

My phone rang.

"Danny, it's Matt—"

"And Bonnie." They had me on speakerphone. "Are you okay?"

I wished that wouldn't be the first reaction of my friends to hearing from me. But I supposed after this past year it was understandable.

"I'm fine. Really. I didn't mean to scare you. I'm not plugged in to the grapevine the way I used to be—" Or at all if I was honest. Hadn't been from the time it became clear my ex intended to dismantle my career. It had been too painful, knowing the grapevine was buzzing about my fall. "—and I hope you can fill me in on something, Matt. Someone."

"Who?"

"Dell."

"You want *me* to tell *you* about Wardell Yardley? Nobody knows him better than you do. Nobody has had less of the sharp side of his tongue than you. In fact, isn't he out there visiting you?"

"Yes, he is. Is that all over the grapevine?"

"I wouldn't say all over, but a few folks know."

I heard a hint of reserve in his voice. "Matt, is he in trouble. His job?"

"You know Dell. He's burned more than a few bridges. It's left him with fewer directions to take and fewer supporters."

Damn.

"What's going on, Danny?" Matt asked.

"I'd tell you guys if it were my business to tell, but it's not."

"Okay," Bonnie said. "Then tell us about your business. You're staying out there?"

I remembered a conversation with Tom Burrell not long ago at a gathering at his ranch when I'd made the distinction that I wasn't leaving.

"Yeah, I'm staying here. At least for now."

"If they matched that offer from Chicago, I'll be on the next plane to join you," Matt said.

"You will not," Bonnie shot back.

We all laughed.

"They came nowhere near to matching the offer from Chicago—in money. But what they did offer was a lot more freedom."

I explained, including the late-breaking negotiations Mel had pulled off while I was at Yellowstone.

"But…"

"What, Bonnie?" For so long I'd dodged questions, especially theirs, that it seemed only fair now to encourage them.

"Are you making a life there? Are you making friends?"

I looked down at Shadow, stretched out on his bed in the middle of the floor, lying between me and whatever was beyond that door. I thought of Diana—and her kids—taking me in and giving me a place to live. I thought of Mrs. P and Aunt Gee. Of Jennifer. Leona D'Amato. Penny at the supermarket. Even Deputies Shelton and Alvaro. Of a confounding little girl named Tamantha. Of her father and of Mike.

"Yeah, I am. I am making friends. And I am making a life."

Bonnie cleared her throat. "Okay, then. But don't forget your old friends."

"Never."

WEDNESDAY

Chapter Twenty-Five

I WAS BACK on the phone at the crack of dawn—my definition of the crack of dawn. Not by choice. This time I couldn't blame my mother.

"What?" is not the most welcoming way to answer the phone, but it matched my mood.

"Guess who just arrived at the café?"

"What?" I repeated.

"Elizabeth, wake up. There's no time to waste. We're on our way to pick you up. The VisageTome crew and a gray-haired couple just got there."

"Mike?"

"Yes. Did you hear me? Tansy called to say they're there and no deputies are in sight."

"Who?"

"Tansy. Remember? Penny's niece who works at the café in town. We've got to get there before they leave and bolt back to the bed and breakfast. We're coming to get you."

"I'll meet you there."

"No. This way we can go straight on to O'Hara Hill. Besides, I don't want you driving while sleeping. We'll be right there. Be ready."

Driving while sleeping. Very funny.

I stumbled from the bed directly into the shower and turned it on full-blast.

That's step one of my quick-response routine, honed to a science over many years. No luxuriating in the shower. Hair up. Strategic makeup. Go-to attire.

Having a minimal wardrobe to select from made that part even faster than usual. Jeans, shirt, blazer. Then outerwear, layers that could go from 55 to zero.

Shadow and I were out the door the minute Mike's SUV pulled up.

As I climbed in, the front-seat hog who was not driving asked, "What's that?" Then jerked his head toward Shadow, who had given the SUV a careful look, apparently recognized it, and headed off toward the barn.

Mike muttered "Careful" under his breath.

"That," I said, "is Shadow. He's my dog. I'm his person. Want to make something of it, bub?"

"All right, all right. I forgot what a grouch you are in the morning."

"**THEY'RE ALL STILL** there." Mike squinted through the windshield and front window of the Sherman café. "The gray-haired couple's on the left, but I can't see them well enough to know if they're the same people. The VisageTome group's at the big table over on the right side."

We'd decided during the drive not to split up to tackle them separately because we wanted to make sure nothing was missed. I suspected Mike also feared I was still asleep.

"The couple first," I said.

"Why?"

"If we can eliminate them as having any connection to what happened, it won't take long."

"Also groups take longer in a restaurant," Dell said. "The VisageTome group will still be there when the couple's walking out."

"Just in case, though, Mike, position yourself so you can keep an eye on the VisageTome table. If they start to leave, alert us. Dell, you and I should keep our backs to them. No reason to make it easier for them to spot us and give them incentive to hurry out. Here we go."

It went perfectly.

Joel and Ariel were seated face to face at a square table, their plates nearly empty. Mike went past the table, Dell and I stayed on the near side. We each grabbed an empty chair and sat down simultaneously.

Ariel jumped. Joel blinked at us with his mouth open. He hadn't finished chewing.

"Joel and Ariel, right? Remember us?" I asked in the friendliest tone I could muster at that hour of the morning.

"You're that woman who—" Ariel cut off her own words as she looked at Joel.

He shut his mouth.

"That's right," I said. "We were all there at Yellowstone Park to hear that elk bugling. It was you, Joel, who told us how rare that was this late in the year. And how much we should appreciate it. Great to have that information. We wanted to thank you for that."

I gave him half a beat for a "you're welcome" that didn't come, then went on.

"And now you're, staying at the Wild Horses Bed and Breakfast. I would have said hello yesterday morning, but you'd left when I came downstairs. Imagine you being here in Sherman. What brought you here?"

Ariel looked at Joel, but he didn't appear to be functioning. She said, "It must be the same as what brought you here—an easy day's drive after leaving Yellowstone. And such interesting history in this part of the world, don't you think?"

"I do think so. Though we happen to live here, so it's not the same." I had the feeling that hadn't surprised her. "And now you're staying at the B&B." I shook my head in wonder. "How did you even find out about it?"

"We heard good things about it and had to try it," Ariel said.

"Did you? I'm sure the owners will be gratified to hear that. They'll be thrilled word's getting out at places like—Oh, where did you hear those good things?"

"We checked so many sources while we were planning this trip last spring. So many details…" She rubbed her forehead. It was a good move—play the absentminded gray-hair to the hilt. Had she been playing a role Friday afternoon at Yellowstone, too? "I just don't remember anymore."

"And after all that planning to have the trip marred by this terrible tragedy," I said with great sympathy.

Joel came to life. "Trip of a lifetime. Planned every detail. Had it all mapped out since last spring. So, yes, it sure is marred by—" He cut a look toward Dell. "—a death like that. We tried to move to the Hoover House Hotel, but they said they're full up. And that redneck sheriff insists we can't leave. He won't even let us go to Cody to get a decent room. And I do remember you now. You weren't as apprecia-tive of my expertise at the park. You were disrespectful."

Of an elk? Or of him?

"I'm sorry to hear you felt that way. But at least you have company in your misery in remaining at the B&B. And with people you already know, too."

"People we know? We don't know anyone in this town, much less the B&B. Except, of course, now we've run into you all again." Ariel did do this role well.

"Oh, but surely you recognized the group from VisageTome," I said.

"VisageTome?" she repeated. It sounded less like confusion than stalling.

"That group of young people at the table at the opposite end of the restaurant. Also staying at the same B&B as you are. You must have recognized them from Yellowstone, since they were there too, listening to that rare late elk bugling."

Her eyes widened. "Are they some of the same people who were there that afternoon? I didn't realize... Oh, but you all know each other, then?" She looked from me to Dell.

That was a mistake. It indicated she knew there was some connec-tion between Dell and the VisageTome people. Yet how could she know that when she was disavowing all knowledge of the VisageTome group.

Dell said, "New acquaintances."

"So you happened to be staying at the B&B with those people from VisageTome, too?" That was better. Making the point that if it was strange that they were staying at the B&B, it also was strange that

Dell and the VisageTome people were.

He'd caught it, too, I could tell by his slightly feline smile. "I happened to mention I'd be staying there."

"Happens all the time," Joel said abruptly. "Why I run into people from when I was in Harvard Law School. And in the strangest places. Met one on a tour of fjords. Another in Buenos Aires, right there on the street. We cross paths all the time with people we've seen before and probably just don't realize it."

I widened my eyes. "I suppose you're right. For example, you crossed paths with Darryl Justice at Yellowstone Park, then he turns up dead at the B&B you're staying at." I kept it bland, so they couldn't claim I was accusing them of something and use it as an excuse to end the conversation.

"Horrible, horrible." Ariel covered her eyes.

"A tragedy," Joel said mechanically.

"Did you see him at the B&B?"

"He wasn't staying there," Joel said.

Had he learned that since the murder or had he known before?

"We hardly spent a minute there except to sleep," Ariel said. "We didn't see anyone. Oh, except for that young woman who runs the B&B and her husband. But no other guests. No one was down for breakfast before we left yesterday morning. When we came back after dinner—well, it was a shock. A great shock. All those horrible questions from a deputy and having to sign a statement. And then to not be able to leave… On top of all that, this morning, we were told there would be no breakfast because they were doing another search of the kitchen."

That was interesting. Searching for what? And why would they expect to find it in the kitchen?

We had agreed beforehand not to push this encounter. It was, first, to see if this truly was the same couple. Second, to try to get basic information.

I glanced toward Dell. He didn't return it, but I knew he'd received the message when he stood.

"We don't want to intrude on your breakfast any longer, but it's a pleasure meeting you officially, even under these awful circumstances. I'm Wardell Yardley. Ariel." He extended his hand. They shook briefly. He turned and extended his hand. Joel met it. "Joel and Ariel Williams from—where did you say?"

There was a quarter beat while Dell held on to his hand before Joel said, "Pennsylvania."

"Well, Mr. and Mrs. Williams—Ariel and Joel—I hope to see you soon at the B&B."

It was unlikely Dell would be staying there, but it was a nice touch. Sounded so pleasant, yet held a hint of threat.

Mike and I also stood, all saying good-bye pleasantly.

We started for the table at the far end, led by Dell.

As we passed the last table separating us from them I could hear a sort of high-pitched reverberation, like anxious hornets.

It was the VisageTomers. Hunched over their plates, buzzing at each other in low voices.

Elaine sat at the end of the table on our left. What with her positioning and the sound, it was hard not to think of a queen bee.

Gordon Kelvin was on Elaine's right, with Varney, the long-faced guy with the short hair, on her left. Next to him sat Nelson, Peekaboo Baldspot. Hart, with the bowl cut, sat at the opposite end from Elaine.

Elaine spotted Dell only when we were almost to the table.

Her face went blank. She said low and sharp, "Shut up." Then she saw me and she grimaced for an instant before focusing back on Dell.

"Hi, Dell. Glad you're out of jail," she said.

Heads came up all around the table. Kelvin, with his back to us, jerked around.

As we had with Joel and Ariel, we each grabbed a chair. Dell nudged in at the corner so he was between Elaine and Kelvin. I did the same between Hart and Nelson at the opposite end, and Mike took the empty spot next to Varney.

Nelson's head was down, but his hands weren't twitching. Sitting near him like this, I could see they were working rapidly over the screen of a phone he held below the level of the table. He'd made me think of a trying-to-quit smoker at times at Yellowstone. But he hadn't been craving nicotine. He'd been suffering connection deprivation.

"I am delighted that you are pleased, Elaine," Dell said smoothly. We'd agreed he'd take the lead with the VT group as long as things were cordial. If anything sharper was required, I'd step in. Mike was our reserve. "However, while I was at the sheriff's department, I was not in the jail. Nor does what is colloquially understood by the phrase *in jail* describe my status."

Kelvin blew out a breath, apparently to denote disgust.

"Did they tell you anything?" Elaine asked Dell.

"Nothing. What has happened at the bed and breakfast since my unceremonious departure?"

She hitched one shoulder. "Police all over the place asking questions."

"All over the place," repeated Landon Hart. He got glared at by several at the table. "What?" No one answered his question.

Dell took the heat off Hart by asking, "What did the sheriff's department ask?"

Another shoulder hitch from the diva. "You know, the usual stuff. If we saw anything—which none of us did."

Head shakes all around. "Nothing," Hart said. Even that drew a couple glares, from Gordon and Varney. He grimaced at them.

"They didn't ask you where you were Monday night?"

"We were all in bed—and *we* were alone," Elaine said sharply. Apparently she'd heard about his alibi.

It didn't pierce Dell. "You didn't hear anything during the night? Any of you?"

He addressed the whole group but looked only at Elaine. Mike and I were surveying the rest.

"Nothing," she answered for everyone.

"Who saw Darryl Justice while you were at the B&B?"

"None of us." It was more an order to the others than an answer for Dell. "We had no idea he was there until the sheriff told me his identity and asked for my help."

That sure didn't sound like Russ Conrad. So, it was either spin for our benefit … or for her own. Did her ego demand that even in this situation she was the rock star, the dispenser of information?

"So you didn't expect him to come to the B&B?"

"No."

"Do you know why he came—to the B&B or to Sherman?"

"No idea."

Dell backtracked in a deceptively easy tone. "The sheriff's department must have asked what you were doing in Sherman, why you were all at the B&B. What did you tell them?"

"Enjoying the charms of Sherman." Not only did she smirk, but it seemed to be contagious, as most of the others joined her.

"The charms of Sherman and each other?" Dell asked.

"Sure. We really got in to the team-building last weekend at Yellowstone."

"Why not stay at Yellowstone, then."

"We wanted to get away. Have some time on our own."

Then Hart said, "That was so lame at Yellowstone. First, making us go out into the wilderness with those wild animals and totally inadequate connection. Then pitting us against each other with our presentations. Throwing everyone in and seeing who survives. They're always doing crap like that. Constantly going for the throat."

"You said it was a great place to work," I reminded him.

"I lied. We were all lying."

"Don't be an idiot, Hart. He's pulling your leg, Wardell." Elaine stared at him down the table, and something happened under the surface, because the table jumped about an inch. "He's our token idiot. Every group has to have one."

The table jump couldn't have been her kicking him. Her legs wouldn't reach. Nelson, sitting closest to him, could have kicked him easily. But he never looked up—big surprise—and any of the other three could have done it in a pinch.

Hart flushed. "Yeah, yeah. Pulling your leg."

"You don't have to be such a bi—" Varney started at Elaine.

"Shut up," she snapped.

But I didn't want them to shut up. I wanted to keep them stirred up. So, I tossed in another match.

"I can see this group might need extra work on team-building," I said dryly. "It's harder to believe you'd have the sense to see that you need it. Yet there you all were the night before last at the Wild Horses Bed and Breakfast, having a special meeting. Even ordering in takeout because you didn't want to disrupt your meeting in the second parlor. That must have been an important meeting."

"Team building," Kelvin said, unconvincingly.

"Oh, but more team building couldn't have been important enough for you to twist Krista Seger's arm to let you stay at the B&B. Because that's what you did, wasn't it, Gordon? You knew she didn't want you there, but you forced her. And then she *really* didn't want you there."

"What, she thought she'd get rid of us by crying to a big-time investigative reporter?" Elaine's tone dripped scorn. On me. On my career. On the idea that either could scare her.

Then she smiled.

It was a little unsettling and it took a moment to realize why. The way her cheeks pulled and—especially—her open-mouthed, closed-teeth expression looked more like a wolf baring its teeth than a warm and sunny smile.

"Yes, I heard her talking to you." Elaine's scorn was still turned on full. "She was all whispery on the phone and her husband was lurking around like he was ready to jump up and shout, 'Ah hah! I've caught you in the act.' Like one of those hokey melodramas. Don't make me laugh."

Interesting.

Not that Elaine could laugh, although that was worthy of a Breaking News crawl.

No, what was interesting was that Krista had been worried about Dirk hearing her mention VisageTome on the phone.

It made sense if she hadn't wanted the VT people to know she was unleashing the media on them, but why keep her husband in the dark?

Unless...

But... I glanced around the table again.

Oh.

"Finally figured it out, have you?" Elaine's smile had turned even nastier.

Everyone was looking at me, including Mike and Dell. I gave a tiny head shake. I'd tell them later.

Elaine had other ideas. "Krista and Darryl were—" She used a course term where I would have said "having an affair."

"They were?" Hart asked. Varney gaped. Even Nelson's head came up.

"*Elaine, don't*—?"

"Shut up, Kelvin. They were going to figure it out eventually."

So that was the leverage Kelvin had used on the phone to get Krista to let them stay at the B&B—the threat that they'd tell Dirk. Not only that she'd had an affair, but with whom.

"It was ridiculous his drooling over her." Elaine's voice matched her smile. "The way men always do over anything with big boobs. That's all it takes for men to fall all over themselves. She'd wear this white sweater and my God, she looked like a walking marshmallow on sticks. But guys would follow her, panting. Men don't have the brains to see past mammary glands."

Why did I have the idea that Elaine had taken a shot at Darryl and missed?

✧   ✧   ✧   ✧

WE CALLED DIANA and Jennifer, so they were waiting for us when we pulled into KWMT-TV's parking lot. Limber Jennifer climbed into the third-row seat.

I'd kept Mike and Dell from discussing the ramifications of what we'd heard until we could update the others.

We told them about Joel and Ariel first.

"Our friend Joel didn't want to share where he was from."

"I noticed how you held onto his hand," Mike said.

Dell smiled slightly. "An old trick but a good one. Sometimes that will encourage people to give information they don't want to share."

"Smart," Jennifer said in admiration.

"Yeah, but, *Williams*. That's not helpful," I said. "One of the most popular last names in the country. And Pennsylvania. A nice, big state with lots of Williamses in it."

"I'll get on it," Jennifer said.

I sighed. "I'd bet you'll have to go beyond Pennsylvania to get anything."

"Try the neighboring states," Dell said. "A lot of people try to keep their lies close to home."

"Thanks, Dell. I'll do that."

Uh-oh. Looked like Jennifer was developing a journalism crush on Wardell Yardley. Few people out of the business developed crushes these days on journalists, but inside the biz, some newbies still swooned over the flexing of reporting muscles.

"Elizabeth caught them in at least one lie for sure," Mike said. "They said they'd planned this trip way in advance and planned every detail, but they couldn't have planned to stay at the B&B when it's not even officially open now and clearly wasn't last spring."

"Did you notice how Joel and Ariel changed roles?" I asked. Dell and Mike nodded. "She wasn't nearly the downtrodden little wife she'd been at the elk sighting."

"Enough of them," Diana said. "I want to hear about Elaine and the VT guys."

Dell related the conversation.

"Elaine must have tried to kick Hart under the table and missed," Dell said of the table jumping.

"Not Elaine," Mike said. "I think Varney was trying to play footsie with me. Besides, she doesn't need to kick them. That Medusa glare will do it. No offense, Dell."

"None taken. Medusa glare is apt, as is your observation of how the others respond when she is present. We need to divide to conquer," Dell said. "If I get Elaine alone, you could talk to—"

"Not a good idea," I said firmly. "Definitely not a good idea."

"We don't necessarily have to have sex. Though it could be good if—"

"Please. No visuals. Seriously, Dell, if you were reporting this story instead of in the middle of it you'd never consider that as a tactic. And it's an even worse idea with you being involved. I can imagine what Sheriff Conrad would make of that."

My gaze slid toward Diana. I guess the others' did, too, because she looked around and said, "All right you guys, this stops now."

"What?"

"Looking at me to see if I'm speed-dialing the sheriff to tell him what Wardell Yardley just proposed. Look, I'm either in this or I'm not. If I'm in, I'm in it all the way, as I have been before. And you have to trust me and not keep reminding me not to share things I've never blabbed about before. If you can't trust me about that because I'm with Russ, then I'll be pissed as hell, but I'll get over it. I won't even take my revenge by zooming in so tight on you all the time that every pore is visible."

"Okay, okay," Mike said.

I went farther. "You're right, Diana. We—*I* haven't been fair. Worrying you're going to tell the sheriff things we learn when you never..."

"Elizabeth?"

"What? Oh. Yeah. Sorry. The answer is yes, of course you're in. All the way."

"That speech would have been more convincing if you hadn't gone off to the clouds in the middle of it."

"I didn't—"

"Ha," she scoffed. "You got the same look last night when you were talking about what Krista Seger told you."

"Which wasn't much. All she said was..." I heard her voice again, heard the words. But this time I really listened. "I'm an idiot."

"She said you were an idiot?" Jennifer asked.

"Why?" Mike asked.

I ignored both. "A total, complete, and utter idiot."

"We can't agree with you unless you tell us why," Diana said.

"How did Krista Seger know the man found dead in Dell's bedroom was not one of the VisageTome people checked in to the B&B?"

They all frowned at me.

"She said he didn't have a room, she said he wasn't staying there, she said he didn't come with the other VisageTome people. But she said all that after she'd also said she hadn't been anywhere near the room after Dell found Darryl Justice."

"Maybe the sheriff told her the name." Mike used one hand to rub out his own suggestion. "No, no, you're right. He wouldn't."

There was a moment of silence.

"So, you're thinking she knew the dead man wasn't checked in to the B&B because—what? She killed him?" Diana asked.

"That's a possibility. Say she knew because she'd seen him dead in that bed, whether she did the deed or not."

"Or her husband killed him and told her," Jennifer said. "He *wanted* her to know he'd killed her lover. You said her eyes were puffy from crying."

"True. It sounded like the affair was over, but if the lover showed up on his doorstep could that drive Dirk to murder? Maybe," I answered my own question.

"Why do you think Elaine told us about Krista and Darryl?" Mike asked.

Dell said, "It cost her little. We already had the affair part. We could have gotten the answer to the other part by digging at VisageTome. Elaine saved us time."

"And sent us in a different direction," I said. "But if that was her purpose, it's not something we can ignore. We've got to talk to Krista again. And soon."

"Not now," Mike said. "We should have left already for Mrs. Parens' and Aunt Gee's. I'm not taking the risk of being late."

Chapter Twenty-Six

I WAS HEARTENED on the drive to O'Hara Hill when Dell nodded toward cattle in a field and said, "I think I met their cousin in the Hoover House Hotel."

"Haber House," Mike and I corrected, but mine was perfunctory. It was good that he was getting back to himself. Wardell Yardley subdued and even a bit humbled wasn't what I was used to.

But I was mostly occupied with fretting about spending this time going to O'Hara Hill when we had less than two days before the network crew arrived.

"Dell, could you work your magic with your crew and persuade them to keep what's going on to themselves for a while? At least over the weekend, say."

"No."

"Because the people coming in aren't—?"

"That's not why. The producer would do it. I don't know who else she's bringing, but there would be a chance. But I can't. It's bad enough not informing them now. Come Friday I'm telling them everything. Exactly where everything stands."

"Then we need to be sure you can tell them who the murderer is by Friday," Mike said.

"That would be ideal," was all Dell said.

Right. All we needed to do was figure out the murderer in less than forty-eight hours.

I was back to fretting.

Arriving in front of a pair of ultra-neat houses on one of the few side streets O'Hara Hill could boast, we went up the walk of the house on the left and knocked, precisely at ten-thirty.

Mrs. Parens swung the door open.

After introductions, she led us to what would be the living room or parlor in most houses. In this house it was a museum. Wardell Yardley won a truckload of brownie points by his reaction.

First, he didn't recoil.

Mike seemed to fight that response every time he walked in the room. Though that might have been flashbacks caused by the pointer she kept by the door. Hard to blame him, since he'd had her as both a teacher and a principal in his academic career.

Second, Dell went immediately to a wall covered ceiling to floor with photos from the history of Cottonwood County.

"Teddy Roosevelt. We heard about his 1903 trip to Yellowstone," he said. "But this looks earlier."

A lesser woman would have beamed. She nodded in approval. "That photo is of President Roosevelt in Buffalo, Wyoming when he was ranching in the Dakotas. That young boy—" The pointer came into play and Mike stifled a flinch. "—is my grandfather."

"Amazing that the history is so close to the present here in Wyoming," Dell said.

If he kept this up, she was going to break down and beam.

They were quite a pair to look at. The tall, elegant African-American man who lived in the doubly heated hot-house where journalism and the presidency intersect. And the petite, white-haired retiree who nurtured learning and brooked no breach of discipline.

"If you should care to discuss the history of Cottonwood County or, more generally, of Wyoming at some future time, I would be pleased to welcome you again, Mr. Yardley."

"Please, call me Wardell, ma'am. I would be honored and delighted to take you up on that invitation, if circumstances allow."

I had seen Wardell Yardley woo any number of women. Never like this. He was rather sweet.

"Speaking of circumstances…" Mike said.

"Yes, Michael, you are right to remind us that there is not adequate time to indulge our other interests at this moment, although that reminder borders on the redundant with Elizabeth standing under the class photographs and fidgeting with impatience."

Fidgeting? I'd shifted from foot to foot a few times. So what? These shoes were new.

I defended myself with, "As you said, there's not a lot of time. And I have questions."

"In this situation I am unlikely to be able to give you background, since it is my understanding that neither the victim nor any of the people staying at the bed and breakfast establishment where this unfortunate incident occurred is from Cottonwood County."

The wily old fox. She'd worded it perfectly. And I suspected that if I hadn't already known what I already knew she wouldn't have volunteered it.

"That's true. Those people have no connection to Cottonwood County that we know of. However, one of the owners of the bed and breakfast does." As Mrs. P had told me herself. "Her husband is connected to it through her and the B&B."

"Indeed." Her eyes glinted. I'd passed the quiz. "Krista spent a considerable amount of her childhood vacations here."

My hopes sank. "Vacations? Only vacations?" That would mean she hadn't been in the school system.

"She did spend several school years here as a child. In addition, after her parents' deaths, she finished high school at Cottonwood County High School."

I meant no disrespect to the dead parents, but thank heavens.

"Has she talked to you about strains in her marriage? Were she and Dirk having—?"

Her upright posture froze.

What was I thinking? Of course Mrs. Parens wouldn't tell me something like that. I'd learned that last spring. And here I was trying to rush her into territory I knew she'd never venture into.

I pulled in a long breath and started over. "Is her picture here on the wall?"

"It is." She raised the pointer and went to a section of photos about a decade old. She pointed to a portrait of a girl who appeared shy, yet determined. Her top was baggy, which emphasized her bust even more, though she'd probably meant it to disguise. She'd refined her hairstyle and makeup since then.

Krista had definitely improved with age. And perhaps with confidence.

"She looks intelligent," I ventured.

"She was an excellent student. Indeed, I would describe her as exceptional. She graduated at the top of her class at Carnegie Mellon before obtaining dual graduate degrees from the Massachusetts Institute of Technology."

And now she was changing sheets and cooking breakfasts to run a B&B. How had that happened?

No use asking that directly. But Mrs. P's comments on the phone had signaled which area she was willing to talk about.

"VisageTome prides itself on hiring the best of the best," I said.

"They had that in Krista."

"It's unfortunate they didn't value her the way they should have." A flicker of her eyes indicated I was on the right track. "What impressions about her career at VisageTome would help to give us an accurate picture of her time there?"

"Working for a company that underwent explosive growth from a startup to where it is now was at the core of her experience there. She found it challenging, exciting, and frustrating. Leaving the company was wrenching for her. However, she has said she would have preferred being there during its years as a startup, despite the financial uncertainties. She has expressed interest in launching a small startup herself. However, her employment contract forbids that for a period of years that has not yet been met."

Was the B&B a way to earn a living until she could launch her own company? Or, perhaps a venture for Dirk to run once she could pursue other opportunities?

"Has she talked about what kind of startup she's interested in?"

"If she has, it was in the form of a confidence entrusted to me and I will not answer. If she has not, I cannot answer. In either case, there is no answer for your question."

I was making no headway with this. I glanced at Mike, but he spread his hands. He had no ideas, either.

"Did Krista know these people from VisageTome before they checked in to the B&B?"

"She has not told me."

"Does she know what their meetings are about?"

"She has not told me."

"Is there anything you can tell us that might help us?" Frustration might have come through on that one.

"I am not aware of any further information that could be of benefit to your inquiry that I will share with you at this time."

"Okay. That's clear enough. Then we might as well go to you aunt's house, Mike, so we can resume our inquiries as soon as possible."

"Elizabeth." Mrs. Parens made it a reprimand.

I wasn't prepared to sit still for a reprimand. "What?"

"Use your considerable intelligence to its best advantage. In addition, use all your resources, including your human resources."

Did she mean… I looked at her. She gave a quick nod, but before I could respond, she turned and said, "Wardell."

"Yes, ma'am."

She reached up—a long reach for her—and put her palm on his cheek. "You need not fear. Your friends will help you."

Dell didn't get tears in his eyes. He did, however, look touched. "Thank you, Mrs. Parens. Thank you for everything."

She was back to her brisk self when she said, "You all go ahead to Gisella's. She expects you now. I will be there in a moment."

Mike led the way. We walked down Mrs. Parens' perfectly straight front walk. Along the sidewalk a short distance, then up the drive of Aunt Gee's house.

"We couldn't have walked across?" Dell asked.

I left Mike to answer. I was frustrated—by Mrs. Parens, by the lack of information, by the ticking away of the clock, and by my uncertainty of which way to jump.

"Not across the lawn. Never across the lawn. Wait until it snows. If a rabbit leaves a print she brings out the bazooka. Aunt Gee won't even have a sidewalk put in because she says it ruins the lawn."

"That must have been a popular statement with Mrs. P, since she does have a sidewalk," I said.

Mike covered his laugh with a cough. Behind the hand he brought to his mouth, he said, "She's watching us from the door."

"Which one?"

"*Both.*"

"And you think they can read lips?"

"I *know* they both have hearing like bats."

"THAT IS A meal I will never forget," Dell said as we drove away. "Not even after I digest it, which might never happen."

"I'll tell Aunt Gee—the first part only. She'll like that. She was really down, you know." Mike looked at me as he said that. "She feels bad she can't help us."

"I know. And I get it that with Sheriff Conrad around she could be fired for giving us information."

"It's not only that. She believes in law enforcement doing its job." He added more cheerfully, "She did say she'd let us know anything she could."

"Yeah." I wasn't as optimistic as Mike about any information coming from Aunt Gee. I was also disappointed in what I'd gathered from Mrs. Parens on the Segers. Other than a great meal it felt like a waste of time when time might be our most precious resource.

Dell said, "I have a question I've been waiting to ask, since you two warned dire consequences if anything untoward was said in front of the ladies."

"What's that?" Mike asked.

I would have made Dell volunteer it. Mike is too easy on him.

"Since Mrs. Parens is adamant that only bison roamed Wyoming, why hasn't she insisted the town be renamed from Buffalo to Bison?"

"Ask her that," I begged him. "Just let me be there when you do it."

MIKE AND DELL had dropped me off at the bunkhouse to get my SUV.

I was going to question Krista again. Specifically to see if I could get Krista to admit she'd seen Darryl Justice. Mike and Dell were going to try Round 2 with the VT group.

I had hit the edge of town when my phone rang.

"I hear you're wondering about Krista Seger's background." It was Leona D'Amato.

How had she known… Mrs. P? Surely not. She wouldn't have used a proxy. She'd either tell me herself or not at all. Aunt Gee. It had to be. But I knew better than to ask Leona her source. "I am."

"Buy me a cup of coffee and we're on."

"Station coffee? I—"

"No way am I drinking that sludge. Meet me at the Haber House. Think you'll get me a slice of pie along with that coffee."

I texted Dell—since Mike was driving—that I was taking a detour to get more background before tackling Krista.

Leona, with coffee and pie, was sitting on a bar stool at the short end of the counter where it curved after a long run down one side of the dining room. She had her back against the wall for comfort and a 180-degree view of the bar, the dining room, the lobby, and, through the front windows, a major slice of the front sidewalk. With nobody nearby to overhear.

My kind of woman.

Except she'd left me to sit facing her and with my back to all that prime real estate.

I asked the man behind the bar for coffee as I headed for her. While we said hello, I dragged the next stool in line at the bar and placed it next to hers, also against the wall.

The bartender glowered as he handed over the black coffee, but didn't say anything.

"You know who Krista Seger is?" she asked after several bites of pie.

"A former VisageTome employee, I know."

"That might matter out there." Her nod indicated the rest of the globe. "But here in Cottonwood County what matters is she's Val Heatherton's niece."

"Heatherton, as in the owners of—"

"Our happy little playground. That's right." My stomach sank.

That explained the puff piece they'd tried to get me to do. It also meant this inquiry might not be great for job security—for me and others—if it revealed Krista or Dirk was the murderer.

"How did I not know that?"

She gave a bark of laughter. "Ha. There's more that you don't know than could ever be reported. Because people don't want you to know. That's your handicap. You're reporting things people don't want known. That's where Mike and I are the same. We report what people most *want* to be on TV. Of course the stuff they don't want out there that he and I know, they *really* don't want out there."

Another bite of pie.

"Oh, sure, you report some things people don't want out there, but that's head stuff—business, legal, ethical. But what Mike and I deal with is the gut—relationships, winning or losing, identity. It's emotional."

"So, what do you know that's emotional and that can't be reported on air?"

"Krista's marriage was in trouble. That's why they came back here—well, back here for her. He's from someplace on the West Coast."

I lost half a beat to astonishment that she'd answered without trying to extract some benefit for herself. I might have been hanging around Wardell Yardley too much.

"How was coming here supposed to get their marriage out of trouble? And has it?"

"No idea on the second part. The first part was officially because she was working long, stressful hours at VisageTome."

"And unofficially?"

"Hey, there are things I won't report but am willing to tell you, and then there's plain old gossip."

I appreciated the distinction. I also appreciated the heck out of her calling me to offer this information. It was possible Mike's asking around yesterday sparked this. But with the timing, my money was on Aunt Gee.

"But I will tell you this, she didn't want to leave VisageTome."

"He said leave the job or leave me?" I asked Leona.

"Not exactly. He called in the big gun—Val Heatherton."

I felt my brows rise. "He went to his wife's aunt for marital help?"

"That's right. And it was a smart move."

"She's gung ho on the sanctity of marriage, against divorce, and thinks the little woman should stay home and make beds," I guessed.

She hah'd a short laugh. "She'd never be able to look herself in the mirror in that case. No, geography was the card Dirk played by calling Val Heatherton. She never liked Krista living out there anyway. She does a good amount of traveling herself, but insists Cottonwood County is home base for everyone in the family. So she got a hold of Krista and said enough of this being away. Get yourself back here. Fix your marriage or end it. But either way, do something and do it here."

"Wow. That must be a close-knit family for the aunt to be able to lay down the law like that."

"Close-knit isn't the first term that comes to mind. But there are other considerations."

"Such as?"

"Krista is one of Val Heatherton's primary heirs. For now."

I had a few more questions for Leona D'Amato, but the answers didn't add much to my knowledge except for one.

"Does Les know about the Segers' relationship to the Heathertons?" I asked her.

She gave me long look, then shrugged. "Don't know. Never heard him discuss it. If I had to guess, I'd say no."

"Ah. Or he'd have assigned multiple stories on the Wild Horses Bed and Breakfast ages ago."

"Exactly."

I thanked her and paid the tab, while she headed out.

I, on the other hand, wasn't going anywhere.

Chapter Twenty-Seven

LOGIC SAID THAT unless Bunny had taken off, there was a good chance she was in this hotel. Not only were there limited options in Sherman, but there was that glimpse yesterday.

The hotel would ring her room if I asked, but I had a better idea than asking at the front desk.

I went up the stairs from the lobby, looked around, and walked along the hall to the bottom of a stairway to the next flight up in this rabbit warren of a hotel.

I took out my phone, called the Haber House Hotel number and asked to be connected with Bunny Ramsey Sterakos' room.

"I'm sorry. We have no one here by—Oh, wait. Did you say Ramsey? Here she is."

Bunny answered before the second ring. Her "hello" was low and hesitant.

"Bunny! It *is* you." I infused as much enthusiasm into my voice as I could without being so loud I could be heard in any of the rooms, in case hers was nearby. Didn't want to confuse her with this call in stereo. "It's Elizabeth. Elizabeth Margaret Danniher. What a delight that you're here in my town. Now we finally will have a chance to get together. Tell me you're free tonight. We'll have dinner. Us and your delightful son, Christopher."

"How did you—?"

"Oh, Sherman's a small town. You know how that is. Like the one we grew up in, where everybody knows what everybody's doing. No secret's ever safe."

She sucked in a breath, not quite a gasp.

"So, what time do you want to have dinner tonight? We can eat in the hotel, but if you're tired of that, there's another place I like. Is seven okay with you?"

"Uh, yes. Okay. Seven."

"Great. I'll pick you up at the hotel. Right out front at seven. It'll be great. We can really catch up."

"Yes. Okay. But I have to go now, so…"

"Sure, sure. See you tonight."

She'd hung up before I'd finished.

I'd just slipped the phone into a handy pocket when a door down the hall opened and Bunny rushed out.

That was lucky. I'd thought if she and her son had a suite together I'd have to wait until they finished packing.

In fact, it was lucky all around, because his room was closer to me than her room, so she cut the distance I had to sprint to get right behind her as Christopher opened the door.

She pushed past him, so preoccupied she didn't even notice me on her tail. He did, raising his eyebrows in confusion.

Below those eyebrows, his eyes were red and puffy. His young, healthy skin had the week-old-dough look of someone who'd been crying. A lot.

Sorrow? Remorse? Fear? Could have been anything.

Bunny grabbed his bag as she went by, tossing it on the old-fashioned bed with the same spread Dell had objected to.

"We have to get out of here. Right now. I don't care what you say. We're getting the first flight out and that's the end of it."

She was throwing in whatever came to hand, including an old fash-ioned windup alarm clock that I strongly suspected was part of the décor.

"Mom—"

"No more of this. I don't care that you paid for your own room, you're still my son. We're going. Now."

"Where?"

She spun around at my question, both hands to her heart.

Gripping the edge, I took the door from Christopher's unresisting hold and swung it closed behind me. "I'm hurt. You're not even staying for dinner?"

"I… I should have told you, but your call… It, uh, took me by surprise. You didn't give me a chance to tell you, we have to leave and—"

"Give it up, Mom. She played you. She wanted to see if you'd run."

"Why would I run? Don't be ridiculous."

"She knows," he said flatly.

"Knows? There's nothing to know. Absolutely nothing. We need to get home, Christopher and I. I would have called you from the airport."

"He's right, Bunny. I know."

"There's nothing to know," she repeated.

"About your special program in high school. About the baby—"

"No. No. No. You will not say these things. Not to my son."

"For God's sake, I know, too." He was disgusted as only a teenager can be with a parent. "I've known for months."

"You can't." It was the same hoarse tone coming from that same white face as I'd seen at Yellowstone.

"I do. I found papers in the attic."

They seemed to have forgotten me. I stayed still and quiet.

"There are no papers in our attic. Nothing about that, not a word or hint about it anywhere in our house. I made absolutely sure your father would never—"

"Gran's attic. When I was helping her clean out the place before you made her move to that depressing cell they call an apartment."

She'd started to regain color. "I did not make her. It was for her own good. To make life easier for her."

"Easier for *you*. So you didn't have to help her with things around the house. *Her* house. She didn't want to sell. You know she didn't. And I didn't want her to sell. I loved that house. I hoped someday—"

"So you're doing all this—coming out here, talking to that… that person, insisting on coming here with me when I told you and told you to go home—all to punish me because your grandmother sold that crumbling old house and moved into a condo?"

"Geez. Paranoid much?"

"And why shouldn't I be when you nosed around into my private affairs—"

"Affairs is right."

"—and dug up what had nothing to do with you."

"It does have to do with me. He was my brother. My half-brother. At first, I just wanted to know..."

For the first time he faltered and looked away from his mother.

Wanted to know or wanted something to hold over his mother?

I tried mental telepathy to get Bunny to ask my question or to say anything to keep the exchange going. Nothing doing.

I asked, "How'd you find him, Christopher?"

He flashed a look at me. Might have been grateful for the question, for my interest. Less charitably it might have been an opportunity to show off.

"Papers in the attic. Not the diaries, but—"

"Diaries? You read my diaries?"

He ignored her outrage. "The official papers listed his adoptive parents. It wasn't easy to find them, because they'd moved a couple times. But there are services online you can buy that will tell you who else is associated with somebody as long as you have one name. And I had both their names. That's when I saw they'd named him Darryl."

Great. Now even kids knew about those invasion-of-privacy services.

"I dug up everything I could about him. When I started, I thought just knowing would be enough. But it wasn't. I wanted to meet him. Only he didn't want to meet me. When I wrote to him I thought it would be like you see on TV all the time, with him being curious about what happened and where he came from and he'd be happy I'd found him. It wasn't like that at all. He wrote back and said he wished me a good life, but he had his own life with a great family and he had no interest in the woman who'd given him away. Or in me. He didn't want any more to do with me than you do."

That last was a shot at his mother.

Bunny went white again. It was like her face was a stoplight with only white and red as options. "I don't know how you could possibly think I don't want to have anything to do with you."

"Everything for you is all about you and Dad. It's like I don't exist for you. Me or the girls," he added belatedly. "Only him. I used to dream about you two getting divorced and—"

"Did you hear something? Did he say something about divorcing me?"

"—I'd go with him and then he'd remarry and maybe I'd finally have a real mom."

"He said something to you?"

I wasn't sure Bunny had even heard the rest of what her son had said.

"No, Mom. It was a dream. All a dream." The sarcasm was thick. But maybe it needed to be with Bunny.

"So you contacted Darryl Justice," I prodded him.

"Yeah, but like I said—"

"Don't tell her anything, Christopher. Not another word."

"—he didn't want to have anything to do with me. He wasn't interested. I even tried saying there was money in the family, so he'd be smart to get me on his side and I could help him. He didn't want it." He gave a harsh laugh that was far too old for someone his age. "Guess he didn't get that gene from you, huh, Mom."

Apparently the harsh laugh was a gene Christopher *had* gotten from his mother because hers now sounded identical. "Oh he wanted money all right." She jerked her head around to me. "You heard him."

"I heard him say something about money, but—"

"Right. Blackmail. Blackmailing me."

"I don't believe it," Christopher said. That had a tinge of desperation to it. Had he built up his unknown half-brother to hero status already? "He wasn't interested. Not in the money. Not in you. Not in me. He said he didn't want to meet me. There was no purpose to it."

"Yet you went to Yellowstone to meet him," I said.

"No," Bunny said. "Christopher was there for a special program for school. But he was supposed to be at the Mammoth. Assigned to the Wooly Mammoth area."

"Yeah, the Wooly Mammoth area," he said with full-out sarcasm, "and I magically got reassigned to the Lake Yellowstone Hotel, which happened to be where Darryl was." Some boys' voices break from soprano to tenor at his age. His broke from nice guy to smart-ass. "Get a grip, Mom."

"A program for school," Bunny insisted.

"A 'special program.' You didn't even catch it was the lie you told when you went away to have that baby—Darryl."

"A program." This came out as a whimper.

"No program. I lied. Do you hear me? I lied. And you fell for it. Like always. You don't even think about what I'm saying. A special program at Yellowstone Park from a school in Illinois? At the start of November? Why? But you never even questioned it."

"How'd you know Darryl would be at Yellowstone, Christopher?" I asked.

His grin bordered on a grimace. "VisageTome, of course."

"He posted where he was going—?"

"No. He's not—He wasn't stupid. But he said something about a trip and I cross-searched with other people connected to him and one had a map of Yellowstone and someone else mentioned they were going to miss their college homecoming game, so I found out when that was, so I knew the date."

I was impressed. "That's good digging. But what did you hope to accomplish by going to Yellowstone when your half-brother—

"Stop saying that," Bunny muttered. Her son and I ignored her.

"—would be there?" I asked.

"To see him. To meet him. As a person. I wasn't going to tell him who I was. Not unless... But there never was a chance."

"But you did talk to him at Yellowstone?"

"Yeah. A couple times. He was nice to me. We talked a little. About VisageTome, the park, football. He had no idea who I was. He was a nice guy."

The boy looked close to tears again.

It struck me that he was the only one in Sherman who truly

mourned Darryl Justice.

Presumably Darryl's family and friends back home did and would, but here it was only a teenager who'd wanted a connection but had taken a few nice words.

"Why are you still here now?" I asked evenly.

Bunny sent a baleful look toward her son.

My gaze followed it. "You didn't want to leave, Christopher?"

His doughy face had gone stubborn. "He was my *brother*—half-brother. Somebody killed him. Hell, no, I don't want to run away and pretend none of this happened. Not like *her*."

Before the acrimony underlying that could explode, I quickly spoke. "So you followed him here to Sherman to try to get to know him better, but how did you know he was coming here?"

"I heard him talking to somebody about coming to Sherman."

I guessed him to be old enough to drive, but not to rent a car. He'd needed Bunny, whether he liked it or not.

"It was all your idea? Your mom didn't know Darryl would be here?"

"I—"

I cut across her attempt to interrupt. "Let Christopher answer, Bunny."

"That's right. I told her. She didn't know until we got here and saw him."

"What? You saw him? When? Where?"

"On the street out there. I knew what he drove—" He'd certainly done his homework. "And spotted it when he drove by, even though it was getting dark. He pulled in and went in that place down the block. Some museum or something. I followed him. He was asking for directions to that bed and breakfast."

Now that daylight savings was done it got dark about five. Darryl must have gotten in to the Sherman Western Frontier Life Museum shortly before it closed.

"Did you talk to him?"

"For a minute. He was real surprised. I was saying maybe we could have dinner. Then *she* came in." A head jerk indicated his mother. His tone was bitter. "He didn't want anything to do with me after that. He walked away."

"You didn't follow him to the B&B?"

"How could I with her crying all over me?"

"He was trying to *blackmail* me." It might have been more motherly if she'd gone with the angle that she was trying to protect Christopher from having contact with a supposed blackmailer.

"He wasn't."

"He was. *She* heard him." *She* was me. "He said the money wasn't enough. He never would have been satisfied. He—"

"Christopher, who was he talking to?" I interrupted.

"Huh?"

"When you heard them talking about coming here to Sherman, to the B&B."

"Some park ranger."

That threw me off stride for a beat. I'd expected him to name one of the VisageTome people.

"Was the ranger telling him about the B&B, or was Darryl telling the park ranger."

"Darryl was telling him. Saying he needed to deal with a snake."

"And you didn't see him again?"

A loud knock stopped the boy from answering.

"Now what?" Bunny demanded of the universe that was refusing to play by her rules.

I can't say what made me step back and to the side so the door partly masked me. Perhaps caution, perhaps intuition.

She opened the door, and the crack along the doorjamb gave me a view of the new sheriff of Cottonwood County, Wyoming.

Chapter Twenty-Eight

"BUNNY RAMSEY STERAKOS?" The sheriff advanced to the threshold, presumably to block the door if she tried to close it. He'd spotted the packing in progress. He presented his badge. Not one of those lightning flashes, but giving her plenty of time to look it over. She didn't take advantage of that. She'd gone white and numb again. "I'm Sheriff Conrad. We'd like to talk to you. May we come in?"

Through the crack, my eyes met those of one of the "we"— Deputy Wayne Shelton.

"Sheriff," Shelton said. Not quite a warning. Surely not a *Danger, Danger, Will Robinson* caution.

Still, the sheriff's hand went to his gun as he stepped in, apparently taking her silence as an invitation.

"Hello, Sheriff," I said.

He pushed the door more fully open. He didn't say *You*, but he looked it.

I smiled at him.

He didn't smile back.

"Deputy Shelton, will you escort Mrs. Sterakos and her son to the station? I'll be right there."

I smiled again. He thought he'd stymied me by not questioning them in front of me.

"I don't want to. I don't have to. I won't," Bunny said.

"If you don't come down and talk to us voluntarily, we can arrange other circumstances, ma'am."

Wild-eyed, she turned to me. "Elizabeth?"

"Either go with them and tell them everything or call your husband, tell him everything, and ask him to get you the best lawyer he can who can be here in a day. You and Christopher might have to spend the night in jail, but—"

The sound she made should have insulted the Cottonwood County jailers. Except I thought it might have been directed at me for the suggestion to call her husband.

"You should listen to your friend," the sheriff observed.

She fumbled for her purse. "I don't know anything. I have nothing to tell you. This all has nothing to do with me or my son. I don't know why you'd want to talk to me."

"Yes, ma'am," Shelton said calmly, moving in and gesturing her to the door in a way that reminded me of a herding dog. "We'll discuss all that." He looked at Christopher. "Son?"

The boy followed his mother.

Shelton exchanged a look with the sheriff and headed out without looking at me. But I'd seen one corner of his mouth twitch. The old softie.

Not waiting for the sheriff to start, I said, "Should you be in here without the occupant's permission?"

"What about you?"

"I was permitted."

He grunted. "I'm not here to search. I'm here to tell you—again—to stay out of sheriff's department business."

"It's not sheriff's department business I'm interested in, it's my friend I'm interested in."

"Is she your friend?"

I'd meant Dell. But I was walking a thin line. I did not want him questioning my status with Bunny, because that would make him question my being here. Yet I didn't want him considering me an authority on her. He might decide I should answer more questions and I didn't have the time. "It's hard not to call someone you knew as a child, someone from the same small town, who went to the same schools, a friend isn't it?"

His eyes narrowed. "What do you know of her since?"

"We ran into each other at Yellowstone Park for the first time since high school graduation." I didn't feel the need to share what I'd learned from Mom's spy network. "She was staying—no, I don't know that. I don't know that she was registered at Lake Yellowstone Hotel. I only know I saw her there Saturday and Sunday evenings, as I told you."

Yes, I was convinced I'd heard her on Friday night, too, but I hadn't *seen* her.

DELL HAD TEXTED that they were treating the VisageTome group to a late lunch and questions at Hamburger Heaven.

I wished them good answers and said we'd each report later on what we'd found out.

I went straight to the B&B from the Haber House Hotel.

A deputy sheriff's car was parked outside. A deputy sheriff was parked inside.

Lloyd Sampson.

"Ms. Danniher, ma'am."

"Hi, Lloyd." I breezed past, heading toward the kitchen.

"Ma'am." He not only said that louder than I'd ever heard him speak before, but he touched my arm. Not a grab, but a definite get-your-attention.

Darn. Bad enough Dwayne Shelton was intent on ruining Richard Alvaro. If Sheriff Conrad had infected Lloyd Sampson with law enforcement fervor, who was next? Randy Hollister of Sherman PD?

"Sorry, ma'am, but nobody's here."

"Oh." I hoped that didn't betray my relief that he'd stopped me out of politeness, not out of law and order derring-do. "Guess I'll try later."

He nodded.

I could join the confab at Hamburger Heaven, but if Mike and Dell had any sort of flow going, my arrival could throw it off. Not to mention that Elaine wasn't likely to open up in my presence. So what was the point?

I went to the Sherman Western Frontier Life Museum.

Clara was sitting at her desk in the narrow back room, finishing her lunch.

We weren't precisely friends, considering that the last time I'd been in here I'd wondered if she might be a killer.

"I've got five minutes," she warned.

"I wanted to thank you for confirming Dell's whereabouts the night before last."

"It's the truth."

"It's not always easy to tell the truth. Not with Sheriff Conrad questioning you."

She huffed out a breath in agreement.

"And not when it means your personal life might be on display."

She gave a faint, wry smile. "What have I got to lose? At least it reminds some people around here that I'm capable of having a sex life."

Yeah. I didn't need that reminder of my *lack* of a sex life.

But then I remembered that she'd had it worse than I ever had or would, because she'd been driven to the extreme of dating Thurston Fine at one point. She'd recovered her sanity quickly and now detested him.

"Besides," she said, "Dell is a good ... guy."

I had the feeling she'd intended to say something else.

"Uh-huh. Doesn't hurt that he'll do a national report that will include your museum. Which he couldn't do if he were behind bars."

She met my gaze. "No, it doesn't hurt. But Wardell Yardley was with me all night. In my house. In my bed."

I believed her.

I think I even would have believed her if I hadn't already believed Dell, who was saying the same thing.

"Sheriff Conrad seemed to believe you?"

"Less that he believed me and more that he believed finding the room key on the floor near the chair where most of our clothes ended up."

That was more than I needed to know.

She was continuing, "What I don't get is why the network sent him on this assignment now. It will be ages before ownership of the gold is resolved. But I'm not complaining."

Good thing. Because I wasn't about to explain the absurdities of Big Bosses politics in network television.

"I also wanted to ask if you know who was at the ticket desk at closing on Monday."

"I was. Why?" There was a lot of wariness in that question.

"Did, uh, anything happen then?"

The wariness mushroomed. "Why? What—"

"I don't want anybody to say I gave you any ideas, so, please, just answer. Did anything happen?"

"A young man came in and asked for directions to that new B&B." Her head jerked up. The penny had dropped. She closed her eyes. Possibly in the hope that I would disappear, but I prefer to think it was in an effort to aid her memory. "While I was looking it up—it's so new I didn't know the details yet—a kid came in. Teenager. They seemed to know each other. As I was starting to give the directions, the door flung open again and a blonde woman came in and said—"

She shook her head.

"No. Sorry. What she said was too disjointed. I couldn't quote her. But she was crying and trying to drag the kid away. The young man looked fed up and said something to the kid about not being who he thought he was."

"The guy who came in asking directions to the B&B? That's the murder victim."

She groaned.

"You have to tell the sheriff. It's not a big deal, but it does help with the timeline. Tell him I sent you."

I'd considered for half a second not telling her, but the downside was too steep. On the flip side, I didn't have to wave a red flag under the sheriff's nose about Bunny and Christopher's activities. I still had some questions for them.

A MESSAGE FROM Needham Bender was on my phone. He was putting together a story for Friday's edition of the Sherman Independence, would my friend Wardell Yardley care to comment? I texted him to talk to James Longbaugh, who was representing Mr. Yardley, for comment.

He texted back: Eventually?

I replied: Hope so.

No text from Dell or Mike.

I went back to the B&B.

As I pulled up, Lloyd Sampson opened the front door and shook his head.

I still had one more stop on my agenda.

Time to stop putting it off.

I put the SUV in drive and headed west, then north before turning west again, up into the beginning climb of the mountains.

As I drove, I made a phone call.

Chapter Twenty-Nine

"**MOM, DO YOU** remember any details about Bunny Ramsey when we were in high school?"

Immediately, she came back with, "What are you up to, Elizabeth?"

"Cat," Dad protested, "she's asking about an old friend."

I hated it when Mom knew me better than Dad. Sometimes he gave me too much credit.

"They were never really friends."

"They played together all the time as little girls. Don't you remember?"

"That was because they were the only two that age in the area. Elizabeth would have preferred to trail around after her older brothers. To keep her from getting trampled and to give them a break, I arranged for her to play with Bunny. When they started—"

"I didn't get trampled. I kept up with—"

"Broken arm," Mom said.

All right. A little trampled.

"—school," she picked up as if neither she nor I had said anything in the interim, "Elizabeth immediately found other friends more to her liking. Bunny surely did, too, since most of their play sessions had ended with Bunny in tears and Elizabeth saying she hadn't done anything."

"I *hadn't*." Could I help it if her Barbie doll was practically made of glass? Besides, who gives a Barbie doll to a pre-schooler? Not only one, but a sequence of them. Just because the previous one got a little

messed up, with grape and dirt stains on a ball gown, lost some hair, or
a leg. Shouldn't her parents have wanted their daughter to learn that
people didn't have to be physically perfect—or perfectly coiffed—to
be loved?

Mom ignored my denial. "By high school, they barely spoke when
they passed each other in the halls."

"How could you possibly know that?"

Mom ignored my question, too. She was a great ignorer.

"Bunny didn't even write to Elizabeth once that year she was
abroad. I thought the least she could do would be to send a birthday
card and Christmas card. But not a word."

"That's right." I wasn't lamenting the lack of birthday or Christmas
card. I was confirming Mom's memory. Now that she mentioned it, I
remembered there were rumblings about what a surprise it was that
Bunny left after most exchange students. Something about her going in
place of someone who'd dropped out. "Where was it she went?"

"Austria."

"No, it wasn't anywhere she'd have to speak another language. I
remember she hadn't taken any languages, so—Australia. That was it.
She went to Australia."

"Why all this interest?" Mom asked.

"Oh, you know." That wouldn't satisfy her. I don't know why I'd
wasted the breath on it. Quickly, I added, "Seeing her at Yellowstone,
uh, brought back memories. But there were gaps. I saw her son at
Yellowstone, too. Christopher. Good-looking kid. I guess seeing him,
and he looks so much like her at that age it made me think about, be a
little curious about…"

"He's a reliable kid," Dad said. "He mows several lawns in the
neighborhood. I tried to get him to do the leaves, but he said he was
going to Yellowstone for some special program."

There was that phrase again.

Mom made a sound.

"Now, Cat," Dad objected. "He *is* a good kid. You're the one who
said he was so good to Muffy Ramsey, including—"

"Muffy?" No wonder she'd had no compunction about calling her daughter Bunny. How had I not known this? I suppose because she'd always been Mrs. Ramsey to me. My parents had always referred to her as Mrs. Ramsey. I wondered if this was some kind of rite of passage—you're finally an adult when your parents use other adults' first names in front of you.

"—helping her with the move to the senior living center."

"That place," Mom said disparagingly.

That place was how she always referred to the senior living center on the edge of town.

"You know some of the folks there like it. There're lots of programs and events and that house was getting to be too much for Muffy. Besides, that's not the point. Christopher helped her a lot with the move. Helped her sort through her things, decide what to take, and you saw how he was with her at the yard sale."

Mom *humphed,* which was darned near a complete surrender.

"Dad," I said quickly, "did Christopher say anything about knowing that his Mom would be at Yellowstone, too?"

"Don't remember anything about that."

"So which trip do you want to know about," Mom complained. "Yellowstone or Australia?"

"Australia. How long was she there?"

"She left right at Halloween, because Muffy was telling me all about it when I saw her in the grocery store when she was buying ingredients for her popcorn balls. She came back… Let me think… A little past the middle of May. We were driving down to Champaign for Steve's graduation from college. You were in the back seat moping because you'd wanted to stay home alone—"

"I didn't mope. And I had a major project—"

"—and we drove past the Ramseys' house, and they were getting out of the car with all her suitcases. I'd have expected her to have been tanner after being in Australia."

End of October to the end of May. Seven months. She could have been three months pregnant when she left. That would have given her time to gestate, deliver a baby, plus a month for getting back to normal.

"Did you hear any, uh, rumors about her trip?"

"You know I don't listen to gossip." No, only the reports from her spy network.

"But people tell you things." That was true. She was also good at prying things out of people who didn't volunteer it.

"There was some chatter among the less charitable that it was odd that she didn't have a single photograph to show for her months there. Though Muffy explained that her suitcase with the photos in it was lost by the airline."

And the dog ate my homework.

"Certainly that was all forgotten when she became engaged to a Sterakos. You know they're the sixth-richest family in Illinois?"

Just a guess, but I suspected Muffy as her source for that factoid. How many people do you know who have the list of richest people in their state memorized?

"I didn't. I knew they were well off, though. I'm sure you've mentioned that." At least the frequency of those mentions had slowed down in the past couple decades. "Do they have more children than Christopher?"

"Two younger girls. Twins."

"What's her husband like?"

"Rich."

"I know that. But what's he like?"

"Ordinary. He's about ten years older than her. They wanted a young bride for him so they could mold her."

"They?"

"His parents—really, his mother and the grandmothers. They're quite old-fashioned." Coming from Mom, that pushed them back to the Century, possibly several centuries earlier. "He'd been dating someone, but the parents and grandparents didn't approve. They wanted the whole virgin bride thing, like he was a prince or something."

Maybe keeping her husband in the dark was reasonable.

"How do they get along now, Bunny and—what's his name?"

"Stelios."

"He's fairly discreet," my father said.

"James," protested Mom, but she didn't dispute his implication.

"Any rumbles about a divorce?"

"Never," Mom said firmly.

"It would dilute the Sterakos family holdings."

That drew a scolding, "James" that clamped off the pipeline of information.

TOM BURRELL'S RANCH isn't deep in the mountains, though some of it clings to slopes on the eastern edge of the dense range. The ranch also includes enough level land and gentler valleys to have kept it going for four generations now.

Tamantha had declared her intention of being the fifth. Though she might mix it with being president, curing cancer, and single-handedly bringing class to reality TV. Nothing is beyond this girl.

Tom was getting out from behind the wheel of his work truck.

His head came up as I drove in. As soon as I'd parked beside his truck, he came around it quickly, cutting me off before I could get anywhere near meeting him halfway.

"Have you been talking to Mrs. Parens?" I asked.

His eyebrows rose. "Yeah. Talk to her every few days."

"About me?"

"No."

That stopped me. I'd thought her line about using all my resources had been a prod to enlist Tom. But if he hadn't talked to her about me...

And since he said he hadn't, he hadn't.

I asked another question. "What do you not want me to see in the bed of your truck?"

He's rarely quick to speak, but this time he took an extra two beats beyond his quota. "A dead cow. Killed by a wolf."

My urge to look in the back was gone. "I thought they mostly hit when the herds are grazed up on the mountains."

"You are learning." His expression wasn't so much a grin as a lessening of the tightness around his mouth. "Wolves might come in this close after a hard winter, but this time of year it can mean one's got a taste for beef. One—or more."

"You shoot them?"

"Not many commit suicide as an alternative to killing and eating my cattle."

"I didn't—" Well, maybe I had. Though it didn't seem a reasonable reaction now.

"But I won't do the shooting. I'll show this and the pictures I took where I found the cow to U.S. Fish and Wildlife folks in Cody."

"You take the corpse to their offices?"

"Mostly we call it a carcass," he said with that same lessening of the tightness around his mouth. "Wouldn't usually, but if this wolf or its pack are rogue... Be best to make an impression. Hope for fast action."

"They'll shoot it?"

He shook his head. "USDA's Wildlife Services."

"But first the people in Cody have to approve?"

"Pretty much."

"You said it can mean it's gotten a taste for beef. What else could it mean?"

The tightening was back. "There was a surplus kill of half a dozen elk a couple weeks ago."

"A surplus kill?"

"Pack kills a lot of elk and leaves much of it uneaten. If they do it late winter, sometimes they'll come back and eat more later if they can't hunt. But this time of year? This weather? It's worrying. But you didn't come here to talk about wolves. And since you already asked about Emmaline Parens, what did you come out to talk about?"

"I came to talk about..." I lifted my hand, but the gesture didn't go any farther than my sentence. Words are my business. It's hard when they disappear.

He looked at me. Fat lot of help he was.

Where was Tamantha when I needed her?

"It was—" I coughed, cleared my throat. "It was something Diana said."

At least this time when I stalled he asked a question. "What was that?"

"I guess we'd been riding her a bit—"

"You guess?"

"Okay, we had—I had been riding her about the sheriff."

I lifted my brows in question. He nodded. Of course he knew about the sheriff and Diana. Why did I even wonder?

"And she said," I continued, "that she was either with us or not, that she was one of us or not. In other words, we'd have to trust her unless she proved she couldn't be trusted or preemptively kick her out."

"Uh-huh."

"That's what I did to you. Preemptively kicked you out."

"Uh-huh."

"I'm sorry."

There was silence for several beats.

"What?" I demanded of him.

"I'm waiting for the *but* before you list all your reasons for not thinking I could be trusted."

"I'm restraining myself."

"Impressive."

"*But*," I said with deliberate emphasis, "it's not only trust. It's knowing you've hated being involved in some of these cases. That resistance drags down everybody else."

He considered that, looking somewhere over my left shoulder. Do you know how hard it is not to turn and look when someone does that?

At last his gaze came back to me.

"Fair enough. If more of these situations come up—and they seem to with regularity since you hit the county—"

"Hey, it's not like *I'm* killing people," I protested. "I'm finding out who did."

"—I can't say there won't be times I won't participate. But I'll tell you at the start. If I commit, I'll see it through."

"Even if someone you care about starts showing up as a suspect as things develop."

"Even if." He looked directly into my eyes. "I don't back out when I commit."

I swallowed. "Okay then." I put out my hand.

He enveloped it in his, then took one step to the side and a second in to me. "Are you Mike's?"

"I'm not anybody's. Even if we were … I'm not … anybody's." It had started so strong, then disintegrated.

"You and Mike aren't together?"

"No. Not that it's anybody's business but ours and—"

"He wants to be."

A vise squeezed my lungs. "I … He thinks he does."

"He does. You?"

"I … don't know."

"You don't know about me, either."

"No. Not you, either."

A stream of breath came out through his teeth. I looked up. Mistake. I couldn't look away.

"When you know—for sure—you'll tell me." It wasn't a question. "Straight out."

I could have no more have not answered than I could look away. "Yes."

"Okay, then."

I thought he'd back off.

I was wrong.

He reeled me in. I can't say how, because his hold on me didn't tighten, and he still touched me nowhere but my hand, yet somehow I was drawn in closer and closer, until I was pressed against him, looking up, with him looking down, and the brim of his hat enough to drop us into a shade of intimate connection.

"Okay, then," he said again. Solemn, but with a hint of humor and a lick of heat.

He kissed me.

I kissed him back.

Then he ended the kiss.

I blinked up at him.

He gave me one of his eye-crinkles-only smiles. "Yeah, I want more, too. But not until you get straight on whether it's Mike or me. And not then—not ever—if it's Mike."

"That's... That's ridiculous. And bossy. What makes you think anything's going to happen between me and Mike—or between you and me. Besides, who says I want more?"

Eye-crinkles gone, he slowly dropped a hand down, the back of it grazing my breast with an electrifying touch on the way to gesturing to part of his anatomy that had undergone an impressive change. "This says we both do."

I'll argue a lot of things, but sometimes facts are facts.

"I get it. You've got things to figure out. Mike, for one. He's a good man. He'd treat you right. But—" His eyes narrowed and I could only be grateful he appeared ready to change the subject. "—maybe it's not only Mike. Maybe it goes back to your ex and—"

So much for gratitude.

I stepped away, retrieving my hand. Found a fence rail across my back and side stepped. "Fine, fine. And I probably have father issues and childhood psychoses. Let's get back on track here. So, when—if—another investigation comes up, we'll count you in unless you count yourself out."

His eyes never left me. I wasn't looking at him, but I knew that anyhow. I was sure he would pursue the personal fork of this conversation.

He said, "What about this investigation?"

I did my best to mask both that I'd guessed wrong and how much I hated being wrong. "But... You're friends with the sheriff."

"You making up my mind for me, Elizabeth Margaret Danniher? Thought we agreed how this would work. And how that would be different from your coming to the construction trailer to invite me in, then deciding to shut me out."

Damn him. Of course he'd known what was up and why I was there. "That was to spare you having to make a difficult decision about loyalty."

"It was you being pissed that I knew something you didn't."

"Me being pissed that you didn't tell me when you knew—"

"You wanted to beat Thurston on being the first to talk to the new sheriff." Before I could dispute that charge, he continued. "And you did. Without me helping. But now I want to help."

I came out of the corkscrew turns of those statements demanding, "Why? Why would you want to help now when Sheriff Conrad is someone you—"

"Because Wardell Yardley's your friend and you're worried."

Chapter Thirty

As I drove back, I was thinking about Tom...

He'd asked if there was anything he could do. When I couldn't think of anything short of picking up Sheriff Russ Conrad and shaking him upside down until he told us everything he knew, he said he'd get Tamantha squared away at a friend's house for overnight and be at Diana's for our scheduled discussion tonight.

...and his words about friendship.

Wardell Yardley was my friend. Even if the evidence hadn't backed him I would have believed him when he said he had nothing to do with the death of Darryl Justice.

What about Bunny?

Others considered her my friend because the accident of childhood addresses had put us in contact for years.

But I didn't believe her. Not about anything.

Bunny was so unsure of her husband and her marriage that apparently she would do anything to avoid letting him know about the son she'd had as a teenager.

Could that extend to killing that son?

She'd thought Darryl Justice was blackmailing her. Thanks in part to me, had she missed the drop Saturday and Sunday nights? She'd certainly been fearful those nights.

And then she'd come here, where Christopher knew Darryl Justice was coming,

Because Christopher had asked her to? Without him telling her why? They didn't seem to have that kind of relationship.

Which meant he'd lied. Because, despite their differences, he was protecting her. Because he thought his mother needed protecting.

So she'd known about Darryl coming to Sherman. She'd overheard the directions from Clara.

Then she'd demanded a tour of the Wild Horses Bed and Breakfast.

Casing the joint?

Could the girl who'd wanted to keep her dolls pristine have done to Darryl Justice what I'd seen?

Sometimes I wish I wasn't so good at asking questions.

LEONA D'AMATO CALLED as I neared Sherman.

"Can I borrow that tomato colored jacket in your studio closet?" That's what KWMTers called the backup clothes we all kept at the station. After my wardrobe was destroyed—I've told that story—I was glad to have those pieces to tide me over on-air. The studio closet did me less good off-air because it was almost all jackets and tops—what's seen above a desk.

I wore a lot of black off-air—it always matches, doesn't show dirt. It started with my first newspaper job. Not only did black help hide newsprint smudges, but I had an editor who used to call me his tragedy writer, like that was an official beat. All the stories about kids being snatched or a family wiped out in a car crash or the high school cheerleader slashed by a psycho. I'd wear black because I never knew when I was going to a funeral.

As I progressed up the TV ladder, though, execs thought it was too severe and wanted "a dash of color." After they'd dashed in with magenta, fuschia, and puce, I settled on red and enough Kelly green to get me through St. Patrick's Day. That worked fine with all the black, although sometimes I looked as if I had gone into mourning at Christmas.

"Sure."

"Thanks. What's the opposite of a sleeping tiger?"

"Uh. An awake tiger?"

"Nope. Maybe a sleeping sloth. That's the second reason I called you. Our very own sleeping sloth has finally blinked his eyes open, and guess what he's seen."

"Sorry. I'm not—"

"A story. A news story. Right in front of him."

"Oh." As in a murder at the local B&B. He was a day and a half behind. "I'll be right there."

"Good."

BEFORE ENTERING THE station, my worry about how a story on KWMT-TV might affect Dell had abated.

After all, we were dealing with Thurston Fine. As Leona had intimated, rousing a sleeping sloth didn't stir much fear.

KWMT-TV's anchor and news director stood in the hallway between the mini-break room and Les's office door.

As I approached, Haeburn saw me first and his face turned a shade of red I would never wear on-air. Or anywhere. "You didn't tell us."

Thurston spun around. "Just like I said. She kept it a secret, planning to take the story herself."

His idea of a secret is anything that's not spelled out in a news release thrust under his nose. And even then...

"What secret, Thurston?"

"There's been a murder at—"

"Oh, that. It's—"

"You're not getting away with it this time. You're not going to lie about it being a nothing story in order to steal it way from me. Not this time." Not any time. But trying to reason with him was a windmill too far, even for Don Quixote. "It's my story. *My* story. It's the lead, so I get it."

I focused on Haeburn. "There are so many unknowns about this—"

"You can't take it away this time." Thurston's voice was screeching toward a Wicked Witch of the West register.

"Think about this, Les," I said. "Do you want to jump on the air with this when there are, uh, factors that could come back to bite you?"

He looked at me blankly.

So he had no idea how the B&B owners were related to the station owners.

Thurston crowed, "She doesn't want us to report it because it's her friend who's murdered somebody."

And neither of them had any idea that my friend was Wardell Yardley, network White House correspondent or they both would have been stalking him with methods that would make paparazzi look like stand-up citizens.

Since Sheriff Conrad had not released Dell's name and since Thurston wouldn't do any actual reporting on the story, most, if not all, of the danger to Dell had been eliminated.

Plus, I'd spotted potential upside to leaving them to their own devices.

Alas, that darned conscience Cat and James Danniher had done their best to instill in all of us rose up.

I kept looking at Les. "Do you want to take the risk of him going on air and saying a man has committed murder? A man who not only hasn't been convicted and hasn't been charged, but has, in fact, been *released* by the sheriff's department? How do you like defending lawsuits?"

"Now you're *threatening* us," Thurston boomed from behind me. "Threatening to sue us?"

"Not me. You wouldn't be saying anything slanderous about me. It would be my friend who would have the slam-dunk case."

"Not if he's guilty," Thurston said triumphantly.

"If it's said on-air before a conviction, slam-dunk," I repeated. "Ever wondered why every—" I amended to make allowances for him. "—almost every journalist uses 'allegedly'? Not to mention you'd be accused of messing with the jury pool."

"You're trying to protect your friend. You're—"

"Thurston, let's go in my office." Haeburn so rarely interrupted Fine that it stopped him long enough to let the news director add, "As you say, she's not reporting the story, so why should she be privy to our discussion of the coverage."

"Les, please. Listen—"

Thurston shot a triumphant look at me as he put an arm around Haeburn's narrow shoulders and led him off. "Good point, good point. But we'll go in *my* office. It's bigger."

When I turned toward my desk, I saw Leona with her hip propped on a nearby desk, where she'd clearly been eavesdropping. "You didn't fill them in, huh?"

"Nope."

"Good. I can't wait to see what happens next. But I had the distinct impression you were going to spill the beans. What made you decide against it?"

Primarily, I'd realized that I couldn't stop them from airing a story. If that story came later it was more likely to include the name Wardell Yardley, but if they went on-air now...

"I had a vision of what might happen after they do the story."

"Oh? You think the owners won't be happy?"

"That and I suspect Thurston might get off on the wrong foot with the two new law enforcement leaders in Cottonwood County."

NEXT CAME A brief side-trip to the Sherman Supermarket. Yes, this investigation was tough on my Pepperidge Farm Double Chocolate Milano cookies supply, but I also wanted to confirm a point with Penny.

That meant buying something as a reason to go by her register. So cookies were strictly utilitarian.

I checked my phone as I followed the familiar path to the cookie aisle.

Mike had texted that he was heading to the station because he had to do the five o'clock sports. His backup's truck broke down and he wouldn't make it in time. We must have just missed each other.

Where's Dell? I asked.

Errand, he responded.

Amid Penny's flow about Deputy Wayne Shelton being harder

headed than the sculptures at Mount Rushmore or he'd listen to her for once, I slid in my question. "Was Krista having an affair with a VisageTome coworker? Is that why she and Dirk came back here to Sherman?"

Every syllable of that overlapped with her words about failing to let go and moving on and learning from dogs about living in the now. At least that's what I thought she said.

But apparently she heard my words with no problem. "Yes, indeed. That poor boy that got himself killed. Not that it was true love or—"

"How do you know? Krista—?"

"—anything. It was a case of being lonely. Working all the time and getting caught up in that job and competition and all. Emmaline Parens. I hear working there is like a cult. Why, Jennifer was telling me—"

In delayed reaction I said, "Mrs. *Parens* told you they were having an affair?"

"—they have a compound and some people never leave at all. Bye now, Elizabeth. Well, hi there, Renata."

There was nothing left to do but try to find Krista Seger again.

Chapter Thirty-One

THIS TIME I succeeded.

Not through any brilliant reporting stratagems.

As I approached the Wild Horses Bed and Breakfast, I saw a small pickup heading the opposite direction and recognized it as one that had been parked by the B&B, then recognized Krista as the driver.

I did a U-turn and followed her. To the parking area between the sheriff's department and the back of the courthouse.

Maybe she had business at the courthouse. Maybe she was going into the sheriff's department for a brief chat.

I wasn't willing to wait to see how either *maybe* turned out.

I climbed into her truck before she even realized I'd opened the door. She'd been in the process of pulling her purse off the passenger seat. Since I now sat partially on it she wasn't going anywhere for the moment.

"Oh," she said.

It's the kind of opener a reporter likes. So many ways to go with it.

"I've learned a number of things since we talked last, Krista."

"Like what?"

"For starters that you didn't want to leave VisageTome. Why say you did? Was that for Dirk's benefit?"

"Wh—" She licked her lips. "What do you mean?"

"You left because of your affair with Darryl Justice. Because Dirk wanted to get you away from there. I suppose it was politic to let him think you didn't like it."

"Huh. Politic." I thought I'd lost her. I'd meant to jolt her but I might have gone too far. Finally, after three slow breaths, she started talking. "We were told on the first day that there's no politics at VisageTome. That's not true. There is politics there. All sort of politics."

She sounded disillusioned. I refrained from saying that any effort that involved more than one person involved politics. Heck, after my few riding lessons with Tom and Tamantha, I'd say anything involving a human and a horse involved politics. Dogs, probably, too. Though Shadow was so self-contained it was hard to tell.

"There's this feeling about the users like they don't really count, like they're not very bright. It's... It's..."

"Disdain?" I supplied, recalling the tequila-fueled discussion at Lake Yellowstone Hotel.

"Yes. That's a good word for it. They say it's all about creating the best product, but it's what *they* decide is best, not what users want. They don't care about what users want. They say they do. Over and over and over they say it. Like that will make it so. They send out these articles about how great it is to work at VisageTome, and everybody has to read them. You're reading and thinking, nobody can believe this stuff."

"That can certainly make it frustrating to work for a company. But a lot of times it's the more personal elements that cause issues. A boss who's unpredictable, say. Or plays favorites."

"Oh, yeah, we had that, too. Though most of the time management isn't around that much. In some ways that's worse."

"Worse?"

"*Lord of the Flies.* Peer pressure that goes way beyond peer pressure." She shook her head. "Being professional is frowned on. You're supposed to be as open and revealing as you would be with your best friends. There are no boundaries. There's pressure—a lot of pressure—to socialize with coworkers. And they don't want outsiders around. That's all part of it."

"Your husband."

She nodded unhappily. "But the worst thing is I got sucked into it and went along. No. More than that, I threw myself into it. I wanted to be part of it. It was like a drug. Truly, like a drug. And I couldn't kick it. And Dirk didn't understand. He kept saying *it's only a job, Tell them no, they can't make you.* Which made me tell him less and less.

"I think that was part of why... Well, and Darryl is—was one of the nicest people there. Genuine. He should have gotten out of there. There's a saying that VisageTome wraps its arms around you. Feels like a hug until it squeezes the life out of you."

"Do you think Darryl Justice came here to Sherman to see you? To try to start things up again?"

"No." The single word was decisive. "It was over. He knew that. He agreed. Completely over. I don't think he even knew how it happened—us, I mean."

"Could he have come here to make trouble between you and Dirk?"

Her head shake was also decisive.

"Or to make you cooperate with something for fear that he would?"

"No. Not only because it wasn't like him, but because he wasn't the one who called about the group staying at the B&B. I never heard from him at all."

"Who did call?"

"Gordon. It was Gordon Kelvin. He said they wanted to come here for meetings. Someplace out of the way, he said. Private. I said no. But he got kind of... I don't know how to describe it. You know that smile he gets? I'd bet everything I have he was smiling that way when he said refusing to let them stay would call attention to ... *everything.* And it would be such a shame if, after I moved so far away, Dirk found out what had happened at VisageTome."

"Dirk didn't know?"

"He knew there'd been ... someone. Not who."

I reserved judgment on that.

She didn't appear to notice my silence as she went on. "I thought for a moment that Darryl must have put Kelvin up to it for some reason, because I didn't think anyone knew about us at VisageTome. I was sure of it. But after... Well, none of it made sense. At the time, though, it gave me chills. The more I thought about it over the weekend the weirder it seemed. And when they arrived Monday afternoon, it was the worst of VisageTome taking over my home. All I wanted was for them to *go*.

"It was horrible. Our first night and we were completely full and I wasn't sure I could handle it and Elaine and the rest were demanding this, and wanting that, and all the while these sly little digs about how they could tell everything any time they wanted. And then Dirk acting so strange..." A tear slid down her cheeks.

"That's when you called me."

"Yes. When my aunt said you weren't coming, she said she'd get somebody better to do a story on the B&B, to get the right attention. I knew if you came and did your kind of story there probably wouldn't be that other story. But I thought it would be worth it if your nosing around scared them off."

"When Kelvin called to make the reservation, did you think Darryl was coming?"

"Yeah. Yeah, I did. He was the team leader. It wasn't until they were here that I realized they were meeting without him, so something was going on. They counted on threatening to tell Dirk to keep me quiet."

"Do you know what they're up to?"

"No."

That was a lie.

Or at least a fudge. She at least had an idea.

Would forcing her on this be my best bet? How badly did I need to know what Elaine and Co. were up to?

Better to stick with the lead story of the murder before tangling with sidebars.

"Did you call him—Darryl?"

"*No.* Absolutely not. I didn't want him here. I never knew he was here. Not until—"

"Until you went in the room."

"No. No, I never—"

"Krista. You did. You said Darryl didn't have a room at the B&B.

You said he wasn't staying there. You said he didn't come with the other VT people. You told me all that yesterday morning right after he'd been found. Before you should have known anything except that someone was dead upstairs. When you shouldn't have known who it was. But you did. You knew. Which means you had to have been in that room."

She gulped. "Not in. Not all the way in."

"Krista."

"I was ready for bed when I thought I'd put fresh bath towels in the bathroom before Wardell returned. I knew he'd showered and I knew he'd gone out, but I thought it might impress him and he might, you know, talk about us on TV."

In between reporting the doings at the White House.

Sometimes even people with connection to TV news had no idea how it works.

"I went down there—our rooms are in the attic. I went down really quietly and—"

"What time?"

"I don't know. About eleven? I could hear the TV in the Williamses' room as I went by and it was that late-night show with the comedian."

"Were the others in their rooms?"

"Oh, no. They didn't break up their meeting until almost two. There was no one around. I used the key. Oh. There's a spare key—"

"On top of the doorframe. I know. Three-quarters of the population of the world knows. What did you see when you went in?"

"Nothing. I mean, a few of his things were around. Very neat."

"The bedroom. What did you see in the bedroom?"

"I didn—"

"You did. We've been through that."

"For a second. To be sure everything was okay. And I saw—I thought I saw Darryl. I couldn't believe it. I thought I was imagining things. I closed the door right away, thinking it must have been Mr. Yardley, but... I knew it wasn't. I knew it was Darryl. At first, all I could do was pray he hadn't seen me. I ran up to our room and tried to think. But... it didn't make any sense. He wasn't supposed to be there. Not at all. And I was afraid there'd be a fight and then it would come out about him and me, because I knew Elaine would tell Dirk out of spite. And if she didn't Kelvin would."

"Why didn't you call the police?"

"The police?" Her eyes widened. "Why?"

"A man beaten in a bed in your establishment. What if he hadn't been dead yet?"

"Oh, but he wasn't—he was sleeping. There wasn't any blood. I know there wasn't. The light from the bathroom... I'm sure I would have seen."

I wasn't prepared to say I believed her, but that could account for why she'd been so shocked to hear he was dead, why she'd said, "He's *dead.*" She'd known who was there in that room, but she hadn't known he was dead. Maybe.

"So you went to your room."

"Right. And tried to think it all through. I kept waiting to hear him going downstairs to the parlor to confront them. Waiting and waiting and it never happened. And then I heard them coming upstairs, really late, like I said and I thought, oh, God, now he'd come out and they'd have the fight... But they didn't. They went to their rooms and it got quieter and quieter. And it seemed to me it *couldn't* have been him. And why in Mr. Yardley's room? I told myself I *must* have imagined it. I'd been up since five and I'd been crying and I must have fallen asleep. Then my alarm was going off and everything else was like I told you."

I was reserving judgment on whether I believed all that.

But not reserving judgment on believing that she was very worried about her husband.

"Oh, I'm late," she said. "The sheriff asked me to come in to talk to him. I don't think he wants to talk with all those VisageTome people around." And without her husband around, too? Was that the trend of Sheriff Conrad's thoughts? "I said I'd be there by now."

Taking the hint, I freed her purse, opened the truck door, and stretched a leg down toward the pavement.

"Elizabeth."

I turned back.

"Darryl. He's—he was—a good guy. Decent. I don't think he ever would have done what you said—hold it over me, try to make trouble. Not for me, not for anybody. And I know—" She swallowed, started again. "I know he didn't deserve what happened to him. I should have come forward right away."

I couldn't disapprove of her sentiments.

Still, I could curse to myself that it probably meant she would tell Sheriff Conrad everything she'd told me.

The fact that she'd told me first was small recompense for the fact that what she'd said meant Darryl Justice had to have been beaten in that bed in a much narrower window of time than we'd thought. Because if she heard the VTers going to bed at two, surely she would have heard the beating before that, while she was waiting on tenterhooks for what would happen next and straining at every sound.

So it had to be after she fell asleep.

Though why no one heard it during the night was still a question. Krista might have been worn out from her early-to-rise routine, compounded by worry and tears, but what about the guests. Why hadn't they heard?

No one had an alibi, unless Ariel and Joel alibiing each other counted.

And all that complicated this investigation. Dimming hopes that it could be resolved before Dell's crew arrived in—despite my efforts to stop it, my head did the math automatically—forty-two hours.

Then I had a more cheerful thought.

She might be lying about everything and this wouldn't be so complicated after all.

DEX HAD CALLED while I was talking to Krista and left a typical Dex message: "Call me."

I did.

"Danny, I've looked at that video."

Full stop.

"And?" I prompted.

"In fact, watching the video came later."

"Later than what?"

"Later than asking a friend who is adept at such matters to refine the visual elements of your video. He succeeded. I'm sending you the new version."

"He did? That's great. Since you could see it better could you tell how long it had been dripping? Maybe from the size of the stain on the floor? Or whether parts had started to dry? And that could tell you time of death, right? Or at least a ballpa—" No. Dex didn't like ballparks. Far too imprecise for him. "A range of times."

"It depends."

Of course it did. Sometimes how long I could talk to Dex without screaming also depended. Even though I loved him. But I know my role. "What does it depend on, Dex?"

"What was your purpose in sending me this video? Was it to ascertain the specific variety?"

"It's a particular variety?" Sure there were blood types and in the old days that was used to eliminate people if their type didn't match what was found. But outside of a hospital you hardly heard about blood types anymore because DNA was so specific.

"If forced to conjecture and judging from visuals alone, I would say it was Bikavér."

"Bikavér?" I repeated, doing my best to duplicate his Bee-kah-vehr pronunciation. It didn't sound particularly forensic science-y.

"An alternative would be Agiorgitiko—" I didn't even try to repeat that one. "Possibly Cabernet Sauvignon. Or there's—

"Cabernet—? Dex."

"—a Slovenian wine that—"

"*Dex.*" My insides were twisting.

"What?"

"You're saying that wasn't blood? It was *wine?*"

"The viscosity alone tells you that. Blood is expressed as point zero zero three to point zero zero four. For comparison, water is point zero zero zero eight nine. The viscosity—"

"So blood truly is thicker than water?" Great. My brain was whirling around trying to get a handle on this and my mouth could still come up with smart ass comments.

"Point zero zero three versus zero—"

"Right. Sorry."

"As I was saying, the viscosity of a specific wine will depend on varietal, as well as temper—"

"I'm sorry to cut you off, but it's vital that I understand this." Since I clearly hadn't understood *anything* up to this point. "You could tell that it was wine, not blood from my video?"

"Yes. I cannot, however, tell you which variety. The favorite of the Forensic Vampires is Bikavér. Some consider that it has a metallic undertone that adds to a resemblance to the taste of blood. The flaw is viscosity. For visual purposes they add corn syrup, though not for drinking, or course."

"Of course. What are Forensic Vampires?"

"Who are Forensic Vampires," he corrected. "It's a group of like-minded individuals exploring vampire mythology through forensic science."

"Are you—Would it be rude to ask if you're a member?" And here I'd thought his favorite pastime was feeding squirrels.

"I am not. I have, however, been a guest speaker at four of their meetings. A most convivial group."

It took every bit of my will power not to ask more. Convivial how? What were the dues? Did they only meet on moonless nights? Was garlic allowed at the meetings?

But, as what this meant began to sink in, I had far more important questions.

"Was the wine used to poison him? Could you tell from the dripping, did they try to pour it down his throat?"

That explained why no blood spray—or in this case, no wine spray. Dumb. Dumb. Dumb.

Dell had mentioned the absence of blood spray. I'd agreed, yet still pushed this investigation along the beaten-to-death track.

"Until the autopsy results and the analysis of the liquid are performed and compared it cannot be stated that it had any bearing on the death."

"Could it have asphyxiated him?"

We'd been looking at the entirely wrong things. Instead of blood stains, we should have been looking for empty wine bottles. Sheriff Conrad must have known from the first, because he'd been able to turn on the lights to look at the scene.

"Until the autopsy results and the analysis of the liquid are performed and compared it cannot be stated that it had any bearing on the death," he repeated.

"But if it didn't have any bearing on the death, that would have to mean someone poured red wine on him after he was dead?"

"Until the autopsy and analysis—"

"Okay, okay. I've got it, Dex."

Chapter Thirty-Two

I HAD IT but I had no idea what to make of it except for the fact that I had fallen headfirst into a deep, wide assumption and I'd dragged everyone else trying to help in after me.

We had to make a brain U-turn.

Not blood.

Wine.

Not beaten.

Poisoned?

Possibly.

Or… sedated, perhaps, then smothered. The bedclothes…

Thoughts raced through my head faster than I could hope to catch them.

So it must have been instinct deeper than thought that had me out of the car and chasing after Deputy Richard Alvaro when I spotted him heading across the lot for a sheriff's department vehicle.

Before I knew it, I was holding onto his arm and saying, "C'mon, Deputy, there must be something you can tell me."

"Nothing." It was a blend of Shelton and the new sheriff coming out of Richard's mouth. It didn't even sound like his voice.

"I'm not asking for a comment for a news story. Anything you tell me now will be entirely confidential. We don't have much time. You know we've done good work and—"

"Sheriff Conrad said the sheriff's department needs to take back—"

I groaned. "I can imagine. Don't let his old-fashioned ways blind you to the fact that not all crimes are solved behind the blue wall of law enforcement, Richard. There are plenty of instances when law enforcement messed up by keeping that wall between them and the outside world. You know we're just trying to get to the truth. You know we're not the enemy. You're too smart to fall into the trap of that kind of thinking."

"I was going to say he said we need to take back our self-respect."

Oh. "You've never had cause to feel anything but pride in your work, Richard. You and most of your fellow deputies. I know it's been hard with the sheriff and others leaving under a cloud, but—"

"Hard in some ways, working more and all, but even then it was a lot better than when Sheriff Widcuff was in charge." This he was glad to talk about. Eager, in fact. "And I think it's going to be even better with Sheriff Conrad. You know what he did these past days? Well, until this murder case came up."

Performed a miracle? Walked on water? Parted a sea? Turned the sheriff's department brew into something resembling coffee?

I gave a *hmm?* with the lowest qualifying amount of interest.

"He did ridealongs with a bunch of us. Just got in the vehicle and did the shift with us—that's after he'd worked all day as sheriff. Didn't say a whole lot at first, which made me kind of uneasy. But as the night went on, we got to talking. Not him giving rules and such, but like *colleagues*. His experiences and mine—and even though he has a lot more he didn't try to lord it over me or anything."

"And he asked you questions?"

"Sure. Some. But not like a grilling or anything."

Sheriff Conrad was probably too wily to stoop to grilling. Yet I'd bet he picked Richard's brain to a fare-the-well. His and those of other deputies he rode with. His own little focus group.

"Did he ride with Shelton?"

"Not yet. But I'm sure he will. We all told him Deputy Shelton's the... Well, you know."

I knew all right. Conrad was gathering information before he took on Shelton.

"That's great." My big smile didn't feel believable and I strongly suspected it didn't look that way, either. "Look, Richard, I will grant you the premise that Sheriff Russ Conrad is the best there is at applying standard law enforcement methods to a crime. But you have to admit he has not wrapped this one up, and we're fast approaching the end of those golden forty-eight hours. So there's at least a strong possibility that standard law enforcement methods are not the answer this time. And the problem is that if this isn't resolved before the network crew comes in Friday, Wardell Yardley's career is going to be flushed down the toilet. Through no fault of his own. None. Solely because standard law enforcement methods aren't fast enough. You won't be able to live with yourself if that happens. I know you won't. Not when you know from experience that we—Mike and Diana and Tom and me and the rest—might be able to pull this off. If we have the information the sheriff's department already has. Please, Richard. Please."

For an instant, I thought... Then he cleared his throat and said, "I can't, Elizabeth. I'm real sorry if your friend gets hurt by this. He seems like a nice guy. But we've got to do it the right way to get a conviction. That's our duty to the citizens of Cottonwood County."

Sheriff Russ Conrad was one hell of a ventriloquist.

"Richard—"

"No." He backed up two steps. "I can't." Then he turned and went.

I WAS STILL staring after Alvaro's departing vehicle when a grip on my arm jolted me.

The grip also turned me to face a young man with a fierce expression.

"I didn't know where else to go, even though—Is it true?" His words sounded like they hurt his throat. "Darryl—Darryl Justice is dead? He was murdered?"

"Yes, it's true."

I might have avoided answering in other circumstances. But even people who only got their news from KWMT-TV knew that much from Thurston, despite his getting pretty much everything else wrong.

Plus, this man's desperation was noteworthy. Also, there was something familiar about him.

"Oh, God."

He started to sink toward the pavement. I hooked my arm under his arm pit holding him up. No easy task because he was solid.

"Come on. You don't want to do this in the parking lot. Come sit in my SUV."

He didn't resist, but he didn't help much. By the time I maneuvered him into the front passenger seat, I was panting.

I hurried around to the driver's side and, as soon as I was in, clicked the doors locked and added the child protection.

I wouldn't have kept him in the vehicle against his will. Not for long. But I sure wouldn't be against slowing him down some if he decided he wanted to leave before I found out his connection to Darryl Justice.

"I'm sorry for your loss. You must have been very close."

He cut me a look. "It's not like that."

Rather than trying to pin down what it wasn't like, I decided to ease in with a more wide-angle approach. "You clearly knew him."

"Yeah, I knew him. I... I can't believe it. Are you sure? Sure it's Darryl Justice, who worked for VisageTome and was—?"

"I'm sorry, but yes, it's verified. Is that how you knew him? Through VisageTome?"

"No. And he was at Yellowstone Park this past weekend?"

My radar lit up. Wasn't sure what it was showing, but it had detected something new in the skies.

"Yes, he was. Did you know about his VisageTome event there last weekend?"

"Yeah."

"And that he was coming here?"

"Yeah. But how did this happen?"

"That's what everyone's trying to figure out. What—"

"Who killed him? Why?"

"We don't know either of those answers yet. Do you have any ideas?"

"No." He said it fast, like he'd been saying it in his head for a while.

"But you knew he was coming to Sherman and going to the bed and breakfast?"

"Not specifically, but he'd mentioned going to the modern version of Colter's Hell, so—"

Ding, ding, ding. "That's where I saw you. You're the ranger who talked about the geysers and thermal things Saturday. And you know Darryl Justice? How did you know him? What's your name?"

"You ... you were there." He suddenly looked frightened. He tried to open the door. Immediately turned to pin me with a glare when it didn't cooperate. "You better let me out."

I raised my hands in innocence, which also delayed the process another second. "I just want to know what your name is, and how you knew Darryl."

"Now. Open it now."

He was trying to get the door open. He clicked to unlock, but I reclicked it.

"If you'll give me a moment. The fact that you know Darryl Justice could be so important. You could know information that—"

"Now." He turned his torso toward me, bringing his right arm around, as if to cut the distance it would have to travel to throw a punch.

And he'd seemed so nice at Yellowstone.

I clicked the button to unlock the door. He swung it open immediately.

"Hey, wait," I tried, but he was already out, closing the door behind him.

I got out, too. He had a good head start.

"I just want to talk. If you'd only—"

A sudden urgency to go after him grabbed me. I stepped back from the SUV door, preparing to slam it and take off.

"Lose somebody?"

Sheriff Russ Conrad. From right behind me.

If I showed too much interest in the departing park ranger, Conrad would pounce on him.

The ethical question was whether I had an obligation to tell the sheriff—what? That I recognized the guy as a park ranger who'd lectured on thermal features?

I wasn't sure even the strictest ethicist could withstand the horse-laugh that would elicit.

"Sheriff," I said neutrally.

"Looks like he didn't want to talk to you." Beneath his facial impression of a rock, a glint of satisfaction showed. I hadn't thought he was that vindictive. My mistake. "Fancy that. Want to tell me about it?"

"No. Because if we share the same experience—someone not wanting to talk to us—it might be a real bonding moment." I got in the driver's seat. Before I closed the door, I added, "Don't want to risk that."

❖   ❖   ❖   ❖

I DROVE AWAY.

I circled back only after I was out of sight of the sheriff's department. By the time I got to where my circle around the sheriff's department intersected with the mystery ranger's path, he was long gone.

I called Mike and wasted no time in telling him "We have to talk. Right away."

"Oh, yeah, we have to talk. But all hell's broken loose at the station. Don't come back here, you might not get out alive."

Was I imagining it or was he fighting laughter. "Why? What's going on?"

"I'll tell you at Diana's. I'll get some food. We'll all be there right away."

"Mike—"

"I gotta go."

His words were dire, but there'd been something else in his voice.

Chapter Thirty-Three

I SPOTTED THE rental car parked in front of Diana's. Wardell Yardley was behind the wheel, on his phone. So getting the car back had been his errand.

I parked my SUV in front of the bunkhouse then walked the short distance to the main house. Shadow, who'd been on Diana's porch, came to meet me halfway, then turned and accompanied me back.

Dell, seeing me out the side window, held up one finger, wrapped up his call, then climbed out.

Forcing far more cheer into my voice than I felt, I said, "Hey, look at you. You've got wheels again."

"That's putting it too strongly. They did, however, release my rental car. Can you ask your dog to back up? I don't trust him."

"Hey, don't pick on Shadow. He's a wonderful dog. He—"

"I know, he saved your life. But he peed on my rental car."

I laughed.

Surprised the heck out of me, but I did.

I held up teeter-tottering hands. "Saving my life, peeing on your rental car, gee, which matters more?"

"Fine. And to some degree, I share his opinion of the thing. But with all the dust around here, it's created a pee and mud slide down the side panel."

"It's a sign of affection. He's marking it—and you—as one of his herd he's protecting."

"That's what I'm afraid of." He eyed the dog. "How do I resign from his herd?"

"You don't. It's a one-way gate. He lets you in, he never, ever lets you out. That kind of loyalty's worth a little pee."

Dell shifted his gaze to me. "I'm not sure which is scarier, the dog or the new Elizabeth Margaret Danniher."

Was I new?

He must have read my question in my face. "Yes, you are a new Elizabeth Margaret Danniher. Still see the old one in there, but not completely."

"Which…"

"Hah! See? You were going to ask which one I liked better. The old Elizabeth Margaret Danniher never would have asked that."

"Too secure to ask."

"Too scared to hear the answer. You're stronger, Danny. Still raw, but stronger underneath. I don't know if it would have happened if you'd stayed back East, I think it would. But some of it might be from coming here. Either way, it's like you've shaken off layers of baggage."

He might not tie it absolutely to moving to Wyoming, but I did.

Coming to Wyoming was like a chemical peel—removing the accumulated dead skin of years past and leaving you with a fresh new complexion. It looked better, but the newly exposed tender skin was also vulnerable.

I looked up at him.

"Yeah, you're right," he said wryly. "You've never heard me talk like this. And I doubt you ever would have if I hadn't come to damned Wyoming."

I could only pray his chemical peel turned out well. So far I'd accomplished little to promote its healing.

✧   ✧   ✧   ✧

MIKE, JENNIFER, AND Tom came in the door, all carrying takeout bags.

"Met these two on the steps," Tom said. "They're about to burst."

"It was the best moment of my career at KWMT-TV and I was just watching," Mike said.

"Epic. Totally epic," Jennifer said.

"You should have seen it." Mike spread his arms to encompass the room. "You all should have seen it."

"You can tell us about it as soon as we get the food out." Diana said.

"No. This first. Food second."

Diana and I turned and stared at Mike.

"No kidding," Jennifer said, "you have *got* to hear this."

"I'm wrapping up my last package before we go to break before the bye-bye." That meant Mike was finishing up the sports report, which would be followed by a commercial break, then weatherman Warren Fisk and Mike would each do a mini-stand-up recap of their reports before Thurston did the solo sign off from the anchor desk. "First thing is we can see the people in the control booth showing the whites of their eyes. You know how they do when Thurston's gone totally off the rails. But he was just sitting there, fidgeting like he does when anyone else is on-camera. And there was all this excited talking in the booth. Of course we can't see anything outside the studio, but we can see the hallway on Thurston's NannyCam. And there's Les with his arms spread wide like he was going to stop whatever's coming, except he's backing up and backing up and backing up."

"Only it's not whatever, it's *whoever*," Jennifer said.

"Right. It was a whole lot of whoevers, because everyone from the newsroom was following—"

"Following whom?"

"Wait, let me tell it, Elizabeth. So, I finish the package and we're clear and I hop it to the door and open it."

"And Les just about falls in," Jennifer said, "Because he was back against it with his arms out like that would stop anybody from going in. Mike had to grab him by the collar to keep him from going all the way to the floor."

Mike's nodding and grinning. "So, Thurston's still sitting at the anchor desk, shouting 'What is the meaning of this?' in his super-anchor voice and he steps over Haeburn and—"

"Who?" Diana and I demanded.

"Sheriff Conrad. He steps over Haeburn and strides around to

Thurston, who's scrambling to stand up, only he gets all tangled in the chair and Conrad says, 'I want to talk to you.' And Thurston's telling Les to call the police and Les is babbling. So I said. 'He is the police. In fact, he's the sheriff.' "

Through laughter, Jennifer said, "I thought Thurston was going to barf."

"And all the while, Conrad is saying calmly. 'I want to talk to you about what you said on-air.' "

"What did he say?"

Mike successfully interpreted my concern, immediately saying, "Nothing about Dell. Really, not much of anything. It was his usual hatchet job of half-understandable puff, except twice he attributed stuff to Conrad—"

Diana sucked in a breath.

"—and he took a shot at the B&B as not the sort of establishment wanted in Sherman."

My turn to suck in a breath.

"And Conrad repeats that he intends to talk to Thurston, who's screaming for Les, who's suddenly answering his phone during all this. Nobody—"

"It was Val Heatherton," Jennifer said. "He had me program a special ringtone for her on his phone and I recognized it."

"Of course we didn't know that then," Mike said. "Nobody could hear what he was saying or who he was talking to, but then he faints away."

"Fainted? Les fainted? In the *studio*?"

Mike nodded. "And the control room's screaming that we were coming back."

"Mike was heroic," Jennifer said. "He calmly says to the sheriff that we're going to be back on-air in a few seconds and it would be best if this was taken out of the studio or it was going to be on live TV. Then he scoops up Les and sort of shoves him toward a bunch of us in the hallway. And then—"

"The sheriff takes Thurston's arm and escorts him out of the studio and says he was sorry to disrupt, but he was pressed for time and needed to get some things straightened out. So I sat at the anchor desk and did all three parts—mine, Thurston's, and Warren's, because he was a statue, frozen in front of the blue screen."

"Then the sheriff took Thurston into Les's office and we got Les into his chair," Jennifer picked up. "The sheriff told the rest of us to get out. He was only in there a few minutes and we couldn't hear a thing and you know how you can hear if anybody's shouting in there. Then the sheriff came out, totally calm, but I swear when he came out, one of them—Les or Thurston—was *crying*."

"I came out of the studio just in time to see the sheriff exit the building," Mike concluded.

So that's what the sheriff's satisfied glint had been about. Not vindictiveness—which was a relief for Diana's sake. But satisfaction.

Under the circumstances, a glint showed great restraint. I wouldn't have begrudged him a bonfire.

"Let's eat," Mike said. "I'm starved."

Chapter Thirty-Four

I REGRETTED BEING a downer after that, but I had to tell them two things right away.

First, I broke the news about Krista's relationship to the owner of our station.

"She's a suspect. If she ends up being more, our digging could put us all out of a job. Mike should be able to go somewhere else. I hope I could, too. We could get Jennifer a job at another station. But, Diana, with your kids in school and owning the ranch, you don't want to go anywhere else... If you want to step back, we'd all understand."

She sat silent a moment. "I'd like to say that if Val Heatherton fired someone for reporting the truth I wouldn't want to work for her, but you're right. It would be hard to lose this job." She huffed out a breath. "It's easier to deal with a lost job than lost self-respect. No step back."

"Attagirl," Mike said.

"On the other hand, if we know Krista or Dirk is about to be exposed as the murderer, we could toss that assignment to another shooter, huh?"

"Absolutely," I said. "Next, I have to tell you about the video of Darryl Justice's blood ... which wasn't a video of Darryl Justice's blood."

I explained my screw-up. After their exclamations, I pointed out errors in our thinking that stemmed from that assumption.

"...so we're left with a big fat nothing from the video," I conclud-ed. They'd all been eating while I talked. "When we were thinking it was a beating, it probably narrowed when the murder could have been committed to when people weren't in nearby rooms because they likely would have heard something. Now it's wide open. Also, the killer wouldn't have had bloody clothes to dispose of. It's worse than a big fat nothing because it's wasted time."

I took a burger from the Hamburger Heaven bag. I had managed a few fries during my recounting.

"It strengthens the idea that he could have been drugged and then killed another way or poisoned, and we've considered those," Diana said.

"Sure, that's right," Mike said. "Otherwise, why introduce the wine at all."

"Somebody spilled it by accident," I proposed morosely. Then I sat up. "That much wine? Would anyone spill that much wine by accident? It had to be most of a bottle to drip that way." I groaned. "I should have realized from the way it was dripping—"

"We all viewed it. We could have seen it, too," Diana said briskly. "It is possible to spill a whole bottle by accident, though what seems more likely is that it was a way to get Darryl Justice to ingest something else."

"He was a red wine drinker." I listed the times I'd seen him with a glass at Yellowstone.

Diana nodded. "The spill seems to indicate someone tried to get more of it into him. Maybe they really wanted to be sure he was incapacitated. Or, if there's poison in it, to be sure he got enough of it to kill him."

"Maybe they wanted him to choke to death on the stuff," Jennifer said.

"Could the stains on that pillow be from holding it over his face?" Mike asked.

"Yes. But they could have come back anytime during the night to do that."

"Not necessarily," Dell said. "Those floors creak like crazy. I can't imagine anyone taking that risk."

"So, we're looking at drugging him before eleven, then killing him between eleven and two. But since everybody was moving around, that doesn't help much."

Silence fell for a moment.

Tom broke it. "Elizabeth, what are you thinking?"

I could feel my forehead contracted in a frown, so I supposed I was thinking, but I had to search for it. "Without the autopsy and analysis, we can't know. But the sheriff's department is doing all that. So we're speculating on what they'll eventually know for sure and way before we do."

"Don't we always do that?" Diana asked. "But our speculation gets us there faster."

"Not fast enough. Not this time. But ... but, what we do have is our experience with people. We need to focus on what we have. What we can do—talk to people."

"Good. Because that's what I did today," Diana said. "First, I collected a lot of negatives. The sheriff's department would not talk to me. At all. Krista does not have help. No one cleans for them. The neighbors didn't see or hear anything of interest Monday night or early Tuesday morning. But then it gets better. I think I know why Russ seems to be accepting Dell's alibi from Clara without trying to break it the way you said he might."

"He told you?"

"No," she said with drawn out emphasis. "And I didn't ask him."

Chastised, I nodded. "Sorry."

"Next, I—"

"Wait a minute, Diana." Jennifer looked at me. "Still on Krista. Did you ask her for that couple's license number?"

"I forgot. I'll—"

"That's okay. I went back and talked to Dirk and got it. I checked, and they are the Williamses and they do live in Pennsylvania—near Pittsburgh—and he did go to Harvard Law School." She sounded bored with those confirmations. "They've got money, but they sold a bunch of stock and stuff this fall."

Did I want to know how she'd found that last part? No, I didn't.

"Getting cash for this trip?" Diana said.

Jennifer shrugged. "I'm working at finding out how much."

"Good job and sorry I forgot," I said. "Did Dirk say anything else?"

"He bitched about how much the VT people are drinking. He said one guy drank more than a bottle of tequila. He had to go get more. That's all I got. Back to you, Diana," Jennifer concluded in a good impression of Leona.

"While I was in that neighborhood, I walked past Clara's house," Diana picked up.

Clara Atwood lived in a house Sherman considered historic, most places on the East Coast would consider merely old, and Europe would consider new. In other words, from the turn of the Twentieth Century.

"Uh-huh." I had no idea where this was going, but wanted to be encouraging.

"The second I stepped in front of the house next to hers—the one anyone going from Clara's house toward the B&B would pass, the neighbors' dog started howling like crazy."

"Was it out that ni—?"

"It's left out every night. Apparently the neighborhood parents love it and the neighborhood teenagers hate it. I talked to several neighbors and they all said they'd already told the sheriff's department that there was no way anyone left Clara's house that night after ten o'clock."

Good dog!

"That dog I like. Yours I don't," Dell said to me.

Though would this be enough to satisfy Dell's network? Specifically the Baby Big BossBaby BB bent on ousting him? I doubted it.

"What about the video?" Tom asked abruptly. "You said your source said he had it cleaned up. Anything interesting on it now?"

I stared at him for a half a beat then grabbed my phone. "Where are my brains? I never even—"

"Here, give it to me," Jennifer ordered. "I'll make backup copies first to be safe."

When she was satisfied, she sent copies to each of us. As we had last night, now with the addition of Tom, each of us viewed in silence, with Dell and me sharing my phone.

When it was over, the mood was somber.

This wasn't as gruesome as our imaginations had made the original version, but Darryl Justice was just as dead.

And the consensus was that we'd seen no new clues.

A lull hit. I hoped the rest of them weren't as depressed as I was.

"Since it's an open field," Dell said, "is there any way we can pin this on the CEO of VisageTome?"

Mike was game. "He wasn't anywhere near Sherman—or Yellowstone last weekend, for that matter. At least not that we know of. Unless you know something different?"

"I'm devoid of knowing anything. Simply a longing to pin it on him. After all anyone who could create a business that incubates monsters like the ones we've met—as well as the ones hiding behind all that anti-customer service—surely is capable of murder."

I said, "I share your longing, but fear we'd need a little more to persuade Sheriff Conrad that the CEO who wasn't here is the murderer. Besides, I know what your real motive is Wardell Yardley— it would be a great story and you'd have the scoop."

He smiled. Sharks would recognize that smile if they had mirrors. "Yes, I would."

Feeling slightly less depressed, I asked what he and Mike had learned this afternoon from a second round with the VisageTome group.

"We split up to cover more territory."

Mike shot me an apologetic look, and I knew exactly how they'd divided the group, despite what I'd said about it not being wise for Dell to be alone with Elaine. My glare at Dell bounced off his imperviousness.

"I hope whatever you got was worth the risk you're running of having Elaine sell her I-slept-with-the-White-House-correspondent-murder-suspect story to the tabloids."

"It was."

"What was it?"

"I shall share at the appropriate moment."

"For Pete's sake, Dell, this isn't—"

Mike cleared his throat.

"I'll tell you about my conversation with the guys. Started by going over the times with them. They were all in line with what we'd already learned. I asked more about why they were here in Sherman. Got pretty much the same song and dance as before. I tried asking about the meeting. They clammed up. I tried softening them up, talking about what they'd done at Yellowstone. Kelvin said it was stupid, boring, and everything bad. Hart disagreed, Varney was neutral and Nelson said nothing.

"Next, we shifted to Darryl Justice. Hart said he was an okay guy, Kelvin disagreed, Varney was neutral and Nelson said nothing. On the topic of Elaine, Kelvin said she was brilliant, Hart disagreed, Varney was neutral and Nelson said nothing.

"In desperation, I brought up Krista Seger. That got different results—not good ones, just different. Hart said he barely knew her. Kelvin said almost nothing. Varney said Krista was wasting herself at the bed and breakfast. That was about the only time Brant Nelson spoke. He said she wasn't as good as she thought she was."

"Did he stop with the phone?" Dell asked.

"Nope. Didn't look up, either. After that, it was mostly Kelvin and Hart sniping about, uh, tech stuff."

"Speaking of Krista…"

I told them what else I'd learned about our employer's niece today, and then our conversation at the sheriff's department parking lot.

"So," I concluded, "if Krista's telling the truth and she saw him around eleven, sleeping as she thought, someone must have met him before that and drugged him."

"And had to be in the room at least one more time to try to pour more wine down his throat."

"But that could have been any time before Krista got up the next morning."

"Could have been, but most likely was before the VisageTomers' meetings broke up. It would have been a lot riskier to be in that room then, because there were people in the rooms around to hear something. Also, the later it went, the higher the risk that Dell might come back."

Tom slowly nodded. "Fits in with the scene, too. It was like the murderer got impatient. Or anyway they had to hurry things up."

"That's good," Mike said. "The murderer gives him the first drink before eleven and it puts Darryl to sleep. Then he goes back to check—maybe more than once—and Darryl's still alive. So then he comes back again, say, right before he or she thinks the meeting's going to break up. And tries to get Darryl to drink more. Only it doesn't work. Little of the wine ends up in Darryl, so the murderer smothers him with a pillow."

"Before we get too involved in discussing that, there's something else that happened today," I said. "And, unlike some people, I'm not waiting for the most dramatic moment."

"Appropriate," Dell murmured.

I told them all about encountering the ranger from Yellowstone Park this afternoon.

✧   ✧   ✧   ✧

"WELL, THAT HAS a lot of potential implications, doesn't it," Dell said when I finished.

I'd included not going after him because my interest would alert the sheriff. Didn't matter that Burrell kept his mouth closed, I could still practically hear him telling me to trust Conrad and work with him.

Diana also gave me a disapproving look.

Mike, bless him, did not comment on that. What he said was, "Is this one of those situations where you had a feeling something weird would pop up and here it is?"

"I had no feeling about something weird coming and certainly not about this. If I had maybe I would have recognized who he was sooner and he wouldn't have gotten away."

"What were you going to do? Drive off with him?" Diana asked.

"Maybe."

Diana coughed several times. Among those coughs I think she said something about kidnapping.

Mike had been thoughtfully munching potato chips. "What do you mean about the implications, Dell? You mean this ranger could have something to do with Darryl Justice's death?"

"Possibly. On one end of the scale he could be the murderer, though…" He looked at me.

"He'd have to be a really good actor. But Dell's right, there are implications. He could be totally surprised about the end result, yet know the causes that led to it. We need to find this guy."

Tom cleared his throat.

I braced for him to say we should call the sheriff, then forced myself to relax. No pre-judging.

He said, "It's interesting he was on the spot when another VisageTome guy nearly died. Could he have had anything to do with the one who fell at the hot spring?"

"I didn't have a good angle to see it," Dell said.

I looked at Mike. He was looking at me.

"Think about it before you answer," Diana said. "Run it back through your minds."

There was silence for a long moment. I was staring at where the fireplace met the ceiling, but without seeing it in any detail, because I was trying to see the scene at the geyser.

"He moved in that direction," Mike said in a half dreamy tone, so I guessed he was mentally revisiting that sequence, too. "He'd been in the middle, then he moved that way. That was before the guy nearly went in."

"Before," Diana repeated. Too neutral to be a question, yet making us question our memories.

I dropped my chin. Mike wore an unfocused frown.

"Yeah, definitely before." He shifted his shoulders and looked around, back with us now. "But too far away to have had anything to do with it."

"Elizabeth?" Tom asked.

"I agree."

Mike nodded emphatically. "Unless he had a line or something that tripped the guy, but somebody would have seen it, because people sort of pounced on the guy to help."

"Agreed again. And I didn't see any strange gestures or motions from our mystery park ranger, which you'd think there would be if he were manipulating a trap somehow. He might have moved that way to point something out better, but ... I had the feeling he was reacting to—maybe an instinct to stop trouble he sensed brewing in that direction."

"What trouble?" Tom asked.

Until he asked I hadn't been conscious of using the word *trouble*.

"I couldn't see clearly because of people in between. Mike, could you see over them better?"

"Yeah," He drew it out, making it tentative.

Or maybe that was because he'd gone back to unfocused frowning. We all remained still and silent.

In the end he shook his head. The frown remained, but he was focused again. "There was a sort of shuffle on that side of the circle. People moving, like something had made them uneasy, but it was too quick and—No, I didn't see exactly what happened. And what did happen came fast, so I can't say for sure if it was quick reactions to Kelvin starting to fall or reactions to whatever made him fall."

"You have to pick one or the other, Mike," Tom commanded. "Right now. Which is it?"

"Reactions to something that made him fall. But really, it's a guess."

"I'd bank on that guess," Tom said. "Most people pick up cues they're not conscious of, but for an athlete like you, it's ingrained. Lets you anticipate other players' moves—your teammates' and opponents."

"That's true. Like driving and you can tell another car's going to pull into your lane even though they haven't made the move yet. Like subtle body language."

"Exactly. Your park ranger might have picked up similar cues, moving in because he sensed something."

"Possible," I said. "It's also still possible that he was involved with what happened even if he didn't—literally—pull a string to cause it. No matter what happened Saturday at Yellowstone, it's clear we need to track this guy down and find out more about him. Jennifer, see if you can find out which park ranger was giving a talk at Norris Basin then."

"You want me to get into the National Park Service's computer system?"

It would have been more reassuring if she hadn't been so eager. "I was thinking along the lines of social engineering. Getting people to share information with you. It's what used to be called reporting."

"Ha. Ha. But how?"

"Try calling them up and saying you were so impressed with the ranger's talk that you want to write a complimentary email about him to his boss, but you need the names of both the ranger and the boss."

"But I don't need the boss's."

"That's why you ask for it. It masks your true goal. Also backs your story and makes it more believable."

"It's called being sneaky," Mike said, clearly approving of the prospect.

"Okay. I can do that. What else?"

Chapter Thirty-Five

I HAD NO answer.

I had no ideas.

Worst of all, I had no questions.

To my surprise, Tom had one. "Dell, do you have any enemies?"

"Thousands," he said immediately. "But the worst of them is in D.C. right now, trying to take my job."

"Why?" I asked Tom at the same time.

"A possible angle that it wasn't happenstance that Darryl Justice was killed in that particular room."

"You mean they staged the murder in Dell's room to implicate him? They'd have to know he wasn't going to be there. That would mean Clara was involved. Dell, did she make any phone calls, send any texts after you got to her house or—"

"Whoa. Hold up on the conspiracy theory there, E.M. Danniher. I never said a thing about Clara being involved. From what we know none of these people have connections with Cottonwood County," Tom said.

"Except Krista and Dirk Seger. Besides, Clara's not from here. It could be a connection in her past or—"

"Or it could be someone taking advantage of learning that Dell wasn't going to be there that night."

"Well, we know *that*. That doesn't help because everybody knew he was going out. And easily could have checked if he was back by using the hallway key to the bathroom, then checking the connecting door."

"Look at it from the murderer's perspective," Tom said. "If they're planning to meet Darryl Justice and kill him, why pick Dell's room? Right there in the B&B with lots of other people around. There had to be a benefit over, say, meeting him on a lonely road—we've got plenty of those around here—and killing him there."

"Why in the B&B," I repeated. "Spur of the moment or because the murderer had to be there. Krista or Dirk or the VisageTome people."

"Then why in Dell's room?"

"Some of the guys did seem unhappy with Elaine being around Dell, talking to him," Mike said.

"Jealousy."

"No, Dell, Mike's right. There was definitely an edginess about that at breakfast, at least from Kelvin," I said. "Okay, so Darryl and the murderer meet in the hallway, the murderer says, c'mon in here, I happen to know it's empty. We can talk in peace. But they could have talked in peace in the murderer's room, since everybody had a private room. But the murderer wouldn't want to kill him in their own room. But an invitation to another room would have made Darryl suspicious if it was someone he wasn't friendly with. But if it was someone he was friendly with, he'd wonder even more about why they were going into another room. So the murderer let Darryl think it was their room or— What?"

Tom was fighting a grin.

"Sure makes it easier on the rest of us when you argue with your-self."

Everyone chuckled. Yes, even me.

"What if," Mike said, "the murderer wasn't staying in the B&B, so they'd need a place to meet."

"Again, why not a lonely road?"

"Because … because there was something in the B&B they needed for this discussion?"

"Or someone?" Diana offered.

Mike brightened. "Yeah. Or someone. They're supposed to meet with someone at the B&B. The murderer says he—or she—will tell the third party, but never does. Instead he—or she—tells Darryl to meet in Dell's room and does the deed. And the third party's none the wiser."

"How does he—or she—know Dell's not there?" Tom asked. "The VisageTome people knew he was leaving. Maybe the owners and the elderly couple, but how could someone not staying there know?"

Diana said, "Someone in the B&B called the murderer and told him. And now they're not coming forward because either Darryl being dead suits their purposes or they're afraid of the murderer."

"That means we're basically talking about Bunny or Christopher and there's no sign that either of them knows any of the people who were staying in the B&B. No sign of any connection or—" Mike interrupted himself to say, "What, Elizabeth?"

"It's a long shot. A wild, wild long shot, but who else might be involved in whatever was going on involving Bunny, Christopher, and Darryl—whether it was really blackmail or whether that was Bunny's delusion and he was trying to get them to leave him alone?"

"Her husband," Jennifer said.

I turned to her. "Oh, good one. I hadn't thought about that. But, yeah, we should definitely check where he's been these past few days. But I was thinking of—"

"Darryl's biological father," Diana said.

"I'll check them."

"The husband's name is Stelios Sterakos. As for the birth father ... I wonder if it was on those papers Christopher saw."

"Joel's the only one old enough, but... You don't remember who she was seeing then?" Mike asked.

"Remember who a non-friend was dating twenty-five years ago? No, I don't." Though my mother might. Or I could get her to ask Muffy on her next walk or...

I flopped back in the chair. "This is crazy. We're way past the grasping at straws phase. We're grasping at nothings. Phantoms. Twenty-five-years-ago gossip. There's—"

"You're tired, Elizabeth. Don't be so hard on yourself," Mike said. "You need some rest."

"We're all tired. We all need rest. But there's no time. Not with the crew arriving in thirty hours. And I have nothing. Absolutely no—"

Tom interrupted. "Hold up, Elizabeth. You've been pushing through things fast. Have you considered everything you've been told? Not alibis, but the other things you've picked up. Things the sheriff's department wouldn't necessarily know."

"You mean like being told that I totally jumped to the wrong conclusion about the liquid on that video and dragged everybody else with me?"

"Among other things," he said calmly. "Who else have you talked to? Who else has told you things?"

I could have argued. But I'd admitted to being blank. There's nothing worse than sitting back and taking pot shots at someone who puts forth an idea—no matter what it is—when you have none.

"Bunny told me she was being blackmailed—not in so many words, but that's the gist of it. Christopher said he tracked down his half-brother through papers in his grandmother's attic."

"What else?"

"Lots of things. Darryl said he wanted nothing to do with the family, but was pleasant to Christopher at Yellowstone, not knowing who he was. Christopher saw him here in Sherman and spoke to him. Darryl seemed surprised. When Bunny arrived on the scene, Darryl recognized their connection and got away from them."

"Go on. What about the B&B and VisageTome."

"Mrs. P told us Krista had worked at VisageTome."

Jennifer contributed, "Dirk sort of said Krista was having an affair at VisageTome. And the VT people were going through a lot of liquor."

I nodded. "Leona said Dirk turned to Val Heatherton to get her niece to leave VT and end her affair. And I suspect the person who told her to tell me about the connection was Mike's Aunt G. So at least one good thing came out of that lunch."

"What do you mean?" Tom asked.

I told him about Mrs. Parens insisting on our having the early lunch in O'Hara Hill today—well, technically yesterday, since it was past midnight.

Tom frowned. "Mrs. Parens got you up there today, then told you nothing?"

"Well, not nothing. She said Krista was a great student and she talked about her working for VT, but we already knew that, so—" I sat up. "Startup. She kept talking about a startup."

"Who?" Jennifer asked.

"Mrs. P. Or Krista, as quoted by Mrs. P. How she was interested in a startup, how she'd had opportunities, but wouldn't pursue them because of her employment contract. Oh, my God."

"What?"

"I even thought about how VT has had trouble with employees leaving and starting competing companies." I looked around at them. "That's what Elaine and the others are doing. That's why the meetings. That's why the secrecy. That's why quiet, out of the way Sherman. They're planning a startup."

"And this," Dell said in his grab-the-room voice, "is the appropriate moment."

He drew out a device smaller than a pack of gum. With his finger poised over a button on it, he said, "This is the edited version to eliminate, ah, distracting sounds before and after this conversation. There was an introduction to this topic, but I'm certain you'll all pick up the context."

He pressed the button.

Elaine's voice came on. "They're the tech and I'm the brains."

Dell said something that was muffled, though I thought I caught the phrase employment contract.

"So what?" Elaine said. "It's how startups get going all the time. It's business. No big deal. We needed to get some final things in place. Now we've got what we wanted from VisageTome. We don't need them anymore. I'll be running it, and there won't be any of these stupid ass retreats and groups and all that shit."

"So you plan a little spinoff business," Dell's recorded voice said.

"Nothing little about it. My company—the company—will be a sure-thing success. Worth more than you'd ever think of making."

I raised my brows at Dell. He shrugged elegantly—taking a hit for a good cause.

"I can't imagine VisageTome would be happy about that. You seem casual about having signed a non-compete agreement. I've heard VisageTome is clamping down about that since, as you say, a number of startups have sprung up from VT employees departing with more than a few pens tucked away in their pockets."

"Let them try." Her defiance sounded brittle.

"What about Darryl? He wasn't part of the group, was he?"

She sounded sulky when she said, "He was stupidly stubborn."

"Was that the plan? To bring him to Sherman—"

"I didn't—"

"—in order to talk him around? Or to keep him in the dark."

"You're so smart, you figure it out."

Dell's smooth voice responded as if she hadn't been trying to be a smart ass. "Keep him in the dark. Which means you hadn't invited him, so what was he doing here? It certainly must have been an unpleasant surprise when he arrived."

"*I* didn't know he was here. Not until he showed up dead in *your* bed." She made that an accusation. "And there's no proof that his being here had anything to do with me."

"It's going to be awfully hard to prove you didn't know he was here. And his being here for a reason that had nothing to do with VisageTome tests one's credulity."

"We're not talking about this anymore," Elaine's voice said. There was a rustle, then silence.

Dell clicked it off.

"You could take that the sheriff. You were a party to the conversation, so it's legal in Wyoming," Diana said. "Don't look so surprised, Elizabeth. Just because I tote a camera doesn't mean I don't know the laws."

Dell said, "I prefer to hold on to it myself for now. It could be considered a conversation with a source, which I would not share with the sheriff."

"It could be motive," she said. "Darryl Justice wasn't part of their group. If he found out what they were planning and came here to confront them, they could have killed him to protect their plan."

"But it hasn't protected their plan because everybody's digging into what they're doing here," Mike said.

"They—or an individual murderer—might not have foreseen that in the heat of the moment."

"But it wasn't just a moment. They drugged him and then went back some time later and tried to get a lethal dose down him. Having failed that, they smothered him."

"That's all conjecture. Besides, we're not focusing on means, right, Elizabeth?" Diana asked.

"I don't know." I hadn't really followed the argument. My mind had been on another track. "Did you hear when Elaine said *They're the tech and I'm the brains?* That left out one more necessity for a startup."

"Money," Dell said promptly.

"Exactly. Who's funding this startup?"

"What if Bunny was right? What if Darryl Justice was blackmailing her and he was going to use that to fund them?" Mike asked.

"Sure didn't sound like he was involved," Jennifer said.

Mike persisted. "It would explain why they ended up at the Wild Horses Bed and Breakfast. What do you want to bet that they didn't go there out of the blue? They knew it was Krista's. It was ideal for them."

"But that could also work without Darryl being involved or blackmailing Bunny."

"Right. They could use the affair to threaten Krista," Diana said. "If Krista said she didn't want them there or if she told anyone what they were up to, they could tell Dirk about the affair."

I was nodding. "Maybe they were using the threat for more. What if they wanted Krista to join them. What Alan Varney said about her wasting herself, remember?"

Mike started to nod, then gave a small start and reached to his pocket. The telltale response of someone whose phone was vibrating. He stood and went toward the kitchen to answer.

"You're saying they came to the bed and breakfast to maneuver Krista into being part of their startup?" Jennifer asked.

"Possible. According to her they left her alone, but we can check—"

"No." We all turned toward Mike at that single word spoken into his phone. He sounded shocked.

He was listening intently, not focusing on any of us.

"Okay.... Got it. ... Thanks. Thanks a lot."

He clicked off and turned to us. "That was a, uh, source. There's been another death at the B&B."

Before I could ask "who?" he said, "Gordon Kelvin."

"How?" Dell asked.

"They don't know yet. No obvious wounds or injuries."

"Like Darryl Justice?"

He nodded, but added, "But in his own bed."

FRIDAY

Chapter Thirty-Six

LIGHTS SET UP by the sheriff's department glared-white and unreal, glazing the lower two-thirds of the exterior of the Wild Horses Bed and Breakfast, washing out its gray siding, and reflecting blindingly off the windows.

Tom had driven Jennifer home from Diana's, then joined us.

Mike, Dell, and I had come straight to the scene, responding to the gravitational pull of a news story. Diana had checked on her kids, found both sound asleep. Wrote them each a note, saying she'd be back to get them breakfast, then came back.

Needham Bender from the Sherman Independence was here, too.

We all stood outside, shivering. At least I was shivering. Dell stayed in the SUV and the rest of them were dressed for the Arctic Circle.

Eventually, Sheriff Conrad came out and said a few words. A very few words. A male had been found dead on the premises. No name would be released until notification of the family. An investigation was proceeding with no assumptions made about cause. He would contact the media when there were further developments suitable for public consumption.

Needham left. The rest of us rejoined Dell in the SUV, with Mike occasionally turning on the engine to reheat the interior. No one even suggested going anywhere.

I realized I wasn't reacting as strongly to this death as I had to Darryl Justice's. Yet Gordon Kelvin had also been a young man. A smart young man. Was it his fault he was annoying? Well, yes, but it wasn't a death-penalty offense.

Into the silence, Mike said, vehemently. "Damn. I was sure he was the murderer."

Dell snorted. "You wouldn't have wished him dead, but you did wish him incarcerated for life."

He considered. "Yeah, that's about right. He was a—a jerk. Though I suppose that's not why he was killed, or it would have happened a long time ago."

You might ask why we'd come here, since the chances of us being told anything more by the officialdom swarming the area had passed slim an hour ago and were firmly into anorexia now.

But there was something tugging at me, just beyond the fog that encased what used to be my brain.

At least Diana got footage of swarming officialdom—well, swarming by Cottonwood County standards. Footage like this has a short shelf life. And since it couldn't get on KWMT-TV air until the five, it was likely to hit its expiration date before it ever aired.

Still, viewing the footage had allowed us to confirm that the Segers, the VT people, and the Williamses were all inside. Yippee.

I'd tried Bunny, only to have the excited operator/night clerk at the Haber House Hotel inform me that Deputy Richard Alvaro had taken both her and her son to the sheriff's department.

The only possibility not caught in the sheriff's net was the Yellowstone Park ranger who'd shown up today—now, yesterday. Although this second murder of a VisageTome employee sure made it less likely he was involved. Unless he had a vendetta against them for some reason—say, he'd tried to get customer service from the company.

That, however, didn't match with his reaction about Darryl Justice's death.

"Unless he killed Gordon Kelvin in revenge, because Kelvin killed Darryl Justice," Mike said, not for the first time.

He was not letting go of Kelvin as a murderer easily.

"Why would a Yellowstone Park ranger avenge the death of Darryl Justice? Not to mention how would he know who killed him since he didn't know for sure he'd been murdered until a few hours ago."

"You don't want to think he could have figured it all out faster than you," Dell said.

Mike was more tactful. "He could have inside knowledge."

"And we'll be sure to ask him that when we talk to him," I said tartly, reminding them of the little hitch that we had no idea where he was.

✧   ✧   ✧   ✧

WITH THE LIGHT hinting that the sun was going to come up again today, we adjourned temporarily, agreeing to meet back at the café for breakfast.

Diana and I went to her ranch for showers and fresh clothes, for her to get her kids off to school and me to see to Shadow. Tom checked in with Tamantha, who apparently was reorganizing the kitchen at her friend's house, to the friend's mother's delight. Mike took Dell back to his house so they could get refreshed.

We all looked cleaner but no more rested when we rendezvoused at the café, sitting at the same table the VisageTome group had had yesterday morning.

We also didn't look cheerful.

A mood I put into words once we'd all ordered. "What we do best is talk to people and ask questions, but all the people we could ask questions of are at the sheriff's department."

With twenty-six hours left until the crew arrived and Wardell Yardley told the network BBs of his tenuous position in a murder investigation.

Though there was something... Something tugging at me from just past my consciousness. Something...

"If we're thinking it's the same murderer, we should be able to look at these two deaths and see similarities," Dell said.

That started a long, wide-ranging discussion that I mostly listened to as we all ate breakfast and I tried to grab on to that slippery piece of fog at the edge of my mind.

When a lull hit, I said what had just popped into my head. "Maybe we shouldn't be looking for similarities."

"Two murderers?" Diana asked.

"Not necessarily."

"Then why not look for similarities?"

"The wolves."

"What wolves?" Dell asked.

"The ones—or one—that killed a cow on Tom's ranch."

Everyone stopped looking at me and looked at Tom. He hitched one shoulder in a don't-ask-me gesture. He asked me, "What about them?"

"What you said about a surplus kill. I wonder…"

"Surplus kill?" Dell asked.

I waved to Tom and he explained.

Mike nodded. "There was that really bad one—what twenty?—a few years back."

"Yeah, we've got two people dead, that's not the same as a surplus kill of half a dozen elk or even two dozen, so I don't get the connection, Elizabeth," Diana said.

"I was thinking about how the wolves view killing elk—or Tom's cattle—as the best solution to their problem of hunger. But if the wolves have a surplus killing, then it's not solving a problem, and that's like a serial killer."

"So what problem is this killer solving?" Diana asked.

"Exactly. That's what we need to figure out. But the other part with the wolves is they can still have the problem—being hungry—but they found a solution to it that was easier than hunting in the wild."

"My cattle."

"Right. And once they've done that you have to watch carefully because they'll tend to keep doing it, because they're looking for the easy solution to their problem."

"So, you're saying," Mike started slowly, then picked up speed, "that the killer murdered Darryl Justice because it seemed like the only solution, but killed Gordon Kelvin because it was an easy solution."

"I'm not sure it was that clear in my head, but, yes. And that could mean the motive for killing Gordon might not be as compelling as the motive for killing Darryl." I looked around at them. "I say we stay focused on Darryl's death."

"Okay," Diana said slowly. "But that brings us back to no one to ask questions of or—"

I was saved from having to admit I had no solution to Diana's objection by the door opening, propelled by Jennifer Lawton.

Was I hallucinating or did she look excited.

Mike pulled up a chair for her between him and Dell.

"That's gross," she said of the remains of Mike's breakfast eggs.

"If that's all you're here for—"

"No. I found something. I couldn't call up Yellowstone like you suggested because it was night, so I went into their computer system— not the big official one," she said quickly, apparently because she'd seen my mouth open. "A local system they use for communicating about local deals and stuff. Sort of a bulletin board for employees. Anyway, I got the list of employees they use to make sure people are allowed in this closed group. And I cross-referenced it with search engine references to Yellowstone rangers by name to get a lead on which ones were rangers as opposed to some other job. And..."

"And what? You found him? The ranger? But how did you know which one?"

"Not that way."

Our groan came out in harmony.

"That was kind of cool, all of you together." Receiving only glares in response to her appreciation for our unintentional musicality, Jennifer shrugged. "But I did find him. At least I'm pretty sure I did."

"Spill it, Jennifer, before Elizabeth and Mike bust," Diana said. A wise woman.

"The names from the employee list were scrolling by and one caught my eye. Justice."

I sat straight. "Justice? The same last name? Spelled the same?"

"Yeah, but—"

Mike interrupted. "Brothers. They have to be brothers."

"Not unless their parents named them Darryl and Darrell." Jennifer looked downright smug.

Mike said, "Darryl and Darryl? Like on the Newhart show? 'My name's Larry and this is my brother Darryl and my other brother

Darryl'?"

"Exactly." She beamed.

"How on earth do you know that show—Never mind, never mind. Reruns, I know."

"Streaming," she corrected me. "But these two spelled their first names differently. D-a-r-r-y-l—that's the guy who died. And D-a-r-r-e-l-l—that's the park ranger. And I have his picture."

She pulled out her phone and showed us a portrait of a ranger in uniform, but without the hat.

It was the same ranger. The one from Norris Basin, the one I'd encountered outside the sheriff's department.

"You've got to see if you can find out where Darrell—the live one—is from. In fact—"

"I know, find out everything about him." Was it good or bad that she could finish my sentences? "Already on it. Computer's running a program I created to cross-reference the available phone number references with databases that—"

"Quit explaining and give us a chance to say 'good job,' " Mike said. "Way to go, Jennifer."

Diana, Tom, and I agreed enthusiastically. Mike added, "This is a breakthrough. A major break."

I started to say something more, then a memory shut my mouth.

A memory of Darryl Justice and another figure walking away from me in the hallway of the Lake Yellowstone Hotel, and of my thinking it reminded me of something else, of someone else.

I thought I'd connected Darryl Justice to Bunny because the view of him walking away from me reminded me of the view of her son, Christopher.

But I'd been wrong. Partially wrong.

The walk *had* reminded me of Christopher. But it hadn't been him walking away from me. It was him walking toward me.

And it hadn't been the VisageTome employee's walk. It had been the park ranger's. As he walked toward Darryl Justice and me on the dim porch at Lake Yellowstone Hotel.

"Damn. I *should* have kidnapped him. *He*'s Bunny's son."

"What?" came in another chorus.

It took a while to explain my thinking and I had to admit my memory of walks wasn't exactly DNA. "We have to find him. He's got to be staying somewhere."

"Unless he went back to Yellowstone," Dell said.

Diana said, "The rest of us will make the calls, but you have to tell the sheriff about this. You have to, Elizabeth."

"You're right. But I also need to talk to Bunny. Jennifer, are you up for a little game of chicken?"

As we stood up to leave, my gaze went to the table where the Williamses had sat yesterday morning.

"Hoover House." I looked around at the others. "Joel Williams called it the Hoover House Hotel yesterday, the same way Dell does. But the Williamses couldn't have heard it directly from Dell. They must have heard it from Elaine. Unless—"

"She repeated it to one of the others."

That let some of the air out of my balloon. "Yeah. But either way, that indicates they have a tie with the VisageTome people. If we could confirm a connection—"

"I'll get on it," Jennifer said.

Another piece of fog slid away, making a potential connection. And I gave Jennifer a name to start on.

Chapter Thirty-Seven

SHERIFF CONRAD WAS all for throwing me in jail unless I told him what I said I wasn't going to tell him until he let me talk to Bunny Ramsey Sterakos.

Jarvis Abbott had to negotiate to make it happen without jail time for me. So it was a good thing we'd had to meet in his office.

I'd tried the sheriff's department first. I was turned away at the door and told to go to Abbott's office in the courthouse, but not before I'd seen the waiting area was wall-to-wall suspects. They filled benches on two walls, and folding chairs had been brought in for the overflow.

The result of having only two interview rooms and a surfeit of suspects.

Ferrante closed the door on me, and I headed for the courthouse and the eventual negotiations that kept bogging down as the sheriff or county attorney received numerous phone calls.

First, Abbott asked me if what I had was useful and legitimate information. I said it was.

He sternly told me I should cooperate with law enforcement. I said I would as soon as I had half an hour with Bunny.

Then, he pointed out to Conrad that he'd already questioned her with little reward, so could it hurt for me to talk to her?

Only after several hours in Abbott's office and a tuna fish sandwich on stale white bread, was I promised twenty minutes with Bunny. I called Jennifer to come in from the parking lot where she'd been waiting in my SUV while continuing to work thanks to a mobile hotspot.

While we'd come here, Diana, Mike, and Dell tackled the phone calls. Tom said he had another line he wanted to pursue and wasn't sharing what.

"I got it," Jennifer said triumphantly as soon as she heard my voice on the phone.

I said as casually as I could, "The one we talked about?"

"Yup. I can show you—"

"As long as it's only me." The sheriff looked around at me at that.

"I don't... Oh. Because I'm coming in there?"

"Precisely. You're going to come on up to the County Attorney's office and show him and the sheriff what you found out overnight."

"It's okay, Elizabeth. I won't tell them about this. I've got things separated and hidden. They won't be able to see anything I don't want them to see."

"Great. Come on in, then, and meet Sheriff Conrad and County Attorney Abbott."

After all, Darryl and Darrell was her bombshell to explode.

✧   ✧   ✧   ✧

"BUNNY, TELL ME the truth. Tell me if you're being blackmailed."

She stared at me, which was not the response I'd hoped for after still more delay. First, Conrad had wanted me to be there when he and Abbott first talked to Jennifer.

When they started into a second round of super detailed questions with her and the sheriff called in Richard Alvaro to get him started on tracking the information from their end, I gently suggested it was about darned time I got to talk to Bunny.

He put Deputy Ferrante on the case.

It took almost an hour and a half.

I listened to a voicemail from Tom at the start.

He'd talked to someone he knew who worked at the liquor store. Dirk Seger had been in the store Tuesday to replace a good bottle of red wine he said had gone missing. He'd been back yesterday for tequila.

That didn't mean he'd poisoned the two bottles.

Necessarily.

Then Tom said he had an angle he wanted to pursue and he might be out of touch for a while.

I couldn't complain too much about being out of touch after the chunk of time I'd spent with the sheriff and county attorney.

I tried to catnap in the waiting room, but the clock in my head kept ticking, subtracting minute after minute from the time when Dell would inform his network.

Finally, I was called to Interview Room Two for my time with Bunny.

I could hear the strain of the wait in my next stern question. "Did you go to the Wild Horses Bed and Breakfast Monday night? Or last night?"

"I don't know what you're talking about."

She clearly wasn't going to confide in me.

I sucked in a breath. "I have something to tell you, Bunny."

I explained about Darryl and Darrell and that I suspected her real birth son was not dead. I explained it three times.

At the end, she said, "So that makes it all okay."

"Excuse me?"

"I mean I don't have a motive. Christopher doesn't have a motive, either."

"How do you figure that?"

She made a sound. She might as well have said, "Duh" because that's what the sound meant. "He wasn't my son. So he couldn't make trouble for me."

Could the woman truly be that stupid or was it her version of playing possum? Either way, it wasn't going to work.

"First, you didn't know he wasn't your son."

"I sort of sensed it. You can't know this, but a mother has an instinct for her children. A mother knows these things."

"All your actions and statements have made it clear that you thought he *was* your son."

"Well, I couldn't entirely rely on my instinct, so I was, uh, you know, stringing him along until I could prove it."

Stringing him along? More like she thought she could string me along.

"Second, Christopher certainly didn't know the man he met wasn't his half-brother."

"He must have." Her face brightened. "In fact, I told him."

The urge to call Sheriff Conrad and say, "here, you deal with this woman," hit like a tidal wave. I had to wait a moment for the rip current of temptation to subside.

"Third, you said he wanted money from you. Blackmail, you called it. If you didn't think he was your son, what would he have to blackmail you about?"

"My husband is rich. Some people think that means they can gouge everybody in the family."

"To blackmail you, he'd've had to have had a hold on you, Bunny. That's how it works. Not just random, oh, there's a rich person, I'll tell them they have to give me money and they will."

"I didn't say blackmail."

"You did. Many times."

"You're wrong. You always used to make up things when we were kids and you never stopped."

I opened my mouth. Closed it. She was right that it would be her word against mine.

Who would my friend the sheriff believe more readily?

In my favor, I had mentioned it to Mike and Dell at the time. On the other hand, Dell wasn't exactly in a position to be a character witness.

The other thing I'd have in my favor was that Sheriff Conrad would be listening to and watching Bunny in action when she said it.

I leaned in close, caught her gaze and held it. "I know and you know that you told me he was blackmailing you. I know and you know that you thought that man was your illegitimate son. Right up until I told you otherwise a few moments ago."

Another sentence floated through my head. *Sure am glad I didn't tell you that the young man who actually is your biological child is here in Sherman.*

Ah.

I believed Bunny Ramsey Sterakos was capable of murder.

This might end badly for friendly neighborhood relations back home in Illinois.

Chapter Thirty-Eight

I HAD LEARNED one helpful bit of news in the hours of misery getting to Bunny, then talking to her.

The sheriff had let Christopher Sterakos go.

After having dinner last night with his mother in the Haber House Hotel dining room, he'd been playing an online video game with a waiter until well after the time Dirk Segers had called the sheriff's department saying he'd found Gordon Kelvin dead in his bed.

As I headed to the Haber House to find Christopher, I got busy signals for Mike and Diana. Messages that they weren't available for Dell and Tom.

I texted Diana.

She responded that she and Mike failed to reach Darrell at Yellowstone and were still calling hotels and motels. Still no luck. Still no word from Tom. Dell had been asked to go to the sheriff's department.

Conrad must have done that by text while we were negotiating. The sneak.

If we'd traded Dell for Christopher we better make good use of what we had.

I texted Diana to meet me. She was the mother of a teenage son, and I didn't want to miss anything in this conversation.

"Mike has to do the sports at five," Diana said when we met outside the Haber House. "Pauly's truck still isn't running. He can use his dad's truck to do the ten, but can't get in for the 5."

Great. Just great. Jennifer still being debriefed, Dell at the sheriff's,

Tom out of communication, and now a chunk out of Mike's time.

"It'll be okay, Elizabeth," she said. We both knew that wasn't likely.

Diana asked the front desk clerk if she's seen Christopher, when I would have gone straight upstairs. The clerk said he was in the employee's lounge with Nico.

They were playing their game again. Or still.

Christopher's head came up fast. "My mom—?"

"Is still at the sheriff's office. I have to talk to you. Sorry to interrupt," I said, not sorry at all.

"That's okay," Nico said. "I've got to get ready for the dinner shift anyway."

Christopher had added worried and red eyes to his doughy skin.

Nico left. Christopher started to get up.

"You're not going anywhere until you tell the truth, Christopher."

"You can't—"

"Sit," Diana said. He sat. So did I, on a coffee table in front of him so we were practically knee to knee.

I wasted no time, but I also didn't want to hit him with the big question first.

"You said that when you followed Darryl into the museum he said something about you not being who he thought you were. That must have hurt you. Were you angry at him?"

"No. No way. He didn't mean it like that. It wasn't about me."

"And then your mother came in. How did she know you were there?"

"How do I know? She must've seen me go in or something. The bank's right near there."

The bank. "Your mother went to the bank?"

"Yeah. Said she had to get there before it closed."

I wanted to grill him about that, but if I put too much emphasis on it would he realize the implications and avoid answering the bigger question coming up? It wasn't worth the risk.

"So you say Darryl Justice wasn't angry at you and you weren't angry at him. Yesterday I asked if you went after him when he left and you said, 'How could I with her crying all over me?' That's what's known as being evasive. You had no reason to evade unless you *did* follow him, which is what I will relay to the sheriff unless you tell us right now what happened, what you saw and heard, when you followed him to the bed and breakfast."

"I… I didn't."

I stood.

"Where are you going?"

"To the sheriff. I told you. You evaded a question about following Darryl Justice. There was no reason to do so unless you have something to hide. Since he was killed not long after—"

He jolted. "I didn't—You can't think I—"

"Then tell us what happened. Right now," Diana said in the voice of authority. "You followed him to the bed and breakfast."

"I didn't follow him."

This evasiveness didn't slip by me. "But you did go there."

"Yeah. Eventually. Mom was all hysterical, like I said, all through dinner. Then all of a sudden she says I should go to my room. Like I was a kid or something. She left in the rental, so I had to walk. He was there. Standing across the street, looking at the house. I tried to apologize for Mom going all crazy on him. He said not to worry about. That it would all get straightened out, but that he couldn't talk because he was meeting somebody. So I left. That's all."

"What time?"

"About ten, I guess."

Diana gave him the mother-of-doom voice. "Christopher." When he didn't immediately respond, she added. "That wasn't all. You left, then what?"

"I went around the block."

"What did you see when you got back to the B&B?" I asked.

"I didn't go all the way back. I stopped a few houses away."

"What did you see?"

"Somebody came out the back door. It was real dark, hard to see, but there was kind of a light, like a flashlight only small. I saw Darryl heading that way. Then they both disappeared. I saw the light again from a window on the side of the house. Just for a second, then it was gone."

"...**SO THE MURDERER** used a small flashlight to escort Darryl up the dark back stairs to Dell's empty room," Diana said, "then offered him wine."

"Yeah." I was tired. So very tired. I closed my eyes. We were back at the station parking lot, in my SUV for now. The residual warmth would run out soon and we'd have to go inside ... and do what? I didn't have any idea. "Not an accidental meeting. Which meant Darryl had trusted whoever he was meeting."

"What do you make of Bunny and the bank?"

"More blackmail cash."

"That's what I thought, too." There was a pause, then. "What are you thinking, Elizabeth?"

"I'm thinking I'm an idiot."

"That again? Now why?"

"Because I've been playing the sheriff's game and dragging all of you along with me. Alibis and evidence—it's why I took that video. Why I let it absorb me. No more. No. More. Okay, pretend Sheriff Russ Conrad doesn't exist. It's back to Sheriff Widcuff's reign. We don't have access to evidence or alibis—not because the sheriff is holding on to the information and has scared everybody out of sharing it, but because the sheriff was too incompetent to do ordinary police work."

"I think you're sleep-deprived," Diana said.

I didn't open my eyes. "Shh. It's back to the earlier time. And we're trying to figure this out. And we're ... of course, asking questions. But which questions? Things that didn't fit. Things that make me wonder—" I opened my eyes. "How did they know Darryl had been Krista's lover?"

"Who?"

"Elaine and Gordon Kelvin. Elaine said it at the café. But Kelvin already knew, because he used it to force Krista to let them stay at the bed and breakfast. One of them might have told the other, but one had to know somehow to start. Krista certainly didn't confide in either of them. Darryl didn't either. So how did they find out?"

"Gossip? Saw a text from one to the other? Overheard a conversation?"

"I need Jennifer. I need her now." I was out of the SUV and heading inside the station.

Diana caught up with me at the doors. "I'll check the ladies' room and editing bays, you look in back for her."

She meant by the studio, possibly in the booth, since the broadcast at 5 had started.

"Has anyone seen Jennifer?" she called out as she did a quick survey of the bullpen.

I keep going, heading for the studio. As I did, Thurston Fine's image and voice came from ceiling-hung TVs dotted throughout the building.

"...and the dead man came from Seattle, so he and these other strangers brought their violence and gruesomeness to our wonderful community, leaving our fine, upstanding law enforcement representatives to clean up this outside mess. Reporting live from the office of Cottonwood County's fine new sheriff and new county attorney, I—" He held and emphasized his favorite syllable. "—am Thurston Fine. KWMT-TV."

I turned the corner to the hallway that led to the studio.

There were so many things wrong with that sign off, starting with the small fact that the sheriff and county attorney had separate offices. In separate buildings. About half a block apart. Then graduating up to the "strangers" in town, whether Dell, the VisageTome people, Bunny and Christopher, or the Williamses, were responsible for the murder.

Heck, he'd even blamed the victim.

But the worst was that as I listened to Thurston Fine proclaim he was reporting live from the courthouse, I could see him down the hallway, standing outside the studio door, waiting to boot Leona out of the anchor seat after the commercial break.

And he could see me. I knew that because I could see him smirking at me.

I headed for him. The broadcast went to commercial break. But I was fast. I slid in, and leaned back against the studio door, barring entry.

"Get out of my way," he yelled.

"Are you crazy? Or just unethical?"

"How dare you. I am not crazy."

Did he not hear my alternative? I prefer to think that a stray strand of truthfulness kept him from disputing that.

"I heard shouting. What's going on here?" Les Haeburn demanded, coming around the corner from the direction of the offices.

"What's going on is that Thurston just announced he was reporting from the County Courthouse and the sheriff's department, simultaneously. Not being satisfied with what so many thought was the unachievable feat of being two places at the same time, he went for three by reporting he was *live* at those two spots, while actually standing *here*."

"Your report said you were live?" Les asked. Not in anger or disapproval, but apparently simply to gain information.

"Well, I *was* live there when I reported it."

"When you—" I swallowed a curse. "Live means you're live when the viewers are watching it, not when you're reporting it on video. You lied to the viewers. And now you think you're going to go out and sit in the anchor desk and *prove* to them that you lied."

"Maybe you should give it a few more minutes," Les said. "So it's reasonable that you could have returned from the courthouse."

I might have made a sound that my Irish ancestors would recognize as a banshee. "Reasonable? *Reasonable?* Try unethical. Try unprofessional. Try lying to the viewers. But, yes, yes, by all means cover up the lie better."

Leona opened the studio door. "What's going on? I thought I was doing one segment. You need me to do more?"

"No," Thurston said immediately. "I'm the anchor. Danniher is having another of her fits over nothing."

"It's called a 'look live,' Thurston. It's unethical, underhanded, unprofessional, and slimy."

"That's your opinion—"

"And the opinion of all ethical practitioners of broadcast media."

Mike came up behind Les. "What's up?"

"Thurston did a look live," Leona said.

Mike groaned and muttered a curse word.

"And," she added, "now he wants to anchor the next block, even though his package just said he was signing off live from the court-house."

"In other words, he lied," I said.

"You will not call me a liar—"

He took a step toward me. Mike started to come around Les.

I moved toward Thurston. He retreated, making Les the middle of a Mike-Thurston sandwich.

"You told the audience you were live at the courthouse when you weren't. Along with making assumptions about a case that is wide open and implications against people who could sue you and the station every day for a year. And—"

"You could wait another block, Thurston," Les said in another show of great leadership.

Leona nudged me in the side.

She was right. I should leave. There was a far better chance of this going well for the station if Thurston didn't have to back down in front of me.

I still wanted to chew him up and spit him out.

Leona resolved the standoff, grabbing Thurston's arm with one hand, while pushing me past him with the other, as she said, "Thurston, I wanted to ask you a question about something in the C Block. In the studio. You, too, Les. Mike, why don't you take Elizabeth for a nice, refreshing drink somewhere."

With her tugs and pushes, plus a bit of cooperation from Les and Mike, she accomplished a separation of the combatants, leaving Mike and me in the hallway while the rest of them went in the studio.

"What was that about a refreshing drink?" Mike asked. "I have to go on air soon."

"She meant it metaphorically. She was telling you to make sure I cooled off."

He laughed.

"What?"

"Like I could. Or anyone could."

"And there's no reason I should cool off. It's unethical, unprofessional, and unacceptable. It's lying to the viewers. The people we're supposed to be giving the facts and truth. It's deception. It's pretending you're somewhere you're not. It's pretending you're someone you're not—"

I stopped with my mouth open.

Someone you're not.

I'd gotten the quote wrong.

...something about you not being who he thought you were...

He didn't mean it like that. It wasn't about me.

That's what Christopher's response had meant.

"Elizabeth?"

I turned toward Mike's voice but I didn't see him. My brain had hijacked my eyes. "Oh, my God. We have to get out of here."

"Well, that's what Leona was saying, because—"

"No, no. Not because I'm going to kill Thurston. Because I think I just figured out who killed—Well, maybe not that, but a chunk of it. An idea. And if that, then... Oh. *Oh.* Or maybe—"

"Elizabeth, you're killing me here. Who killed who?"

I shook my head. "Not yet. We have to go."

"I can't. I'm doing the sports block. But what chunk? What idea?"

"It's too ... fragile. I need Jennifer. Yes, absolutely, I need Jennifer. Diana was looking for her. Where's Tom? And Dell?"

"No word from Tom. Dell, remember, he's at the sheriff's department. With all the rest of them."

"Oh. *Oh.* That's good. That's really good. We'll all meet at the sheriff's department."

"The sheriff's department? Why the hell—"

"Because there are only two interview rooms. And lots more suspects than that. Oh. But first I need to talk to Christopher again. And I wish to hell someone would find Darrell with an 'e.' "

DIANA SAID SHE had to swing home to check on her kids, then she'd be back as soon as possible.

Still no answer from Tom's phone. I left a message saying things were heating up and he should meet us at the sheriff's department— outside or inside, depending.

I got with Jennifer before I left the station and told her what I wanted her to look for, what I expected her to find, and when I needed it.

"I don't know… I mean, I'm sure I *can*, but I don't know about that fast."

"It has to be that fast. It has to be."

"Can I get help? Tell somebody some of what's going on so she'll help?"

Urgency topped caution. "Yes."

"We might have to… You know."

I closed my eyes a second. "As long as you protect yourself so you can't get in trouble, go ahead."

Her eyes went wide. "Wow. Okay. I'll get right on it."

"As soon as Mike finishes the 5, come with him to the sheriff's department. I'll see you there."

I found Christopher Sterakos in his room at the Haber House Hotel, looking worried and young when he yanked open the door to my knock.

"Mom—? Oh. It's you."

He didn't invite me, but I walked in anyway, closing the door, while he wandered back to the rumpled bed and sat on it.

"I don't know what to do," he said. "The sheriff is still holding my mother, and I don't know what to do."

"You should call your father."

"She'll kill me—" He broke off and went white, strengthening his resemblance to Bunny. "I don't… I didn't mean…"

"I know. Listen, things might get cleared up soon." I sure was hoping they would. "If they're not, I'll give you the name of a lawyer in town. He's already representing Wardell Yardley, so he can't represent Bunny, but he can help you. And I mean it, you have to call your father. Tomorrow, if not tonight. But that's not what I came for."

He wasn't interested enough to ask what I'd come for, so I went ahead on my own.

"Did you make your mother come here or did she come for some reason of her own?"

He licked his lips, but said nothing.

"Okay, then I'll say it. Your mother was coming anyway. You didn't force her to come."

"Yeah. I guess."

"Okay. Now—Christopher, are you listening to me? When I asked you about something Darryl said to you in the museum when he was asking for directions, you said 'He didn't mean it like that.' What did you mean?"

He stayed blank for a second, then he got impatient. "It wasn't anything. It's not important—"

"Tell me."

"Geeze. Fine. You said he was angry about me not being who he thought I was. But that wasn't it."

"What was it, then?" I could see his impatience and double it.

"He said *he* wasn't who I thought he was."

Ahhh.

Chapter Thirty-Nine

I BROUGHT CHRISTOPHER to the sheriff's department with me. He went inside to check on his mother.

I transferred from my SUV to Mike's when he pulled in moments later, with Jennifer in the passenger seat.

She didn't raise her head from her keyboard.

"Diana and Tom said they'll be here shortly," Mike said.

Mike tried to pester me about what was in my head, but I was too busy trying to sort it out to start explaining. I ordered him to keep a watch on Ferrante and let me know when he left the waiting area.

Watching through his phone's camera zoom, Mike informed me Officer Randy Hollister was also with the overflow suspects in the waiting area. That was okay. As long as we could get in and established…

I hoped.

Diana opened the back passenger door and climbed in. "What's going on?"

"Shh." Mike said. "Elizabeth's being brilliant and Jennifer's researching."

"I don't need quiet," Jennifer bragged.

She twisted around and looked at me, her eyes bright. "I've got it. What you thought."

I released a breath that partially unclamped my shoulders. It seemed to let more blood flow to my brain, too, because I was seeing how this came together. Maybe even clearly enough to explain it to other people.

I have no idea how much time had passed before Tom knocked on the driver's window. Mike lowered it. "C'mon in, we're waiting for Elizabeth's head to come to a boil."

"Got room for two in there?"

Tom had a hand wrapped around Darrell Justice's upper arm, though the ranger didn't look as if he planned to bolt.

"Where on earth did you find him?" Diana asked. "We tried every motel in three counties."

"Figured a ranger wouldn't go to a motel. I put out the call about anybody who'd shown up since yesterday, then checked a couple spots folks reported. He was at the fourth one."

"The fourth one what?"

"Camping site. Well up in the woods."

"YOU KNEW HIM," I said to Darrell.

"Yeah. I knew him."

"More than that. He'd traded identities with you—at least as far as your birth mother and half-brother were concerned."

"What?" Diana and Mike demanded in unison. We'd shifted seats around. Mike and Tom in front, Diana and Jennifer in the third row, Darrell Justice and me in the middle.

"You're the Darrell Justice that Bunny gave birth to," I said, never taking my eyes off him. "Aren't you?"

"How'd you…? Yeah."

"How did the switch happen?"

"It started as a joke. Well, kind of a joke. A friend from college works at VisageTome and she said she'd met another guy there with my same name. She introduced us at a party and we hit it off okay. He said it was good to talk to somebody 'normal.' It was kind of weird having this guy with the same name. Our backgrounds were pretty similar, too, even being born in the same hospital in Portland. Except I was adopted and he wasn't. Plus the tech thing for him and me being a ranger. Then I got the job at Yellowstone—I'd been trying for a couple years—and came out here early spring.

"My friend and I would email back and forth, talk sometimes. One day, three and a half weeks ago, she got me on a video chat out of the blue and he was there with her. And he says, 'I think I got a message on VisageTome that was intended for you.' I couldn't see how, because I'm not on VisageTome, but he sends it to me right then as an email, so I can read it while we're talking, because I can't always get on the computer and... Anyway, it was from... from that kid."

"Christopher Sterakos."

"Yeah. Him. I was... It was out of nowhere, you know. I didn't know what to think. Saying he was my half-brother and he wanted to meet me and be brothers and all that stuff. They said Darryl could write back and say he had the wrong guy. But then the kid would keep looking. It was—" He swallowed. "It was my idea for Darryl to write back as if he were the right guy. Thinking that would end it right there. He agreed as long as I wrote the message. It took a while, but that's what we did. I tried to be really straight about not wanting anything to do with this kid or the woman who—or any of it, but without being mean. And Darryl sent it. We were all on a video chat when he did it— him, my friend, and me."

I remembered Darryl's voice talking about taking up smoking again after *someone has a great idea... Dysfunctional, but brilliant.*

I'd thought he meant VisageTome's retreats. Could he have meant this?

"Then, bam, here comes back another message practically the second Darryl hit send and it was clear the kid wasn't going to give up. And then Darryl said that from a couple things in that second message it seemed like the kid had been digging into *his* history—thinking he was me, I guess. I mean he knew things about Darryl's parents and where he went to school and stuff. And Darryl said maybe if *he* wrote to the kid's mother as if he were me and said to please leave him alone that that would do it. So he did."

With those three words he seemed to run out of steam. He rubbed his forehead with his fingertips.

"When was that, Darrell?"

"Uh, two weeks ago. Yeah, two weeks ago today, so a little more than a week before VisageTome came to the park."

"You'd known Darryl was coming?"

"Oh, yeah. We were going to get together for dinner. Then he got a message to me and said not to come because the woman—the kid's mother—was there at the park and she was acting crazy and there was no sense both of us having to deal with her."

The fog was nearly gone. Adrenaline had replaced exhaustion.

"What about Christopher?" I asked.

"What about him?"

"Did Darryl tell you he was at Lake Yellowstone Hotel, too?"

"Was he? The kid was there?" That seemed genuine. He started shaking his head. "I don't think Darryl knew. I'm sure he didn't. He would have told me. Especially—"

"Especially after you met Sunday night."

He was going to deny it. For two, three heartbeats he was determined to deny it. Then he breathed out through his nose and his shoulders dropped. "Yeah. That was you on the porch?"

"Yes. Why did you get together then? And whose idea was it?"

"It was mine. I kept thinking about that thing Saturday at Norris Basin. It … bothered me."

"You saw something."

He shook his head before adding a firm, "No. I didn't see anything I could pin down. That's what Darryl asked, too, and when I said I hadn't, really. Just some guy putting his phone in his pocket. He said I was making a mountain out of what wasn't even a molehill. He said everything was fine, it was one of his klutzy geeks. I couldn't shake the feeling it wasn't that. It kept going through my head that if he hadn't stepped one way and that guy who almost went over hadn't gone the other way when they made room for the little kid, that it would have been Darryl going over and none of the people close to him would've been fast enough or strong enough to hold him the way he held that guy. I'm not saying he'd have been killed, because the boardwalks aren't close enough to the really dangerous spots, but would somebody who'd meant him harm—meant me harm thinking he was me—have known that?"

Probably not. But I didn't say what he already knew.

"What happened next?"

"He was going to stay over another day so we could have that dinner we'd planned. But then there was a mess from work he had to clear up and he had to cancel. But he might be able to connect with me when he drove back through when he returned from Sherman.

"Next thing I know, rangers and my bosses and everybody start contacting me left and right yesterday asking if I'm okay, because some guy with my name was killed in Sherman. I asked for a couple days off and drove straight here and went to the sheriff's office. When you told me I couldn't believe it, couldn't make sense of it. I had to think. Had to figure things out..."

So, he camped. Of course. We'd been looking for a ranger in a motel. Tom looked for him in the woods.

"It's my fault he's dead," Darrell said. "I should have never let him help me. I should have handled it. I should have said it all had to end. I should have faced down that woman myself."

"You think Bunny—your birth mother—killed Darryl?"

He looked up, his face haggard. "Who else could it have been?"

Chapter Forty

MIKE HAD ALERTED us when Ferrante left the front desk. He was nowhere in sight when we walked in.

I waited until all of us were inside, then looked around those seated on the benches along two walls and folding chairs. The missing were Bunny and Dirk Seger. "Hello, everyone. Glad you're all here. We—"

"Ms. Danniher," Hollister tried. So he knew my name.

I kept going. "—should be able to clear this all up fairly quickly now if—"

"Ms. Danniher, you can't." He looked pleadingly at Mike, then Tom. Neither returned his look.

"—those of you not guilty of murder or—"

Over Deputy Hollister's shoulder I made eye contact with Dell. He lifted his eyebrows, asking about progress. I crossed my fingers and held them up.

"Ms. Danniher. *Please.*"

"—double murder will cooperate and—"

Hollister turned and ran two steps toward the back, then apparently thought better of deserting taxpayers, not to mention a hometown football hero, to a roomful of potential murder suspects. Or, possibly, vice versa.

He pulled up and shouted, "Help! Sheriff, help, help!"

"—tell us what we need to know to wrap this up. Your secrets truly aren't worth being involved in a double murder investigation. You have a better chance of—"

The door of Interview Room One jerked open. Sheriff Russ Conrad took one step out with his weapon drawn, then stopped.

I thought that showed remarkable judgment and restraint.

Judgment, because he instantly took in the fact that there was no physical threat to a member of law enforcement or anyone else. Restraint, because there was no doubt he was tempted to pull the trigger when he saw me standing in the middle of his waiting room.

Seeing I was accompanied by the friend who'd helped him get the job, the woman he intended to make his own, and the hometown football hero might have dimmed his urge to shoot.

"What the hell is—" The door to Interview Room Two squawked open. We couldn't see it, but could gather what was going on when the sheriff interrupted himself to order, "Stand down, Alvaro. And put down that coffee, Ferrante," before resuming, "what's going on here?"

"I need a couple quick questions answered, and then—"

"You're not asking any—"

"—we can clear all this up." I left no gaps in my words. "Elaine, you and your cohorts plan to leave VisageTome and create a startup, despite the non-compete and other agreements you signed as condition to your employment, correct?"

"What are you? The VisageTome police? I knew they had spies—"

"Correct?"

"Yeah, so what? They don't own me. I can—"

"You said you were the brains, your colleagues were the nerds—" If she hadn't been impervious, she would have felt the venomous points of sharp looks directed at her from her fellow VisageTome employees. Soon to be ex-employees. Wasn't sure if it was because she claimed the brains or because they objected to being described as nerds. "—but you still lacked the money."

"You said—" started Hart.

"Shut up," she snapped.

"What does this have to do with—?"

Proving I was far more controlled than Elaine, I did not snap *shut up* at Sheriff Conrad. Instead, I interrupted firmly but kindly with, "A piece of the puzzle. And we're here to introduce you to another piece of the puzzle." I gestured toward Darrell, still with Tom's hand as an accessory around his arm. "He is a ranger from Yellowstone National Park. He knows all about geysers and—"

The sheriff's face had gone magenta. Not because he didn't know who I was talking about, but because he surely thought we—I—had been hiding Darrell. Conrad took two steps forward, bringing him to the spot where the hallway opened into the waiting area. Behind him crowded deputies Shelton, Alvaro, and Sampson.

But it was Diana's voice that stopped me. "Elizabeth."

I cut short the intro. "Sheriff Conrad, meet Darrell Justice. Tom just found him."

Over breaths sucked in and gasped out from the assembled, Krista demanded, "Is this your idea of a joke, because—?"

"No joke. D-a-r-r-e-l-l Justice."

"That's enough—"

"Not quite, Sheriff. It's important they all meet him, because he's someone you're not. Not *you* you, Sheriff. Still, he *is* someone you're not. Actually he's not Darryl Justice, D-a-r-r-y-l. Or more accurately Darryl with a y isn't Darrell with an e."

Tom turned his head toward the sheriff. "It's the way her mind works."

He didn't sound apologetic. Simply stating a fact. I could have kissed him for that. Well, maybe better not. Not until some other things were straightened out.

But first, this.

"It started because of Thurston doing a look live." The sheriff pulled in air. I spoke fast before that air came out in a command that would stop me in my tracks. "He pretended he was live, but he had actually done the report earlier. So when he was saying he was live at the Courthouse, he was really at the station. That made me think—"

"There aren't any alibis where someone could be somewhere else," Shelton growled.

"Actually, it made me think about someone *being* someone else, rather than being somewhere else."

Everyone looked at Darrell Justice.

"Exactly," I said. Quickly, I explained the deception Darrell and

Darryl had used in response to Christopher's attempts to establish a relationship.

Christopher's eyes welled. From another layer of rejection by his half-brother or from realizing his half-brother had not died?

"But... But..."

I recognized that confused vocal effort to catch up with events too fast for her. I'd heard it a lot as a kid when Bunny Ramsey had tried to absorb that Barbie was not going to prom, but instead had been sent to the Amazon to retrieve the secret code that would save the planet.

Bunny apparently had come out of whichever interview room she'd been closeted in when her interrogators exited. And had piled up in the hallway behind the law enforcement guys.

Now Richard Alvaro, ever polite, stepped aside so as not to block her view of the waiting area. Deputy Shelton didn't need to perform the same courtesy for Dirk, who was behind him, because Dirk could see over him. Not that Shelton would have anyway.

Ferrante wasn't as fortunate. I could just make out the salt and pepper at the top of his head as he shifted back and forth, presumably trying to see around the logjam at the doorway.

"But that means the blackmailer's not dead. You're not *dead*," Bunny wailed.

From the corner of my eye, I thought the sheriff, Shelton, and Alvaro looked at her in a way that indicated they knew she was lamenting that her first-born son was not dead.

But I was more interested in other reactions, so I kept my eyes on the waiting area.

Bingo.

At my shoulder, Diana cleared her throat. She'd spotted it, too.

The jerk of a shoulder. The twitch of a hand.

I breathed a little easier. But there was still a long way to go.

"No, he's not dead, Bunny. And the blackmailer's not dead. But Darrell Justice—either spelling—has never been blackmailing you."

"Yes, he has. He *has*. Or the other one... I gave them money. And then they demanded even more money."

"Actually, you gave your second son money." I turned. "Didn't she, Christopher?"

His head jerked up. "Are you crazy? You think I was blackmailing her about having a kid before she married my dad?"

"No, I don't think that."

"Wait a minute here—"

I held up a stop sign hand to the sheriff and looked at Christopher Sterakos. "I think you took the money out of the trash can in the hallway at Lake Yellowstone Hotel where your mother had left it in response to a blackmailer's demand. You said you were broke at Yellowstone, but you had money to pay for your own room at the Haber House Hotel. You didn't make the demand, but you took the money." Silence. Quietly, I said, "Didn't you, Christopher?"

"I didn't know it was blackmail."

Maybe. Maybe not. He must have thought there was some reason his mother had put a stash of cash in the trash. In fact, he must have had some suspicion or why look in the trash can at all? Especially, why linger there after I and then his mother left that hallway Sunday night.

"You took the money," I repeated evenly.

"It wasn't like stealing. It's my family's money. My dad's. So it's—"

"With that money gone, the blackmailer demanded more. That's why your mother came here to Sherman. You'd heard Darryl with a y telling Darrell with an e that he was coming here, so you were all for a trip here."

"He made me come here," Bunny said. "Him—" She flapped a hand toward Darrell. "—or the other one or both of them. They demanded more money."

"The blackmailer demanded more money, but that wasn't either of the Darrells."

"It *said* it was."

"What said it was?"

"That message thing. The private one. The one VisageTome advertises all over the place."

I turned. "Jennifer?"

"It's easy. It's a variation on spoofing email. VisageTome really should have better security."

"You can't—" Elaine started with a sneer.

"I did." That stopped Elaine temporarily. Then Jennifer gave the icing on the cake an extra swirl. "To prove it could be done, I sent the sheriff a private message from Sgt. Ferrante. The sergeant asked to work nights and weekends from now on."

A squawk came from the back of the clog in the hallway.

"I—" Jennifer stopped when I gave a little head shake.

"I want to be sure everyone understands what happened." I was pretty sure Bunny was the only one completely lost, but a few were farther along than the rest. "Christopher was looking for his half-brother, the baby his mother bore when she was in high school, but—"

"I didn't. It's a lie. She's always been jealous of me." No one even looked at Bunny.

"—he got tripped up by the Darryl and Darrell issue. How did that happen, Christopher? The papers you found in your grandmother's attic—"

"No papers. There are no papers." Bunny was essentially muttering to herself.

"—must have had the right spelling."

"When I searched, the only Darryl Justice on VisageTome had a 'y.' I figured he'd changed his name or the papers were wrong or something."

It was probably a sign of the decline of our civilization that this kid had not even contemplated the idea of someone simply not being on VisageTome.

"The person spoofing—and spying—on Darryl Justice's VisageTome account saw the communication from Christopher. Now, why would anyone be spying on Darryl Justice's VisageTome account? Because he was the roadblock between them and potential startup nirvana. If he knew what they planned, he'd tell the higher-ups. He might even stop them from taking proprietary information with them when they went so—"

"It's not worth much. Their code is sh—"

"Shut up," Elaine said.

Alan Varney shut up.

"—they wanted to keep track of his communications, so one of them set up as a spy. The spy reported back to the rest of the startup conspirators that the coast was clear. But in the meantime, the spy had found other fascinating things, like messages that revealed Darryl and Krista had been more than coworkers." Nelson lost color from his face. Hart went red. "That information was used to force Krista to let them use the bed and breakfast for this meeting before they made the final break."

I looked over all the VisageTome people.

"After intercepting and stopping Darryl's message to Bunny, the spy saw another way to make use of his backdoor into Darryl Justice's account. Blackmailing Bunny over her illegitimate son."

"I didn't—" Bunny started.

I talked over her. "The spy sent a very different message, demanding money. The money trail is going to be interesting. I'll leave it to the sheriff, but I suspect we'll find out that our kindly gray-haired elk bugling lovers had already put a lot of money into the startup enterprise, persuaded by a relative who was involved, and with hopes of reaping huge rewards. But they became worried about their investment and decided to see for themselves.

"Other than letting me get a glimpse of Ariel at Norris, you did an impressive job," I said to the Williamses. "It was Gordon who gave you away. At least he gave us the first hint we needed. He used the phrase *going by way of Altoona*. The only people I've ever heard use that are from Pittsburgh. Jennifer confirmed you are from Pittsburgh." I nodded to her.

"Then I found family photos on archived Leafs. They showed you with Gordon Kelvin. Your sister's son."

"Thank you, Jennifer."

Ariel started to speak. I talked over her, too. "But let's get back to our blackmailing spy. Non-cash was too easy to trace and the spy couldn't have Bunny send cash to Darryl, because he lived away from VisageTome. How would it be intercepted? The retreat at Yellowstone provided the perfect opportunity, so the spy ordered her to deliver the cash in person.

"Things started to go wrong from the start. The first night, Bunny tried to plead with Darryl. He thought she was nuts, but what if he stopped dismissing her as a nut job? Darryl looking into the messages was the last thing the spy wanted. The spy indulged an unwise impulse to try to get rid of Darryl by pushing him off the boardwalk at Norris Basin. Not only did he give himself away—though we didn't know that until we had Darrell's account of the episode—"

I glanced at him. He looked confused. He hadn't known he'd identified the pusher.

"—but the spy also almost took out Gordon Kelvin, the one person the spy had told about Darryl and Krista. But the spy, wisely, didn't tell Gordon or anyone about the blackmail. The second night at Yellowstone, Bunny was scared off from the drop by a chance encounter with an old acquaintance. Me. I noticed the door to the group's meeting room was partially open as it had been the night before. Wardell Yardley and I had observed and heard some of that meeting Friday night. How much could someone inside observe through the same reflection of a reflection, through the same partially open door?

"The spy needed to wrap this up fast, so another message went to Bunny, this one scaring her even worse. She made the drop this time, though the spy didn't know that, because someone—Darryl, was it?— closed the door to the hall. Then the money went astray ... right into Christopher's hands, though the spy didn't know that, either. So far the spy had zilch. But the group was moving operations to Sherman, so the spy could try again here, without Darryl or other interference. The spy ordered Bunny to come to Sherman and bring more money.

"Except then Darryl Justice showed up, clearly suspicious. If Christopher—or Bunny—talked with Darryl enough, the blackmail by proxy scheme was sure to be exposed. Darryl had to go. To protect the startup, sure, but more urgently to protect the blackmail money."

I was guessing Darryl had been seen talking to Christopher outside the B&B that night. Maybe the murderer had just planned to talk, but after seeing that and with another drop from Bunny either just having happened or about to, the decision to kill Darryl was made.

"A quick offer of red wine, courtesy of the B&B owners—" A sound came from Krista. "Purportedly from them. Doctored first with—sleeping pills? Something stronger? Keep him talking until they could take effect and—"

"It was his room." Elaine jabbed a finger toward Dell.

"How would Darryl know whose room it was? The killer—or at this point, the drugger—opens the bathroom with the spare key you all knew about, leads Darryl in to the bedroom and offers him the wine. It knocks him out. At least for a while. On one of the spy's trips back to check on him—everyone left that meeting to go to the bathroom multiple times—was Darryl stirring? Is that why more wine was poured down his throat. Clumsy. Very clumsy. And then, thinking about the danger of Darryl being found and possibly revived… That was when the decision was made to smother him and—"

"No, wait. Not sleeping pills. The spy used those drugs Gordon had. The ones you talked about, Landon."

"Me? No, I never said anything."

"Yes, you did," Alan Varney said. "You told me—"

"Shut up," Elaine said.

"You shut up," he snapped back.

I resisted the urge to cheer and said, "I bet the sheriff can track that. As for Gordon's murder, that was a combination of fear and panic. Gordon knew too much, starting with the drugs, whether they were taken without Gordon knowing or whether he contributed them. Plus the spy had told him things and Gordon talked too much. The spy couldn't have that.

"All this to protect the blackmail money. Was it going to be kept for the spy? Or was it to give the spy a bigger ownership stake in the startup?. Outside money would demand a stake in this enterprise and every rapacious startup entrepreneur knows the trick is to keep it all in the spy's own hands. And now we know whose hands those are. Jennifer?"

"I found the spoofed blackmail messages sent to Bunny Sterakos," she picked up smoothly. "And traced back to who sent them. The cyber fingerprints are clear. It was—"

That started two surges forward.

Mike stepped in to the male trying to reach the door with a shoulder block to the ribs that sent Brant Nelson crashing and his phone spinning out of his hand.

Tom and Darrell Justice latched on to either arm of the other surger, which seemed overkill for a woman in her sixties.

"*You*—you killed my Gordon. You killed him. I'll kill you myself."

Ariel must have counted on Harvard Law School alum Joel to get her off.

Chapter Forty-One

IN THE IMMEDIATE aftermath, I found myself on the sidewalk in front of the sheriff's office, standing next to Bunny.

There'd been so much going on inside, that the sheriff had ordered several of us noncombatants outside with orders not to go far and with Lloyd Sampson keeping a careful eye on us.

Mike, Dell, Tom, Jennifer, and Diana were just past us, and Christopher and Darrell Justice were behind us.

"It's over? It's finally over?" Bunny demanded.

"Yes, it's over."

Over the way a marathon must be over for an amateur runner. With relief, with exultant accomplishment, and with the knowledge that what's behind you is going to make itself felt for days and days and days to come.

"Thank God," Bunny said. "What a nightmare this has been."

I looked at her, the woman version of the little girl I'd once played with. "Is that your only reaction?"

"What else? This has been horrible for me."

"Don't you feel any—*some*—grief for the two young men who died. Especially for Darryl Justice?"

You're not a fan of VisageTome sending its staff to the wilderness?

Oh, that. That's survivable with a good dose of humor and cabernet sauvignon.

Poor Darryl Justice.

"Grief?" she repeated as if I'd spoken a foreign language. "I didn't know him. He was a stranger. A stranger who—" She cut off her own words with a gesture.

"You thought he was your son."

"I didn't know him."

"Sorrow then." At least. "Sorrow at the death of a young man with so much ahead of him. A young man who seemed quite nice." Her face went blank. I kept trying. I felt I owed it to all those Barbies. "A young man whose family and friends love him and will miss him so much."

"Sure. It's a shame." She had displayed more emotion about the loss of each Barbie than she did now. Because she'd learned to hide her feelings? Or she felt less? "But I have to look out for Christopher and myself. I've got to get us out of here and fast."

"Fast? Why, when the murderer's been found?"

"Of course, fast. Do you have any idea what could happen if my husband finds out about this mess? And he will if we're stuck here much longer."

"Do you ever think about anyone other than yourself?"

She sucked in a sharp, audible breath. "You can't talk to me like that. You always were nasty, even as a child. Nasty and spiteful and jealous. Jealous of me now that I have a rich husband, just like you were always jealous of my Barbies, because they had such tasteful wardrobes and beautiful hair. That's why you tried to destroy them all."

She smoothed down the fabric of her exquisitely cut and entirely inappropriate jacket. And then—I am not making this up—she did the hair-plump I'd only previously seen in cartoons.

"Yup. You caught me. Jealous to the bone."

Mom had often chastised me for sarcasm when playing with other kids, but it sailed right over Bunny's head. Or under her ego. Hard to tell which.

"I knew it," she said triumphantly. "I knew—"

"Oh, for heaven sakes. I was never jealous of you or your Barbies. I thought they were hare-brained and idiotic, worrying about their clothes when they could have been exploring the rain forest."

She huffed in indignation.

I turned to get away from her and here came Christopher and

Darrell.

"You could come home with us—"

Christopher's words caused simultaneous stillness in his mother and his half-brother.

"—get to know me—us—the rest of the family. Just as friends. No obligation or—"

Darrell put a hand on his half-brother's shoulder. "No. Thanks, but no. My family's coming in and so's Darryl's. I want to be here for them if I can do anything. And when that's over I want to go home with my family for a long, long time."

He'd given the *mys* a trace of emphasis. Subtle but telling.

The teen tried again. "Maybe we could talk. Text. Just to, you know, get to know each other."

Darrell looked at him for a long moment. "You seem like a good guy, Christopher. And maybe, someday. But this isn't the day."

Bunny stepped forward and took Christopher's arm. "Come, Christopher, we have to get to the airport."

She and her first son never made eye contact.

"Ma'am, nobody can go anywhere right yet," Lloyd said. He sounded like Sheriff Conrad.

✧ ✧ ✧ ✧

ALAN VARNEY AND Landon Hart, faced with the possibility of being implicated in the blackmail plot, fell over themselves to say that Elaine had said she and Gordon would take care of the money angle.

Hart asked if we thought this could be kept quiet. Maybe VisageTome wouldn't have to know. Maybe they could just go back to work next week.

Jennifer cackled derisively.

Wardell Yardley, in full reportage mode, said, he'd like to talk to all of them tomorrow to get their side. Because if they explained to him on camera what had happened, surely VisageTome would have to listen.

And darned if he didn't line them up to be interviewed when his crew arrived.

The sheriff had made it clear none of them—none of us—were going anywhere until he was satisfied he'd wrung out every drop of information.

Dell demanded to see the sheriff, and came out with the news that he had been excused.

"What did you do, threaten a lawsuit?" I asked.

"I did point out how my network might view my being detained further after I had been fully cooperative for days and requested only that I be allowed to go home—well, to Mike's home."

"I'm surprised at you bringing out the big guns now," Mike said.

"It was time for the big guns. Crew comes tomorrow. Got to get my beauty rest."

He waved to us and was off.

My opinion of Sheriff Russ Conrad improved when Elaine came out of that interview room looking puffy-eyed and devoid of self-satisfaction.

It dipped when he announced she was being held as a material witness and would not be available for interviews or questions.

Some people are just so selfish.

Some people are also thorough.

I had to go through my account twice for Conrad and a third time with Jarvis Abbott sitting in.

That time, I fleshed out some of the things that had made me suspect Brant Nelson.

The fact that he was in security certainly didn't hurt. Darrell's mention of the pusher at the geyser putting away his phone first. Nelson's shocked reaction at the café when Elaine referred to Darryl and Krista's affair, because he'd told only Gordon and hadn't known Gordon had told Elaine.

But I don't know that I would have been alerted to any of those if there hadn't been that moment at Lake Yellowstone Hotel when Gordon Kelvin bragged about messing with customers' accounts and Brant Nelson said with both disdain and outrage for someone taking credit for what Nelson had done, *You*.

Nelson wasn't talking, but the Williamses were filling in enough hints shared by Gordon Kelvin that the investigation was perking along nicely.

By the end of Friday, Sheriff Conrad had persuaded Bunny to tell her story. It included following orders to drop another wad of cash behind a shed at the back of the B&B Monday night. When she'd looked back, she'd seen a small light heading that direction as Brant Nelson and his phone went to collect the money.

They also confirmed the cyber fingerprints from Darryl Justice's account. It was easy after they knew whose fingerprints to check.

THE ENDING

WE SAW LESS of Wardell Yardley over the next several days.

He was reporting the gold coins story he'd been assigned while also doing reports about his brush with murder. He also did a gracious interview with Needham Bender for the *Sherman Independence*, which the *Washington Post* picked up as a special.

Wardell Yardley was back on top.

Unlike past murder cases we'd worked on, there would be no special for KWMT-TV on these murders at the Wild Horses Bed and Breakfast.

Mike and Jennifer grumbled, but didn't put much heart into it. After all, the scene of the crime was the fledgling business owned by the niece and nephew-in-law of the station's owner.

There was trying to get a story and then there was beating your head against a brick wall outside the unemployment office.

Besides, maybe laid-back Wyoming was dulling my edge, but I didn't see a good reason for making their B&B more notorious than it was.

On top of that, who needed another story centering on the Wild Horses Bed and Breakfast when the word had spread around the newsroom on Monday that Thurston Fine was slated to do a special live—truly live—report from its official Grand Opening the following weekend.

Its success was still up in the air. As was the future of Krista and Dirk's marriage.

Krista hadn't said it explicitly, but had acknowledged to me—off the record—that with Dirk never coming to bed that night, she'd initially feared he'd "been involved in" Darryl's death. That's why she'd been less than forthcoming to me and the sheriff.

How much Dirk knew of her doubts was unclear.

He had cleared up one point. He'd found Bunny in the B&B's backyard Monday night and assumed she was interested in a room, and that's why he'd given her a tour. Bunny had just deposited the blackmail money behind the shed and went along with the tour to get Dirk away from the spot.

Poor Bunny. Zero for three in making blackmail drops unobserved.

Mom had reported that she'd learned from Muffy that Christopher had had a long conversation with his father. That resulted in a sort of three-pronged approach. Bunny's mother-in-law was back on the scene along with the surviving grandmother-in-law, trying to reshape her to their image. Christopher was being allowed to spend more time with Muffy. And the whole family was going in to counseling.

I wondered if there would be role-playing dolls for Bunny.

After yet another debriefing with Sheriff Conrad and County Attorney Abbott, the sheriff said as we left the courthouse. "It's looking like you got the right guy, but you could have blown this for good." He was stern, but not outraged.

I nodded. "We also left you to do a whole lot of corroborating work. I know. And I'd do it all again to clear Dell before it could really hurt him."

"Don't do it again. Ever," he ordered and walked away.

That Monday night, with Dell leaving the follow day, we gathered at Diana's. Outside this time, around a large campfire, where, joined by Tamantha, Jess, and Gary, we roasted marshmallows and tried to stay warm.

Only after we repaired inside and segregated—the girls watching a movie in Jess' room, Gary doing homework, and the rest of us in the living room—did the conversation turn to the murders.

"I have an announcement," Dell said. "I will be returning to Sherman, Wyoming next summer."

Amid the "greats" and "look forward to seeing you agains," I asked, "Vacation?"

"No. I'll be presenting an hour-long episode of the network's prime time crime show on these murders."

"Wow," Jennifer said. The rest of us echoed that.

I added, "Could this be a stepping stone to a permanent prime time gig?"

"That's the plan," he said with satisfaction. "Can't spend the rest of my life chasing presidents."

"See what a trip to Wyoming can do for you?"

That drew teasing jeers from the others, yanking my chain about being unsure about Wyoming when I'd arrived.

We talked about how the legal cases might proceed. Eventually the conversation swung around to lingering questions.

"What I want to know is how you recognized Darrell with an 'e' as Bunny's son," Jennifer asked me. "I never got that."

"His walk."

She demanded more explanation. When I finished, she said, "And from that you figured out Nelson was hacking into Darryl's VisageTome account?"

"It sure wasn't a direct line. Nothing in this was. But I'd already been wondering how they'd found out about the affair between Krista and Dirk. And then the idea of Darryl and Darrell. Plus, there'd been those comments about getting into customers accounts."

"Does VisageTome really know details about us like Gordon Kelvin said that night at Yellowstone?" Mike asked.

Jennifer rolled her eyes. That relieved me.

Until she added, "Of course."

"How can we safeguard against that?" Diana, mother of two, asked.

"You can't. It helps if you don't give them any more information that you absolutely have to—no listing your birthday or giving them your phone number or address. Just don't do it."

"You're saying we should all get off VisageTome?" Mike asked.

"Yeah. But I know you won't. Well, except for Elizabeth, whose account is still frozen. But the least you should do—in addition to never giving them any data you don't have to—is to lie. Make things up. Tell them you're an eighty-year-old man who can't drive, but owns a LandRover. For any real thing you do on there, do three or four fake. Searches, talkies, smiles. Any of that stuff. Mix it up. Screw up their data as much as you possibly can."

"I love it, Jennifer. Our very own data guerilla warrior," I said.

"I could do a lot more if you'd let me—"

"No hacking."

~ *THE END* ~

If you enjoyed Look Live, I hope you'll consider leaving a review, to let your fellow readers know about your experience.

For news about upcoming books, subscribe to Patricia McLinn's free newsletter.

www.PatriciaMclinn.com/newsletter

Caught Dead in Wyoming series

SIGN OFF

With her marriage over and her career derailed by her ex, top-flight reporter Elizabeth "E.M." Danniher lands in tiny Sherman. But the case of a missing deputy and a determined little girl drag her out of her fog.

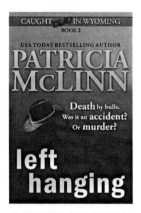

LEFT HANGING

From the deadly tip of the rodeo queen's tiara to toxic "agricultural byproducts" ground into the arena dust, TV reporter Elizabeth "E.M." Danniher receives a murderous introduction to the world of rodeo.

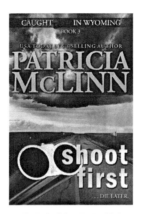

SHOOT FIRST

Death hits close to home for Elizabeth "E.M." Danniher – or, rather, close to Hovel, as she's dubbed her decrepit rental house in rustic Sherman, Wyoming.

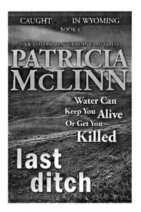

LAST DITCH

A man in a wheelchair goes missing in rough country in the Big Horn Basin of Wyoming. Elizabeth "E.M." Danniher and KWMT-TV colleague Mike Paycik immediately join the search. But soon they're on a search of a different kind – a search for the truth.

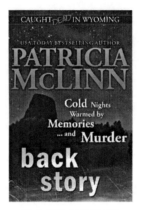

BACK STORY

Mysteries from the past threaten Elizabeth "E.M." Danniher, her friends and KWMT-TV colleagues.

What people are saying about the
CAUGHT DEAD IN WYOMING series

"While the mystery itself is twisty-turny and thoroughly engaging, it's the smart and witty writing that I loved the best."

–Diane Chamberlain, bestselling author

"She writes a little like Janet Evanovich only better."

"E.M.'s internal monologues are sharp, snappy and often hilarious."

"McLinn has created in E.M. a female protagonist who is flawed but likable, never silly or cartoonish, and definitely not made of cardboard."

If you particularly enjoy connected books—as I do!—try these:
Wyoming Wildflowers series
A Place Called Home series
The Bardville, Wyoming series
The Wedding Series
Marry Me Series

Explore a complete list of all Patricia's books
patriciamclinn.com/patricias-books

About the author

USA Today bestselling author Patricia McLinn's novels—cited by reviewers for warmth, wit and vivid characterization – have won numerous regional and national awards and been on national bestseller lists.

In addition to her romance and women's fiction books, Patricia is the author of the Caught Dead in Wyoming mystery series, which adds a touch of humor and romance to figuring out whodunit.

Patricia received BA and MSJ degrees from Northwestern University. She was a sports writer (Rockford, Ill.), assistant sports editor (Charlotte, N.C.) and—for 20-plus years—an editor at The Washington Post. She has spoken about writing from Melbourne, Australia to Washington, D.C., including being a guest-speaker at the Smithsonian Institution.

She is now living in Northern Kentucky, and writing full-time. Patricia loves to hear from readers through her website, Facebook and Twitter.

Visit with Patricia:
Website: patriciamclinn.com
Facebook: facebook.com/PatriciaMcLinn
Twitter: @PatriciaMcLinn
Pinterest: pinterest.com/patriciamclinn

ISBN: 978-1-939215-65-9

CPSIA information can be obtained
at www.ICGtesting.com
Printed in the USA
LVOW11s2034020317

525958LV00001B/188/P